A Deadly Shade of Green

A Novel

by

P. Willis-Pitts

MiNReF PRESS

Sacramento, California

Published by MinRef Press

This novel is a work of fiction. Names, characters, places and incidents
either are the product of the author's imagination or are used fictitiously.

MinRef Press Fiction Edition, March 2000

Library of Congress Card Number: 99-068161

ISBN 0-9624394-9-5

Cover design by Ron Houghton

MinRef Press Web Address: http://www.minref.com

Manufactured in the United States of America

This book is dedicated to:

Sandy Whelchel for her continued enthusiasm and support
Rick Lawler who made it possible—and who went the extra mile
Artist Ron Houghton for his talent and tolerance
Lou Lambert for keeping the faith
And…
Vima and Cassie, two ladies dear to my heart
without whom nothing would get done or
even be worth doing.

Acknowledgements

Quotes for the chapters entitled, *Autumn, Winter, Spring, Summer* were gratefully taken from *The Great American Forest* by Rutherford Platt (further details in Bibliography).

The poem recited by Miranda in Chapter Ten is *The Garden* by Andrew Marvel, 1621-1678

A Deadly Shade of Green

PROLOGUE

400 million years ago there was no Tree. Only land and water; and a silence broken by the sighing of the wind and the crash of the waves. No bird songs; no insect buzz. The land was low uniform rock stretching to the horizon.

Then nature concocted magic from lignum and cellulose, injected this into the straggly, flaccid plants and ferns at the water's edge and wood was born. Now stiff and erect, the plants reared their heads to the sun and broke their bonds with the seashore forever. Gravity was conquered. Over the next forty million years, these plants strode inland soaring strong and high on their vertebrae of wood.

In its 400 million years upon land, Tree has never ceased being a creature of the sea; its basic cell unit remains unchanged from its ancient form: The cell still has to be constantly immersed in water for the vital interchange of oxygen and energy.

Tree's innovation is to carry the sea within it. In just one hour, a full-grown specimen draws hundreds of gallons of water from the soil. The water is pumped up to dizzy heights, bathing the tree cells with its precious, mineral-bearing benediction. Then the water is flung away from the vast green corona of the leaf tips as waste.

This creature standing vast and silent hundreds of miles from its Alma Mater, the sea, is a miracle of adaptation. It absorbs water, carbon dioxide and the red, blue and orange wavelengths of light. Ninety-nine percent of the water is expelled; carbon dioxide becomes oxygen; and the white light, drained of its blue, red and orange—the components of blood color—becomes a visual marvel: every possible shade of green.

Therefore, it should be remembered that to Tree, green is a waste product—excrement—produced by the absorption of the components of blood.

CHAPTER ONE

It was Miranda who found it; Miranda of the long, blonde hair and the Laura Ashley dresses. Summer Miranda; cotton Miranda; impractical, impossible, dreamy-eyed Miranda. Miranda who spent her whole life in an arcane world of poetry and dance. Yes, it was Miranda who found the house. Practical Peter had been too busy at his machine.

¤

Peter gripped the edge of the foundry door with a moleskin cloth. It hissed and sizzled with the heat. He heaved, but the door remained stuck. He grunted and wiped his nose with a short, muscular forearm and pulled again. The moleskin cloth began to smoke, but the door did not budge. He swore, threw the moleskin aside and stepped out into the sunshine for a breather.

The afternoon light etched its long shadows across the front of a tumble-down house covered in a weather-warped insulation. Peeling strips of insulation dotted the walls like grubby band-aids, giving the building an air of desolation and ruin: the windows were split and cracked; the walls canted over at a crazy angle.

Peter surveyed his domain—rented for an impossible $120 a month from an Estate Agent who'd been glad to have it off his hands. Peter was well satisfied. If Miranda's province was the heart, Peter's was the head—and pocket. The house was a bargain—Peter had fixed the deal.

'Peter can fix it' had become Miranda's slogan and battle cry. And not without reason—Peter *could* fix it; and it seemed he never failed. Even when it came to the phenomenon of Vietnam—so sarcastically termed the 'Asian Vacation' by its survivors—Peter hadn't *had* to fix it. He was drafted, but he never went to Vietnam. Instead, he worked with a group of electrical engineers, learning to strip down generators in North Dakota. Even Peter couldn't fix the Vietnam war—but he never had to. He'd spent his entire enlistment learning More Ways To Fix Things.

Yet this small property, situated on a dusty road between San Francisco and Sacramento, badly needed fixing. The outbuildings were besieged by a profusion of weeds: mint, horehound, melissa and thickly-twining ivy. Odd shapes nestled in the unkempt grass like giant insects; a mysterious conglomeration of tubes and wires whose function was known only to Peter. Angle iron and plastic tubing, glass bottles and fire bricks sprawled in confused array around an odd assortment of tools: a wire-feed welder; a generator; oxyacetylene cutter; refining bottles; clamps; heavy-duty drill presses; and, crouching over it all like a giant predator, the Machine.

Because of the Machine, Pete hadn't fixed the house. The house and the yard were in the same state of disrepair as they'd been when he first moved in. 'The thatcher's roof is always the worst in the village,' he mused, contemplating the ruin about him wryly.

And, as if in answer, the Machine rumbled:

Its forty yards of thick, metal tubing snaked around the house to a squat, black body that shuddered and swayed on its iron supports like a living creature. And like any living creature, the Machine fed constantly. Deep in its belly, a mysterious digestion was taking place. Into its narrow maw Peter would cram film; any kind of film: X-ray; old negatives; unused Lab spools; defunct feature films; cuttings collected from the editing floors of Hollywood production companies. Film—tons of it—crackling and complaining was fed into the monster's mouth.

And, rumbling and hissing, the monster reduced the mass of film in its belly to a lumpy, silver-gray ash. This was re-absorbed and re-digested repeatedly until the final meltdown. Then, miraculously, it produced a substance of a quality that would have made any Medieval alchemist delirious—pure Silver.

Peter stood by the Machine in his stained leather apron. A short, dark, muscular man with brawny forearms and John Lennon glasses perched on his nose, he seemed unaware that from behind a bush, Miranda—tall and wispy—peeked at him impishly.

An odd couple these two. And yet, not an unlikely match.

Peter had that earthy quality attributed to the drubbers of caves and caverns; those solid little men of sweat and iron who refined common dirt into its precious component metals: the gnomes.

If Peter was the gnome, Miranda was the elf—possessed of that quality known to connoisseurs of the Fantastic, as 'eldritch'. Not a quality that has ever aspired to success in the material world, yet Miranda had never been poor. Though she was without guile, her beauty and her childlike nature had always opened doors for her. Women responded to her beauty with a reflexive hostility. But this quickly dissipated when they found, instead of a rival, a sister and playmate. Men responded to Miranda's child-beauty by strutting and preening. But their sexual displays would fall on stony ground and they would retreat, puzzled. The compromise was chivalry. Around Miranda, men became knights, strong but gentle, courteous and romantic. For in some ways, Miranda was a product of a bygone age.

Poor mechanistic Peter. How Miranda troubled him; and how he loved her; and how he tried to understand her as he might a valve or an intricate machine—and how he failed constantly.

Peter squinted off along the dusty road running between the ramshackle gates. Miranda, concealed in the bushes, suppressed a giggle and hunkered down further; Peter was obviously looking for her.

Peter turned to gaze at a postcard pinned on the greasy black wall of the workshop. It was from Miranda's father and its message was clear:

A tall, blonde girl flitted through a stylized pastoral setting of impossible leaves and even more improbable flowers. Gnarled trees reached out thorny, clawed hands to ensnare the maiden but, with an easy grace, she evaded them, her diaphanous garments fluttering in the wind. In her hands, the girl carried a glittering, translucent stone, ocean blue, as big as a hen's egg. At its core was a crimson ruby. The caption beneath the illustration read:

'She is simply a child on the seashore
of Time gathering colored pebbles and
returning them to the sea.'

Peter stared at the elf-child on the postcard, his face set. Miranda was late; she was always late. Miranda seemed to have no concept of personal danger. Sometimes she would wander for miles across the lonely hillsides, as if protected by the Archangel Gabriel himself.

"Goddamnit!" muttered Peter out loud, "That girl…!" Sometimes Miranda's lack of concern for her own welfare frightened Peter…

"BOO!!" Miranda leapt out from behind the bush.

Peter turned from the forge without even flinching. He smiled. "Do you think that you could ever frighten me?" he said slowly, enjoying the dance of her eyes and the sparkle of sun on her corn-colored hair. "I knew you were hiding in the bushes. You make more noise than an elephant." He wiped his hands and looked at her smugly.

"There are more things in heaven and earth than dreamed of in your philosophy, Horatio," she pouted.

Peter groaned good-naturedly, ever aware of the gaps in his literary education that rendered much of Miranda's poetic outpourings unintelligible.

She caught the groan and came and hugged him. "How's the Alchemist?"

"Fine."

"And the Alchemy, the transmutation of base film, the dross of industry, into riches beyond compare?"

"Oh," he said, "That's even better—if I can get this goddamn door unstuck." He pointed at the forge door. "I guess it's warped with the heat. It's almost 2,000 degrees in there."

"How do you know?" She furrowed her brow in bewildered admiration. "How do you know that? It's amazing."

"It's the temperature at which the slag renders down," he shrugged, "I know it 'cos it happens. If it didn't happen, it wouldn't be that hot. Simple."

"Well, I don't think it's simple," she said, "You're a magician. You're wonderful!"

And next minute, she was in his arms and it was all scents and sighs, moans and softness, and foundries, temperature, meltdowns and furnaces drifted far away from Peter's consciousness to be replaced by the feel of the warm earth on his back, fumbling fingers and the delicious tide of expectation surging up from his body.

When they'd finished, he was bewildered—as always. Miranda sat like a naked sylph across his squat, hairy body. His heart ached just looking at her. She was perfect; a woman-child; a fairy with golden hair, delicious lemon breasts and silken thighs. And she was crazy about him. It didn't make sense.

"God!" He sat up and glanced over his shoulder. The road was only fifty yards away, hidden behind the plum trees. "God! How do…how can you do that?!" He laughed—it was all too wonderful, "I mean, look, anybody might've walked up while we were doing it! I—"

"Oh! You're right," she said, "Look, it's the postman! My God!" She jumped up and slipped her cotton dress over her head. In one liquid movement, she was dressed.

Peter tried to move fast but it was all too much for him. Swearing and stumbling, he hopped about, trying to get his pants on. He fell over and managed to pull them on. He heard her laughing. "Oh, Peter! You look so funny! The postman came this morning! There's no one there! I'm only teasing!"

Peter stopped his comic struggles and shook his head, exasperated. "Miranda, you nearly gave me a heart attack!" Then his expression changed. "Hey!! The meltdown!!"

He leapt up, grabbed the thick leather gloves and slipped them on. This time, he didn't fiddle with the jammed door. He took a nine-pound hammer and freed the forge door with a ringing blow of metal on metal, hoping the door wouldn't fracture. It didn't. Then, with deft movements, he slid back the keeper bolt and tipped the entire foundry on its pivot. The molten metal surged towards the rim under a crust of dross, and cascaded into a trough with a sizzling and spitting that brought an acrid smell to his nostrils.

"Hooray!! Hooray!!" Miranda danced around the trough madly, "We're rich! My magician has wrought riches from the bare earth! We shall never want again!"

Peter laughed aloud, partially at her antics, partially because it was true. He threw his gloves off and picked up a cold ingot of silver from a previous pouring. He hefted it in his hand, estimating its value—about $600 at present market prices. Not bad… And he had *three* of these machines leased out to franchises. He glanced up at the derelict buildings, neglected for a year while he'd slaved away at his dream project. It had worked. His heart was full as he looked at his lovely girl-wife. "Here, Mira…catch! Buy yourself a fancy ring!"

She yelped as he tossed the heavy ingot into the air and he laughed when she leapt out of the way without making any effort to catch it but, instead, let it plump onto the grass with a deep thud. "I do not pluck silver from the air when there are riches a'plenty to be had otherwise, sire!" she cried with a false, mocking tone, striking an indignant pose.

"And what, exactly, does that mean?" grinned Peter.

So, she took him inside the house, made him sit down and when she was sure he was ready, with great ceremony, she told him that she'd found a house.

He couldn't believe it when she told him the price of the house she'd found. "God, you're clever," he muttered in her ear. She was so proud. He held her close for a long time and told her over and over how clever she was to find such a bargain. Like a child she giggled and hugged him, never growing tired of the repeated compliment.

In the yard outside, the Machine lurched and rumbled, huffed and puffed, its innards rumbling, ready to eat again. The forgotten ingot lay half-hidden in the grass. Already, insects were beginning to burrow and squirm under the damp rectangle formed by its weight...

CHAPTER TWO

Peter couldn't put his finger on it. Neither could Miranda. But he could see that it certainly affected her.

"God," he muttered, "Must all Realty Offices smell like they've been closed down for two years?" He glanced around the offices of Martinez and Thompson. Everything was neat enough—the desk (simulated wood-veneer) actually shone where it had been regularly polished, but there was a feeling of aridity about the room that was almost tangible.

Miranda could hardly keep still. She kept standing up and looking out of the window at the sycamore trees in the drive, a wistful expression on her face.

Peter glanced at the calendar. It wasn't fly-spotted, but somehow it felt like it *should* have been. And the chairs—simulated brown leather—felt grubby, but on closer inspection they weren't. It was a peculiar sensation; a sanitized, deodorized dinginess—without dirt.

Martinez, a thick-shouldered dark-faced man in a suit, tie and a cowboy hat was not unaware of his customers' restlessness. He rushed through the preliminaries at lightening speed and, before Peter knew it, Martinez was pressing the house keys into his hand. "Of course, Mr. Riley, under normal circumstances I would come with you to the Mission, but I can't."

"Mission?" said Peter. He looked at Miranda; she shrugged.

"It's the old name for the place," said Martinez, "I guess the name stuck."

"Who owns it now?" questioned Peter.

Martinez spread his hands. "It belongs to a Mr. Owen. He lives in San Luis Obispo. A curious tale: his son went off to India and became obsessed with some old guru, Shiva-something-or-other. The old man is a millionaire, and he was glad that his son was off the drugs and into something else." Martinez smiled; a thin smile. "Fate plays strange tricks. The old man bought this place for his son to set up a kind of monastery."

"Ashram," corrected Miranda.

"Yeah, that's it—an ashram for the old guru. To keep the son out of trouble. So, the old guru gets here and dies."

"Dies?" said Peter sharply.

"Yep. He died of influenza, would you believe? He must have been eighty years old. He never got anywhere nearer than New York City. Died in Manhattan. So the property has been left to rot for two years. The old man isn't interested, neither is the son."

Peter shook his head. "What a strange story."

Martinez nodded. "There's always a tale in this business. Birth and death—that's it. Properties always change hands around some big event. We get used to it. Anyway, if you want me to come and show you the property, I'll be free on…" he consulted a calendar, "…Thursday afternoon…" he spread his hand helplessly, "…but not before. I'm sorry…"

"No, no, it's fine, Mr. Martinez, really," said Peter, "We, er, prefer to look over the place alone. Gives us a better chance to size it up."

"Of course," smiled Martinez. He handed them a card. "Unfortunately at the moment, the phone is disconnected in the Mission house. But there's one two miles down the road though." He pulled a long face. "If you have any questions, I'll be here until six o'clock."

Peter stood up and shook the man's hand. The man's palm was cool and Peter withdrew his own a trifle hastily. Peter looked apologetic. "Hot in here," he muttered, wiping his sticky fingers on his trousers.

Miranda exploded from the office in a whoosh of air, as if jet propelled. Peter followed close on her heels.

"God, I thought I was going to stifle in there!" cried Miranda, "It smelled like a flea market that's had been closed for ten years! Let's go! Let's get away! I need to breathe!"

"Right," said Peter slowly; Miranda's sensitivities always surprised him; they seemed so extreme.

"There was something…funny," said Miranda, "Something not quite right back there. Martinez wasn't quite right. There was something going on…"

"I dunno," said Peter. He reached the Jeep and pulled open the door, "He seemed a nice enough guy. Maybe he was just nervous trying to make a sale. Some people are like that I guess."

Miranda shook her head, and as Peter got in the Jeep, she looked back at the low one-storey building that was the Estate Agent's office nestling in the crook of the gravel path. Peter bent forward to start the engine. "C'mon!" he called.

Miranda didn't move. She'd seen something move at the office window. It was Martinez watching them leave, his dark face almost hidden in the shadows.

Miranda got in the Jeep, her face taut. The engine ticked over, but Peter didn't engage the gears. He stared at Miranda, puzzled. "You O.K., Hon?"

"Well, I don't know," said Miranda slowly, "I have this funny feeling …here." She put her hand on her belly.

"Just that stinking old Realty Office," chuckled Peter.

The chuckle fell flat. Miranda didn't react. "It's a deep feeling, Peter," she said, "Really, don't make fun of it."

Peter stared at her bewildered. Give him a circuit and he'd trace an electrical fault; give him a broken engine and he'd have it whirring and purring in no time. But when it came to Miranda's 'intuitions', he was totally at a loss. Peter groaned and said: "Miranda Lacey, are you sure that you're not just off on a wild track?"

Miranda stared at him. "Have you been talking to my father, Peter?" she asked suspiciously.

¤

Mr. Lacey, a piano tuner, always talked when he worked, never once pausing in his deft administrations to the lovely cherry wood piano in the New England living room.

"You see," he said, tightening the piano key with a high-pitched squeak that made Peter wince, "Theoretically, each piano is tuned the same—it's a so-called scientific principle of string length and tension. But, this bugger…" he pointed at the lovely, old piano, "…is going to keep me here all afternoon. You know why?"

Peter responded to the rhetorical question with a cocked head.

Mr. Lacey stood up, brow furrowed. "I'll tell you." He banged his hand flat on the piano top and there was a faint shimmer of noise that died away slowly. "This piano has been tuned. Each string is tuned to the next. Then, by way of compensation, I go back and tune 'em all again. But that's not enough." He pointed at the piano. "Some quirk of resonance, some quirk of age and wood, temperature, shape, humidity—God-knows what—cosmic rays, I bet…!" he grinned, "Means no two pianos are alike. And this one is in tune, theoretically, but, by God, it's not in tune in actuality, and it'll take all hell to adjust it. It's off on a wild track of its own. Listen."

And then, with the damper off, he struck a ten-finger C chord…

The room was alive with the splendor of the sound. Rich and mellow, it blossomed through the air like a living thing, filling the small living room with a surprising sense of presence. Even unmusical Peter could hear its nuances: a shimmering underlay of dissonant and assonant tones that shifted and wove under the richness of the C, each one evanescent and fleeting, but omnipresent, like dust motes in a shaft of sunshine.

The piano was not in tune. It was not out of tune, either. For a long time the chord hung in the air and, as the fundamental note died away, the undertones seemed even stronger on the ear, as if, straining against the confines of its musical identity, the piano had asserted its particular uniqueness.

"Hear it?" Mr. Lacey chuckled deep in his throat. "It's not out of tune, it's just not a *known* tuning. Like I said, it's off on a wild track—just like Miranda."

And at that moment, Peter had gained his first insight into the lovely creature that was his wife…

◻

"I said, you've been talking to my father, Peter Riley, haven't you?!" repeated Miranda sternly.

Peter jerked back to attention and shifted guiltily in the worn Jeep seat.

"Well, I'd be lying if I said no."

"Well, Mr. Fix-It," said Miranda, "My father is just as bad as you. And I tell you, there was something very, very strange back there in that office."

"Yeah, you might be right," frowned Peter. "My own Daddy told me, when a deal's too good to be true, it probably isn't."

Miranda didn't respond.

Peter cast a glance over his shoulder and saw the dark patch of Martinez's face at the window. "Funny," he mused. He revved the engine and the Jeep shot forward in a flurry of gravel and screamed off down the road.

It took quite a long time for the dust to settle in the Realty yard; but Martinez's face was still at the window; watching…

CHAPTER THREE

The man staggered across the road, a flapping bundle of rags, his torn clothes fluttering around his stick-like body. He almost fell, then he righted himself and stood there swaying, his matted hair streaming back from his coarse, stubbled face. His eyes rolled madly and he began to dribble at one corner of his mouth. "Get back!" he whispered, waving thin, gnarled arms like knotted branches, "Get back!" he cried, staring along the empty road...

Arrowing along the glistening tarmac, the Jeep screeched as it turned a bend, then sped into the straight again between the twin rows of pear trees.

Miranda was leaning back against the roll bar, her dress and hair flapping in the wind. "It's lovely!!" she cried into the slipstream, "Lovely! Smell the trees!"

Indeed, Peter could smell the trees; the heavy green; the scent of blossom; and the all-pervading pungency of the countryside. He wrinkled his nose. "Smells like cow shit to me!" he shouted with a grin.

"It's all the same," she laughed, "Trees and cow shit. But it's lovely!"

Lovely it was, with the blue sky shimmering above the moody, dark green of the pear trees and the road glistening ahead with the light pooling in silvered mirages across its distant surface.

"Hey!" Peter began to slow down, "What is that?"

A scarecrow figure staggered out of the trees up ahead and stood in the middle of the road, swaying, black and ominous.

"Slow down, Peter," urged Miranda.

But there was no need to urge him. Peter was already decelerating. The Jeep rolled the last few hundred yards in second gear, the engine straining and protesting its desire to move faster. But Peter kept throttling down—the man showed no sign of moving. Finally, the Jeep had all but stopped and the man weaved back and forth in front of it, his reddened eyes glaring at the Jeep with a barely-concealed hostility.

"Shit!" muttered Peter, "He is gonzo—drunk. Excuse me!" he shouted irritably, "Could you, er, move out of the way *please*?"

In answer, the man let out a cry, rushed forward and began beating the hood of the Jeep with his bare fists. "The righteous road is the only road!" he cackled, "The way of the devil is the way of despair!!"

"Oh, shit!" muttered Peter, exasperated. He scratched his head. "A religious nut! What can we do?" he whispered to Miranda, "The old guy's as pissed as a fart! Do I have to run him over, or what? Look...!" called Peter just a little more belligerently, "We're in a hurry. Now, if you just step aside, we'll continue on our way!"

"Don't you hear me??!" roared the man, eyes aflame. He took out a bottle of cheap wine, drained it off and threw the empty bottle into the undergrowth.

"Look, mister!" hissed Peter, his irritation mounting, "We need to—!"

"Don't!" interrupted Miranda indignantly. She slipped over the side of the Jeep, crossed the hot tarmac in a few light steps and retrieved the bottle.

The man grinned. "Aha! She empty, no dice. Too late—all gone. The cat got the canaries, it's all gone. No one here save Mr. Bear, and he's the one who's not quite there..." He tapped his head and began to sing, "The cat got the canaries..." in a mad, cackling voice.

Miranda marched up to the drunk.

"Miranda," said Peter, half rising from his seat, a note of worry in his voice, "Don't!"

She turned and glanced at him with an expression that made Peter shut up and sit back despairingly in the seat. How well he knew that look!

"What's your name?" Miranda asked firmly.

"Joe Bear. What's yours?"

"Miranda Lacey," she replied evenly.

"Miranda Lacey. A lacy dress for a Lacey girl. Well, I'm Joe—Lazy Joe, not Lacey Joe. I ain't never worked for a long time—" He suddenly lurched against her, and the sudden sensation of her softness and her scent in his nostrils made him look at her anew. He gazed at her, bewildered, as if seeing her for the first time. Hie eyes widened, then, suddenly, he started to cry.

"Oh Jesus!" said Peter, "That's all we need."

"Now, Joe," said Miranda, "What are you doing out on the road all by yourself?"

"Miranda," groaned Peter, who was used to Miranda's 'social work', "We'll be here all day!"

"Ole Joe ain't got nobody. Nobody got ole Joe," sobbed the man.

"C'mon, Mr. Joe." Miranda led him gently to the side of the road and sat him down on a rock. The man continued to wail and blubber. "Mr. Joe, you shouldn't go throwing bottles away in the countryside," she urged.

Peter rested his head on the wheel and sighed. This was it. Somehow, no matter what the situation was, Miranda always managed to get herself involved, right up to the neck. She'd had conversations like this with every bum and wino from California down to Tijuana.

Miranda talked softly to the man for a moment and he seemed to quieten down. He didn't look at her, but stared at his lap, clenching and unclenching his hands. Eventually, she stood up, went to the Jeep and took out her purse.

"Shit! Are you going to give him money?!" hissed Peter.

"Of course. We've got plenty." She returned to the man and handed him a bill and patted him on the shoulder. Peter raised his eyes to the sky.

The man looked at the bill through drunken, bleary eyes then, to Peter's disgust, wiped his nose on his forearm, leaving a streak of glistening mucous across his sleeve.

Miranda came back to the Jeep and got in without looking at Peter. "Bye, Joe!" she shouted, "Be careful—don't get run over!" She settled into her seat while Peter stared ahead stonily and started the car.

The man looked up from his contemplation of the bill and realized she was leaving. The car started forward. "Missy!!" he swayed to his feet, "Missy!! Where you a'goin'?"

The car moved off northwards. Miranda waved gaily and pointed back south. "Go to town, Joe!" she urged, "You can't stay out here!"

"Where you goin'?!" he called as the car gathered speed.

"The Mission!" she shouted.

The man screamed out loud, but it was lost: "Noo!! Nooo!!! The cat'll get the canary, Missy, the cat'll get the canary!!" He was still waving and shouting when the car was a dot in the distance.

As the car disappeared around the bend, he crumpled up the bill in agitation and, throwing it in the bushes, began to trudge north.

Peter drove silently for ten minutes, then he said: "How much did you give that old drunk?"

"Twenty dollars."

"Twenty dollars! Miranda, do you really want to support his drinking habit?! That's no kind of help!"

Miranda laughed. "The twenty dollars isn't what he needed, and that's not what I gave him—and he knows it."

Peter pressed down on the accelerator in a surge of annoyance. "Twenty dollars is twenty dollars! And we're not that rich! What did you give him if it wasn't twenty dollars?"

"A little bit of myself, that's all..."

Peter glanced at her. From anyone else it would have been corny, but Miranda said it with a natural ease. "Oh, hell! You think he'll be satisfied with a little bit?!" muttered Peter, "I know the type—you give them a quarter and they want a dollar; you give them ten minutes and they want an hour; give them a blanket and they wanna move into your house!!"

"This house is big enough," laughed Miranda, "Wait'll you see it!" Peter stared at her. "Look out!!" she called. He swerved around the corner, narrowly missing the bank. "Keep your eyes on the road," she giggled.

He took a deep breath. He could never stay mad at her for very long.

Five minutes later they were singing 'Ten Green Bottles' with enthusiastic but discordant harmonies as they rounded the bend towards the Mission.

"Don't believe this! I do not believe it," complained Peter as he shifted the Jeep into four-wheel drive.

The going was so painfully slow because, at this point, the road was barely wide enough to take the Jeep. The road snaked around the side of a sheer rock butte that was jagged and split with fine, horizontal cracks. Its crumbling had scattered the road with geometric fragments like hundreds of small dice.

"It's lovely," cooed Miranda, "Look!"

To the left of the track was a fifty-foot drop onto a river bed strewn with a morass of branches and stones. Peter assayed a quick glance. "Looks like someone just threw all that down there." He grinned, despite his complaining, "It's a mess, isn't it?"

"It's a lovely mess," said Miranda happily.

Despite his querulous tone, Peter was happy too. Here they were, going to 'inspect a property with intent to buy', and only a few months ago they'd barely been able to pay their PG&E bills.

"Floods!" yelled Peter, glancing down at the river as the Jeep whined and protested around the bend.

"How do you know?" asked Miranda glancing at him with her usual admiring expression.

"Look down there, at the trees trapped in the rocks—no foliage. It's old growth. Why, I bet you that little trickle down there is a muddy torrent in the winter."

Miranda nodded, looking down at the torn limbs of trees wedged carelessly between the sun-bleached boulders. The stream was little more than a trickle, snaking and twisting and, at times, disappearing altogether under the rocks.

"Yeah. Remember, Healdsville was flooded completely last year," yelled Peter, "And that's only fifteen miles from here. I saw pictures of the townspeople wading waist high in the Main Street. Remember? A kid was drowned in his own garden!"

Miranda nodded, awed. It was difficult to think of floods at the height of the arid north Californian summer. The sierra grass was baked to a golden brown on hills dotted with scrub oak and manzanita struggling for survival.

"Here!" she yelled so sharply that Peter nearly drove off the road. "Stop, Peter! Look!"

As the motor died, the sounds of the valley suddenly sprang into life: the distant gurgle of the stream; the faint soughing of the wind as it sifted through the branches of the pepperwoods clinging to the steep slopes of the river.

Miranda was over the side of the Jeep before the dust had even settled, her sandals scrunching on the gravel. Peter followed her, coughing and fanning the dust from his eyes. "Nice place to stop!" he complained good-naturedly.

"Oh, it is! Look!" cried Miranda, and pointed. "Impressed?"

They stood on the crown of a road which descended steeply to the valley below, ran up to a stone buttress, took an abrupt right, then disappeared around the corner. Framed by the rock buttress, was the Mission.

Peter nodded—it *was* impressive. Behind the property was the smooth dome of a hill, rearing up like a huge golden beast, sparsely dotted with oak and black walnut. It was an artist's dream. The vast golden mound of the hill formed the backdrop for the Mission lands nestling in the foreground. The bright silver necklace of a river ran around the base of the hill, separating the mound from the Mission. In the foreground was the Mission itself, hewn out of an ancient mossy stone like an ancient castle, with that lovely greenish hue which only time can bring. The grounds were encircled completely by an ivy-infested wall that ran along the front of the property, took an acute turn on the west side, then was lost to sight.

But it was the Tree that made Peter gape.

From this distance, Peter assessed the height of the two-storey Mission to be at least forty feet—and the Tree towered above it; a huge, dark-green mass that obliterated most of the front of the building.

"God! Look at that Tree!" he muttered, "It must be ancient! I've never seen anything like it!"

Miranda was dancing up and down, beside herself with joy. "It's wonderful, isn't it?!"

Peter had to concede that it was.

Miranda pointed. "See that?" To the east of the Mission was an L-shaped wood-frame building. "That," said Miranda, "Is—guess. What?"

"An aeroplane? A UFO? A gold-manufacturing machine?" joked Peter.

"No, silly. It's a theater, a real live theater. And the other building by it is a workshop. Oh, Peter!" She did a little twirling dance, kicking up clouds of dust, "You'll be able to build lots of wonderful machines, and I'll be able to dance on the stage!"

Peter faked a coughing bout as the dust devils whirled up around him. "Hey! I agree! I agree! Stop it or you'll choke me with positivity!" Miranda settled down to an agitated skip while Peter studied the property with a shrewd, craftsman's eye. "One…two…three…" He counted the windows of the Mission that were visible before they were lost to sight, obscured by the huge Tree. "Let me see… Mmm, I bet there are at least thirty rooms!" he said, surprised.

"And a library and a study. And look…!" Miranda was still jumping up and down as if she had ants in her pants, "That building behind the main building—to the north of it. That's where the animals were kept. Oh, my goodness!" she twirled again.

"Thirty bedrooms?!" frowned Peter, "Theater, animals?! God, Miranda, what are we going to do with this?!"

"Do?! Oh, my goodness! Do?!!" Miranda looked like she was about to explode with excitement, "Don't you see? It's going to be an Artist's Retreat!

It's what I've always wanted—a place where people can come and be alone and work on their books or their paintings, or whatever, in the right kind of atmosphere. Do you like the idea?"

So her secret was out. As much as he wanted to tease her, Peter kept a straight face, though it was an effort. "A retreat? Mmmm. I'll say it is—it's almost inaccessible." He pointed at the main building, "God knows where they got that stone from. And that..." His finger traced out the heavy outline of something that glinted like a spider's web, arching over the Tree in a dome, "What in tarnation is that?!"

"Oooh, no more words! C'mon, let's see now." Miranda jumped into the Jeep and hopped up and down until Peter climbed in and, with deliberate precision, began to ease the Jeep forward so slowly that Miranda couldn't contain herself. She wacked him on the shoulder: "Hurry!!" she urged

"Right, Miss," teased Peter with a mock, deferential bow, "At your service..."

"Oooh!" cried Miranda in exasperation, never taking her eyes off the Mission.

The Jeep rumbled down the road trailing a vast plume of grayish dust, completely obscuring its own tracks...

CHAPTER FOUR

"Look at this," said Peter as he fiddled with the Mission gate lock. As thick as a man's forefinger, the key was a scrolled antique of hand-beaten iron. "And this…" said Peter as he hefted the padlock in his hand. "Worth twenty bucks in scrap metal," he joked.

Miranda was silent. She was staring at the sign above the gate arch; a sign fashioned from the same blackened and pitted oak as the huge double gate. "Look, I never noticed that before." She pointed.

The sign spanned the two heavy pillars of the gate portals in a stylized wooden arch, supported at either end by rusted iron bolts an inch thick. The sign was cracked and mottled, bleached by sun and rain, but some of the words could just be deciphered.

"A…L…A…V…E…R…A," Miranda spelled out, "What a lovely name. Like Aloe Vera—that's so green and healing."

"Sounds Spanish," said Peter, "Wonder what it means?"

"Alavera Mission," chimed Miranda, "We're going to be monks and nuns!"

Peter was busy trying to push open the gate. He heaved against it with a brawny shoulder. But though it wagged inwards a little, it didn't give. Puffing with the exertion, he stopped. "However did you manage to get in last time?"

"I didn't," said Miranda, "I've never been in."

"But how about all this info you're clued-up on? The workshop, the theater?"

"Oh, I read about that in the Estate Agent's handout and drove down to take a look at it from the hill. Do you realize that we're both setting foot on *our* property for the very first time!"

"Our property?!" echoed Peter. "Oho, so you've decided already?"

"Well haven't you?" said Miranda, her eyes sparkling.

"Mmm, I dunno," said Peter cautiously, "We've got to look at the place first." But in his heart of hearts, Peter had already decided. "One, two, three…" He thrust at the gate again and, with a squeal of metal on wood, it swung back and they stepped into the Mission yard.

"Oooh!" gasped Miranda.

"Well look at that!" said Peter overawed.

Dominating the courtyard, crowding out the entire Mission, seeming to take possession of the very sky itself, was the ancient Tree…

Behind the Mission, a dark shape stirred under the privet hedge surrounding an empty swimming pool. A pair of blue jays perched on the house eaves watched the movement with beady, glittering eyes.

The shadowy shape, discernable only as a slight parting of the grass, began to worm through the thick undergrowth towards the house. It paused, then suddenly flitted across the yard and down some crumbling steps to a weathered cellar door. The door squeaked open, rending the silence, and the blue jays took to the air shrieking madly. The door slammed shut with a jarring thud. The birds settled back into the branches of a fig tree but hopped back and forth in agitation, watching the closed cellar door warily...

Peter looked up. "What was that?"

Without taking her eyes off the Tree, Miranda muttered: "Squirrels. Blue jays always fight with squirrels."

Peter nodded and craned his neck in wonder, staring up at the Tree. "My oh my," he sighed, shaking his head, all thoughts of squirrels and blue jays thrust out of his mind by the impressive sight before them:

A tangled mass of green almost as long as the Mission, the Tree's canopy was at least a hundred and twenty feet wide. Dwarfing the building, it was close to seventy feet in height. Gnarled branches twisted through the air like grotesque, oversized human limbs; the massive trunk itself sat squat and low, black roots driven into the earth like a baleful insect about to arch up and spring on its prey.

"My God," whispered Peter, craning his neck backwards, "How does it manage to support its own weight?"

He walked around the base of the massive trunk, puzzling over the Tree's identity. Madrone? No, too big. Oak? No, the bark was wrong for oak—too smooth. Yes, it was more like madrone with its flesh-like texture patterned at the branch intersections like the whorls and wrinkles of human skin.

"It's a bit like madrone, isn't it?" muttered Peter. Miranda did not answer and Peter remembered ruefully how upset she'd been when they'd chainsawed a madrone tree back home and found it stained red at its heart—just like a severed human limb. Madrone? He didn't press the point. It was madrone-like, but it couldn't be a madrone, the branch configuration was all wrong—and the size!

A noise from Miranda broke into his reverie and he trotted around the huge bole to see her kneeling and pointing silently.

Peter gasped.

Like the multi-taloned claw of some giant bird, the gnarled roots of the Tree coiled and gripped around a vault half-sunken into the black earth.

"My goodness! It's like a mythical bird guarding a box of treasure," whispered Miranda.

The vault, hewn from the same greenish, moss-covered granite as the Mission walls, was almost hidden from sight by the snake-like root sections that encoiled it in a death-tight grip. Just above ground level, two squarish openings peeked blindly out from between the roots. The vault's surface hinted at ornate, carved patterns, blurred hieroglyphics and gargoyles, but they were weather-worn, almost lost to sight beneath the clutching limbs.

Peter shook his head in wonder. The vault was old; very old. Who would build such a thing? It had obviously been constructed at the base of the Tree, then, in time, the Tree had overgrown it, surrounding the vault with its roots. Now thrust deep into the ground, the roots had trapped the vault forever in a gnarled and woody prison.

He turned and realized that Miranda was kneeling by the tree bole with a strange expression on her face, soft and dreamy. She let her cheek rest a moment on the ground, then lifted it slightly, fragments of dirty leaf adhering to her smooth skin. "This is a holy place," she whispered, "Can't you feel it? The Tree is the Life-Force of the Mission."

Peter shifted uncomfortably as he always did in the presence of Miranda's esoteria, but he was unusually silent. Even he had to admit the Tree was quite something.

Miranda rose to her feet, took a step back and stared upwards as though searching for something.

Beneath the gloom of the Tree's vast canopy, everything was tinged green. Even Miranda's hair was bleached of its natural gold; tinted the green-gold of russet. Palimpsests of light danced across her face like jewels. She swayed like a sea anemone caught by a faint, undersea current and, for a moment, she was like a creature from another world where sorcery and magic, spells and witchcraft held province and science and reason had not been discovered.

"Look… Look at the leaves," she whispered dreamily, "They're like umbrellas."

The huge leaves spread in a green shroud above the dark branches; the limp, green flags of new growth, each almost two feet across.

"I don't get it," said Peter, "I've never seen a tree like this anywhere in America. It's more like a tropical tree and those look like Paulownia leaves. Y'know, from the tree that old Mousey Tongue asked his loyal subjects to plant in China in 1958. But, it's not Paulownian…"

A slight breeze ruffled though the leaves and Miranda cried out: "There! Look!" She pointed.

Peter spotted a flash of crimson. "What is it?"

"Flowers!" she cried, clapping her hands, "I knew it would have flowers! It's a wonderful, wonderful Tree!" And, impulsively, she ran up to the huge bole and spreadeagled herself against the silvery-green bark, her eyes closed in ecstacy; like a willing human sacrifice. "It's the heart and soul of the land," she whispered, "The spirit of the Mission, older than time. It's felt the heat of the sun and the bite of the cold; the dirt and decay of hundreds of years have rotted and fed its roots. And it knows the land and the air like we'll never know them." And then, with a gesture that Peter would have found comic in anybody else, she turned, dropped on one knee and bowed to the Tree.

Peter, embarrassed, moved uncomfortably from one foot to the other and looked anywhere but straight at Miranda. Alright, he thought, it was a truly amazing phenomenon and he'd have to read upon it, try to find out the Tree's species. But enough was enough and *he* wanted to explore the rest of the property. He began to edge away from the silent Miranda and the gloomy green. "Miranda," he said hesitantly, "I'm going to, er, look around a bit more…"

As though hearing him from a great distance, Miranda lifted her head, slightly dazed. She seemed to notice Peter for the first time and smiled a friendly but bewildered smile. "Peter! What is it?!" she called. She began to follow him. "Where are you going?"

There was a sudden rustle of wind through the Tree and Peter stopped abruptly, feeling the ground tremble. The huge canopy swayed slightly, then was still again. "My God," muttered Peter, "The roots must go on forever! Did you feel that tremor?!"

"Oh, look!" cried Miranda delighted.

Like a tropical bird, a huge blossom detached itself and drifted down towards them, crimson and black. It settled on the ground, fluttered, then was still. Miranda ran forward and picked it up. "God, it's beautiful. Look!" She went as if to sniff it.

"Careful, Miranda," warned Peter, "It could be poisonous."

"With a scent like that?!" cried Miranda. She shook her head. "No, siree."

Peter could smell it already. Like a rich wine, it held a deep tawny musk, with another odor beneath that—pungent, alien. It stole across the intervening space, redolent of ancient rain forests and vegetation-dense landscapes that had flourished and died and flourished again long before man was on the Earth. "Phew! It's strong!" muttered Peter, "How come we aren't knocked over by the smell of the rest of them?" He craned his neck and searched the green canopy for other blossoms.

"It's the first, that's why!" said Miranda, clapping her side with glee, "We got the first blossom of the year!"

"It's hard to believe there's only one," muttered Peter eyeing the green canopy quizzically.

"Well, there is," pouted Miranda, "And I've got it. Look!" She fixed the huge blossom behind her ear and struck a Hawaiian maiden pose, "How's this?"

"More than a man can bear," said Peter dryly. This time, he wasn't kidding. "C'mon, let's look around." He spun on his heel and strode away.

Miranda held her nose between thumb and forefinger, plucking her throat in a comic imitation of a Hawaiian guitar, and ran out into the sunlight after Peter.

As Peter emerged from the gloomy green shade, the sun hit him full in the face and he realized dimly how much he'd missed it...

By the time they were ready to go, it was almost sunset.

They stopped the car once on the brow of the road—the same point at which they'd stopped on the way in. This time, they didn't get out.

Peter sat half turned in his seat. The sun was setting to the west of the Mission, flooding the buildings with golden light. Long shadows stole across the landscape and an occasional glint of fire winked off one of the Mission windows. "I don't get it," he muttered.

"What?" asked Miranda, eyes half closed, enchanted by the idyllic scene.

"A thirty room house, a swimming pool—albeit nonfunctional—a workshop, a theater and eleven hundred acres of good land—some of it still producing grapes—for $68,000. What's the catch?"

"There isn't one," said Miranda softly, "It's ours and we can buy it. Isn't that just wonderful?"

Peter was silent. He felt uneasy about the deal; something didn't ring true. Even for the land alone, the price was too low; and the buildings were sound—at least, the main building was. "I don't like it," he said, biting his lip. He shrugged his shoulders and started the engine. "Well, we'll check it out with Martinez."

"Oh, Peter!" cried Miranda, "We're going to buy it, aren't we?!!"

Her voice was suddenly so pathetic that Peter laughed out loud. He gave her hand a little squeeze and sighed. "I guess so."

"Oh, Peter!!" she cried, hugging him tightly.

He revved the engine and eased the Jeep around the bend, acutely aware of the steep drop to their right. "Hey, Miranda, let go, or we'll both be over the cliff!" Miranda relinquished her grip, but rested her hand affectionately on his knee.

The dust from the departing Jeep had not settled on the mountain road when, far below in the Mission, an upstairs window was abruptly closed.

CHAPTER FIVE

The bee hovered over the crimson and black flower which stood in a glass vase on the window ledge. The morning sun etched the dark pistils sharply against the crimson petals, each pistil laden with maroon-black pollen. The bee approached the pistils, hung suspended for a moment, then backed away without touching them and, veering off into the courtyard, zoomed out of sight.

Miranda sat by the window reading a book. She buried her teeth into a green apple and began chewing and reading simultaneously. "Mmmm…" she said through a mouthful of apple, "Here it is, O.K.…?"

Peter was pacing up and down restlessly amidst a pile of boxes and packing cases, clasping and unclasping his hands.

"'Of the genus of succulents with basal leaves and spicate flowers, Aloe Vera is renowned for its balm; used extensively in preparation for the skin and hair; it is soothing and healing…' What do you think?" asked Miranda brightly, "Aloe Vera Mission?"

Peter didn't respond.

"What's the matter, Pete?" asked Miranda gently.

Peter gazed out into the courtyard at the decaying ruin of a once-productive vegetable garden. "This, I guess." He pointed to the packing cases. "You know, I've been working my tail off for two years in the silver-refining business, building machines, getting the contracts for the film—and so on…"

Miranda nodded. "Yes—and I'm proud of you. Without all your work, we wouldn't be the owners of Aloe Vera Mission."

Peter plumped down onto a packing case. "I dunno. It's just that I've spent two years working on the machines, we've lived like church mice, struggling to pay the P.G.&E. bills each month, with everyone saying 'why don't you get a job?' or 'don't ask *us* for money, we'd like to be hippies, too'—and all that crap…" Miranda dropped her book and gazed at him sympathetically. "It's always the same," he continued fiercely, "No one gives a damn when you're not making it. They're ready to criticize, to put down what you're doing and say it's a dream, it's an illusion—why don't you grow up? Remember my father? Those were his exact words: 'Why don't you grow up?'"

"But you didn't," said Miranda. She hugged him. "Dear, dear Peter. You're so lucky. You're so practical, so scientific, so down-to-earth. But in another way you're more of a dreamer than me—except your dreams are dreams of the stars while I dream of the spaces between the stars. Don't you see why we fit so well, honey?" She slid her fingers together in a fluid motion, like a hand into a glove. She stared at him for a long time in silence, a worried look on her face.

He broke the silence, waving his arm in an agitated gesture. "I don't know what it *is* really. I've never been good at explaining my emotions. I've *done* it. We made it. Three franchises are pulling in enough money to keep us for the rest of our lives—even if the price of silver hits rock bottom. We'll never have to struggle again and yet I'm not happy, though I feel like I should be. It's something to do with this…" he pointed at the packing cases, "…the stuff we lugged over from the old place. You know, for the last two years, I never bothered about where I lived. I never even fixed the faucet!" He laughed. "God, I build these machines, each selling at $20,000 and never once did I get around to fixing the faucet. It was still leaking when we left! The toilet didn't flush properly!" He raised his hands up in the air. "I've *never* bothered about where I lived or what it looked like. And now I've got to worry about packing cases and bookshelves and desks and curtains and all that! It just seems so useless! Like a weight around my neck!"

Miranda's face cleared. "Oh, Peter," she laughed, and she hugged him and jiggled him up and down until his glasses fell off his nose.

"What? Why are you so happy suddenly? I don't get it."

"I do!" she exhorted, her eyes bright, "You're so funny! Did you ever hear the tale about the great astronomer who was so busy looking at the stars that he fell into a ditch?"

"Well??!" said Peter, still perplexed.

"Don't you realize what's happening?" asked Miranda mischievously, "You've had your nose so long to the grindstone and now suddenly the grindstone has stopped turning and you look up and, blowee!!, there you are!"

"Where?" said Peter even more perplexed.

"Here!!" shouted Miranda doing a little run and a ballet step, "Now! With me!!"

"And??" queried Peter.

"There's no *'and'*. That's it," said Miranda. "Peter, listen, you poor scientific nitwit. Kahlil Gibran talks about a man who spends his whole life looking for God and one day he finds God's house, walks up to the door, raises his hands to knock then, suddenly, instead of knocking, he runs like hell!"

"Why?" asked Peter mystified.

"Because the meaning of his life was the search itself. If he'd got what he wanted there would be no meaning. And that's what's wrong with you, my lovely Alchemist."

"So what?" said Peter sourly, "I still don't want to bother with all this crap." He pointed at the packing cases, "Or sorting out these bedrooms or…" He groaned at the thought of having to make the house livable.

"But you don't have to!" cried Miranda, "That's exactly what I mean! You don't have to do anything you don't want to! You're so used to doing things that suddenly, faced with the prospect of nothing to do, it all seems so much!" She knelt and put her golden head in his lap, "Suddenly my Astronomer's world is not bigger than a few packing cases and empty rooms, and he doesn't like it. He wants to reach for the stars again."

"I guess you're right," said Peter running his fingers through her hair appreciatively, "God, aren't I an ungrateful wretch?! I've got more money than I ever had in my life and the most beautiful girl in the world and I'm complaining!"

"Peter," said Miranda looking up at him with her eyes shining, "Do you ever remember as a kid moving house with your parents?"

"I'll say," said Peter, "Tell me about it! The American disease—mobility. We did it at least four times."

"Yes," said Miranda, "And while you ran around as a kid exploring and excited, making castles out of the packing boxes and finding hidden treasures in dirty attics and muddy cellars, you parents bickered and got bad-tempered and argued about where to put this and what to do with that…"

"Yes," said Peter, "How do you know?"

"'Cos parents always do," said Miranda with a grin, "That's the way they are. The point is, to the kids it was a big adventure. To the parents it was a job—a big drag. What I'm saying is we can afford to be the kids!" She spread her hands, "We don't have to do *anything* with this place. We'll just play in the packing cases and explore the attics and find hidden treasures in the cellars. And we'll live out of cases like we're camping out, just passing through! We don't have to unpack!! We're free!!"

Peter couldn't help but laugh. He stroked her head and shook her good-naturedly. "Do you think for one minute that I could do that? That's you, not me. You're the only person I know who could spend $68,000 on a place then camp out in it!"

"Why not? When it's time, we'll do things—and not before. Look, there's no proper heating or cooling system, for instance. But we don't have to do anything about that until we feel like it."

"Mmm, Christ, the winter is coming…heating? I never thought of that." Peter mused for a moment, lost in his own thoughts. Then he muttered half-aloud: "You know, with solar panels this place could…" He suddenly had a vision of a house he'd read about in Montana that had no fuel bills, recycled its water, that even made a slight profit on the vegetables it grew in hydroponic tanks. "A closed ecosystem—that's an idea!" He pulled a pencil out of his top pocket and began to make sketches and calculations on the top of a cardboard box. "Yep, and the water from the river… Well, we'd have to check the public rights on that one…" He muttered to himself and began to sketch even more furiously. Soon he became so absorbed in his task that Miranda was completely forgotten.

Miranda stood back and smiled a slow, secret smile. She wet her finger and traced in the dust on top of a packing case 'I love you, my Alchemist' where Peter could see it when he looked up from his labors. Then she went to the door, where she called softly, "Want something to eat, Kahlil?" a winsome smile on her face.

"Eh? What? No thanks," muttered Peter absorbed, "Later…later…"

Miranda glided out of the room and looked back at him once more, her face soft with affection. So, while her man once more reached for the stars, Miranda went off to build castles out of packing cases, find sorcerer's secrets in dirty attics and to prepare magic meals out of tin cans.

CHAPTER SIX

Miranda shifted in her sleep and turned over. Her arm fell across Peter's chest. He snorted in his sleep and moved his head, but did not wake.

They were lying on the floor on a makeshift mattress in one of the Mission rooms. Except for their mattress, the room was bare. At the far end, moonlight poured through a nave-like window grille, throwing a distorted black and silver pattern on the stone floor.

Miranda was awake, puzzled, aware of a rich, heady scent. The heavy pungency seemed to crowd against the very walls; to beat silently against the floor and ceiling like a physical presence. Miranda took a deep breath and smiled. It was delicious. She snaked one foot out from under the sheets and touched the cold floor with her toe and withdrew it with a shiver.

Then she heard it: At first, just a faint murmur, but slowly it grew louder. She held her head cocked, listening intently. Then her eyes widened and she sat up gently, careful not to wake Peter.

The checkered puddle of moonlight shimmered and blurred on the floor as a faint breeze stirred through the Tree outside, and a fresh wave of scent assailed Miranda with redoubled strength. She could hear the singing more distinctly now—faint, but clear. Men's voices, rising and falling in a sonorous rhythm like an old Gregorian chant.

Miranda's mouth fell open in delight. She slipped out of bed and padded silently across the floor in her bare feet. As if to greet her, a faint breeze fluttered through the window, billowing out her cotton nightdress and wafting her hair in a cascade of silver around her shoulders.

Gently, she unhooked the hasp of the iron shutter and swung it inwards. Long unused, it opened with a grating squeak. She held her breath and glanced over to the patch of darkness that was the bed. Peter grunted in his sleep, but did not waken.

Miranda turned her face to the window.

Moonlight poured onto her in a silvery munificence, and the heady blossom scent was thick in her nostrils. Inundated by the twin assault of light and scent, she swayed as these silent assassins threatened to steal her senses. For a moment, she felt like she might fall…and keep falling and falling into a sea of silver-green. She struggled weakly against the overpowering sensation, but it stole through her senses until, with an inner thrill, she let go and surrendered to the sensation as if to a lover.

The singing grew louder. Deep and sonorous, it drifted through the Tree, resonating in the spaces between the shadowy foliage. In a counterpoint of light, the moon dappled through the latticework of leaves, dancing across Miranda's wide-open eyes in motes of molten silver.

The sonorous booming grew, accompanied by the clink of livery and the thud of horses' hooves; metal on stone. With a lazy smile, Miranda slowly lifted up her arms, slim and silvered, palms upturned to the sea of light. Shadow and scent, silver and sound beat down on her relentlessly and soon she began to sway with the rhythm, caught in the undertow of a deep, mellow chant.

A single blossom silently detached itself from the Tree and drifted downwards in a liquid, spiralling slow motion that seemed to defy the tug of gravity. Its color, oddly vibrant, untouched by the moonlight, was blood red. Down, down it drifted until it touched the ground. It quivered then fell sideways and settled against one of the huge gnarled roots, twitched slightly, and for a moment was lost in the gloom. Then the shadowy canopy of the Tree shifted as in a faint wind, and a beam of moonlight probed between the dark flags of the leaves, its shaft lancing down to strike the blood-red blossom.

For a second, the blossom seemed to flare with an inner intensity, then its color ebbed away like blood running into sand, and the blossom lay glistening in the beam of moonlight, white as bleached bone.

Miranda stood at the window, arms outstretched in supplication, her eyes wide, pupils dilated; seeing and yet not seeing.

As the color drained from the blossom, the mellow chant boomed once, twice, fell back with a haunting echo; then all was silent.

A strange sadness pricked Miranda's breast. She blinked and shook her head, dazed, and when she looked again, the blossom was gone, lost in the gloom beneath the dark mass of the Tree.

The moon slipped out of sight behind a shifting mass of leaves, darkness rolled across Miranda's face like a heavy black fog and she cried out in distress. She stood for a moment, helpless, then she dropped her arms and turned away from the window, heavy with a sense of loss. She padded towards the mattress and slid in between the sheets.

Peter half woke in the darkness to feel Miranda slide into the bed, ice-cold. He muttered to himself and instinctively wrapped his arms around her icy body.

Miranda shivered and her teeth began to chatter. It was a long time before she felt warm again. But Peter did not notice. He was deep in a heavy, unnatural sleep…

Peter was drowning; deep down beneath a bottle-green sea. Strange fish-like shapes glided and brushed against him in the icy-cold, greenish gloom. Shafts of sunlight probed wanly but failed to penetrate the depths. Peter kicked and struggled upwards, but the surface was still too far away. His chest began to heave and he fought the urge to open his mouth and swallow huge lungfuls of greenish water. He began writhing and struggling madly in a desperate attempt to reach the surface, to break out into the light; to fill his lungs with life-giving air. His chest was swelling; bursting. In a final frenzied paroxysm, he jetted upwards, broke through the dappled surface of the water and... There! His chest heaved; he tore at his eyes; bright sunlight suddenly blinded him; and he was taking vast lungfuls of life-giving air.

"What!!!???" Peter cried, and Miranda was suddenly jerked awake as Peter tore the filmy green thing from over his face and took in great lungfuls of air. Panicked, Peter gazed around, blinded by the bright light, not knowing where he was. He squinted. He seemed to be laying in a vast pool of green. Sunlight shafted from a bright shape above him, forming a distorted rectangle on the pool's surface.

"Peter!" cried Miranda sitting upright, all harvest-gold hair and creamy white skin against the green.

"Jesus!!" cried Peter, still swallowing air, "Who opened the shutters?!"

The bedroom was carpeted with a thick layer of the huge leaves; limp, green flags that lay across everything—including the bed, Peter and Miranda.

Miranda cried out with delight and clapped her hands. "How lovely! Our home is being blessed by Nature!"

"Phew!" muttered Peter, still a little breathless, "I don't know about blessed." He glanced about. "No wonder the shutters were locked! Look at those leaves! One of these things landed full on my face! God, I couldn't breathe! I felt as though I was drowning! You know, one of those funny waking dreams."

Miranda looked at him cat-eyed and hugged the sheet around her nakedness. "You know," she said slowly, "I had such a weird dream last night..."

Peter wagged a finger at her. "Too many psychedelics in the Sixties."

"Peter!" she said shocked, "Drugs!! I never did that!"

"Only joking," he yawned, fully recovered from his rude awakening. He lay back and clasped his hands behind his head. "Mmm," he said thoughtfully, "I wonder what time breakfast is served in this establishment? I'm starving."

"Well, I guess it comes when you make it," grinned Miranda. Then she suddenly flopped a big green leaf down over his face and leapt out of the bed and ran, screaming in mock fear, as he bellowed and snatched the air where she'd been a second before. A moment later, she peered around the door and extended a long, smooth, naked leg seductively. Then she popped her whole head around the door and said: "Sire, if it would please ye, would ye give your slave the pleasure of servin' your Lordship's breakfast while 'e's a'bed all mornin'?"

"Oh, two eggs over easy, mushrooms, tomatoes and a pork chop," said Peter unperturbed by her scenario.

"Pork chop! Eagh!" said Miranda in disgust, "Animal eater!" She was an ardent vegetarian.

But she made the breakfast anyway.

Peter was pulling on his jeans and buckling his belt when she came back with the tray. "Miranda!" he cried in gratitude.

And there was breakfast, set out perfectly. Especially for the occasion, Miranda had donned a fresh white smock edged in tiny lace flowers. Behind her ear perched a huge crimson blossom. She curtseyed whimsically and set the tray down besides the bed. "Zorry, Zire, oi didna' get it ready a'fore ye was out of bed," she said humbly.

Peter grinned. "Your Medieval accent sounds like a cross between German and Irish." He scratched his head and looked at the tray appreciatively.

Nestling on the plate were two perfect eggs—firm whites, soft yolks—neatly-diced tomatoes; plump, grilled mushrooms; a cup of rich, dark coffee; a glass of orange juice; and, in a white vase, a freshly-picked bunch of daisies, buttercups and honeysuckle. "Why, it's lovely, Miranda," said Peter genuinely, "What a great start to the day…"

She gave him a huge, full-mouthed kiss and snuggled up to him. "You deserve it," she said, her face glowing.

"So, I'm going to be a vegetarian whether I like it or not?" he asked picking up his knife and fork. Then he added hastily, "Not that I'm complaining."

She looked puzzled. "What do you mean?"

"No pork chop," he said through a mouthful of egg.

"But there wasn't any. I was going to make two for you, even though I hate it—just as a treat. But I couldn't find any."

"Hey," he said, putting his fork down, "I put a packet of pork chops out on top of the fridge last night—a barbecue packet. There must have been twelve chops there! I put them there to thaw out for breakfast, knowing…" he grinned, "…that *you* wouldn't touch them."

"Nope," said Miranda, "No siree. You check it out."

So, a puzzled Peter got up and went to look in the kitchen.

"Hey!" Miranda called, "Your breakfast is getting cold!"

"Miranda!" he shouted. Something in the tone of his voice made her leave the bedroom and follow him into the kitchen.

Peter was standing by the open kitchen window. "Look," he said, pointing.

On the window sill was a scuff of fresh dirt and below on the worn linoleum, a sprinkling of damp soil.

"We've had intruders."

"Oh, Peter," she said alarmed, "Burglars? Vandals?!"

Peter laughed. "Out here?" He looked up through the kitchen window at the vast golden bank of the sierra. He swept his arm out to encompass the landscape. "Huh! If someone had enough spunk to go creeping around this

area in the dark, I'd give them a medal. It's too isolated, honey. Nope…" He
eyed the marks on the floor, "Must have been an animal—racoons, maybe. So
we'd better keep the doors closed and the windows barred, or else…"

"Or else what?" asked Miranda with a fearful expression.

"Or else…" Peter suddenly pulled a horrible face and hooked his fingers
into talons and began to advance on her, "Ze monster will coom and bury his
fangs in your soft, white body!"

Miranda gave a yelp and raced out of the door into the sunlight. He ran
after her, roaring and growling horribly as she screamed and ran around the
yard in mock agitation.

They were so intent on their game that neither of them heard the scrape
of wood on stone as the cellar door was hastily pulled shut.

CHAPTER SEVEN

Peter scaled the last few feet of the aluminum ladder, blinked in the afternoon sun, and swung a leg over the parapet of the roof.

Below, Miranda anxiously clutched the light metal ladder and stilled its thrumming. "Be careful, Peter!" she called, "It seems so shaky!"

"It's O.K.," he called back, "Go and play in the attic."

She smiled and waved back lovingly, and ducked out of sight into the kitchen.

Peter turned and walked gingerly across the roof, not too sure of the stability of such an old roof. He stopped, taken aback by the sight in front of him:

It was as though he were on a huge square raft floating on a green sea. The Tree was to the right of the roof, but it was so big—stretching almost the whole length of the Mission house—that the roof.seemed to hover beside it like a boat anchored to a green shore, drifting slightly in a gentle current.

The Tree was now covered with the crimson blossoms, like daubs of blood on a shifting green shroud.

Peter tested the roof by easing his weight onto one foot then the other, and took a hesitant step forward. Dried leaves crackled underfoot, making him uneasy. The whole roof was covered with them.

Peter could smell the heady blossoms now. The scent hit him with a pungent blast. Vaguely, he wondered why he hadn't noticed it before. The heat of the sun, the searing crimson of the blossoms and the vivid lime green of the fresh leaves seemed to glare angrily into his eyes. The sensation was so strong that it made Peter sway. He instantly regretted leaving his sun hat below, but he'd only slipped onto the roof for a moment just to make a few preliminary measurements for his solar panel project.

With an effort, he pulled his eyes away from the shifting sea of green and took a hundred-foot tape out of the small bag over his shoulder. With his foot he scraped a path through the leaves close to the parapet, choosing the side furthest away from the Tree. Close to the parapet would be an area of maximum support, he reasoned, and he shuffled through the dried leaves, kicking them aside gingerly, until he'd made a pathway exposing a narrow strip of ancient black pitch.

Peter smacked an eight-penny nail into the crumbling masonry of the parapet, hooked the steel eye of the cloth tape over the nail and began to back away slowly, paying the tape out as he went. His peripheral vision caught the field of green and its crimson smudges to his left, while to his right beat the brassy gold of the sun.

He shuffled backwards through the crackling leaves. The tape etched a line between the two worlds, bright in the yellow sunlight: leaf-green one side; sun-gold the other.

Eight feet, nine feet, ten feet… He had a sudden odd sensation as he paid the tape out; as if the swaying length of the cloth tape was a rope and he was lowering himself into an abyss further and further away from the safety of the wall into a dangerous quagmire of crackling, dead leaves. He stopped and realized that his shirt was damp with sweat. He shook off a feeling of uneasiness and tried to concentrate on his task, muttering to himself about the effect of heat.

Twelve feet, thirteen feet… With renewed confidence, he quickened his backward pace.

Fifteen, sixteen, seventeen… A wind rippled through the Tree and the blossom smell was suddenly overwhelming in his nostrils.

Peter resisted the impulse to take a deep breath of the cloying air. He began moving backwards more slowly. Then he stopped and listened again. He could hear a noise. 'Putter putter', it went, coming from nowhere in particular. He shook his head, muttering at his own stupidity for not covering his head. The 'puttering' increased—and then he recognized it: Rain!

Startled, he glanced up to the sky. A mistake: the sun jabbed into his eyeballs like two sharp gimlets. He clapped his hands to his temples and fell, blinded. He dropped down to one knee, fireballs dancing in front of his tightly-closed eyelids; white and orange. He scrabbled blindly in the leaves, somehow fearful of losing the tape. Then he stopped, his eyes still tight-shut:

The leaves were wet.

It was raining. He could feel it; pouring down his head, plastering his hair to his forehead, running down his neck.

Puzzled, he blinked open his eyes and assayed a cautious look. The lights still danced before his eyes; bright spots that bloomed and span. He winced in pain, shut his eyes and re-opened them to peer out between fluttering, wet eyelids. And saw cobalt gloom and…dark shapes looming in the driving rain.

He shielded his forehead with a cupped palm and squinted into the dense blue-black of the downpour. He was surrounded: stiff, unmoving shapes circled him in the gloom. A patch of red or white gleamed occasionally through the somber shadows. One of the shadows detached itself from the others and glided forward. Peter glimpsed a short, squat body clad in animal skins, a broad, leathery face surmounted by a nodding black and white feather and two daubs of orange paint on the man's cheeks.

The man raised his right hand. He held something in it; he pointed this at Peter and uttered a single word in an unknown tongue: The world flooded a reddy-orange and Peter realized that the hissing and crackling in his ears was his frantic scrabbling in the dry leaves. He opened his eyes cautiously, wary of the pain behind his eyelids.

The tape stretched out, thin and yellow, across the brown leaves, but the nearest end was twisted and contorted like a long snake, the leaves around it raked and scattered where Peter had scrabbled frantically. The sun beat down in a merciless yellow flood. Everything was sun bleached; bone dry. There was not a trace of rain.

Peter rewound the tape warily and made his way back to the ladder. The light hurt so much, he had to close his eyes frequently. He straddled the parapet, found the ladder with his feet and inched his way downwards, cautiously reaching one foot down behind him and finding a firm footing before he moved the other.

In this way, he descended very slowly until, halfway from the ground, he felt the light metal frame thrum beneath his clenched fingers. The ladder slipped sideways and with a yell, Peter was pitched into the air and fell twenty feet, twisting and writhing. Then, 'whump!', there was the ground and he blacked out as the impact drove the air from his lungs.

He fought to retain consciousness, then Miranda was kneeling over him, frantic with concern. "Peter, Peter! Why didn't you call me? You know that ladder's not safe! Oh, Peter, are you alright?!" She clenched and unclenched her hands in agitation until he sat up slowly and examined the damage.

His shoulder was bruised and he had a gash in his right knee, but otherwise, nothing serious. Peter tried a conciliatory smile but it hurt so much that it turned into an ugly grimace. "I gotta go to bed," he muttered, "My head hurts."

Miranda nodded, whitefaced, and helped him to his feet. Together they staggered into the Mission building.

The cool gloom of the interior cut across the pain in Peter's eyes like a soothing balm. "Phew," he muttered, "Made a bad mistake. This sun is not to be taken lightly. We should wear hats, Miranda. It really got to me."

"Sshh, sshh," cooed Miranda, "It's O.K. First things first." She eased him onto the mattress, then dashed to the fridge to return with a bag of ice.

She spent the afternoon running her cool fingers through his damp hair, administering to his knee and shoulder and putting fresh ice packs on his hot forehead until, eventually, Peter fell into a feverish half-doze.

His sleep was haunted by images of short, squat natives dressed in skins and feathers, dancing in strange patterns and circles as meaningless to Peter as the dream itself.

He awoke hours later. It was dark.

Miranda lay next to him, long and cool, a white, naked blur in the gloom. "Peter?" she whispered fearfully, "Are you better??".

He squeezed her hand. "It's O.K. I had a touch of sunstroke, that's all. I'm feeling O.K. now."

"I'm glad," she whispered.

He looked up at the window and, for a moment, saw the moon through the crisscross pattern of the grille and the moody silhouette of the Tree. Then the leaves shifted and the room was plunged into gloom; a restless gloom…a shadow prison of shapeless blurs.

Peter shivered in the dark involuntarily. "Goddamn fool," he muttered to himself. But he held onto Miranda tightly until they both fell into a troubled sleep.

SUMMER

'Tree patterns are three dimensional and tend to be symmetrical because they are traced in the air by radiations of light. Each day, the radiant energy of the sun first strokes a tree from the East, then floods it from a constantly higher angle as the sun travels up and over the tree. Then, descending, it paints the opposite side of the tree with sunlight, until the light is suddenly shut off at the western horizon. A tree is molded in the open air by the curving torch of light... Chlorophyll performs life's most majestic feat by trapping the weightless energy in light— the sunlight is stored, ready to be released at any later time. Man, in his most advanced science, is unable to duplicate this storage of energy, neither in its simplicity nor its enormous latent power...'

Rutherford Platt
The Great American Forest

CHAPTER EIGHT

Peter crunched away on the piece of toast, stared at Miranda and chewed in redoubled irritation.

He was displeased.

Not with his labors or the progress of the farm—during the last two months a great deal had been accomplished.

He was displeased with Miranda.

She held the fruit between her palms. A curious combination of grape and mulberry, the berries clustered plumply together around a central stem, deep purple in color. Rich and heavy.

"Miranda, you've no idea what that Tree is. Neither do I," said Peter in between furious bites on his toast.

"I know it's O.K.," she said, dangling the fruit in front of her mouth sensually, her eyes half closed dreamily. "Mmm, I can smell it. It's like a cross between raspberry, blackberry and pears. It smells lovely."

"Yeah? And so will you if you eat it and keel right over on the floor. You know as well as I do that you shouldn't eat fruits or berries that you're not sure of!"

They sat at a rough-hewn wooden table outside the kitchen, shaded by a canvas awning from the morning sun. Peter had erected a scaffold on the roof to aid him with his labors, and this had been extended into an awning so that they could dine outside.

Miranda was now a golden brown, her face thickly dusted with freckles. Peter was almost mahogany; his face brown and leathery with the sun. He scowled at Miranda and his tan looked even darker.

Miranda dangled the heavy fruit in front of her nose, then said with a regretful sniff: "O.K. Peter. *But* I'm going to get some books and read up on it. The Indians used to live off the land around here. Look…" she pointed at a bush, "…no one eats manzanita nowadays and the word means 'little apples' in Spanish. The Indians loved to eat them."

"Well," said Peter appeased, "If you can find out what the Tree is called and some accurate description of what that fruit is, you *can* eat it—but not before. Look, I'm only thinking of your health." She smiled and squeezed his hand across the table. He caught sight of his wrist watch and cried: "Ooops, I've got to go." He looked up at the morning sun. "I'll get *nothing* done if I leave it much later."

He was referring to his flea-market passion. Peter was a true swap-meet veteran. Miranda hated them. To her, the swap-meet was the 'droppings of a society bent on obsolescence, consumerism and over-abuse of the Earth's natural resources'. Peter agreed heartily, but somehow that abstract belief didn't stop his passion for the old, the bizarre and the occasional bargain that turned up in the mounds of rubbish. Despite their recent influx of wealth, Peter, out of long habit, deemed it unnecessary to pay exorbitant prices for objects which could be bought cheaply after a morning's snooping at a swap-meet.

"Just leave the table to the Animal," joked Miranda.

Peter frowned. She was referring to the unknown animal that stole anything that they did not lock away overnight. Neither of them had been able to locate its 'nest', nor, indeed had they even seen it. Peter had wanted to put down some traps or even poison, but Miranda had raised such a hue and cry that the matter had been dropped. Miranda regarded their table scraps as a form of Natural Welfare. Peter could have sworn that at times she deliberately left some of the tastier morsels on her plate for the 'Animal'.

"O.K.," he shrugged, "Let's leave it for the Animal."

She hugged him, plopped on a huge straw sun hat and, tying it beneath her chin, struck a humble pose. "Thank you, my Lord."

"God, you're so sarcastic when you want to be," said Peter without heat. "Well, Madam Miranda, when you gotta go, you gotta go—and I gotta go." He kissed her on the cheek and went out.

Miranda followed him to the front of the building, holding his arm. He jumped into the Jeep and she kissed him again passionately.

Miranda stood waving goodbye as the Jeep roared out of the gates in a cloud of dust. She stood watching until the Jeep bumped across the dusty field and mounted the road that circled the hill—a minuscule toy vehicle in the distance with a cloud of dust hovering above it. The Jeep slowed as it turned the corner and Miranda heard the horn beep faintly. She waved again. Then it disappeared round the bend.

Miranda remained unmoving, enjoying the silence of the garden, broken only by the buzz of insects. The Jeep reappeared briefly as a cloud of dust further along the road. Then it was gone, leaving only a faint noise that was no louder than the insect hum. Then the noise died away completely.

Miranda gazed wistfully at the huge, green umbrella of the Tree and the luscious, dangling fruits, her mouth set in a compressed line. Then, with an impish expression, she strode up to the table outside the house, picked up the heavy fruit lying on the plate there, and took a huge bite.

It was delicious. She closed her eyes and chewed it slowly, savoring the strange, musty, bitter-sweet taste. Suddenly, she pulled a face as she realized she was breaking her promise to Peter and, with a guilty start, she hastily replaced the fruit on the plate. But her mouth was a stained, bloody gash, and she licked her lips furtively. She wiped her mouth with the back of her hand

and exclaimed as it smeared her wrist with a blood-red streak.

"Oh dear," she said out loud, remorse welling in her breast.

She gazed at the vegetable garden where Peter's homemade irrigation sprinklers blithely threw out jeweled drops of water in a lazy spiral onto the neat, serried rows of freshly-planted vegetables. Miranda went over to the garden and uprooted a handful of the lemon balm that was springing up like wildfire across the sawdust-sprinkled pathway. She knelt at the water sprinkler, wet her mouth and scrubbed her lips clean with the sweet, lemony tang of the bright green leaves.

She threw the soiled rubbings down and inhaled the fresh lemon smell with a satisfied smile, and began to inspect the garden. Eggplant, onion, garlic, squash, tomato and bell pepper stood in geometrically precise rows like soldiers. "Peter," she muttered, "You are so *orderly*." Each row was divided from its neighbor by a two-by-six redwood plank driven edge-on into the soil. And everywhere, Peter's sprinkler system was making great, wet spirals on the sawdust he'd laid down the paths to keep the weeds away.

It was lovely. She pondered how much she valued Peter and, involuntarily, her hand went to her freshly-scrubbed mouth as she realized again she'd broken her promise...

"Well," she shrugged with a rueful sigh, "It *was* only one bite!" And promptly forgot the matter.

She knelt down in the freshly-mulched soil and began a task that she enjoyed immensely: weeding. Her knees made great holes in the wet mulch as she tweaked out the weeds from the beetroot and carrots with her forefinger and thumb. It was slow work and after an hour, Miranda had only cleared a patch about four foot square. It was hot. She glanced up at the sun. She scooped up the picked weeds and, tossing them onto the compost heap, returned to the welcome, cool shade of the house.

She ducked beneath the canvas awning outside the kitchen, then stopped. The table was as she had left it. But the huge fruit was gone. Puzzled, she began to clear the table, only pausing once to cock her ears when she thought she heard a distant vehicle.

¤

Peter threaded his way through the crowd, his eyes darting, examining the rows of ancient flower pots, cutlery and cooking utensils that covered the worn trestle tables in great and inevitable profusion.

Clocks and cameras, old Pepsi Cola signs, ancient boots and shabby overcoats were heaped upon the trestles. Some displays were neat and regimented; others were just piled in mounds or still in their boxes. Bargain hunters clustered around the boxes, rifling their contents furiously as if searching for gold.

Peter's eyes caught something: Machines, ancient spindles, time-worn cogs, remnants of a time when machinery was built to last After a rapid inspection, he chose a device of unknown purpose—a peculiar conglomeration of spindles and wedges—pleased by the solidity of the brass and iron ferrules and the workmanship of the castings.

"It's a leather splitter," said the dour-faced stall owner declining to offer any further information.

Peter realized with a secret grin that it was probably all the man knew of the article; the man had probably bought if off someone who had told *him* that it was a leather splitter. Somewhere back along the line was *someone* who knew what a leather splitter was. By now, the gadget had probably changed hands four or five times.

Well, thought Peter, gazing at its solid yet intricate workmanship, the buck stops here. You've found a home, old leather splitter and *I'll* work out just what you can do.

"So, you like to collect old tools, Mr. Riley?" came a voice at Peter's elbow.

Peter looked up, surprised that someone knew his name in this strange town. Peter stared at the man for a moment before recognition dawned. It was Martinez; but a different Martinez from the nervous, shifting man at the Estate Office. Martinez was now wearing jeans, a fringed buckskin jacket and cowboy boots. Peter stared at him thoughtfully. It wasn't the clothes that made such a difference. Martinez's hair was not plastered back as it had been in the office; it was tucked beneath his hat and hung down his cheeks in two long blue-black plaits. His skin seemed darker, more leathery. It wasn't even the hair, thought Peter, the man's whole bearing seemed to be changed.

"Forgotten me already, Mr. Riley?" laughed Martinez.

"Er, no," said Peter, pulling himself together, "You look different. I suppose I'm used to seeing you dressed for the office." Martinez's manner was somehow looser, thought Peter, more confident; now the man seemed to move with a natural grace. And for the first time, Peter realized how big he was—large hands and broad shoulders. "You don't seem much like an Estate Agent today," said Peter slowly, "If you'll excuse my saying so."

Martinez shrugged. "Not at all. We do what we can to live in this world, Mr. Riley, and its not always what we would do if our choices were wider."

Peter smiled. He like the man. "Hey, call me Peter." He stuck his hand out involuntarily and Martinez took it in a large paw which enveloped Peter's completely. "Nice to meet you," said Peter, suddenly shy as he always was at reaching out to another person.

"Me, too. C'mon, check out my stall."

Peter hesitated: "Hey, what's your name? I can't keep calling you Mr. Martinez, can I?"

Martinez laughed. "Nope. You can call me Miya."

"Miya…" echoed Peter puzzled, "Is that Mexican?"

"No, sir," said Martinez with a proud smile, "It's short for Muyamuya."

Martinez pronounced the name with a sudden lilting meld of syllabic sound that transformed his whole demeanor. Suddenly he seemed taller.

Peter tried to repeat the name, but failed to get his tongue around the liquid syllables.

"That's why I shortened it to Miya," laughed Martinez.

"Miya it is," said Peter with a slow smile at his own ineptitude, "If it's not Mexican, what is it?"

By way of an answer, Miya gesticulated towards the stall behind them. Peter was pleasantly surprised. Unlike the other stalls, this was a splash of vibrant color. Woven baskets were grouped artistically on multicolored blankets. Small wood carvings were arranged in neat, concentric circles: amulets, arrowheads, beadware. And, against the backdrop of the blankets, some of the loveliest paintings Peter had ever seen.

"Not bad!" said Peter enthusiastically, "Not bad at all!"

"Indian work—all of it," said Miya proudly.

"Miya! So, you're Indian?" asked Peter cautiously, fingering a blanket.

"Yep," said Miya with a broad grin.

"Excuse me saying so, but, aren't you kind of tall?" asked Peter, hastily rethinking his preconceived notion of Indians as being 'generally squat and short'.

"Hence the name," said Miya with a twinkle in his eye, "You get genetic throwbacks in every culture, and that's what I am—a genetic throwback." He laughed heartily. "Muyamuya means 'strange being or hairy man giant'—and I guess that's me."

Peter nodded, wondering how the nervous Real Estate man named Martinez had so suddenly metamorphosed into this dignified giant. "But 'Martinez'? Where did that come from?"

Miya shrugged and made a hand motion as if pulling something from thin air. "Protective coloration, I guess. My ancestors adopted it during the Extermination Drive in the nineteenth century. But I am pure, sir, absolutely pure Indian."

"I don't doubt it," said Peter, "And this?" He indicated the stall.

"Society for the Preservation of Indian Culture. Each and every one of these objects was made by an Indian. I'm the president of the local branch."

Peter surveyed the paintings. They were gorgeous: vivid etched lines; huge splashes of bright color crowding to the perimeter of the frame which seemed about to burst, unable to contain the bright energy of the primary colors. Miranda would love these, he thought. Then he suddenly stopped, shocked.

Miya's eyes became alert; he studied Peter's face closely.

Peter felt a roaring in his ears, and the familiar sounds of the swap-meet seemed to fade. The clink of cheap dishware; the bustle of the crowds; the sound of shod feet on gravel became dim and distant and all he could feel was the sun on his head and its light in his eyes; a brassy glare that beat down on life and death alike, millions of years old; older than man; older than the planet.

Peter was shaken to his core. He stared at the painting anew. It depicted a stern-faced Indian, his head crowned with the nodding quills of woodpecker feathers. The man's eyes were daubed with black powder, his cheeks orange. It was unmistakably the man Peter had seen in his 'sunstroke' hallucination.

"Is something wrong?" asked Miya gently.

"No…no…" muttered Peter uneasily. His mind seethed with the possibilities. He must have seen pictures of this man before, he reasoned rapidly: The brain stores millions of such images; no wonder that his 'dream Indian' existed in the real world, for it was from the real world that its images were drawn. Peter calmed himself. Yep, he must have seen this picture somewhere before.

Miya spoke, interrupting his thoughts. "There is amongst some tribes—especially the Pomo—an idea of an ancient figure, a hero figure from whom all spiritual sustenance and principle was derived. This is the basis of the Kuksu legend. And this," he pointed at the picture of the stern-eyed warrior, "Is a description of Kuksu as seen by a Maru, a Dreamer—a woman who claims connection a with the spirits. It is powerful, isn't it?"

"It sure is," said Peter soberly, "Very vivid."

Miya laughed. "Its power is akin to what is called the hypnogogic imagery of your Edgar Alan Poe—a white man who also depicted those strange visions seen between waking and sleep."

Peter looked surprised. "You are extremely widely read," he said in admiration.

"It is wise for the Indian to educate himself in the ways of the white man, for only then can he decide what is worthy and what is not," said Miya with an odd lilt to his voice.

Fearing a sermon—which didn't come—Peter promptly bought the painting, amazed at the low cost. He offered Miya more, but the man wouldn't take it. "It is more a gift. I must pay the artist the full price, but take it as my gift to you."

Peter hesitated, then said: "Perhaps you will come and visit us."

"Perhaps," said Miya. "Is all well at the Mission?"

"Yep. I've laid in an irrigation system from the stream and cleared and planted a vegetable garden. Now I'm working on a design for solar power and water recycling that's in natural harmony with the whole balance of the place. It's really exciting."

Miya chuckled and nodded. "Good, good—it sounds good. But be careful. The Indian lived in harmony with America for ten thousand years without disrupting the flow of one stream or the fall of a tree, and in just two hundred and fifty years alone this balance was upset by the Anglos. It seems that progress isn't always upwards." He put his thumb down with a sly grin.

"Don't worry about the Mission…er, it's all ecologically sound," spluttered Peter defensively.

Miya clapped him on the shoulder. "Only kidding. Don't let me get on my high-horse about the Indians."

Suddenly the sky was blue and the noises of the swap-meet re-emerged, familiar and mundane. The brassy, ancient sun seemed to abate and Miya, the ancient Indian, became a little more of Martinez, the 'Mexican' Estate Agent. Peter took a breath of relief and shook himself as if emerging from a bad dream. "Well, thanks a million," he said shaking Miya's hand. "Please come and see us. Like I said, I know that Miranda would really like to meet you." Miya nodded. Peter had a sudden thought. "Miya, what does Alavera mean—in Spanish?"

Miya frowned. "Alavera? I don't know the word. Perhaps it's slang or dialect. Why?"

"Oh, nothing," said Peter, "I just wondered. I can't find it in the dictionaries. 'Bye now!" Hastily, Peter slipped into the crowd, embarrassed by so much contact so soon, and was soon lost amongst the piles of old crockery, kettles and clothing.

Miya stood watching Peter leave. Towering above the heads of the men in the flea-market crowd by almost a foot, his face was as impassive as weathered stone…

¤

For a long time, Peter lay awake on the mattress listening to Miranda's even breathing.

The room was dark save for the crisscross lattice of light thrown on the floor from the barred window. Peter stared at one patch on the wall that was darker than the rest. It was the Kuksu painting.

Miranda had gone into shrieks of ecstasy over the painting and insisted that they hang it opposite the bed.

Peter could not see the picture in the gloom, but he strained his eyes staring at it and once, by a trick of light, he thought he saw the flash of eyes and the orange daubed cheekbones as in his waking dream on the roof.

He lay awake for a long time, sifting the images of the last few days through his mind: the swap-meet; Martinez cum Miya; and rain—a grayish-black downpour; the jangle of harnesses; squat figures looming out of the gloom. Eventually, exhausted, Peter fell into a restless sleep.

Miranda opened her eyes sleepily and sat slowly upright as if listening. She smiled like a child that has been awoken to receive a gift. She cocked her head and listened. There! Faintly she could hear the sound of voices rising and falling in a sonorous chorus. She slipped out of the bed and glided across the floor, her cotton shift pale and fluttering in the gloom.

She stood at the window grille, a checkerboard of shadow thrown across her white face and shoulders. The gauzy checkerboard solidified into vivid black squares as the moon rode high, and Miranda sighed gratefully as the pungent odor of the tree blossom stole across the yard.

With the slow movements of a dream-dancer, Miranda undid the window hasp, swung the grille open gently and slid over the sill. She landed on the hard soil in her bare feet with barely a sound. Without so much as a glance backwards, she loped across the yard, her figure wan and ghostly in the moonlight filtering through the vast arching umbrella of the Tree.

CHAPTER NINE

Cal O'Donnell rubbed the stubble on his chin, squinting through the windshield into the truck's headlights. The thin ribbon of road snaked towards him; a jerking, twisting strip of rutted rock and impacted gravel that was laughingly termed 'the County Road'.

"Shit," he muttered as the truck bounced, swerved and bounced again. But he didn't ease his foot off the pedal, even though he was driving too fast.

On either side, the brush whipped past, a uniform gray, drained of color by the truck's lights. On the distant horizon was a faint, whitish corona of light thrown up by the town just behind it.

Cal drove without thinking. In fact, Cal did most things without thinking. There was some excuse for his mindless driving, as Cal had driven this road every day for nigh on ten years and knew its every twist and turn. If a car approached, he would see its lights a mile before it reached him.

One of the old breed, Cal had a thirty-ought six slung over the windshield of the car, and at his side, a twelve-gauge shotgun. "Never take chances," he had confided to one of his cronies, an equally gnarled fifty-year old, "There's still some mighty peculiar people living around these parts."

Cal's cautiousness was not without foundation. The County was severely economically depressed and this sometimes bred a desperation which led to sporadic attacks on unwary travelers.

The truck slewed around a corner in a cloud of dust and Cal saw the log too late. He cried out involuntarily and, in a reflex action, wrenched the wheel hard over. The tires squealed sideways across the hard dirt and missed the log. The truck rolled, its lights stabbing into the air, bounced and miraculously landed right side up. The spinning wheels caught the road with renewed traction and the truck shot forward, impacting a boulder with a sickening scrunch.

The night sky jolted savagely as Cal's chest impacted the steering wheel, driving the air from his lungs. He gasped for air and slumped over the wheel, semiconscious.

He opened his eyes slowly. He could taste blood, metallic and salty in his mouth, and there was no sensation in his chest, though it was as tight as a drum.

"Ribs…" he muttered. "Goddamn ribs…"

Not knowing what he was doing, he pushed at the door. It swung open and he tumbled out sideways into the cold night, feeling the hard stab of stones on his knees and palms. He raised himself up, stood upright, staggered clutching his ribs, then regained his balance. A noise made him turn around and his eyes suddenly widened. He raised his arms weakly. Before he had time to cry out, something suddenly clamped around his throat and he was forced to the ground, struggling weakly.

After a few moments, a shadow detached itself from Cal's inert form and glided lightly off into the windswept darkness...

CHAPTER TEN

Peter was crouching down over a flat piece of metal propped across two piles of angle iron. The sun was high and sweat ran down his forehead, staining the green-black protective goggles; it ran down his nose and dripped onto the hot metal and sizzled. The blue and yellow flame of the cutting torch hissed malevolently as it drew a neat, glowing line across the flat bar. The metal suddenly parted as a perfect rectangle detached itself, canted over and fell smoldering into the dust. Peter grunted in satisfaction and pushed back the goggles. Wiping the sweat from his eyes, he turned off the torch with a 'crack!' and a puff of blue smoke.

Miranda, ravishing in brief shorts and sun top, leant over and fingered the red bump on his nose where the goggles had perched. "That'll get to be a permanent fixture," she said with a smile.

Peter nodded. The work was progressing well. He had the bit between his teeth and he was really going for it now. Miranda gestured towards the hill. "There's a car coming."

Peter could hear it. A plume of dust appeared briefly over the road, coiled around the distant hill and disappeared around the bend. They waited in silence as the car appeared at the base of the hill and rolled towards the Mission in a cloud of dust: Their first visitor.

The car turned off the hill road and bounced onto the dirt track that ran up to the Mission gates. Peter suddenly recognized the black and white markings. "Jesus, it's a police car."

Miranda gazed at it thoughtfully, wiping her hands on the weeds that she'd just pulled.

With a purr, the large black and white car eased into the courtyard and stopped. Miranda wrinkled her nose as the smell of oil and hot metal mingled with the drowsy smells of the country.

The cop eased his bulk out of the car and sauntered up, thumbs hooked in his belt. He was a short, fat man; trousers tucked into fancy calf-length boots; a shirt splotched with sweat. His face was round, pinkish, like a bland moon, surmounted by the two dark circles of sunglass lenses. As he strolled towards them, he continuously doffed and donned a Stetson, smoothing his balding pate with a pudgy hand in a nervous motion. His jaw moved incessantly and he paused once to spit out a narrow stream of yellowish liquid onto the dusty road.

Both Miranda and Peter disliked him instantly.

The man stopped in front of them and gazed at them from behind the black windows of the sunglasses. "Sheriff Dooley's the name," he said slowly in a drawl tinged slightly with the South. He rocked on his heels, thumbs in his belt. Miranda's eyes fell onto the worn gun handle jutting at a cocky angle from the shiny black holster, and she could not hide a grimace of distaste. Miranda hated guns.

The man stared at Miranda. She could feel his eyes boring into her, hidden beneath the dark lenses and, instinctively, she folded her arms in front of her breasts.

Peter felt distinctly uncomfortable. "Peter—Peter Riley," he said slowly without proffering his hand, "This is my wife, Miranda. What can we do for you?"

Dooley ignored the question and glanced about the Mission yard, chewing methodically. He let his eyes rove over the barn, the workshop, the sprinkler system. "New in these parts, ain't yah folks?" he said.

Peter bristled. Somehow the man managed to make every question sound like an accusation, so in answering, Peter already felt as though he was guilty of *something*. "Yes, that's right," he said coldly.

"You planning on growin' crops...or what?"

Peter shrugged, puzzled. "What do you mean?"

"I mean, it's kinda difficult to get work around here," said the Sheriff. "I was wondering what you folks did for a living."

Peter stared at the man, feeling a tide of frustration at any attempt to describe the whole nature of the silver business and the complex network of supply and delivery of the film. He realized instinctively that any occupation which fell outside this man's terms of reference would automatically be suspect.

Aware of Peter's hesitation, the man stared at him with the blind discs of the sunglasses.

"We're doing O.K.," said Peter churlishly.

"That's not what I asked," said Dooley, just a hint of menace in his tone.

Peter realized he'd tensed himself; his shoulders were hunched and his fists knotted. "Hey, look, what is this?!" said Peter, "We're decent people on our own land, not bothering anyone. What are you doing barging in here with all these questions?!"

The Sheriff let him rail on. Peter's voice tailed off into the air and he realized he'd fallen into Dooley's trap: he was defending himself. The Sheriff smirked in satisfaction. He gazed about and said incongruously: "Nice place."

Peter didn't answer. He realized Miranda had stepped closer to him and was holding him tightly, her fingernails digging into his forearm.

The Sheriff turned his gaze and stared at Miranda's hand. She withdrew it hastily, leaving indentations in Peter's flesh. The Sheriff stared at Peter's arm for a second, took off his glasses and pinched the top of his nose with his thumb and forefinger and rubbed slowly. His eyes were small and beady. He replaced the glasses carefully and the lenses resumed their blank gaze.

Peter felt as if he was going to explode, but he remained silent.

"Do you mind if I look around?" said the Sheriff.

"Yes we do," said Miranda, "Have you got a search warrant?"

"Well now," said Dooley rocking on his heels. He spat out a stream of juice. "There's an easy way to do this and a hard way. Let's do it the easy way. What say I look around without getting a search warrant?" His tone implied that if he was forced to get a warrant, the consequences would be dire.

Peter relinquished. "You poke around," he said angrily, "But mind *how* you poke. Whatever you think, this is my property!"

"Well now," grinned Dooley with a broadening of his pink, fleshy cheeks, "Ah'll poke real gentle now—but poke ah will." And with a rolling motion of his large hams, he began to saunter towards the workshop.

Half an hour later, Peter sat at the rough table outside the kitchen, a full cup of untouched coffee before him. Miranda sat next to him, a reassuring hand on his shoulder. Peter glanced up, seething with anger as the rotund figure of Dooley appeared outside the theater and then disappeared around the back of the workshop.

"Why did you let him look?" whispered Miranda, "It makes me feel soiled. Like someone looking at my personal diary or pawing through my belongings!"

"It's easier this way," said Peter, his mouth clenched, "I know the type. If we get in his way, he'll use anything he can to harass us so that we'd be sorry we stood in his way. Fucking asshole!"

Miranda lay her cheek on his shoulder and ran her hands through his hair. "Don't worry, he'll be gone soon," she said, feeling Peter's bottled anger in the tautness of his body.

Dooley finally came back. He sauntered towards the table. His eye fell on the coffee pot. Shit on you, thought Peter, and took a long sip without offering any. It was childish, he knew, but it gave him some satisfaction. The man was so provocative.

"Well, everything looks dandy," said Dooley, "I'll be on my way now." He made as if to go, then, suddenly remembering something, he half turned. "Oh, by the way, where were you two last night? Do anything special?"

Peter glanced at Miranda, puzzled. She replied: "We were here—we're always here."

The Sheriff nodded. He stared at the distant hill and the road snaking around it. "Reckon it's half an hour from here to the County Road intersection," he said as if talking to himself.

"Half an hour?" said Peter puzzled, "Nope, it's much longer."

"By foot, sir," said Dooley, "By foot. Ah know this territory." He pointed down the valley. "There's Injun tracks down there alongside the creek—it's easier to walk. It's actually longer to go around the hillside by truck on account o' those bends. Think about it."

He sauntered over to the car. The radio crackled. Dooley leant inside the car, jerked out the microphone and said something into it in an unintelligible flurry of syllables. "Yeah, ten four." He nodded, clicked the microphone back onto its hook and eased his bulk in behind the wheel.

He didn't slam the door.

He pointed off into the distance, eastwards. "Ole friend of mine—well, lemme say, acquaintance—Cal O'Donnell...hardy devil, tough as whip cord... was strangled up on the County Road last night, not too far from here."

Peter was taken aback. "Strangled! Murdered?!"

"Looks like," said the Sheriff, "His truck was crashed, but that's not what killed him. No siree. Looked like he'd been strangled with a piece o' rope or something." Dooley drew a finger around his fat neck, "Marks all around here. Coroner put down cause of death as asphyxiation."

Peter stared at Miranda, stunned. "That's terrible!" he said. A numb feeling rose in the pit of his belly at the thought of their pastoral paradise bespoiled by the proximity of such malignancy.

"Yep," said the Sheriff, "Sure is. Reckon ole Cal was dazed or unconscious already or he would put up a helluva fight—an' he was armed." He leant out of the window and spat artfully in the dust. "Take it easy now." He started the engine with a throbbing purr, eased the car out of the yard and bumped across the track.

Miranda and Peter watched the car for a long time until it finally turned out of sight around the last curve of the mountain. Finally, Miranda broke the silence. "Isn't it horrible that people like that are always cleaning up messes? They seem to like it."

Peter thought about the killing with a crawling sensation in his stomach. "I suppose someone has to clean up the mess," he said slowly, "I'm only glad it doesn't have to be me."

¤

Peter sat at the table moodily sipping the cold coffee. He stared across the vegetable garden to the distant stream where it coiled around the base of the huge golden mound of the hill and a black basalt boulder, perched as if it had been dropped by a careless giant. The shadows had already begun to elongate and the scrub oaks were etched out starkly. Peter shifted in his seat and watched the scene, untouched by its beauty. Somehow the Sheriff's visit had disturbed him more deeply than he'd like to admit—as if an unseen and malevolent presence lurked beneath the green and gold loveliness of the surrounding hills.

"The sweetest hours of the twenty-four," said a soft voice behind him. Before he could turn around, something cool slipped over his eyelids. It was Miranda's palm. He could feel her hair caressing his shoulder. Something rustled against the back of the seat. "What's going on?" he asked.

"Keep your eyes closed," she whispered, "And turn around slowly." Despite his mood, Peter grinned. Miranda was always playing these little games. "O.K.," he said from the darkness of closed eyelids, "I'm ready. Are you?"

"Yes. You can look now."

Peter opened his eyes. And there stood a wood nymph: Miranda, wearing one of her dance costumes; multi-layered strips of green and white that swirled and shifted as she rotated on her bare toes like a ballerina. Her hair was festooned with jasmine; behind her ear was a huge scarlet blossom from the Tree. Around her neck was draped a garland of purple Morning Glory and, crowning it all, a green victor's garland fashioned from laurel leaves encircled her golden hair.

"You look like an wood nymph," he said, his voice thick with emotion.

"C'mon," she said, her eyes twinkling. She grabbed his hand and pulled him upright.

"Where?"

"I'm going to give you a show, Mr. Riley. I'm not going to have you sitting around all miserable because of some stupid, fat Sheriff!"

Peter laughed out loud. Sometimes Miranda could read him like a book. He allowed himself to be tugged good-naturedly across the yard. "Why aren't we going to the theater?" he asked, puzzled.

"Because this is a nature show—the Theater of the Wild," she said, tiptoeing across the stones of the yard painfully.

"God, why aren't you wearing shoes?"

"This *is* the Theater of the Wild!" she retorted, "Wood nymphs don't wear shoes!" She dragged and prodded the weakly-protesting Peter until they had circumnavigated the Mission and were beneath the green mantle of the huge Tree.

Miranda had chosen her moment well. The sun, low in the western sky, struck the overhanging mantle of green at just the right angle so that the huge leaves were almost translucent, forming a vast canopy beneath which the light was a speckled pattern of green and gold. As the Tree trembled slightly in the faint breeze, the light shifted and swayed, almost liquid in its movement.

"Look!" cried Miranda, her eyes dancing with excitement, "My Lord's repast!" She pointed. A neat, white square of cloth lay on the compacted soil beneath the canopy. On it was set a feast: crisp, green apples; a bunch of succulent, purple grapes, gray-blue with the yeast bloom; a watermelon sliced in half showing its pinkish-white seeded interior; yellow peaches; a bottle of Burgundy, two glasses and a fruit that Peter did not recognize.

"What's that?" he asked, examining the glossy exterior of the unknown fruit.

"It's a nectarine. Taste it."

He did. It had a delicious taste, somewhere in between that of an apple and a peach. "Mmm," he said cheekily, "No meat??"

"This is a very, very special meal," said Miranda wagging a finger reproachfully, "No dead animals parts, my Lord. And when you see the show, you'll see why."

Miranda made Peter taste each of the fruits in turn and then swill it down with a sip of wine. After a while, he realized there was something more than vegetarianism behind her choice of food.

"So..." she said mysteriously, "The subject is prepared. Now for the show." She disappeared around the corner and reappeared with the portable tape deck.

"Looks kind of out of place!" shouted Peter as she propped it near the base of the Tree, "All that technology! Shouldn't you have a band of pipers and a lyre or something?"

"We do what we can," she called back unperturbed, "We do what we can. Now, no more interruptions. The show is about to begin." She pushed the start button on the machine and retreated a few steps, flexed her toes and bent her knees a couple of times.

There was a sudden hiss of tape noise and, on cue, Miranda stood absolutely still, waiting in the balletic pose known as 'en bas'; her palms uplifted, her eyes closed; her green and white garments fluttering in the breeze.

It was a rare moment. Sun spots, speckled gold and green, danced across Miranda's face, casting prisms of amber light onto her golden hair.

Gently, the music began: a quiet splashing of piano notes in a silvery cascade. Miranda began to dance; and as she danced, she intoned a lovely poem that Peter did not recognize. Sipping the red wine, its pleasant glow warming his belly, Peter soon realized the reason for his preparation.

"*'What a wondrous life is this I lead'*," intoned Miranda, half singing, half speaking. She raised her hands further and let them fall. "*'Ripe apples fall about my head...'*" She mimed the fall. "*'The luscious clusters of the vine...'*" She opened her mouth, soft and sensuous, "*'Upon my mouth do crush their wine.'*" Miranda did a lilting step and spun closer to Peter and stared into his eyes, reaching out her open palms:

"*'The nectarine and curious peach*
Into my hand themselves do reach.'"

She raised herself up on tiptoe and began to turn in slow spirals, her arms outstretched. The green and white costume fluttered as she turned, showing her bare, golden-tanned thighs. Her hair streamed out behind her and some of the flowers fell from it and cascaded around her feet. She slowly sank down to the ground with one leg half under her as she said softly:

"*'Stumbling on melons as I pass*

Ensnared with flowers, I fall...on...grass.'"
Miranda lay crumpled forward, her hair a streak of gold across her back; her arms open wide; her head down across her leg. The music lilted softly and Miranda lay still for a long time, until Peter grew restless, thinking that the dance was finished.

The wind stirred in the Tree, carrying the musty odor of the tree fruit. Peter, mellowed by the alcohol, inhaled it deeply. Somehow it all blended: the green and golden girl-child; the tawny, red wine; and the deep and rich tangy fruit smell.

Peter felt a little drunk and he put the wine glass down hastily. His head was spinning with the images and scents of green apple and yellow peach; golden hair and russet leaf; shadow and song; the sensual juices of the pink-seeded watermelon dripping with rich life; and the blood pounding in his ears, rich and red as the tawny wine; the crimson of the tree blossom. Beneath it all, the pungent odor of the tree musk.

Peter tried to stand, but he lurched awkwardly, his head spinning, and he sat back down with a bump.

Then Miranda moved:

Slowly, like a flower unfolding at the touch of the early-morning sun, Miranda unfolded her body and lifted her arms.

Peter settled back and squinted a trifle blearily as Miranda turned her face to the sky. Her eyes were huge and dark; her movements slow and dream-like. The moody green of the Tree washed over her face and for a moment it was as though she were drifting in a deep, green sea with an occasional shaft of sunlight finding its way to the glassy depths. Her face had changed some-how and when she spoke, her voice seemed to come from a great distance.

Peter pushed his glasses back on his nose, still dizzy, wondering if the oddness of Miranda's voice was him or her. Miranda stood up swaying like a sea anenome caught in an undersea current. Then, one by one, she began to throw the blossoms to the ground as she hummed deep in her throat. Like a bride divesting herself of her clothes in front of her lover, she threw off each layer of blossoms until only the laurel crown and the crimson flower of the tree blossom remained.

She turned on her heels, and, with the slow stride of a sleep-walker, she padded across to the tree base, took off her victor's garland and laid it rever-entially on the roots of the vast trunk. She took one step back, raised her head and stared up into the shifting green umbrella of foliage.

Then she began to take off the white layers of her dress. As she cast aside each layer and it fluttered to the ground, she intoned:

"'Meanwhile, the Mind from pleasure less*
Withdraws into its happiness
The Mind, that ocean where each kind
Does straight its own resemblance find.'"

Peter half rose, then stood up, a little shaky. Miranda's voice seemed to come from a great distance. As she threw off each streamer of white, she became less distinct against the green-gold of the Tree. Her body, a splash of green surmounted by the cascading gold of her hair, gradually began to blend into the moody, shifting green of the leaves and their golden pattern of sun-speckles.

Finally she stood with her head thrown back, the last strip of white fluttering in her hand. Now she was almost indistinguishable from her surroundings, save for the crimson splodge of the blossom and the fluttering, white streamer in her hand. Peter had to strain to see her. Head back, Miranda stared wide-eyed into the canopy, her throat mottled, vulnerable in the shifting light, and crooned softly:

> "*Yet it creates, transcending these*
> *Far other worlds and other seas...*"

She dropped the fluttering strip of white and, for a moment Peter lost her against the shifting matrix of green and gold. Her voice wafted softly from within the distorted colors:

> "*Annihilating all that's made*
> *To a green thought...in a...green shade.*"

There was a shift of light and for one hazy moment, Miranda seemed to disappear completely.

Peter cried out involuntarily: "Miranda!" He scrabbled up painfully and began walking with leaden feet over the hard ground; so difficult was the motion, Peter felt as if he was walking through a thick green sea. "Miranda!" he shouted, his lips thick and dry.

Then he saw her. She was laying in a heap like a fallen leaf, green and lifeless, crumpled across a thick, gnarled root.

Peter knelt down. "God! That was indescribable!" he said, licking his dry lips, vaguely wishing he hadn't drunk so much. "Incredible! Miranda, you're marvelous!"

Miranda did not answer.

"Miranda...?!" He reached out and touched her bare shoulder. It was cold; ice-cold. "Miranda!!" His head cleared a little with the shock and he gingerly cupped her head and turned her face upwards.

Her eyes were open wide, purple-black and luminous. She gazed sightlessly into the canopy, her face stained an unearthly green, blank and expressionless.

"Miranda?!!" breathed Peter huskily. His heart was pounding. He slapped her gently on the cheek. She did not respond. "Miranda!!!" This time, it was a cry of agony and desperation. He felt her neck with a quivering finger and could not locate her pulse. He took her limp wrist between his thumb and fingers and probed gently.

There it was; weak and flickering, but, nonetheless, a pulse.

"Oh, Jesus!" he muttered in relief. His eyes filled with tears. He swept her up in his arms. Though short and stocky, Peter was strong, and he carried her easily to the Jeep. He lay her gently down beside the Jeep and swung open the door. He stood for a moment, uncertain, staring at the outline of the hills laced with the red fire of the setting sun.

Then he made a quick decision. He raced into the house, grabbed all the cushions and pillows he could find and dashed back to the Jeep where Miranda lay, her face chalky-green in the dimming light. Gently he eased her onto the rear seat, on her side in a foetal position. He positioned the cushions around her and jammed some of them against the back of the seat. Then he roped it all down with a length of half-inch nylon rope, careful that the rope didn't touch Miranda's inert body. He worked quickly and efficiently, ignoring the frantic buzzing in his brain, glad of the action.

He finished and tested his handiwork by rocking the Jeep back and forth on its suspension, one foot on the fender. Miranda swayed back and forwards in her cocoon of cushions, but the movement was slight. Peter let out a sigh. It was O.K. No matter how much the Jeep bounced—providing he didn't drive too crazily—Miranda would bob and sway, but not too much.

He jumped into the seat and fired the ignition. As the Jeep bumped out of the yard, he glanced behind to check Miranda. She stared waxily and sightlessly into the sky. Fear coiled itself around Peter's heart and he fought back the urge to jam his foot down on the accelerator. Instead, he clenched his teeth, forcing himself to drive slowly.

Something caught his eye beneath the thick, black bulk of the Tree on his left. He glanced at it briefly. It was a crumpled heap of white rags marred by a splotch of crimson. He gripped the steering wheel rigidly and drove out of the yard, his face set.

He forced himself not to think until he reached the hospital…

CHAPTER ELEVEN

Peter sat on a grubby, green plastic seat in the poorly-lit corridor of the small hospital, clutching an empty coffee cup. He stared at the notice board and had to tear his eyes away in order not to read the notices on 'Smoking', 'AIDS' and 'Safe Pregnancy' for the fiftieth compulsive time.

Eventually, the Sister came; a plump, homely woman in her late forties. "The doctor would like to see you," she said softly. "Don't worry, he's a good man—your wife is in good hands."

Peter thanked her, grateful for the sympathy, and she ushered him into the doctor's office. The doctor—a thin man aged about fifty with close-cropped, iron-gray hair and the fine hands of a surgeon—stood up and gestured to a chair. "Please take a seat, Mr. Riley."

Peter looked about wildly. Where is she? he thought.

The doctor read his expression. "Don't worry, Mr. Riley," he said in a thin, soft voice that barely concealed his fatigue, "Your wife is sleeping."

"Is she going to be O.K.?"

"I think so," said the doctor.

"Think so?" said Peter menacingly, "You think so?!"

The doctor held up his hand. "Whoa, Mr. Riley! Don't jump to conclusions. Your wife will…survive. I hesitate simply because I need to ask you a few questions before I decide exactly upon a final diagnosis—O.K.?"

Peter subsided. "Sure," he said wearily, "Fire away."

"Well, first I'd like you to repeat the story you, er, told us when you first came in—not in elaborate detail, just the events leading up to her…fainting."

Peter recounted the details of the picnic; the dance; and Miranda's eventual collapse.

The doctor toyed with a pen. "Had she eaten anything you don't normally eat—or at least, which she doesn't normally eat?"

"Nope," said Peter, "We only ate fruit. I don't know what she had earlier in the day, but she is a vegetarian. I'm the one who usually gets food poisoning, you know, I'm the carnivore."

The doctor nodded. "Mmm… Look, Mr. Riley, I'm going to be frank with you—and you'll help your wife much more if you're absolutely frank with me. Now, I *do* have to write out a report, but reports don't interest me. I'm interested in people's health. So, whatever we say here is just between us.

D'you understand?"

Peter stared at the doctor, not knowing what he was driving at, but recognizing a sincere desire to help. "Sure, Dr. Prescott," he said puzzled, "Of course I'll tell you anything you need to know."

Prescott pulled a wry face. "Now, look, do you—or does your wife—take any drugs?"

"Oh, no," said Peter sharply, "No—especially Miranda. She hates artificial things. She won't even take aspirin."

"Well, I meant more 'natural' drugs. I mean, a lot of people won't take aspirins but they will smoke marijuana or use fly agaric or psilocybin mushrooms. They are, in a way, perfectly natural substances," he sighed, "And drug-taking is a sign of the times, it seems."

"Well," said Peter slowly, fighting the urge to deny and denounce the doctor's claims, "You're right. Miranda would be more inclined to do something like that. Except that she doesn't. She doesn't even smoke pot. But…"
The doctor, detecting Peter's hesitation, raised an eyebrow. "Well, I'm just being truthful," said Peter, "And perhaps misleading. Miranda does not take drugs—street, legal or natural. But sometimes she's so wild that she just does things on the spur of the moment. She's unpredictable," he said unhappily, and not a little embarrassed at his inept description of the girl he loved.

The doctor chuckled sympathetically. "Don't worry, I see what you mean, and you've answered my question in a way, because what I'm asking is, if she may have, spontaneously or otherwise, taken a drug prior to this unfortunate event?"

"Only alcohol," said Peter, "Two glasses of wine. That's all I know about. Now, can you tell me—why these questions?"

"I'm sorry that I had to probe with these personal questions, but you see, a lot of people your age do come in with bizarre symptoms and then won't admit that they were taking drugs. It makes our job very difficult sometimes. But," he nodded, "I can see you're telling the truth. As for your wife, her symptoms are rather atypical and that's why I have to ask. Her blood pressure is down, her heart beat is irregular, and her motor reflexes are all haywire. My first diagnosis—very preliminary—was narcolepsy. But none of the tests show any indication of a known drug in her blood stream. Your wife was in a coma…" Peter's expression changed. "Let me reword that," said the doctor, "You wife *was* in a coma-like state. It appears to have shifted into a more natural sleep. She's going to be alright, I'm sure."

Peter exhaled.

"But we have to do a few things like a CAT scan and an MRI, just to ensure that there's not some mild temporal lobe disturbance that we can't detect with our rather primitive equipment." The doctor held up his hands, "Though, quite frankly, I'm as puzzled by it as you appear to be."

"Thanks for being frank, doctor," said Peter, "I really would tell you anything I could to make her well again. She's…she means a lot to me."

"I can see that," said the doctor gently, "So, just as a precaution, we're going to keep her in overnight and send her for some tests tomorrow. It would help if you stuck around. Do you think you could stay in town? The Vita Motel is just down the road. It's not the Ritz, but it's comfortable."

"Oh, sure, sure doctor. Can I see her?" asked Peter hesitantly.

"Of course," said the doctor, "But don't expect anything. She's asleep and it would be best to let her sleep it off—whatever *it* is." The doctor suddenly smiled broadly and, coming from behind the desk, he shook Peter's hand. "Anyway," he continued, leading Peter to the door, "As you well know, we can't take too many precautions with someone in her condition."

Peter looked at the doctor, puzzled. "I'm not quite sure what you mean."

The doctor stopped and looked closely at Peter. "You mean, you don't know, Mr. Riley?! Your wife is pregnant."

CHAPTER TWELVE

"Goddamnit!" said Dooley, striking his large, fat thigh with his hand. "The Lord'll have your tongue for breakfast if'n you keep using His name like that!" said Jeb Stonson.

"Goddamn the Lord, too!" growled Dooley, resisting the temptation to spit all over Jeb's shiny floor, "An' if you paid as much attention to the living as you do to the dead, Jeb Stonson, I'm sure the Lord would be mighty pleased!"

Jeb was a fifty-year old negro with a thin, mournful face and white hair that would have made him look distinguished except for his continual air of worry. The net result was comic; he looked like an ebony Stan Laurel. He busied himself over his administrations to the corpse. Cal O'Donnell's body lay out on the slab as naked at the day he was born. The rest of the room was in darkness; the only source of illumination was the neon strip over the body.

Jeb, ignoring the Sheriff's taunts, studied the body on the table with his perpetual, worried look. "Sometimes you can tell more about a man when he's dead than alive," said Jeb slowly, letting his eyes roll down the length of the naked corpse.

"I know I can crack this one!" said the Sheriff, ignoring Jeb's remark. He slapped his thigh. "I just know it!"

"Shouldn't you be callin' in outside help?" muttered Jeb.

"Outside help?! Shee-it no! I'm gonna get this one all by myself!" retorted Dooley standing up, clenching his hands. "People getting killed in mah territory—it's kinda *personal*, like they don't give a shit about the Law." He jabbed a thumb ferociously in his own chest. "An', dammit, ah'm the Law!" Dooley turned and saw Jeb staring at the corpse. "What in hell you lookin' at like you'd just won it in a lottery?!" he growled, realizing that Jeb had paid no attention to his own impassioned performance.

"Him."

"*It* man. It's an *it* when it's dead, ain't it?" said Dooley, breathing heavily.

"Got the body of a young man, ain't he?" said Jeb proudly.

"So what?" snarled Dooley putting on his hat and stomping to the door.

Jeb continued talking, unconcerned, "An' he was eating fruit just before he got snuffed… Yep, strange…"

Dooley turned slowly, walked across to the table and stared down at the corpse. "Strange? Why?"

Jeb pulled open the man's mouth. "See? Blackberries. Beats me!"

Dooley peered at the purple-stained mouth and tongue. "Don't look like blackberries to me. Funny thing is, his hands ain't stained."

"Maybe he wiped them," said Jeb with a shrug.

"Maybe he did," said Dooley acidly, "Clean hands is the kinda thing Cal was *very* particular about, you know, especially gunnin' along at seventy miles an hour on a bumpy track." He stomped to the door.

"You being sarcastic?" asked Jeb slowly.

"Would ah do that now?" said Dooley pulling the door open. As he left, he gave Jeb a withering glance.

CHAPTER THIRTEEN

Peter sat staring at the flickering television screen. The reception was lousy; the desk clerk had apologized in advance, saying it was the surrounding hills blocking the signal. Nevertheless, Peter stared at the screen. Not that it mattered too much. He didn't see a thing, lost in his own fears.

He stood up and began pacing up and down the motel room. He just couldn't relax. Despite the doctor's reassurances, he was still worried about Miranda. With a muttered curse, he threw himself on the drab coverlet of the bed and, for the third time, dropped thirty-five cents in the slot attached to the little bedside table that made the bed hum and vibrate. The humming started, although the vibration seemed minimal. Perhaps it wasn't working properly, he thought with a frown.

He stared at the ceiling for a moment, wondering how such a new building could have so many cracks in it. His eyes fell onto the picture on the wall—probably painted by an enthusiastic amateur using a 'paint-by-numbers' kit.

Dingy. Brown. Depressing. Doleful. The words plopped into his consciousness like dead fish as he surveyed his dingy, brown, depressing, doleful surroundings. God, the place was only five years old. Perhaps motels hired interior decorators that specialized in 'Dingy Motel Decor'.

He swung off the bed realizing that, for once, solid, calm, ride-along-with-it Peter Riley was being affected by his surroundings. Normally it was Miranda who complained about the dinginess of motel rooms and their soulless paintings. Well, he thought with a grimace, tonight *he* was the sensitive one.

The phone rang, making him jump. He snatched it up and said, "Yes, room 27."

"Is that Peter Riley?" asked a hesitant, male voice.

"Yes it is. Who's this?" said Peter slowly.

"Dr. Prescott…at the hospital."

Peter's heart started racing. "What's the matter?" he asked, "Is Miranda O.K.?"

"She's gone," said the doctor.

"Gone?! What do you mean?!!"

"She's gone. She must have got up and left when the nurse was in the main ward."

"Is she O.K.? I mean, did she talk to anybody?" asked Peter.

"Well, that I don't know. No one saw her…leave."

"If Miranda woke up and felt O.K., she probably phoned the Mission to see where I was."

"No, she didn't use the phone—the night nurse would know," came the doctor's faint voice, "You can't phone without going through the switchboard."

"What do you think's happened?!" asked Peter hoarsely.

"Well, she may have just headed home. People do that sometimes. But she didn't ask for her clothes. She's just wearing a flimsy nightdress and a hospital dressing gown and no shoes. Have you been out tonight, Mr. Riley?"

"No, I've been indoors since I left. Why?"

"Well, the wind is up and it could be one of those rare ole nights—not the kind of weather for a body to be out half-dressed."

"No," said Peter softly.

"Anyway, I've notified the police. But I thought I'd ring you personally, in case you can throw any light on the situation. Besides, I knew you'd want to know."

"Thank you," said Peter, "I can only think that she might be on her way home." He pulled the curtain back to see the thin saplings bending against the wind and cigarette cartons and litter whirling across the ill-lit car lot. "You're right, doctor, it's a helluva night for anyone to be out. I'm going back home, too. If you get any news, I'll be there in a couple of hours…"

"I hope she's O.K., Mr. Riley. We'll keep you informed."

"O.K."

"And Mr. Riley, I'm very sorry, really, I—"

"That's O.K.," cut in Peter, "After all, she wasn't in prison. It's not your fault."

"Thank you, Mr. Riley, you're very kind."

"Thank you, doctor." Peter put the receiver down in its rest and swore quietly. Then he snatched it back up and waited for the sleepy desk clerk to answer. "Come *on!*" he said in irritation.

"What was that, sir?" came the clerk's voice.

"Oh…nothing. Excuse me. Look, could you get me the Sheriff's office, please?"

¤

A huge tumbleweed sailed across the road into the truck's headlights, then bowled ponderously out of sight, like a great ball of candy floss.

The wind caught the truck in huge buffets and it shuddered from side to side, forcing the man at the wheel to clutch it more tightly. He let out a cackle. "Yea ha!! That's what we call Valley weather around here. Y'go to bed with a clear night sky and next thing you know, the wind is a'whirlin' and a'whappin' and throwing trees an' barns all over the place!"

The girl did not answer. She sat staring ahead stonily, her face pale in the half-light of the cab. As the truck bounced over the rough surface, the girl swayed waxily in her seat, making no attempt to steady herself.

Clutching the wheel tightly, the driver divided his attention between the road and the girl's breasts, half visible where her dressing gown had fallen open.

A thin, scrawny man with a prominent Adam's apple and blue-veined arms, he eyed the girl salaciously. At one point, he took his eyes off the road for just a moment too long. The truck whipped across the road and he jerked the wheel hastily to straighten it up. "Jesus, what a night!" he exclaimed.

The girl did not answer. She had not spoken since he'd picked her up on the unlit road five miles back.

"Mah name's Ferris—Ferris Ansell," he said, glancing down at the expanse of long, smooth thigh that poked out from beneath the girl's night dress.

The girl still didn't answer.

"Don't talk much, do you?" complained Ansell, "Kinda makes for problems, don't it? I pick you up, you don't talk—like, I don't know where you're a'headin', lady, so you'd best speak up soon, hey!" He cackled.

The girl suddenly leaned forward and stared ahead into the gloom at a dim light ahead. It was the broad swathe of a 'County Road' sign looming up on the right. The girl lifted one arm in a waxy, slow motion and pointed.

Ansell didn't follow her pointing finger because her dressing gown had fallen wide open and the girl's breasts were in full view. He gaped openly at her breasts. Licking his lips, he muttered: "The Mission turnoff—three miles. You going to the Mission?"

The girl pointed again as another notice whipped past on the right.

Ansell grinned. "Well, I'll take that as a 'yes', lady. An' if you're going to the Mission, ah'll take you. It's no use a pretty thing like you a'walkin' around in this kind of weather, is it now?"

He drove on in silence, glancing down frequently to feast on the panorama of naked thigh and breast, occasionally righting the truck as it buffeted in the wind. "You from the hospital?" he asked casually. The girl didn't answer. "You seem a little, like, not all here, girl." She gazed straight ahead. "Well, maybe you *are* from the hospital," grinned Ansell suddenly, "You're wearing a hospital gown. Maybe I should get on a phone and call up right now—tell 'em one of them thar mental patients escaped!"

The girl stared bleakly ahead.

"Don't care, huh?" he chortled. "Maybe you can't even talk, eh? Can you even talk?" he asked in a hard, patronizing voice. "Well, if you can't talk, you can't drink." He pulled a quart from under his seat, dexterously unscrewed it with his teeth and took a swig. He offered her the bottle. She didn't even look at it.

In between swigs at the bottle, he eyed the girl shrewdly. "Well, honey," he said, "I guess you are gone—gone with the wind." He cackled. "Maybe you're so gone, I should take you back *after* we get to know each other... Yes siree..." He watched her closely, but she looked neither left nor right. He chuckled throatily and downed the rest of the quart.

He wound down his window. The wind roared louder and the truck swayed as the air buffeted into the cab. Papers swirled across the dashboard and the girl's hair was tossed into a silvery flurry around her face. Ansell threw the empty bottle into the shrieking wind and wound the window up hastily. The noise abated; the sudden drop in volume was almost like silence.

"This is our turnoff!" said Ansell, and turned right onto the dark mountain road. He drove along the road for about a mile, then slowed and eased the truck onto a grassy bank. The truck rolled to a halt and he cut the engine. As he switched off the truck lights, the gloom sprang up around them and the shriek of the wind rose in pitch as the engine died away.

The girl sat blankly for a moment, staring unseeing through the windshield into the gloom. Then she began fumbling awkwardly with the door handle.

"Going so soon?" drawled Ansell. "Why, if you wait just ten more minutes, honey, I'll drop you right at the door and tell 'em you was wandering about, all crazy like. They may even give me a reward!"

The girl ignored him and fiddled with the door lock with a puzzled look.

Ansell pulled his scrawny frame across the worn seat and placed an outstretched hand over the girl's breast. She neither resisted nor responded. "Mmm..." muttered Ansell kneading her soft breast, "Nice, nice..." He dropped his hand down to her knee and slid it up the inside of her thigh. The girl fumbled with the lock, oblivious to his presence. Ansell grew excited. He gripped her thigh with his bony fingers and began fumbling at his zipper with the other hand. "Honey, you are terrific!" he hissed, his chest heaving.

The girl managed to unlock the door and it swung open with a sudden shriek of wind. The girl slid across the seat and extended her right leg out of the door.

Ansell gripped her left calf tightly, still fumbling with his pants. "Not so fast, honey. We got some business," he rasped.

As if puzzled by an unknown obstruction, the girl tugged at her leg. She pulled again and Ansell tightened his grip. "C'mon, beauty," he said urgently, "Won't be more 'n five minutes!"

The girl turned around slowly and stared at her leg where Ansell's hand was clamped. She gazed at his bony hand blankly, then raised her gaze and looked into his face for the first time. Her face was chalky white and her eyes were like two huge, black pits. She dropped her gaze down to his hand again, as if equating for the first time her inability to move with Ansell's grip.

"Honey," hissed Ansell, "I—" He was cut off short as her fist smashed into his face with a force inconceivable from her slight frame. Ansell shrilled as his head snapped backwards. "Jesus!! You fuckin' bitch!!" The girl began climbing out of the truck. Enraged, Ansell launched himself across the seat and grabbed her dressing gown. "Whore!!" he spat painfully through bloody lips, "You broke my goddamn jaw!" The dressing gown tore and he grabbed a handful of hair and yanked the girl's head. Her brow struck the edge of the door with a dull smack, and for a moment the girl's eyes flared with surprise. Ansell managed to get two fistfuls of dressing gown and began pulling her back in, screaming curses.

Her eyes were dark with surprise and pain, the girl fingered a deep cut on her brow. Still puzzled, her eyes fell on Ansell again and, without warning, her fist shot out with terrific force and smacked into his Adam's apple. Ansell slumped backwards and toppled between the seats, gagging and choking.

The girl slipped out of the cab, swayed briefly and made a few hesitant steps forward, her torn clothes streaming in the wind. Then she pressed forward into the darkness, her right arm dangling limply at her side. Her figure grew indistinct in the gloom. Then she turned into a grove of swaying manzanitas and was swallowed by the blackness.

Ansell lay upside-down writhing on the cab floor, his feet up on the seat, the foot pedals digging into his shoulders as he gagged and choked, fighting for breath.

His struggles slowed and he lay gasping hoarsely, the breath rattling noisily in his throat. The left side of his face was a dull, throbbing pain. He touched his cheek bone tentatively with his fingers to find a huge, egg-shaped lump; he could hardly move his jaw.

"Fucking bitch!!" he hissed painfully, "Fucking, crazy bitch!! Goddamn screwball! Mental case! Broke my goddamn jaw!!"

He leaned sideways on the seat and with a grunt reached forward and slammed the cab door shut. The screaming of the wind abated. He hunched forward over the wheel and gazed through the windshield. Ahead was the blue-black of the sky with a dark ridge of the mountains outlined against it; to the right, a flurry of motion in the gloom as the trees were whipped back and forth by the wind.

"Bitch!! he muttered thickly. He flicked the headlights on and off and caught a brief glimpse of bushes bent by the wind and the glitter of the pebbles on the dusty road. No girl. "I'll git you!" he muttered, "Fuckin' crazy! Break mah jaw, heh?!"

He reached up and, with a screech of rusty metal, pulled the sun visor down. He fumbled one-handed and tore away a strip of duct tape which held an ancient .45 in place. "Bitch!!" he muttered as he hefted the gun in his hand. He placed the gun carefully down on the worn seat next to him and started the engine. "I'm a'comin' to get you, crazy girl!" he muttered through his teeth.

CHAPTER FOURTEEN

Peter faced Dooley across the partition.

Still wearing his hat, Sheriff Dooley sat at his desk, his fat bottom squeezed into a rotating chair and his boots up on an old-fashioned, roll-top desk. His gun and holster lay in front of him, black and shiny on the worn wooden surface. "So, you had to come down in person," said Dooley wearily. His piggy eyes looked red and tired. "But for what? I told you, boy, what more can I do?"

Peter gripped the edge of the partition with both hands and contained himself. It wouldn't do him or Miranda any good if he lost his temper now.

Dooley stared at Peter's white knuckles and slid open the drawer at his side with a smirk, pulled out a bottle of scotch and filled a shot glass with whisky. His movements, slow and studied, were deliberately insolent.

"I thought police officers didn't drink on duty," said Peter stiffly.

"It's four o'clock in the morning," said Dooley, "And I'm off duty."

"Sheriff," said Peter desperately, "Look at the weather! Look at the night! My wife is out there wandering around, hardly any clothes on! She's sick, man, sick!!"

The Sheriff, by way of an answer, reached forward and clicked on a desk lamp. Then he reached up without looking and pulled a cord dangling from the blinding white strip of the neon tube and instantly the room was plunged into a soft darkness, except for the pool of yellow light on the worn desk. "That's better," said Dooley, "My eyes feel like they're poppin' out of my head." Peter whirled around and stared at the wall, his jaw muscles tight with anger. "Look," said Dooley in a tired voice, "Don't get me wrong. I ain't getting in your way here, now. It's just that my version and yours don't quite tally. So I ain't as het up as you."

Peter whirled around and stared at Dooley belligerently. "What do you mean 'my' version?!! A half-dressed woman is out at this time of the night in God-knows what kind of state and you sit there drinking! What's 'my' version got to do with it?! Shit, man, this is your job!!"

Dooley's face went tight. "Don't tell me about my job." He swung his feet down and gripped both thighs with his pudgy hands, his legs thrown wide open. He leant forward snarling: "I got an all-car alert out for a junkie—what more can I do?!"

"A junkie?! What do you mean?!!"

"I use the term loosely, Mr. Riley," grinned Dooley mirthlessly, "Don't get too uppity with me, now. Look…" he relaxed and leaned forward confidentially, "…this ain't a big town. Things happen different to the city. I can't work like no city cop. I work with the people I know. An' I can read ole Prescott like a book."

"I don't know what you mean," mumbled Peter.

"The man is always covering up. Why, this state is known as the Marijuana Capital of America. Only last week he fixed up a local guy shot in a drug deal. Prescott's report says it was a hunting accident. I know better. Every day someone goes to that hospital off his head on something or other and the Good Doctor, misguidedly thinkin' he's helping, treats the shit-head and falsifies the report to cover up for him. Goddamn hippies!" Peter was silent. "You hear me? Maybe your girl is sick—but she goddamn made herself sick, I bet! I know the signs. So, what am I supposed to do? Run off into the night after every screwball who messes around with goddamn drugs? No, sir! If someone reports her, I'll let you know. But—" He stopped; he was talking to himself.

Peter had left.

Peter strode down the main street buffeted by the wind. It was a wild night, matching the wildness of his hot, angry thoughts. A slate whirled off a nearby roof and crashed to the ground inches from his feet but he strode on oblivious to it. The road was empty except for newspapers dancing in the gusts of wind. The telephone wires thrummed and howled as if a devil were loose in the night sky. To add to the insanity, the moon suddenly vaulted from behind the clouds, flooding the deserted road with its garish light.

Face set, Peter climbed into the Jeep and started the engine. He glanced upwards once to see a dark cloud streak across the moon, torn to ribbons by the wind. Then he revved the Jeep and shot out of the parking lot with a snarl of rubber on tarmac and headed north towards the Mission.

A patch of yellow in the gloom, the Sheriff's office was the only light on the street. Dooley peered through the window into the howling night, spat, took a swig from the whisky bottle and sank nonchalantly back into his seat.

CHAPTER FIFTEEN

Ansell had left the truck parked beneath some bushes, out of sight of the road. He loped forward along the dusty track in a crouching half run, holding the .45 at the ready. Dust devils whirled up around him and occasionally he balked as a tumbleweed lumbered across his path like a runaway horse—but he kept running.

He cocked his head; he couldn't hear a thing above the wind—it buffeted against his ears, blocking out all other sounds. He slowed and rounded the last bend cautiously, the gun cocked. Nothing. He stopped and peered off into the darkness.

Below lay the Mission and the vast looming bulk of the Tree etched inky-black against the faint white walls. Crouching low, Ansell ran down the dusty road toward the main entrance.

He reached the Mission gate and ducked behind the gate post. He peered around it. There was a light on in one of the Mission buildings. But Ansell knew that didn't mean much—in those parts it was common practice to leave a light burning in an empty house. He cautiously surveyed the scene. The moon was still hidden by the scudding clouds. Way up behind the Mission was the murky half-dome of the sierra hill and behind it, the jagged black silhouette of the mountains outlined faintly against the blue-gray of the night sky.

Blood-hot with anger, inflamed by the throbbing in his jaw, Ansell swore out loud: "Where is the bitch?!!" As if in answer, the moon slid from behind the clouds revealing the ghostly outlines of the buildings.

There! Something moved. He ducked out of sight and squinted. He saw it again. At the far end of the Mission building a figure flitted along the wall furtively and stopped. Ansell bit his lip, quivering with rage, and watched as the figure crouched against the pale adobe glow of the long building. Then it moved again and Ansell lost it for a moment.

He strained his eyes to locate the dim shadow. The wind howled and tore at the huge Tree, riffling the leaves like flags. Its shadow swayed across the Mission front, occluding everything in its gloom. There! He detected a sudden movement; a shadow amongst shadows. There *was* someone there.

Ansell fumbled on the ground until he located a sizable pebble. He stood cautiously and flung it towards the shadow with a jerk of his sinewy arm. He didn't hear the impact, but the shadowy figure obviously did, because it suddenly froze and crouched down. He grinned. It was the girl. Who else would be hiding from him? And, if she was hiding from him, he reasoned, likely there was no one else in the house.

To make sure, he chose a larger stone and threw it at the nearest of the Mission windows, full force. This time, even over the wind, *he* heard the crash; the resounding clang of stone on metal.

There was no response from inside, not even at the lighted window. But the shadowy figure crouching against the wall stood up and fled away from Ansell towards the far end of the house.

Ansell broke from cover and ran across the yard, shouting: "Hey, bitch, you come here!!" The dark figure froze briefly then bolted. "You!!! I gotta gun! Stop now!!!" He ran into the wind, roaring and railing at the girl, but the words were torn away from his lips. "Shit, she's getting away!!!" He sprinted across the dark yard just as the dark shape reached the end of the adobe building. "Bitch!!!" he screamed, and raced forward.

A gust of wind smacked against him with such force that his shirt tore open and he was almost bowled over. He stopped in his tracks and crouched down, swearing. A shuddering squeal rent the air and Ansell gazed up, startled. The rending noise increased, drowning the wind, and Ansell screamed as a huge black mass blotted out the wind-torn sky. He jumped back, but too late. It smashed him into the ground…

He lay half conscious, his ribs and chest crushed, his mind gibbering with terror, struggling weakly to resist the terrible force that pinned him to the ground. Then he realized what it was. He was trapped beneath the bulk of a huge tree limb. He moaned and writhed in pain as a heady, pungent smell assailed his nostrils. He managed to turn his neck slightly to see the Tree waving and thrashing in the wind. The moon flitted in and out of the raging clouds, throwing mad patterns onto Ansell's terrified face. Painfully, he screwed his neck around an inch more to see something glinting on the ground a few yards away. It was the .45, way, way out of reach.

"Help me!!" He beat at the tree branch with feeble blows. The wind tore away his voice and tossed it into the sky; a pitiful, thin sound. "Help me! Please!! I'm hurt! Don't leave me here!!" He scrabbled about frantically, but he couldn't move. The branches of the fallen limb whipped and flailed above his head as if trying to lash its pitiful prisoner with murderous force.

"Please!" screamed Ansell, "Help me!!"

No answer. The pain in his chest spread. Then a merciful numbness began to steal through the bottom half of his body.

For a full hour, Ansell lay there screaming for help. But no one came. And after a while, he drifted into a fitful state of half-unconsciousness, waking with constant, fearful starts at some noise until, finally, he fell into a feverish, pain-torn sleep.

Ansell woke with a jerk. The yard was still. The wind had subsided. He realized with numb horror that he still lay crushed beneath the huge limb. The pain in his chest had subsided, but he couldn't breathe properly except in short, jerky breaths. There was no sensation at all in his legs.

A grayishness in the sky above told him the dawn was coming. He turned his head and peered at the Mission building; it was becoming more distinct in the growing light, but he couldn't see clearly yet. He stared at the patch of ground just beyond where he lay with a sense of puzzlement. Then he realized what it was:

The gun was gone.

He let out a cry of fear and writhed under the massive log. Renewed splinters of pain tore at his chest and he stopped. He craned his neck backwards, trying to see behind him, his Adam's apple bulging. He glimpsed a dark shape flitting across the yard. It dodged out of sight behind the Tree.

"Please...help me!! Missy?!! Is that you?!" cried Ansell fearfully, "Please!!! Miss, I didn't mean no harm. I wasn't going to hurt you! Please!!" he whined, full of self-pity.

The shape detached itself from the shadows. It blotted out the night sky as it bent over Ansell who was suddenly aware of the cloying scent of fruit. Ansell screamed as a hand grabbed his throat but his scream was cut short by a grip of iron. His eyes rolled. He tried to scream again but something wet was forced into his mouth. He whipped his head back and forth to dislodge it but the scream became a choking gurgle. His breath rattled in his throat then eventually died away altogether.

The black shape straightened, head cocked as if listening, then loped across the yard to disappear from sight behind the Mission building.

Ansell lay quiet and still in the grayish light of the dawn, his mouth wide and his eyes staring sightlessly up into the branches of the Tree.

¤

Peter dropped the Jeep down into second gear and swung around the last bend. And there was the Mission, its lands bathed with a pre-dawn glow that tinged the eastern ridges red.

Peter stopped the Jeep and gazed down at the Mission, his heart filled with a mixture of hope and foreboding. It seemed peaceful enough. The light still burned in the kitchen; blue jays darted above the protective nets on the vegetable garden. But there was something different about the Tree. Peter couldn't quite make out what, though he squinted at it for some time...

Then he realized that the Mission yard was full of broken foliage. tumbleweeds were jammed between the buildings; splintered wood and branches lay everywhere—the disastrous aftermath of the storm.

Peter started the engine and began his descent while his practiced eye measured the damage: some of the fruit trees were destroyed and the eight-sided net he'd erected in the vegetable garden had been flung in the air to smash against a Californian Bay some two hundred yards away. A section of the roof scaffolding was down. Apart from that, the damage seemed to be fairly superficial.

There was no sign of Miranda.

Peter bumped over the rutted track and between the large gate posts into the yard, pausing only to frown at the rough sign post and its odd inscription, 'Alavera'.

Then he saw it.

A huge branch had torn off the Tree.

He stopped the Jeep and climbed over the side slowly. The Tree had lost a huge amount of foliage. The yard was a graveyard of torn branches. Some of the limbs had been stripped completely and were stark in the morning light like the gnarled limbs of an ancient and arthritic giant frozen in naked postures.

The fallen limb was still attached to the main trunk—just. It hung on by a yellow strip of raw, splintered wood, exposing a gaping wound.

Peter approached the broken limb cautiously. The leaves were oddly sensuous and slippery beneath his boots. He examined the trunk, which oozed a yellowish puss where the limb had torn it. The broken limb angled down in a shallow curve from the main trunk to where the remaining twenty feet had impacted the ground in a mish-mash of broken branches, leaves and sap. Leaves hung down from the broken branches, limp and dying like wet flags on a windless day.

He wrinkled his nose at the sharp, acrid smell of the oozing sap, the musty odor of the blossoms and the fetid smell of crushed fruit. It made him feel nauseous.

Like a withered, arthritic arm that had over-reached itself, the fallen limb lay twisted at an unnatural angle. The fruit was everywhere; vast gobbets of sticky, crimson under a thin carpet of leaves, like blood oozing up through a pale green bandage.

"Jesus!" muttered Peter, glancing at the Mission thoughtfully. It was a good job that the huge limb had fallen short of the Mission building, otherwise it would have smashed right through the roof.

He surveyed the scene, arms akimbo, grimacing with distaste at the sticky fruit splattered everywhere. He took a stick and raked the leaves, taking care not to touch the fruit with his bare hands. The torn limb was blood red at the center—just like madrone, he thought. The stick encountered something soft and he jerked his hand away instinctively, dropping the stick.

He spotted a broom laying on the ground near the Mission wall, retrieved it and, maintaining a cautious distance, he used it to brush away the leaves.

The leaves slid back to reveal the white face of a man gazing sightlessly into the sky. His mouth was wide open; his cheeks plump, crammed with the crimson fruit.

Peter stood frozen with shock. Then he glanced wildly about as shock was replaced by horror. Without thinking, in a numbed, automatic fashion, he brushed away the remainder of the leaves from the man's face and body and stood back, breathing heavily, staring at Ferris Ansell's corpse.

The scene was etched permanently into Peter's mind: the man's wizened and bony Adam's apple; the carmen fruit dribbling over his blue lips; the stubbly chin and unseeing eyes; and the dark bruises around the neck as though his throat had been seized by steel pincers. The man's back was arched in a death agony against the huge black limb that pinned him to the ground.

Peter recalled the truck he'd seen parked off the County Road and realized it must have belonged to the dead man. But why had he parked so far from the Mission—and walked in? Peter backed slowly away from the body, his mind awhirl with possibilities.

His foot encountered something beneath the leaves. He hopped backwards then cautiously approached with the broom in his hands and pushed the leaves aside to reveal…

A torn garment—a hospital dressing gown.

Numbly, Peter cleared an area around the dressing gown then bent down. One pocket of the yellow and white-striped gown was stained crimson and on the ground next to it was a thin, sticky pool of…? Peter bent over the puddle without touching it and his nose twitched at the acrid smell. Vomit. It was vomit; somebody had eaten the fruit, then retched. Somebody?? A hospital dressing gown?? "Oh, my God!" he muttered.

He jerked upright, ran to the vegetable garden and returned with a rake. He raked the sticky vomit frantically into the ground, stamping it down to erase all traces. He impaled the dressing gown on the end of the rake and carried it around the Mission to the leaf incinerator.

The sun was creeping over the sierra hill like a tide of congealed blood as he poured gasoline over the gown and lit it with a 'whumph!' of smoky, yellow flame. He stood watching the material burn. As the flame licked over the juice-soaked material, it hissed and sizzled. He turned it over a few times with the rake, then threw handfuls of leaves and twigs on top of it until it had burnt to an indistinguishable mass of ash.

Only then did he leave and walk woodenly to the kitchen. After carefully washing his hands, he picked up the phone and called the Sheriff.

Dooley stood over the dead man, staring down. "This un's just like Cal O'Donnell," he muttered. Peter hovered in the background, expressionless, watching the Sheriff's hawk-eyed inspection. "An' they both really liked fruit," Dooley said with a mirthless smile, turning a quizzical eye on Peter.

Peter shrugged wearily, but exhaustion was beginning to take its toll.

The Sheriff, still chewing, walked over to the police car. He looked straight at Peter with a curious expression then, unhooking the microphone, he spoke into it. "Sheriff Dooley at Mission Farm…yep… O.K., an APB for a white, Caucasian female; 120 pounds; blonde hair, blue eyes; name of

Miranda Riley."

Peter went rigid and strode to the patrol car shaking his head in anger. "Hey!! What is this??!!"

The Sheriff continued: "She may be armed; she certainly is dangerous. Wanted in connection with an unsolved homicide. She was last seen wearing a white and yellow-striped dressing gown, bare feet. She may not be in a rational state; please exercise extreme caution."

"Are you going to tell me what this is all about?!!" shouted Peter white-faced.

"Sure will," said the Sheriff, clicking the microphone back into place, "I'll tell you exactly what this is about, boy. Then right after that, I get to call the coroner, the ambulance, the photographer and a whole mess 'o other people in the line of my duty—so ah would appreciate it if you would not interrupt me then. And, just take a step back, boy, you're crowding me." He dropped his hand to his gun and Peter stood back, grinding his teeth.

"O.K., what makes you think that Miranda has anything to do with this??!!" stormed Peter, "She isn't even here!!"

"Well, sir," said the Sheriff tapping one foot, "On account of the fact that we got a report about your girl. Seems someone phoned in this morning and says they saw a woman in a dressing gown get into Ferris Ansell's four-wheel-drive last night—a red Toyota. And, Mr. Riley, that there's what's left of Ferris Ansell, and his Toyota is parked back up there beyond the hill. Ah saw it on the way down. Now, son, I know you're upset, but them's the facts. And one more thing before you get so uppity—are you telling me everything you know?"

Peter dropped his eyes, his voice low. "I don't know anything. What are you getting at?"

"You know what ah mean, don't you?" snarled the Sheriff.

"I told you, I don't know anything," said Peter, his jaw set firmly. But he could not help but look down at the tortured expression on Ansell's face and the crimson fruit rammed into the dead man's mouth.

CHAPTER SIXTEEN

Peter drove down the main street of the town, looking neither right nor left. It was nearly midday with the sun high in the sky above the one-storey buildings and the neat streets with their clipped gardens and yellowing lawns. Peter stopped the Jeep at the Post Office and parked. He was exhausted, but he had to leave the Mission; had to leave the gaggle of police and strangers that had pried and prodded him. Finally, he'd given up and left, sickened at this disaster that had brought in its wake these strange people over-running his beloved sanctuary, like insects on a piece of meat, drawn by foulness.

On the front seat of the Jeep was a small box. Inside the box was a kitchen jar tightly sealed. Inside the jar, a rotten piece of fruit from the Tree. He took the box and climbed the steps of the Post Office. Old Glory, fluttering in the breeze over his head, seemed to mock him with its mundane normality.

Secretaries stood in line, prim-mouthed in their office finery, next to muddy farmers and squat, elderly women propped up on thick canes, clutching their weekly checks.

Peter's eyes fell onto one black-clad figure and the thick, gnarled cane in her hand. Her arthritic fingers twisted around the handle in a bony grip that made him shiver involuntarily. His sleepless brain was addled with the sights and sounds of the last twenty-four hours, and his ears buzzed. He needed to rest. He shook the feeling off resolutely, went into one of the phone booths, closed the door and sat on the minuscule seat.

As he sat down his head spun. "God," he muttered, resolving to eat and sleep soon. He took a deep breath and wearily dialed a number in the Bay area using his calling card. He mis-dialed twice trying to punch in the long string of numbers, but, eventually he got it right and he was connected. "Hi, I'd like to speak to Professor David Gordon… No, at the Department of Bio-Chemical Research… No, this is a long-distance call! Please, it's very important… Peter Riley… Look, I'll wait, O.K.?"

Peter waited for what seemed like an age, then a light voice with a faint English accent came on the other end. "Hello, this is David Gordon, *who* is that now?"

"Dave! It's Peter—Peter Riley!"

"Pete! Good Lord, Peter! How are you? Where are you? In the Bay area?"

74   P. Willis-Pitts

"Dave," said Peter, "I'm in Northern California and there's some trouble going on up here. I can't give the details. But I'd like your help."

"Mm, sounds serious. How can I help? What do you need?"

"Listen, I've sent you—or, at least, I'm going to send you—a sample for analysis. It's a kind of fruit, but God-knows what. I don't want you to identify it—that might take too long. Just do an in-depth bio-analysis of it and send me the results. And be careful, I think it's poisonous."

"Well, I can do that," said David, "And I'd be glad to. But it would help if you told me why or what you think the properties of the plant are."

"I don't know. But I think that Miranda has been…poisoned by it."

"Oh, no! Is she…she O.K.?"

Peter paused. "Yeah, she's O.K. Look, I'll tell you more about that when I get more info. But for now it would really help if you did some of your usual incredibly astute and scientific stuff on this sample."

David chuckled. "I'll do my best. Send it off and… You got a phone number up there?"

"Sure," said Peter giving him the number. For the address he recited the Post Office box they'd rented in town.

"O.K., Peter, I'll do that right away. When are you coming down to the Bay area?"

"I dunno," said Peter heavily, "I'll get back to you on that. Sorry to be abrupt, there's a line waiting for this phone." There was no one outside, but Peter didn't want to talk any more. Though he felt an urgent need to share his burden with someone, he held back; he didn't want to blurt anything stupid into the phone and upset David as well. "Look, I'll write to you later."

"Sure, sure. And ring me when you can. You be careful now!"

"Sure. Thanks. 'Bye Dave." Peter replaced the receiver. And, pushing the door open, he joined the line of farmers and gnarled old ladies with their gnarled and twisted sticks.

¤

Peter lay on the bed in the motel, staring at the same cracked ceiling, eyeing the same dingy walls and depressing pictures. The fact that this was a different room only added to his bad mood; it was indistinguishable from the room he'd stayed in before.

Peter tried to quieten his buzzing brain. He was exhausted and should sleep, but for once in his life he was unable to be practical, to push aside gnawing thoughts and to do the right thing.

Miranda… He kept turning her name over and over in his mind. Where was she, sweet, sweet Miranda? His lovely, natural girl a fugitive from the Law! It was all so insane, so impossible. Within hours, his whole life had been warped and distorted as if seen through flawed glass. Peter clenched his fists at the realization that he was impotent. There was nothing to do but wait, but he could not stand it any longer.

He swung off the bed, grabbed the local directory, opened it and ran his finger down it.There it was 'Martinez', 'Martinez L.', 'Martinez M.'—three of them. Peter hesitated, then, picking up the phone, he got the operator to dial the first number. A man's voice answered. "Is that Miya Martinez?"

"It is," said the deep, resonant voice, "Come over and see me, Peter. I've been expecting you. The address is in the book, first entry."

Peter started: "Hey, look—!" But he was talking into the buzz of the phone. Martinez had hung up.

Peter frowned for a moment, irritated, then curiosity overcame him. Did Martinez know something? Why had he expected the call? Within minutes, Peter was out of the motel, heading for the Jeep.

¤

Peter was doubly surprised. First, at the appearance of Miya when he came to the door of the clapboard house. He wore nothing save a towel around his waist and in the half-light spilling through the door, he gleamed like a mahogany statue, globules of sweat on his massive shoulders. His face was as expressionless as carved teak.

"Oh, sorry, Mr. Martinez—were you in the bath?" said Peter a little over-awed by this transformation of Martinez into an ancient Indian warrior.

"Call me Miya, please Peter," he said. His carved, inscrutable expression disappeared, replaced by a disarming smile.

"Miya it is," said Peter and cautiously stepped into the house.

That was the second surprise: Visions of Indian hides fringed with beads, woven mats and bleak, carved totems faded rapidly. Peter surveyed a neat room surrounded by shelves of books, with a large audio console, tape deck and player in one corner and a very modern VCR in the other. Miya watched Peter's expression with a grin. "It's, er, not quite what I expected from…" Peter gesticulated, wordless.

"An Indian?" Miya chucked deep in his throat. "The Indian has to adapt to his environment or die, Peter. It would be as foolish for me to try to live in this house as if I were in the wild, as it would be to try to live in the wild as if I were in a house. But, come," he said, "Your expectations will not be completely disappointed."

They passed through the house into a back garden which was surrounded by a high, thick hedge of juniper. Peter stopped on the porch and peered into the gloom. He could smell wood-smoke, at the same time acrid and fragrant.

Peter could just make out a shape in the darkness: a low, circular struc-ture with chinks of yellowish light glinting through cracks in the walls. Pale in the starlight, a thin column of white smoke wafted from a central hole in the structure. Peter stood, gazing at the sky and the hills that circled the town—a deep black against the dark violet of the night—not knowing what to say.

"Take your clothes off," said Miya slipping out of his towel, "It's hot in there."

Peter began to take his clothes off. "What is it?" he asked curiously.

"It's an Indian sweat house," said Miya. He draped his towel over the edge of the veranda and stood naked, waiting for Peter.

Peter dropped his pants and stood shivering in the cold night air. He glanced up at Miya.

Side-lit by the light from the kitchen door, Miya stood like a bronze statue, impassive and dignified. An owl hooted and the house and the town seemed to crumble and slip away, and all was wild and all was wood-smoke, as if the town itself had been a dream and this Indian savage was the only reality, standing proud and naked.

Without a word, Miya turned and went into the primitive structure. Peter followed and ducked under the low doorway of the sweat house.

He found himself beneath an inverted bowl formed by bent willows. Branches had been heaped on the walls to seal the lodge. A pit had been dug at the center and into this was heaped glowing red embers. A plume of smoke drifted upwards and found its way out through a small hole in the center of the roof. Objects littered the periphery of the room, but Peter could not make them out in the dull light from the fire.

Miya squatted next to two raised, grass-covered platforms.

The heat was a pleasure after the night air and Peter soon stopped shivering. He sat down on the edge of a platform. The grass tickled his bare flesh pleasantly. He took a deep breath of warm air as he realized how tense he'd been.

He watched the bronze statue that was Miya sprinkle the glowing coals with a handful of herbs. Pungent smoke billowed and swirled upwards, caught in the current of warm air. But Miya didn't allow the smoke to escape; he wafted the currents of air, beating them down with his hands until the smoke filled the lodge. Then he began to sing; a strange, repetitive dirge in an unknown tongue.

The smoke bit at Peter's lungs and he coughed involuntarily. Though acrid and pungent, the sensation was not entirely unpleasant. Peter's eyes blurred and his hands started to tingle. His pulse began to race as the fire flared up, casting a corona of shadow around the kneeling Indian; a shifting half-light that played tricks with his eyes. Miya's face blurred and wavered in the flickering light, giving the impression of darkened eyes and painted cheekbones.

"Tell me what happened," said Miya softly without breaking the spell.

Peter talked. It came out with an unaccustomed rush of words, his tongue seeming to wag of its own accord. He described the house, the Mission, the Tree, the murders, Miranda's disappearance. He even spoke of finding the dressing gown and the pool of vomit at the scene of the second murder. And then, compulsively almost, he went on to describe the roof-top incident, the picture of Kuksu, and his own hallucination. Finally, he told of his fears for Miranda. When he'd finished, there was a silence broken only by the hissing of damp twigs in the fire and the occasional crack as a hot coal exploded.

Peter sank back on the grass mat. He was hot now, very hot. Sweat was pouring down his head and shoulders and running in trickles over his chest and belly. He wondered vaguely at the wisdom of telling Miya so much, but somehow it didn't seem to matter. He began to breathe more deeply and evenly; the knot of tension disappeared from his shoulders; he could feel the pungent smoke warm in his lungs. Everything else seemed very distant: Miranda; the Mission; the murders. All that seemed to matter was the heat, the softness of the grassy bed, the trickle of sweat down his body; and the dull pounding of his heart. He closed his eyes, took a great breath of the hot air and let out a long sigh and with it, he seemed to exhale all his worries.

Miya began to speak, slowly but clearly: "There's something I'd like to tell you," he said in a low, resonant voice, "Something about the land you live on…about the Mission."

Peter opened his eyes slowly. Miya was squatting motionless before the fire, sweat pouring down his gleaming body. Peter felt relaxed, almost drowsy, but his sight and smell were clear and sharp. He watched the play of muscles along Miya's arm as he reached forward and stirred the fire; could smell the wetness in the air as a damp branch sizzled.

Miya began his story: "In 1833, owing to the devastating effect of the secularization of the Californian missions, large numbers of missionaries left California altogether. One such group left by sea in the vessel San Antonio de Padua. They set out from San Diego, a very primitive port at the time. The vessel, equipped with provisions taken from the sadly-depleted stock of the Mission San Diego de Alcala, was headed for the Port of San Francisco de Asis in the north. On board the ship were the crew, two blacksmiths, a carpenter, ten Mission Indians and eleven priests from Mexico City, heading for adventure in this promised land of California. This crew, bewildered by the events that were taking place in the older Missions, was prepared to brave the unknown for the promise of a new life."

Miya paused without looking up and threw a handful of twigs on the fire. His eyes were dark mirrors that gazed beyond the blaze of the fire. He suddenly spoke again:

"The ship rounded the Cape San Lucas and was never seen again. No one knows what happened to that ship. But I do." He looked at Peter for the first time and picked up something from the floor. It was an ancient book bound in worn and cracked leather, the pages yellowed and torn, the edges rough. "This diary was found by my forefathers and kept as a token of great power and magic. It's been with my family for years now. It is the diary which was kept by Father Miguel Morales, one of these unfortunate and wretched men…"

Miya took something from the book's pages and placed it in front of

Peter. It was an aged sheet of parchment. On it was a sketch; a fairly detailed sketch. Peter studied it curiously. It depicted one of those promontories so common to the northern Californian coast: an arch of barren rock, its base girdled by angry white foam. Between the twin uprights of the arch, the sea surged relentlessly, throwing up foam-flecked spumes. "This is where the ship foundered," he said. Then he opened the ancient diary and read in a quiet voice:

> "'Thus into the strange and terrible nave was sucked our ship 'ere it had a chance; with full sail set, the vessel shot into this Devil's mouth. Her masts were snapped off like pipe stems and the hull was jammed irretrievably into this vast maw. As the swell crashed and heaved, the ship began to thump against the roof of the opening like a cork in a bottle. Three crew members were crushed to death by the overhanging roof of rock, whilst others of us hurried astern where ropes and grapnels had been cast over the huge but-tress. There, by dint of Prayer and panic, a number of us, not exceeding twenty, managed to haul ourselves to safety; if that be the word to apply to the onerous alternative of balancing along a treacherous and wind-torn bridge of slip-pery rock, lashed by sea spray. But manage we did and we attained the relative safety of the adjacent cliff top with only the loss of one man, poor wretch, who was buffeted off the rock by a huge breath of wind that nearly took all of us. At our last glimpse, the ship was little more than kindling wood, bobbing on the surface of that malevolent swell.'"

Miya fell silent. Peter closed his eyes. He almost could hear the howl of the wind, the screams of the dying men shrill against the rending and groaning of splintering timber. Miya's voice brushed gently across Peter's thoughts:

> "'Escape we did, but for what, at first, we did not know. Our sad little band struggled through a downpour that was almost as thick as the sea-spray itself. And when this rain abated somewhat, we caught glimpses of an ungracious and hostile country, all rocks, brushwood and rugged hills. Cursed by the cold, saddened by the loss of our comrades, we huddled together for warmth, soaked to the bone with the torrent, some of us already shaking with fever. I con-ducted the sorry band in prayers of hope to Our Good Lord, it seeming that I, by omission and Fate, had been chosen to lead this sorry band, consisting of nine priests (what fate!), four Indians and six crew members, including, as Destiny

would have it, the carpenter and blacksmith.

Second Day: Dawn did not alleviate our misery, but added to it. The cessation of rain was a mixed blessing, as now we had to worry about water. Not knowing where we were, upon the instructions of the Indians, we struck inland.

Third Day: Our band of persons struggles on hopelessly, aided somewhat by our prayers, which, thank God, I had the strength to urge them on. Persons is a somewhat ostentatious appellation for the band of thirsty, scurvy-ridden skeletons that straggled through this God-forsaken country-side. Not knowing the how or why of this land, we were content to follow the lead of the Indians, who managed to feed us by dint of many strange dietary innovations, such as acorns, seeds and, at one stage, grass-hoppers, though I had to decline the latter.

Fourth Day: God be praised! We have fallen on a clement valley sheltered from the winds with as fair an aspect as a cultured garden. Water is in plentiful supply from a gracious river that gurgles; a sweetly-swelling hillock of oak and walnut upon which is placed a huge black rock, so precarious as to suggest the haphazard mishandling of its brooding mass by a careless giant. The greatest of these wonders is a tree, however; a tree which provides us with peace and sanctuary beneath its bows, for such a tree as this I have never seen. So huge is its mantel of branches, so vast its mighty trunk, that the men are referring to it as the Behemoth. Beneath this tree we rest. A fire is kindled on the stony earth beneath its sweeping over-arch and with the advent of a number of fish caught at the expert hands of the Indians from a river which seems plentifully supplied, I can only say that life is beginning to take on a more seemly aspect.'"

Peter was now sitting bolt upright staring straight at Miya whose face was a bronze mask in the glow from the fire. Miya paused, cast a handful of twigs onto the coals and, as they blazed up, he read on by their light:

"'It has been decided by group consensus that, having no tools other than an axe and some knives, no provisions except what the Good Lord provides from the earth, we shall build a humble shelter fashioned out of dry stone by the ingenuity of the carpenter and helped by the muscles and

sinews of all. And here, for want of anything further which can be done, we will build our Mission and we will, band of wretches that we are in this unseemly, unknown landscape, hopefully survive by God's Grace. My writing materials being precious and my life being extended somewhat longer than I could have hoped at first, I will be able, from here on, only to annotate those incidents of great import. I have only four pages left wherein to write...'"

Peter sat quietly, his eyes fixed on Miya, his heart and mind locked in another time, another place.

"'Miracle of miracles, a sign! Affairs, though primitive, are well inasmuch as our humble abode is extended by the ingenuity of the Indians and our two craftsmen. But wondrous to speak, the tree, without a single leaf on it, has blossomed a great flower of crimson hue that fills the air with its heady, pungent odors and bespeaks of the spring and summer which will surely follow this winter as the sun doth rise in the morning to bring us hope and salvation...'"

Miya paused and glanced up at Peter. Peter could not see Miya's eyes— they were lost in pools of darkness. The fire blazed, making two patches of red on his cheekbones. He continued:

"'A strange indolence has fallen over the men with the ready availability of the food. Our plans for a shelter have fallen in disrepair and there is no one who will hardly take the responsibility for gathering the wood for the fire. I have tried to arouse the spirits of the secular members of the group by the songs and chanting so revered amongst those of our calling. But it becomes more and more difficult to arouse them from their apathy. The Indians, who declined to eat the fruit, have long disappeared; gone back to the wild, I dare say. I can only give them my blessing, for without them we would all have perished. Already two of our number have succumbed to the cold and the scurvy and we have laid their bodies in shallow graves, being too weak to do little more. They were, nonetheless, given the Full Rights, although it has sorely taxed my strength.'"

Miya stopped and spoke in a slightly different tone. "The account is almost finished, Peter," he said, "There are only two more brief entries." He glanced down at the last two pages of the book.

"'Two of the men are subject to a strange hallucination or a waking dream that prompts them into greatest terror. Oddly enough, they both claim to see the same thing: a Red Indian, grave-faced and bleak, adorned in skins and feathers, his face daubed with brilliant ocher paint. These men, who are beginning to frighten the others, say we must leave this place; it is a place of the Devil...'"

"Here is the final entry," said Miya quietly:

"'Horror upon horror! It cannot be, but I witnessed it. The Devil's Emissaries stalk amongst us at night, for the dead are walking! It cannot be!'"

Miya stopped.

Peter stared at him, dazed. "Go on," he said thickly.

"I can't," said Miya, "The account ends here."

"And these men? What became of them?"

Miya shrugged. "No one knows. It would seem they just disappeared." He stood up, wiped his brow with the back of his hand and headed towards the doorway of the sweat house.

Peter swung himself off the grass platform and padded out into the night. The cold air hit him with a shock. As he took in a huge lungful, he realized how thick the air had been in the sweat house. He began to shiver immediately; his head spun. Miya handed him a crisp, dry towel. Peter grabbed his clothes up from the floor, stepped inside the house and began toweling himself down hastily.

The sight of the VCR, the books and the tape deck was warm and reassuring. Peter's dizziness faded, taking with it visions of a band of ragged men scratching a fitful living at the base of the huge Tree, beset by unknown terrors. He slipped on his clothes and sat down in a leather armchair, grateful for the feeling of his clothes against his skin. His limbs were relaxed, almost rubbery, and he was overcome by a sense of indolence even though his mind was alert.

Miya came in wearing jeans and a fringed buckskin shirt. He handed Peter a steaming mug of fragrant herb tea. "Here," he said, "Drink this. It'll clear your head."

"Were you throwing pot leaves on the fire?" asked Peter.

"Nope," said Miya with a sudden wicked grin, "But it wasn't pine leaves either!"

"Whatever it was, it did the trick," sighed Peter, "I feel much better than when I went in. Quite a story, though," he said thoughtfully, "These old legends are quite creepy."

"Peter," said Miya, "That was not a legend. It was a diary—a factual account."

"Well, as factual as a half-starved, hallucinating priest could be in the middle of an alien and hostile land," retorted Peter.

Miya sighed. "You are a scientist, Peter. A scientist and a rational man…"

"Yes, of course. Why do you say it like that?"

"Look, my family has followed the Mission's history with some interest ever since the disappearance of that first band of men, and there are some strange facts associated with the Mission lands."

"Such as?" asked Peter sipping his tea.

"Well, for one: The Pomo Indians have always refused its inclusion in their land grants. In fact, they were so violently opposed to it that a site had to be found at some distance from the first site designated in their Land Settlement. You see, the original site would have taken in the Mission lands."

"What was the problem, then?" frowned Peter.

"The Tree…is called the Huk Tree by my people," said Miya. "The Huk is a mythical bird whose quills carry inside them a red liquid that killed people."

"That," said Peter in an abstracted manner, "May be less a myth than a medical fact. That Tree certainly seems to have some toxic qualities."

"Peter," said Miya gently, "In 1901 the land was purchased by one Santos Valasquez, the son of a man who had made a fortune in the Gold Rush. Valasquez came to the United States to realize a dream long promised; a dream of freedom from the religious persecution of Europe. It was he who had the Mission built—built along the lines of the old Camino Real Missions in the south. He wanted to set up a church more akin to the early ideas of St. Francis, an order which eschewed dependence on worldly goods. He thought the Mission in the valley would realize his dream. He ploughed his money into building, clearing, planting the land and when it was ready, he took a Holy Vow, gave the rest of his money to the poor and moved in with twelve other neo-Franciscans, as he called them. They were only there for a year, then they disappeared."

"Disappeared?" said Peter, "How? What year was this?"

"1903."

"Well, it's a little harder to disappear in 1903 than in 1833—a few more folks around California by then," said Peter wryly.

"So the land lay empty until it was bought up by the private owner I told you about before."

"Oh. The guy who wanted it for the Indian Guru who died?"

"Yep. You see, a clause in Valasquez's deed stated that the land had always to be used for religious purposes."

"So, where do we come in?" grinned Peter, "The Aloe Vera Mission isn't exactly a religious organization."

"Oh, we had the original clause over-ruled," said Miya, "Otherwise we could never have sold the Mission. It really did get a bad reputation."

"Haunted!!" said Peter mockingly.

"Peter," said Miya, "I don't want to alarm you, but I think you should take the warning more seriously."

"The warning? What warning?"

"The warning from Kuksu. You got the same warning as those earlier men in 1833. 'Get out!' he is saying."

Peter squirmed restlessly in his chair. "Miya," he said, "I don't want to offend you. I don't dismiss these old legends—there's always an element of truth in them. But the idea of my...sunstroke being a warning is not really something that readily computes."

"Peter, traditionally those who wish to enter into the Kuksu sect have done so by prolonged starvation or near-drowning or even by making themselves sick—even by wounding themselves with knives. The idea is to induce a state of temporary dementia so that a more archaic, deeper part of the mind can function. This puts the initiate in direct contact with Kuksu."

"Exactly!" retorted Peter. "And if Indians induce hallucinations in order to see this Kuksu, small wonder that's who they do see when they do hallucinate! It's quite logical."

"So, how do you explain your seeing him?" asked Miya softly.

Peter shrugged. "I saw an Indian and then I saw a picture of an Indian."

"We all look alike, do we?" asked Miya evenly.

"Hey, Miya, don't! Please! I'm trying very hard not to offend you, but if I try to respect your...your mystical beliefs, please have some respect for my scientific beliefs!"

Miya nodded. "You see, Peter, it's not for me I say all of this, it's for Miranda. She is in danger, I believe. I think she has been poisoned, but I don't know how badly and I really want to help."

"Well, thanks a lot, Miya," said Peter with visible discomfort, "But you see, I'm having the fruit Miranda ate analyzed by one of the country's top biochemists, and on the basis of that, I'll see what can be done."

"No Indian mumbo-jumbo, hey," said Miya flatly.

"Miya," said Peter exasperated, "You seem determined to take offense!"

"No, Peter, I'm determined to save you and Miranda from something terrible—and you won't listen!"

Peter stood up, embarrassed. He paced up and down, waving his arms in the air, apologizing, defending. He was agitated that he'd upset Miya. But he couldn't let some would-be soothsayer meddle with Miranda's health—not even Miya.

Miya listened expressionlessly as Peter painfully dug a pit of penitude with his own words, then fell into it. There was a heavy silence which, mercifully, was broken by the phone ringing.

Miya picked up the phone."Yes, he's here." He turned to Peter. "It's the

P. Willis-Pitts

Sheriff."

"God, how did he know where I was?!" hissed Peter.

Miya shrugged knowingly. "You can't make a move in this town without everyone knowing what you're doing."

Peter took the phone apprehensively and cradled it against his cheek. "Peter Riley speaking."

"Riley," came Dooley's tired voice, "We picked up your wife."

"How is she?" asked Peter nervously, "Is she O.K.?"

"She's fine—she's fine. Don't worry," said the Sheriff. His manner was changed; he seemed less belligerent than usual. "Look, Riley, you should know this. The Widow Jenkins found her wandering on her property last night. Nearly shot her in the dark; said the girl was dazed and confused, crying. Seems she didn't know how she got there or what."

"Oh, my God!" muttered Peter.

"Well, that's the bad news, Riley," came the tinny voice, "The good news is that the Widow kept the girl there, looked after her so to speak, and that kinda clears her of the murder to a large extent."

"How?" breathed Peter. His chest filled with a sudden surge of hope.

"Well, she couldn't kill ole Ferris then make it to the Widow's place in that time. And, according to the coroner's estimate, the Widow was tucking her into bed about the same time as ole Ferris got his. So, she's off the hook."

Peter sat down, tears pricking his eyes. "Where is she?" he asked hoarsely.

"In the hospital. The Widow brought her in just now. Seems that the Widow didn't know anything about the girl being a murder suspect. In fact," the Sheriff chuckled dryly, "The ole bat chewed my ear off when I told her that. Said the girl couldn't harm a fly."

"Is she…O.K.?" asked Peter.

"Well, yeah. 'Cept she's got a broken wrist. Can't remember how she did it. She's been askin' for you."

"Oh, Christ!" breathed Peter, "I'll be there right away." He paused, "Oh, Sheriff," he said, "One thing…"

"Yeah?" came Dooley's voice.

"Thanks, hey."

There was a pause at the other end, then the Sheriff hung up.

Relief swept though Peter with such a painful, sweet flood that he swayed on his feet. Miya grabbed him and made him sit down. "Hey, you take it easy. Are you O.K.?"

"I sure am," said Peter with a wan smile, "Miranda is off the hook—they've cleared her of the murder." He pumped Miya's hand. "I gotta go—I gotta go!"

"Can you drive O.K.?" frowned Miya, "You seem pretty spent."

"I'll be alright," said Peter and, grabbing his coat, he dashed off to the Jeep.

Miya watched the Jeep roar off into the night. His expression was dark and troubled. He stared out of the window long after the Jeep was swallowed by the gloom, fumbling absently with the amulet hanging around his neck.

CHAPTER SEVENTEEN

Peter meticulously sprinkled the mound of vanilla ice cream with grated walnuts, speckling the thick layer of caramel sauce. With the appearance of a magician about to perform his best trick, Peter pulled out a packet of M&Ms and some Oreo cookies. He carefully arranged the M&Ms in neat circles around the huge scoop of ice-cream. Then, as a final touch, he broke two Oreo cookies down the middle and embedded them in the caramel sauce like four, dark butterfly wings. He contemplated his masterpiece for a moment, then handed Miranda a spoon, with the command: "Eat."

Miranda, sitting at the table of the fast-food restaurant, had Peter's jacket thrown around her shoulders to hide her makeshift clothing. Her right hand was in a cast. She smiled at Peter, eyes sparkling, and leant across the table whispering: "Everybody's been watching you for the last ten minutes."

Peter looked up, and the dumpy counter-hand, a middle-aged woman wearing an incongruously short skirt, suddenly looked the other way. A fat-bellied man in a plaid shirt, jeans and cowboy boots suddenly became engrossed by his coffee. The man's wife, a thin, lusterless woman with grayish wisps of hair, began to inspect her tray of french fries and chicken pieces as if they were the last remaining articles of interest in the universe.

Peter laughed. "I don't care about them—I care about you. C'mon, eat up. You know how much you love it."

Miranda protested that it was too much for her. Nevertheless, she drove the spoon into the ice-cream left-handed and, despite her awkwardness, within minutes almost, demolished it.

Peter sat watching her eat, a soft expression on his face. It was a strange and rare occasion when Miranda came to a fast-food restaurant; but the one thing that she'd always liked was McDonald's Caramel Sundaes. So, by way of celebration, Peter had bought not one, but three and arranged them artistically in an oversized container he'd brought specially for the occasion.

Peter ignored the surreptitious stares of the other customers; he didn't care what they thought. He was just overwhelmed with relief to have his Miranda back. Peter watched happily as she spooned the rest of the ice-cream down. A small blob of ice-cream had affixed itself to her nose, but he didn't tell her; it made her look even more waif-like. Peter frowned at the dark lines under Miranda's eyes and the hollows in her cheeks, bespeaking of a long ordeal—an ordeal that she could not recollect.

The doctor had conducted as extensive a series of tests as he could, but, apart from saying that her pregnancy was safe, he'd declined to comment. "Keep an eye on her," was all he'd said.

Miranda leant forward and licked the spoon gleefully like a little girl. Peter frowned again as he saw the scratches and abrasions on her neck.

Again, the Doctor had declined to comment on Miranda's wounds, except to say: "Well, who knows? She's been crashing through the woods all night clad in nothing but a nightdress."

Eventually, the hospital had let her go and this celebration in the fast-food restaurant was the first thing that had come to Peter's mind. It had obviously done the trick—Miranda's cheeks glowed a little. She scraped the bowl and the last of the huge dessert disappeared from sight.

"Careful, you'll take the pattern off the bowl!" laughed Peter.

"Mmm, Peter, that was delicious," she said, closing her eyes in ecstasy. She kept them closed and the pulsing of the blue vein in her forehead and the faint fluttering of her eyelids betrayed that she was still under a nervous strain.

"Miranda," said Peter gently, "We should take you home to rest."

Her eyes shot open and she gazed at him. "Home," she repeated, "Home."

The word sounded odd now. Pictures suddenly crowded into Peter's mind: the Mission yard; the dead man's blank staring eyes; the fruit thrust into his mouth. He took a deep breath. "Well," he said slowly, "At least you should rest until we decide what to do."

Miranda wrinkled her brow. "What do you mean? Aren't we going back to the Mission?"

Peter felt a tightening in his stomach. He hadn't wanted to discuss the details with Miranda; she'd been in such a fragile state that he'd never even mentioned the murder. He made a quick decision. Taking Miranda's hand in his, he lowered his voice and described the incident in a few crisp sentences, making it as matter-of-fact as possible.

Miranda's eyes widened with horror, despite his uncharged delivery. "Oh, Peter," she said, tears springing into her eyes, "Poor you. What a horrible thing for you to have to go through!" She slid out of her booth and came around to Peter's side and slid in next to him, cradling her good arm around his neck. "My poor, poor man. You must be exhausted!"

The fat cowboy and his wife now stared unabashed and Peter thought the counter-hand's eyes were going to fall out of her head. "Hey, c'mon," he said, hugging Miranda, "Let's get out of here." He stood up and dumped the tray, bowl and all into the disposal chute and held the glass door open for Miranda.

The thin, wispy-haired woman stared at Miranda's feet: she was wearing a pair of Peter's boots. Miranda clumped to the door, paused for a moment for full effect and pivoted like a model, allowing the coat to fall open, revealing her nightie. Then she exited with a swanky walk, offset somewhat by the muddy boots.

Once outside, hysteria took over and they both began to laugh. "Christ! Did you see her face?!" roared Peter, "When she saw you wearing my size elevens?!"

Miranda laughed until the tears ran down her face and they stood for a moment clinging onto each other, glad of the relief. Eventually their hysterical laughter subsided and they climbed into the Jeep, still giggling sporadically. Peter had put the soft cover on the vehicle and they buttoned down the flaps carefully.

Miranda gave a sudden groan: "We're not going to the motel, are we?"

"Nope. I've got an idea. Maybe it'll work out. I dunno." And, with a squeal, Peter turned the Jeep and headed towards Miya's house.

CHAPTER EIGHTEEN

Peter stood awkwardly in the light from Miya's doorway, rubbing his hands on his trousers. "I wouldn't ask for me," he said, embarrassed, "It's for Miranda really. But...you see, I think that you were offended when I left you and I didn't want you to get the impression that I didn't...value your friendship..." He tailed off, miserable in his discomfort.

Miya bounded forward, surprisingly light on his feet for such a big man. "Peter!" he cried. He clapped Peter to his bosom in a bear hug that threatened to crack Peter's ribs. "My brother! My son! You do me such an honor! Please come in."

Miya took Miranda's good hand in his own and they entered Miya's home like two street waifs.

Miranda smiled and Peter, though embarrassed, glanced at her and knew he'd made the right decision. "It feels good here," she said looking around the room serenely, "It has a real soft, healing feel about it."

Miya bobbed up and down in front of them, and Peter was amazed to see the transformation. The dignified, somber Indian had disappeared and Miya chattered and chuckled like a ten-year-old, totally beside himself with happiness. "I am so pleased that you came to my house in your need," he said hopping from one foot to the other, "But it is no longer my home. I am just a guest. It is your home now—see?" He flung open a doorway and there was an ancient, brass bedstead sparkling in the light. "This is your room!"

Miranda cooed in delight. But Peter cried: "And where will you sleep?!"

Miya winked. "In the sweat lodge, of course," he said, "I often sleep out there anyway." And, despite Peter's protestations, he went and began to run a bath for Miranda, calling over his shoulder, "I hope you are hungry so I can make you some food!"

Peter sat down in a chair, overwhelmed. Miranda came in from the bedroom, kissed her finger and placed it over Peter's lips. "Well, man of iron," she whispered playfully, "You actually asked someone for help—it's quite a breakthrough!" Peter wriggled in his chair and Miranda added soothingly: "Oh, sweetheart, I'm only playing. I know how difficult it was for you to ask—and I love you for it." And kneeling, she clasped Peter close to her bosom.

Miya stuck his head out of the steamy bathroom and went to say something, but when he saw the couple in a quiet embrace, he gave a broad grin and vanished silently back into the steam. Diplomatically, he yelled from the bathroom: "Bath's ready!"

"And so," said Miranda making a grand entrance from the bathroom, "How does my brave warrior like this?"
Peter stared open-mouthed. In front of him, walking tiptoe on her moccasin-clad feet, was an Indian maiden—an Indian maiden with bright violet eyes and golden-blonde platted tresses—but, nevertheless, an Indian maiden.
Miranda smiled, biting her bottom lip; a personal mannerism which was a dead give-away to Peter, indicating that she was enjoying herself immensely.
"Well?" she said archly.
Peter blinked and stared.
Miranda wore a skull cap patterned with dark blue triangles in a circle around its rim. Her bodice was made of a soft, whitish cloth that Peter could not identify, over which was draped twin bands of beaded material that fell across her breasts from each shoulder. The loosely-beaded ends dangled at her hips, joined to a circular band that encased Miranda's upper arms and back. Beneath this was a brightly-patterned leather skirt that had been split at the bottom; the fringes laced with beadwork.
"You like um squaw Miranda?" she said solemnly.
"Well, er, yes…it's wonderful," said Peter. He turned to Miya. "Where did you get this? It's quite an outfit!"
"Oh, it belonged to my wife," said Miya and, forestalling Peter's remark, he added quickly, "She's dead. Been dead a while."
"Oh dear," said Miranda, "I am sorry. I didn't know. Doesn't it…hurt you to see me like this?"
Miya shook his head. "She never even wore it once," he said.
"What tribe is it from?" asked Peter abashed.
"It's totally fake; something for the tourists." Miya laughed aloud. "Why, if Miranda wore a real Pomo dress, she'd be arrested for indecent exposure!"
Miranda twirled around, admiring herself in the mirror. "Well, whatever you say, fake or not, I think it's lovely." She suddenly turned and gave Miya a hug. "So, Indian brave or brave Indian—whichever you prefer—did you have any children?"
"Oh, yes," said Miya, his face splitting in a wide grin, "I've got a daughter. Your age, I would guess."
"So?!" said Miranda, "But where is she?"
Miya looked away into the distance. "Far, far away at the moment. She is…making a special journey, then she will return."
"Sounds wonderful," said Miranda bright-eyed, "Can you tell us about it?"
"Only to say that she is a Maru, a Dreamer, and it is hoped that she may be one of the great shamans. You see, only a woman shaman can be a healer, and they are all but dying out. My daughter seems to have great powers."

"Oh, my!" Miranda clapped her hands and skipped about in excitement, "Isn't that incredible! An Indian healer! I'd like to meet her."

"Well, when she returns, I'll make sure you do," said Miya beaming.

"Gee, this is wonderful! Thank you for bringing me here, Peter," said Miranda.

Peter nodded happily. The color was back in Miranda's cheeks and she almost looked her old self.

"Do you know any other shamans?" said Miranda to Miya eagerly, "Any healing shamans?"

"There is one—a very old one. Molly Buckskin. She's almost eighty, but she's still as active as a twenty-year-old. She's an old Yurok healer from the north."

"Molly Buckskin! What a funny name!" cried Miranda, "Sounds like a vaudeville act!"

"Well," said Miya slowly, "It's not her real name. You see, part of the Yurok belief is that the shaman's name gives his or her enemies power. So the true name is never revealed. My name, Muyamuya is not my real name—" He suddenly stopped abruptly and lowered his eyes, realizing what he'd just said.

"So," said Miranda curiously, "You, too are a shaman?"

"Yes," said Miya slowly, "But it is not a known fact. I prefer to keep it to myself."

"Your secret is safe," said Miranda mockingly. She placed the back of her hand across her brow like a bad Victorian actress and intoned: "They shall never wrench your secret from my lips! Let them do their worst!"

"Get out!" exploded Miya good-humoredly chucking her under the chin. He turned to Peter and said in mock exasperation: "What can you do with this girl?! She's an incredible teaser!"

Peter spread his hands helplessly. "I've given up, Miya. Maybe you could cast a spell or something."

"Hey!" cried Miranda, "Is old Betty Buckskin still around?"

"Molly," corrected Miya, "Molly Buckskin. Well, she sure is. In fact, she's been teaching my daughter."

"Well," said Miranda slowly, "Maybe she can help me. You know, tell me what's been happening to me. I mean, the doctor at the hospital knew zilch."

There was a sudden silence. Peter gripped the edge of the chair, his face tense.

"Hey," said Miranda, "What did I say?! C'mon, we all know I've been roaming around the countryside all night, suffering from some weird kind of amnesia. Shouldn't we at least do something about it?"

Peter stood up a little abruptly. "Miranda, I *am* doing something about it. I think that you were poisoned and I'm getting some…information from David."

"David!! Oh, that's great! I'm so glad. But, really, I'd like to see this lady Molly Buckskin as well. It would be a wonderful experience, wouldn't it?" Then she noticed the stiffness in Peter's face. "Why, what's the matter, darling?"

Peter looked at his hands and said: "Well, I don't really like the idea, Miranda. You've been very, very sick—more than I wanted to admit to you, 'cos I didn't want to upset you." His expression was agonized. "Honey, please, you've no idea what went through my mind when you first went unconscious. I've been so worried about you. I just can't stand the thought of someone meddling with you who...doesn't..." He faltered and stopped. "Well..." he resumed looking down, "I don't like to say this in front of Miya, because he's been so kind, but I'm scared to have a primitive doctor meddle with you when you've been in such a state."

"Hey, Peter," said Miranda softly. She took his hand. "It's O.K. I know you're only doing this for me. But there's more to this thing than some case of natural poisoning. It's not just poison oak or something like that..."

For the first time since Miranda had broached the topic, Miya spoke. "If there is something more, what is it?"

Miranda sat down and gazed off into the middle distance. "The dreams," she said slowly. "At first I thought they were just that—dreams; dreams brought on by a new environment, a new situation. But now..." she paused and turned to Miya, "...now I think it's something more."

"Perhaps you can tell us why," said Miya glancing at Peter.

Peter looked away.

"There is something..." said Miranda in a distant voice, "Something which I feel here..." She put her hand on her heart and closed her eyes, "Something which is not my sensation. It's a deep yearning; a sense of incompletion; a desire for fulfillment." She opened her eyes sleepily, "It's almost like sex, but it's not sex."

"When does it come, this feeling?" asked Miya.

"With the scent of the blossom," said Miranda, "And at night in the dreams it's very strong. But it doesn't seem like a bad feeling," she said slowly, "It's, like, if I succumb to the feeling all will be well, all will be whole. But there is still a nagging sensation that it's borrowed—like it's not my emotion."

"And the dreams?" prompted Miya.

"The dreams. At first I took no notice. But then they came again and again..." She faltered and looked down at her broken wrist, "For the last two days—the same dreams, the same memories. And that's what frightens me." She suddenly seemed very small. "It's O.K. to dream when you're in bed at night. But I've been wandering around the countryside in some kind of dream state, and that's not O.K.... Miya, can you help me?"

Again Miya glanced at Peter. But Peter would not meet his eyes. "Perhaps it would help if you told us more about the dreams," said Miya softly.

"Voices," said Miranda, "Voices and songs. You know, like the voices of the men at Mass, like a Gregorian chant. It's quite lovely. It reminds me of the voices I once heard as a young girl when I was visiting a monastery. The voices of men—all men—raised in a chant of devotion. And rain," she said, "Wet, glistening, drizzling rain; pouring rain. But…" she closed her eyes, "The rain has a kiss, a benediction; the rain is life and fullness. There is no cold or wet; no desire, no hunger. With the rain comes plenty. Only in the men's voices is there sadness and incompletion…and a calling, a beckoning. Throughout the song there is another voice that seems to whisper under the tones…" She stopped.

"What does it say?" asked Miya gently.

"It is calling. It says, 'come, come, come'."

Miya nodded. He placed one hand on Miranda's shoulder and she smiled wanly, comforted. Miya stood up and looked at Peter. "Peter," he said, "Can I talk to you outside—alone?"

Peter nodded and held his finger to his lips in response to Miranda's expression of concern. "Ssshh now. There's nothing to worry about, Miranda. We'll be back in a moment."

Peter went out to the balcony. Miya was standing silently in the dark gazing at the night sky, his expression serene. Peter, who had expected a confrontation, was surprised by his manner.

"Peter," said Miya, "You are a practical man, a scientist, yes?"

"Yes."

"I, too, am a man of truth," said Miya, "Do you trust me?"

Peter paused and looked up at the solid face of this proud Indian. "In all sincerity," said Peter, "I do trust you. I trust your honesty. What I don't trust is your belief system. I know your intentions are good, but sometimes, that's not good enough."

Miya nodded. "It is enough you trust me. Look…" he pointed to the stars, "…so aloof the stars…each one a mystery." He breathed deeply. "My breath, my life a mystery. Mystery is the daily substance of our being, and it is the most mysterious to those who study a great deal, as your great quantum physicists will tell you." He took a deep sigh. "Unfortunately, much of the knowledge of the Indian has been lost. And the greatest loss is the Indian world view. It is not enough to translate the vast myths, to paraphrase Indian folklore and customs for, you see, the Indian did not have a belief system—he had a world view."

Peter nodded. "Yes, I see that, but what is it you're trying to tell me?"

"Only this," said Miya. "As a scientist you can appreciate that a conceptual system not rooted in time or space or ideas of the difference between natural and supernatural *cannot* be translated into a system which bases everything upon those very factors."

"Agreed," said Peter cautiously, "Which leaves us where?"

"Your great philosopher, Nietzsche, once said that man cannot change until he changes his language. So, let me say this before my meaning is lost in some abstract argument: The Indian viewpoint is a different way of experiencing the world, I won't say better or worse—just different. And it is not available to a person conditioned in Western thought; nor are the white man's translations of the Indian myths anything but pleasant, esthetic experiences—well-intentioned, yes; but, nevertheless, false. A translation of the untranslatable has to be false."

Peter was silent. This made sense to him, even though he would not admit it out loud. He was surprised. He'd expected some argument which began: 'there is an old Indian myth which says…' or some chunk of earthy, Indian, home-spun philosophy which would leave him vaguely embarrassed at his inability to respond. But this was different. This had more the feel of an educated, philosophical discourse. "Quite the philosopher," he said suddenly. It was not a taunt; his tone conveyed that he was impressed.

"Unfortunately," said Miya.

"Unfortunately? Why so?"

"Simply that he who has a foot in two worlds sometimes gets the best of neither."

Peter nodded. He couldn't help but like this man just then, but he was afraid to admit it. "So, where does this take us then?" he asked for the second time.

Miya turned and stood in front of Peter. "Simply this. There is a way of looking at Miranda's situation which says she is in danger and I want to help her. It is not in opposition to anything you might do. It is in the nature of… an investigation; a kind of psychic investigation is the best way I can explain it, and it is, in itself, harmless."

Peter took a deep breath. "It's the psychic thing that worries me," he said. "Miranda is highly suggestible and gullible to these types of esoteria. And I'm worried that it might upset her further, especially as she has been in such a state."

"You're right," said Miya, "That I cannot guarantee. We are dealing with powerful forces."

"I'll say!" came a hard voice.

Peter and Miya looked up in surprise. Miranda stood at the door, eyes ablaze, arms akimbo. Miya covered his eyes and muttered a very un-Indian, "Uh-uh," in the tone that translates as 'here's trouble'.

"Peter Riley!" said Miranda sharply, "And you, too, Miya Martinez! What is this?! Do you think we're back in the Stone Ages so that you men can disappear onto the balcony and discuss the poor, frail woman as if she was an object?!"

"Miranda," said Peter feebly, "I—"

"Yes, I know, you're doing it for my own good. Well, let me tell you that there are men all over this country perpetuating Victorian atrocities on their wives and daughters for exactly these reasons, and it don't wash with me, bub!!"

Miya couldn't help grinning at the fierceness of her tone. But the grin disappeared when suddenly Miranda shrilled. "And what's so funny, Miya?! Don't I get the chance to speak for myself?! Or do I wait patiently while you two great men decide my fate?!!"

Peter and Miya each took a deep breath, and, glancing at each other, exhaled simultaneously. In that moment, an intimacy flowed between them which no conversation could have wrought: a taut acknowledgment of being men—and mere men, at that—in a situation as old as time.

"We are lost, Peter," said Miya with a grin, "Bow to the force of the shaman."

"The shaman?" said Miranda with a sudden change of tone.

Miya shrugged. "It is a feminine trait and it is a power beyond, so…" he spread his hands, "…what would you have us do?"

"Are you shittin' me?" said Miranda suspiciously.

"Miranda!" cried Peter, realizing she'd got the expression from him.

But Miya's face was serious. "Nope," he replied.

"Well," said Miranda, conciliated somewhat, "You can come inside off this silly balcony and tell me exactly what is going on."

So they did.

Peter told her of his hallucination; the dressing gown at the scene of the second murder. And Miya told of the history of the Mission; the disappearance of the priests; the Tree and its connection to Miranda's dreams.

Miranda was not surprised by any of it. She simply said: "Harumph!" with a toss of her head, which indicated she was being told things *she'd* known all the time.

Hours later, Peter lay snoring in Miya's great brass bed. Miranda lay in the dark, clad in a flannel nightdress that reached to her neck. She felt peaceful and serene in Miya's bedroom. She'd awoken once to go to the toilet and found Miya sitting wide awake in a chair in the next room, surrounded by Indian artifacts: feathers; blankets; a bear claw; a semicircle of dried pepperwood; angelica; a bull-roarer; and some hand-made rattles and sticks.

Miranda, knowing intuitively what Miya was doing, touched her fingers to her lips and placed them on his forehead. He, in turn had taken an amulet from around his neck and draped it around hers with a solemn expression.

And now, safe and sound in the large bed, Miranda smiled in the dark and hugged Peter. He turned sleepily but did not wake.

"Thank you," she whispered into his sleeping ear, "Thank you." Her voice echoed around in the room and seemed to float out of the window to mingle with the faint susurrus of leaves in the myrtle tree outside.

CHAPTER NINETEEN

"Hey! Come on, now! Back off!" said Peter, hands in the air. "I mean to say, fair is fair!"

"But, Peter," said Miranda from across Miya's breakfast table, "I'm scared. It's not safe. Whatever our own view is of these crazy events, we all know it's not safe! Two people have been killed!"

Miya crunched on a piece of toast and spooned a very un-Indian over-easy egg into his mouth. "I agree," he said.

"Listen, you two—and especially you, Miranda. I could sock you with all the same arguments that you threw at me last night! Now, you two are quite happy when you're floating off into your world of spirits and demons, so give *me* some room, eh? I've agreed to let Miya call in his medicine woman, even though it's the last thing I want. Now, I've given you your own way, Miranda, so why not let me be?!"

Miranda squirmed about, exasperated, realizing she was trapped by her own argument.

The sun streamed through the open porch door into Miya's kitchen. It was beginning to lose its bite, heralding the advent of the winter months, but its brightness reinforced Peter's down-to-earth attitude. Even Miranda had to admit that the normality of the morning sunshine made murders and miracles seem very far away. But something had clawed at her breast when Peter had said he was going back to the Mission; something akin to panic.

"Look," said Peter, "You're right—two men have been killed and one of them in my front yard. But what do we do? Ignore it? Now, whatever you have to say about…these other things, give *me* credit for my beliefs. I say there is a logical explanation for this. There is a human agent behind it—I know it."

Miya and Miranda glanced at each other.

"Now, wait a minute, you two. I really mean this! I'm not saying that your explanation is all mumbo-jumbo. I'm saying that *some* explanation can be found which maybe overlaps in a more scientific way. I intend to find out who the nut is that knocked off these two men, then we can discuss the finer details." Miranda frowned but was silent. "Look," pleaded Peter, "One thing we ignored when we were at the Mission was the food disappearing. At that time it didn't seem significant. But now… It's something we should have told the Sheriff. It's obvious that something more is going on than we thought at first, so please give me the chance to find out!"

"Peter, please!!" pleaded Miranda, "It's so dangerous!"

"And what else do we do? Abandon the Mission? That place is our dream, our home. Do you think I can just get up and walk away from it?!"

Miya nodded. "I appreciate the way you feel, Peter. But what can you hope to find? The police have been over every inch of the place with a fine-tooth comb and they found nothing. So what do you expect? These guys are trained to look for clues everywhere."

"That I don't know," said Peter dourly, "But at least I want the satisfaction of looking myself. So, I'm going out there."

"But not alone!" pleaded Miranda, "Go with Miya!"

"Some time or other," said Peter softly, "I'll have to face being out there alone. The chances are that if I do go with Miya, I'll find nothing. If someone is hanging around, I stand more chance alone."

"Peter!" shrilled Miranda, "No heroics!"

"Huh! Remember, *I'm* Mr. Anti-Hero, honey. Who do *you* think I am— Clint Eastwood or something? C'mon, Miranda, relax. I've got to do it."

Miya sighed. "O.K., Peter. But let us do one thing. If you don't call back, say, half an hour after you get there, we're on our way out—O.K.?"

"O.K." Peter grinned. "Hey, you two, chill out! It isn't the end of the world, you know!"

"I hope not," said Miranda glumly.

¤

Peter was not a fool.

His presence in the gun shop demonstrated this. He was not given to rushing in where angels-feared-to-tread, and even though it was not his habit to carry firearms, he was not going to allow himself to be vulnerable in a situa-ation where two men had already been killed.

The fact that he'd intended to buy a gun was one reason for his apparent lack of concern about re-visiting the Mission—but he had not wanted to tell Miranda. She hated firearms. She could see no purpose in them, either for self-defense or the killing of animals—she hated hunting.

For Peter, there was no choice. Two strong men had been overpowered and killed and although Peter was not enamored with firearms, he had long ago learnt to handle them as a simple practicality.

The fat sales clerk was sleepy-eyed, but Peter knew he was being sized up shrewdly. The gun store was also a pawn shop and the fat man had all that feral shrewdness beneath his nonchalance which seems to be the trademark of all pawn-shop owners.

Peter gazed around the store feigning calmness, aware of the hardness of the man's eyes. The walls were hung with second-hand articles: guitars with no strings; a dulcimer; an old Appalachian zither; even a full-scale wet suit and an oxygen tank for scuba diving. In the front tray of the dusty counter behind a thick glass case were the weapons: flick knives; butcher knives; hunting knives—and guns.

The clerk, his vast pot belly bulging against the counter, chewed incessantly. He broke the silence and, in a mumbling monotone, began to talk about life and death as if he was discussing planting potatoes. The clerk's nonchalance froze Peter's blood, though he did not react openly.

"'Course," mumbled the clerk, "If it's concealment you want, then it's the .38 in there. Slips out in a minute. But that small barrel makes it inaccurate; you can pump away with that li'l ole thing from ten feet and you'll hit everything but your target. Me, now, I like the ole .45—the Peace-Maker. You know, in the war we used to fire these things with tracer bullets at night, and that goddamn bullet is traveling so slow, you can see it wavering up and down like an ole bumble bee on a hot summer day. But that's the secret of the .45. These modern, new-fangled pistols, why, they don't stop a man! Shoot him point-blank and the bullet'll go right through him an' he'll keep right on coming at you. But with this," the clerk patted the .45 with an evil grin, "Hit the sucker anywhere—even in the goddamn arm—and he'll be knocked right back to kingdom come. You see, the bullet spreads out and—"

Peter didn't want to hear the gory details, so he interrupted hastily. "O.K. Yep, that'll do. And how about a rifle—one with some kind of sight?"

Unabashed, the man launched into equally vivid descriptions of the carnage possible with the different rifles.

After much deliberation, Peter eschewed the sight in favor of ease of use and bought a Winchester .73. "The gun that won the West," the clerk told him proudly. Peter paid the man an inordinate sum (so Peter thought) and left the store as hurriedly as he could.

He propped the rifle between the Jeep's seats and stowed the .45 and its spare ammunition in the glove compartment.

It was nearly noon and, despite the lateness of the summer, the sun still had a bite. Peter donned a wide-brimmed hat and, feeling very much like a parody of a frontiersman, roared off towards the Mission with a rueful expression on his face.

CHAPTER TWENTY

Peter casually slipped over the side of the Jeep and scrunched across the dry earth to the table outside the kitchen window. The sun was high in the sky and as he paused by the rough table, his shadow fell across it, hunched and foreshortened like the shadow of an ogre.

Peter gazed at the table. On it was strewn the crumpled remains of a T.V. dinner: French fries, all congealed fat and flies; ugly in the sunshine. Around the table, the earth was scuffed; covered in scores of cigarette butts where the Sheriff and his men had obviously fed, smoked, argued and eventually left.

Peter had hidden the rifle in the Jeep, but the silver-plated .45 was stuck in his waist band. It gave him a sense of reassurance as he sauntered around the corner of the Mission and gazed up at the Tree.

The Tree's branches arched overhead, black and gnarled. Most of the leaves had fallen, layering the ground with a thick carpet of every shade from deep red to a dull brown. It did have a certain beauty; but Peter shivered when he saw the huge, torn limb, all thoughts of beauty gone. The Sheriff's men had pushed the broken limb out of the way up against the tree bole, still attached by a huge strip of torn bark.

He examined the bole where the bark had been torn so rudely by the falling limb. The wood was beginning to fade to a reddish-brown, in contrast to the gnarled black of the bark sheath. To Peter, it looked remarkably like the scab forming over a rapidly-healing flesh wound.

Peter forced himself to look at the huge, crooked curve of the fallen limb. The Sheriff and his men must have levered it up in order to lift the dead body clear. The image of the dead man sprang into his mind with photographic clarity: the staring eyes; stubbled cheeks; the dribble of crimson fruit; the back arched in a death agony.

His belly contracted, but Peter allowed the mental image to run its course without fighting it. Mercifully, the vision faded, to be replaced by the actual sight of the broken limb and a yard, empty save for the russet and green patch of fallen leaves.

Peter sighed. The man was dead; the body gone. The sun angled down between the Tree's bare branches, and Peter felt better for having come back to the scene of the murder. Somehow, the sight of the empty spot where the body had been helped him erase the horrific image that he'd come to associate with the Mission yard.

Peter made no attempt to search the Mission. Instead, with a deliberate calm, he went to the Jeep and began to unload some of the groceries. Acting far more casually than he felt, he stepped into the cool darkness of the kitchen and emptied a bag onto the table. Out fell three packets of chicken breasts, a clump of broccoli, a bag of mushrooms and a couple of beers.

Peter unwrapped the chicken, cracked a can, placed the chicken in a pan on the stove and poured the beer over the breasts. Soon the pot was bubbling merrily in its beer stew and he threw in the broccoli and mushrooms without even washing them.

While the chicken boiled, he went outside to sit watching the birds flit about the vegetable garden. He watched them for a moment, then rose and sauntered down the path, his boots making deep indentations on the damp sawdust. He knelt over the onions, and, bending the thick, green stems over, began to tie them back 'to send the goodness down to the roots', as his grandmother would have said.

Beneath his nonchalance, Peter's eyes were sharp and his neck tingled in anticipation. He noted that the strawberry patch had been stripped almost bare; the tomatoes had all gone; and that there wasn't a ripe bell-pepper or egg plant left on the bare, green stems.

Someone—or something—had been eating the vegetables.

It could have been the Sheriff's men, of course. But, despite his low opinion of Dooley's manners, Peter felt the man had enough principle to stop his men helping themselves to someone else's vegetables.

Peter stood up and sniffed. The air was rich with the scent of the chicken, broccoli and mushrooms simmering in the beer. He pursed his lips in satisfaction, hoping that the smell was all-pervading, finding its way into every nook and cranny of the Mission.

He stood for a while watching the play of light on the huge boulder over the stream as the sun descended slowly in the sky. The stream was already beginning to swell and widen, fed by the rains that had been making sporadic appearances over the distant hills for the last few weeks. A hint of winter's approach whispered in the moist bite of the air and the thinness of the sun. The heavily-laden fruit trees were beginning to splatter the ground with over-ripe wind-falls. The two fig trees at the rear of the workshop were crowded with ripe green and black figs.

Peter sighed heavily. It was time to gather in the fruits of the summer, bitter though some of them may be, he thought gravely. He fingered the reassuring bulk of the gun unobtrusively and returned to the kitchen. He walked slowly with his head bent, but his ears were ever alert for a strange sound.

Whump! The noise behind him made him whirl on the spot, heart pounding, his hand on the gun. But a startled deer bounded off across the field with impossible spring-like leaps and was gone.

Peter realized he was shaking. With an effort, he controlled himself and strolled into the kitchen. He turned the heat down low under the chicken, picked up the phone and dialed Miya's number. Miranda answered immediately. Peter turned so that he was facing the door, his back to the stove. "That was quick," he said into the mouthpiece.

"Oh, Peter, I've been so worried! Is everything alright?!"

"Fine," said Peter, one hand across the mouthpiece.

"Peter! I can't hear you!" said Miranda, "Are you O.K.?!"

"I'm sorry!" shouted Peter, "It's a lousy line. Look, I'm going to have something to eat, then I'm coming back to town, O.K.?"

"*Is* everything O.K.?!" insisted Miranda nervously.

"Sure is." He hesitated. "The Sheriff and his boys left a mess, but not too bad. Look, I'll be back soon, O.K.?" he shouted, "Hang in there!" He blew a kiss into the phone and replaced the receiver.

The chicken was tender where most of the gravy had boiled away. He fired it up again, turned it a few times to brown the skin, then heaped the meal onto a large plate. He carried the plate to the table outside and sat in the sun.

Peter ate most of the broccoli and mushrooms; but of the six pieces of chicken, he ate only three. He tore chunks off the other three pieces, but didn't eat them, so that there was a substantial amount of chicken left on the plate. He washed his meal down with the other beer, burped, and, crushing the can with his hand, threw it negligently onto the heaped plate. He left the plate on the table, food remnants and all, clambered into the Jeep, started the engine, and, within minutes, was bumping off towards the rocky road that girdled the hillside.

Peter slid down the bank of the river in a miniature landslide of dirt. He fought for balance and came to rest with his feet against the worn surface of a huge boulder.

The Jeep was up on the road above him hidden out of sight. Peter was clambering along the steep river bank where he could not be seen. He listened for a moment. The stream gurgled between the rocks; a flurry of wind shook a buckeye tree, showering the river bed with the dull plops of brown and decaying fruit. The wind subsided and the plopping ceased. He listened carefully, but there were no other noises. He shifted the rifle to a more comfortable position over his shoulder and re-adjusted the binocular strap around his neck.

He began to pick his way across the littered rocks strewn along the bank of the stream. It was a precarious journey; some of the rocks were as wet and as slick as ice. He slipped once or twice, his foot plunging deep into the cold stream. But, all-in-all, he managed to make the opposite bank without any major mishap.

He began to scramble upwards. The bank was so steep that, at first, he made little progress. Eventually, he scrabbled through a shower of dust and shale and he managed to grab an overhanging manzanita and pull himself up onto a plateau.

He lay face down, breathing heavily. He winced as the .45 poked into his ribs. He levered himself up and pulled it free. Propped on his elbows, he glanced about cautiously. Everything seemed peaceful. He could smell the sharp odor of crushed pepperwood; the wind sighed gently; but there were no other sounds save the faint gurgle of the stream. He crawled forward until he reached the russet trunk of a young madrone and peered cautiously through the Y formed by its bifurcated trunk.

Below him lay the Mission.

The sun had descended significantly. Long shadows threw the objects in the yard in dark relief. Peter was looking down at the east end of the Mission building. To its left was the table, diminutive but clear at this distance; and to the right, the thick, moody bulk of the huge Tree. Perfect. Peter raised the binoculars warily and focussed them on the table.

The table blurred and scooted past his vision. He steadied his elbows and adjusted the focus. The table leapt into clarity an arm's length away, it seemed: a slight breeze rifled the remnants of the Sheriff's TV dinner; the sun glinted brightly on the crushed beer can. The chicken pieces still lay on the plate—untouched.

Peter positioned the binoculars carefully in the Y of the madrone, lashing them into place with their strap. All he had to do was to raise himself up slightly and he could see the table without even touching them.

He waited.

He didn't look through the glasses now, but, shielding his eyes from the sun, watched the table with his naked eyes.

The first half hour was the worst. Each second was filled with an expectancy that had Peter rigid with tension, scared of missing something. But soon he slipped into a different rhythm in which he was no long waiting, but simply watching. The patterns of life below began to make themselves apparent: the blue jays flitting from the roof top to the vegetable garden; the sudden, insistent knock of a woodpecker; the flight of a small, furry animal streaking across the dusty yard. At one point, the dappled shadows at the rear of the vegetable garden suddenly moved forward and stopped. The shape moved again. It emerged into the sun—a mother deer and her fawn. They trotted forward, sniffed the air cautiously then, satisfied, began to graze on the strawberry leaves, lifting their heads now and then, keening the air.

Peter pondered… Perhaps it was just the deer that had eaten the vegetables. Then he realized that that wasn't true. The deer were eating all the greenery, not just the vegetables. Without a doubt, the vegetables had been picked. Peter sat motionless, staring down at the deer. The mother ate nervously, constantly lifting her head to sniff the air. The younger one was more preoccupied with the juicy leaves, content to let his mother watch for danger.

Suddenly, the mother went taut and swung her neck around in the direction of the Mission. Then they were both off, bounding across the grass towards the hills in those impossible leaps.

Peter was up in a flash, squinting through the binoculars, just in time to see a large, furry shape lean over the table, snatch the chicken from the plate and bolt out of sight. Peter jerked away from the binoculars to see the figure flit down the cellar steps. There was a faint bang as the door slammed, and then everything was still again.

Peter's heart was pounding crazily; a mixture of fear and jubilation—and confusion.

The cellar?!! But the cellar had been searched by the Sheriff's men!

He waited a few moments. But, as he expected, the shape did not appear again.

What was it? What had he seen? Mentally, he replayed the rapid image: the furry shape; the speed with which it had grabbed the food and disappeared. An animal? But what animal? What animal was that big and that fast? A bear? No…not big enough.

What then??

So, he thought, he had to find out.

Clutching the rifle firmly in his hands, he started to thread his way through the manzanitas towards the Mission, eyeing the closed cellar door with a mixture of trepidation and grim resolve.

CHAPTER TWENTY-ONE

Miranda couldn't tell how old the woman was. Sometimes she seemed no more than twenty as she conversed animatedly with Miya, bobbing her head and waving her hands. At other times her white hair and wrinkled, leathery face made her seem ancient. Miya had said Molly Buckskin was eighty—or 'thereabouts'. Now Miranda realized the reason for the approximation; it was impossible to discern Molly's age from her appearance.

Miya spoke to the woman in a mellifluous language, wrapping his tongue around the syllables as though they were pastilles of honey. She replied in guttural syllables. Miya turned to Miranda.

"She likes you…very much. She says you are of the Power and she wants to help."

Molly nodded, her wrinkled face cracking in a grin, and she put out a gnarled hand and lay it on Miranda's cheek. Miranda started at her touch; it felt warm and tingly. The woman smiled and spoke in a spluttering of syllables. Miya nodded. "She says you are a Maru, a Dreamer, and as such could have great power. But as you are not trained, you are very susceptible."

"To what?" asked Miranda smiling at Molly, "Doesn't she speak any English?"

"I really don't know," said Miya. "Probably. But she chooses not to. It does not suit her purpose."

Miranda understood. She nodded and, taking the old lady's hand, she thanked her. The woman smiled toothlessly and spoke. Miya grinned. "She says you are an Indian in a white girl's body, and this makes her task easier."

"O.K.," said Miranda, pleased by the answer, "I'm ready."

"But," interceded Miya, "She is not. And you must prepare yourself first…"

Three hours later, Miya came back to the house. Naked except for a cloth about his waist, he announced that soon Molly—who was dancing in the sweat house—would be ready.

Miranda sat, awkward in a dress of stiffish maple bark, an animal skin slung over her naked torso. The bark skirt was decidedly uncomfortable and the skin tickled her breasts, but she was so excited that she didn't mind.

Miya sat down and began toweling the sweat off his bronzed body. "I should tell you something about Molly and what she's going to do," he said. "It's difficult, because I don't want to give you any preconceptions, but normally anyone who consults Molly would be well aware of the traditional procedures. You are something of an exception." He gazed at her for a moment and said: "Do you still want to go on with this? You can withdraw if you've had second thoughts."

Miranda pulled her rough shawl closer and said firmly: "I wouldn't miss this for the world."

"Good," said Miya, "You're a brave girl." He stared ahead for a moment without speaking until, just as Miranda thought he'd forgotten her, he suddenly spoke. "To become a healer is a special thing. It can only be truly accomplished by a woman. There are some men who do it, but it's not the same. To become a healer was very arduous for Molly and involved a lot of pain and sacrifice before she was ready to heal." Miya gazed at Miranda long and hard. "It is said a healer is chosen, not made. However, one important thing is that the healer must first acquire something which they call 'pains' or *telogel*. These pains are put into the body by some guardian spirit or another doctor. The healer then has to 'cook' these pains, as it is called, by dancing the *remohpo* or 'kick dance' long and hard in a half-dismantled sweat house. The healer may dance for days before she brings up her 'pain', which is actually a physical object."

"Will I see it?" asked Miranda curiously.

"Perhaps. I do not know," said Miya, "You will be alone with Molly. But don't worry, you are in safe hands."

"I'm not worried," said Miranda, "Just excited."

"Good," said Miya. "So, the healer, having acquired her first pain then dances on one of the stone terraces of a mountain. The next summer, she dances all night, with an attendant or guard nearby. Here another 'pain' is implanted. Then the healer returns to the river or the ocean to dance the Kick Dance to 'cook' the pains again. The doctor may give many pains, but these first two are most important, as is the song—a song which is sometimes sung in nonsense words so that no one else will know the meaning." Miya paused. "Do you think it's crazy, Miranda?"

"No," said Miranda, "I don't think it's crazy. I, too, dance sometimes until I'm drunk with it, and when I do, I feel and see things which I would never see if I was not so."

"You are indeed a Maru," chuckled Miya, "One of the dreamer sect—perhaps even a great healer."

"Perhaps," said Miranda slowly. "Sometimes there are things which I see and feel which I don't like to talk about to other people… But please tell me more about Molly. How will she help me?"

"That, in truth, I do not know, nor do I wish to say. Simply I can tell you the usual methods. But what she will do to you is in her hands; it will be her own way."

"So," smiled Miranda, "What is the usual procedure?"

"Even now Molly is dancing. She has been dancing some three hours and she is in what modern doctors call a trance state. Whatever it is, it enables Molly to 'see' things. For instance, she has told me that sometimes she sees the 'pains' flying over the head of the patient and she tries to catch them in mid-air. Sometimes she sees them like bulbs sprouting in the person's body. They sprout and flower and these she cannot remove. But usually she will put her mouth over the patient's body until it melts the pain carrying the illness. Then she will mix it with the pain she has retched up from her own body and swallow them both. Once it is in her body, your pain is safe. Then she can bring it up and cause it to fly away. Does it sound messy?" he queried.

"A little," frowned Miranda. "That doesn't bother me. But poor Molly. Will she suffer my pain?"

"The word pain is not to be taken literally. It's more like a 'pain object'. Molly will appear to suffer, but in truth her spirit is somewhere else. Don't worry."

"She's so old," said Miranda.

"But not frail. Listen."

And from the sweat house came a ululating chant; the rise and fall of a curious, many-syllabled song so strange that it gave Miranda a delicious shiver.

"It is time, Dreamer," whispered Miya, "Go and dream your dreams."

Miranda stepped out onto the porch. The bark skirt rustled as she padded through the gloom towards the sweat house. Molly's song, strange and piercing in the air, was underscored with the dull thud and slap of the old woman's feet on the dirt floor. The pungent odor of the wood smoke filled Miranda's nostrils, and time and space seemed to fall away behind her as if she were striding back through the years and not along Miya's garden path.

She ducked to enter the sweat house and the ululating song was louder, resonating deep in her belly. And then she was inside; and it was as if she'd never been anywhere else.

Bathed in sweat, Molly Buckskin danced in front of the fire with an energy unbelievable in one so old. She grunted and whirled, slapping her feet on the ground rhythmically, her head flung back, her long hair untied, thick and swirling about her shoulders. She seemed ageless, timeless, sexless.

A small basket and a pipe sat in front of the fire. A circle of dried herbs and leaves surrounded each willow platform bed.

Miranda swung her feet up onto the willow platform, lay back on the soft mat of fresh grass baring her bosom as Miya had told her to do earlier. Sighing deeply, she closed her eyes.

The woman, without opening her eyes, sensed Miranda's presence and danced closer, swaying over Miranda's inert body. Her voice increased in volume and she gesticulated above Miranda, punctuating the movements with rapid trills of the strange song.

Miranda began to sweat; trickles ran down her belly and into the waistband of the maple bark skirt. There was a sizzling hiss from the fire and the pungent smell of the herbs struck Miranda's nostrils. She coughed once, then breathed deeply of the fumes. Time slipped, yawed sideways...and she fell into the ground.

That was the only way she could describe it later: it was as if the ground had opened and she'd dropped down a foot or two.

Molly was suddenly close, very close. She swept her hot breath along Miranda's body, murmuring and chanting. Miranda's belly tingled, even though Molly had not touched her, and she slipped down again—deeper. She was suspended in a deep, warm blackness, floating beneath the surface of the earth. Molly's voice rose and fell. Miranda's breath grew deep and even and with every exhalation she slipped down further.

An infinity above, a tiny, crazed woman was drifting above Miranda blowing smoke down a vast abyss into her nostrils. With a shuddering breath, Miranda let go completely and gave herself up to this woman in total trust. She began to fall again into the warm blackness. Down, down, down she drifted, until, inexplicably, there was the sky rising above her in a vast, blue bowl rimmed with the frozen spikes of blood-red flowers; stiff, unwavering.

A woman suddenly drifted into her sight. Molly?! Or was it? The woman was young; her skin smooth and unlined. She smiled and beckoned to Miranda, intoning a phrase in a strange language that Miranda recognized as 'come, come, come.'

Miranda yawned and stretched, as if waking. She seemed to be lying on the soft surface of the ocean. Like a soft bed, it held and cushioned her. Without hesitation, she stood up and began to stride across its surface, her feet slapping firmly on the glassy water.

The Indian woman, floating above the sea, turned slowly and her black locks cascaded over her shoulder like fronds of seaweed curling languously in a slight current. The woman drifted towards the flower spikes and broke off one of the tall red flowers. With a crystal 'spang!', it snapped like the stem of a wine glass. The sound was strange and lovely, like the peal of a tiny bell. Bowing, the Indian woman offered the flower to Miranda.

Miranda reached for it and laughed out loud at the sensation, for her motions were slow and lazy as though she moved through warm honey. She grasped the flower stem. It was frozen stiff, cold. The woman pointed at her own mouth, showing her white, even teeth. She made a gesture and Miranda knew what to do. She put the flower in her mouth and swallowed it whole.

Miranda cried out loud. The flower slid like an icicle into her belly, piercing her to the womb. She was suddenly cold; death cold. Her senses vaulted and she was back in the sweat house with Molly's hot breath against her icy belly. Molly retched and coughed. Miranda cried out in fear and pain as something icy grasped her heart. She stared down weakly as Molly's fist plunged into her belly and withdrew. Enveloped with slime, the hand clutched an object that dripped red, glutinous blood.

Molly raised her hand to her own mouth and, eyes rolling white and crazy, she swallowed it. Saliva dribbled down Molly's chin, mingled with a reddish, sticky substance. Her face went rigid with pain and she convulsed and gripped her own belly, her eyes rolled up into her head.

Miranda screamed and whipped from side to side, her hair flailing in a wind that sprang up from nowhere, snatching the scream from her lips...

...And she was padding along a wind-torn road at night, looking neither left nor right. The headlights of a truck hit her, but she kept walking, dully aware that her body was ice cold and hot and dripping sweat simultaneously. Miranda fought for control, but her ice-cold body moved of its own volition, giving the curious sensation of being in two places at once. Then the headlights blinded her as the truck stopped and all was hot-oil smells and gas fumes and the stubbled face of a man staring down at her from the cab.

Miranda climbed into the cab aware that she wore only a skimpy dressing gown and that the skinny, stubble faced driver was eyeing her salaciously. But she could not look at him. Her body moved of its own accord as if she were a mere passenger in it.

Sounds battered her ears; crazy sounds: the shriek and buffet of the wind; the roar of the truck engine; the juddering of the wheels along the road. But Miranda could do nothing save stare out from behind the mask of her own face at the wild night outside.

Other sounds brushed her consciousness: the pad of bare feet on an earthen floor; a strange, ululating song in an unknown language; and, in counterpoint, a distant, sonorous cadence—the sound of men's voices, chanting. The sound rose, blending with the acrid, pungent smell of wood smoke, a heady, rich blossom smell and an insistent whisper beneath it all that said...'come, come, come'.

The sky jerked and the image fragmented. Miranda was caught in a spool of Time like a hooked fish. She shrieked and fought to be free, but the images streamed by her like live beings. Her fist drove with terrific force into the scrawny throat of the driver; fire lanced up her arm with a surge of pain. She saw herself leap out of the truck and run. Then she *was* running, crazed by the sounds tearing through the wind: men's voices; a woman's chant; the whisper 'come, come, come'. Then all was pain, tearing thorns and raked flesh; the howl of wind and the glass-sharpness driving into her feet as she stumbled through the undergrowth out of control.

Then she was falling again...into a vast pit which became a woman's young-old face. She heard the lovely 'spang!' of breaking crystal and the bitter taste of the ice-flower surged in her mouth and...

It was dark. Miranda was kneeling in front of the Tree. The cadence of the men's voices soared, filled with such loss and sadness that Miranda began to weep softly. As the cadence swelled, the rich smell of the fruit seemed to resonate with it, filling her mind, filling her body—in her eyes, her ears, her nostrils—so that she thrilled to the scents and sounds as something that could be grasped and held in the palms of her hands.

She reached forward, filled with an indescribable yearning. One palm was open in supplication, the other twisted at an odd angle. A fruit fell into her palms with a juicy plop. Pain seared up her right arm but, with a moan of ecstasy, she sniffed the fruit, ignored the fire lancing up her arm and bit down on the plump juices. Musty warmth slid down into her belly and she fell to the ground beneath the tossing branches that beat and raged like a wild beast.

She was wracked by a spasm of pain. Another fruit fell at her side with a dull thud, but as her hand closed over it, the spasm hit again. She rose to her knees, shoving the fruit in her pocket, moaning. She squirmed, clutching her belly, but she could not stop herself. Her throat contracted and she suddenly vomited up a stream of sticky liquid. Again and again she vomited until her throat was burning.

She fell back, weak and listless and the noises faded to be replaced by the howl of the wind. She heard a guttural growl behind her and she turned her head weakly to see a shape bobbing along the shadows of the Mission wall. Furtive and animalistic, it filled her with a dread so deep that she retched again. The figure stopped.

Panicked, Miranda sprang up, her feet entangled in the dressing gown. She fell down. Whimpering, she ripped off the dressing gown, flung it away and fled.

The shape detached itself from the gloom and followed behind her, gliding swiftly through the grass.

Miranda, oblivious to the pain from her belly and her torn foot, screamed soundlessly into the wind.

Clang! Something crashed against the shutter of a Mission window with a metallic sound. Miranda heard a man's voice shouting unintelligibly into the wind and froze in her tracks. Then she saw a scrawny man running across the yard, screaming in rage. As he drew near, there was a rending sound. He stopped and looked up.

Miranda let out an involuntary cry as a huge limb tore intself from the Tree reared and slapped him down like a giant hand. The man screamed once and then his voice was lost in the howl of the wind.

Miranda snapped out of her fear-frozen rigidity and fled, sobbing, into the night. She ran and ran into the cool benediction of the gloom…

…And there in the distance, waiting for her on a distant horizon, was a ring of frozen red flowers and a woman who beckoned, proffering one of the flowers like a blood-red wine glass, singing in a strange but known tongue: "Come, come, dance on the sky, dance on the sea. You can fly like the eagle, swim like the fish, for I have Seen you and I will take your Pain…"

Miranda jerked bolt upright on the willow couch, her eyes rolling, her breasts bathed in her own thin red vomit, screaming, screaming. The old woman lay across her belly, choking and writhing as she, too, vomited a clear, red stream.

Then Miranda fainted.

CHAPTER TWENTY-TWO

As soon as he entered the yard, Peter felt that there was something wrong. He paused instinctively by the stone wall and glanced about nervously.

The sun hung low and blood-red over the hill, elongating the objects in the yard with a brooding chiaroscuro.

Peter took one step forward then paused again, frowning. There was definitely something about the quality of the landscape that had changed since he'd been there last:

The rows of vegetables, so green and bright in the earlier sunlight, now seemed melancholy and desolate—the green bled away by the ocher sun into a featureless, dusty purple. The workshop listed and yawed slightly to one side as it had always done, but now the blank holes of the windows seemed to stare blindly and the open doorway was a somber, monochromatic sepia against the dun walls; a yawing mouth in a blank, brown face.

Peter gripped the butt of the .45 and eased it out of his waist band, perplexed. His hands were clammy and he glanced about trying to pinpoint the source of his uneasiness. His gaze swept along the adobe wall of the Mission.

A series of slots was cut into the wall at ground level—probably ventilation for the cellars which had once stored dried vegetables, figs and walnuts. The slots seemed to stare back at him like sightless eyes and he felt the hairs spring up on his arms.

He scanned the slots nervously. Was he being watched?! His belly knotted with the sudden desire to piss, defecate and run, all at the same time. With an effort he controlled himself, fighting back the adrenalin surge.

Then he realized what it was.

There was no sound. Not a twitter of a bird or the hum of an insect. The blue jays were gone, as were the sparrows and woodpeckers.

Peter moved forward clutching the gun at waist level. His feet scrunched unnaturally loud on the gravel; he winced and tried to walk softly, but the scrunch, scrunch seemed to tear the fabric of the quiet, announcing his presence. To what…?

Peter reached the Mission building. He rounded the corner and stopped.

The table was as he'd left it, with one difference: Mashed into the ground by the chair was a huge crimson splash of squashed fruit—and the chicken was gone.

Peter circled the table cautiously with the gun trained on the open kitchen door.

He stopped.

To the side of the table was a purple stain. Then another and another. He followed the trail of squashed fruit with his eyes. It led to the ancient stone steps cut into the earth and the oaken cellar door, half underground. From where he stood, Peter could see that the doorway was half-ajar.

It had been closed when he left.

Despite the reassuring weight of the gun in his hand, he felt exposed out there in the open with the sightless slits of the cellar wall staring at him.

Something nestling in the scrubby grass at the side of the cellar steps caught his eye. He gripped the gun firmly and, with one eye on the cellar door, turned the object over with the toe of his boot.

Peter cried out in disgust and took a step back. It was the skeleton of a dismembered human hand. A gold ring rattled on the index finger.

Peter backed away from the hand numbly, circled the table and plunged into the gloom of the kitchen.

A quick glance about revealed it was empty. It seemed unchanged: the large, old-fashioned gas fridge purred away; a fetid odor arose from the dirty dishes in the sink, foul and familiar. It seemed safe enough.

Peter unhooked the binoculars from the strap around his neck. He took the flashlight from the top of the fridge and snapped the flashlight ring on the strap. With the flashlight bumping reassuringly against his chest, he stepped out into the yard.

The sun was now half-way behind the hills. Above the great rock, the sierra was tinted a deep blood-red, etching out the scrub oaks like black crouching dwarves. A chill bit through the air as the light began to fade; already the trees beyond the vegetable garden were becoming fuzzy and indistinct. Peter gnawed his lip. If it were to be done, he had to do it now, before the light failed completely.

Avoiding the dismembered hand on the ground, he strode down the mildewed steps and wrenched open the heavy door decisively. He regretted his impulsive action immediately. The door opened with a horrible screech of metal on wood that set his teeth on edge. He stopped, heart pounding. But nothing happened. With the .45 in his right hand and the flashlight in his left, Peter stepped inside.

He stood in a small, square room with damp adobe walls and a compacted earth floor. A blood-red swathe of light cut across the far end where the dying sun angled through the ventilation slits.

Peter played the flashlight around the room and glimpsed a dark rectangle to his left. He trained the flashlight on it and realized it was a doorless opening. He hesitated briefly then, grimacing, he plunged into it, the hairs on his neck erect…

He was in another square room, the same size as the other. His pulse slowed a little as a quick survey revealed that this, too, was empty. Peter's hand gripped the gun white-knuckled and he realized he hadn't breathed out for quite a while. He let out his breath in a huff of escaping air. It was so cold down there that he could see his breath.

A noise behind him made him whirl, gun at the ready. It was nothing but a drip of moisture from the ceiling.

Peter stood uncertainly in the parabola of light cast by the flashlight, his eyes racing over the room. He made a quick estimate of the room size and guessed that it was half the Mission width. Presumably there was a corresponding series of rooms on the other side of the Mission, with access only from the Tree side.

Fearfully, he squinted into the gloom, shivering in the cold. In the center of the wall there was another dark doorway and to Peter's left, at eye level, a blood-red slit revealed the last rays of the dying sun.

Peter crept up to the wall and peeped through the slit. He realized with a start that though he could see very little inside the rapidly-darkening room, by standing at the slit he could watch the whole of the southern aspect of the Mission, undetected. It was probably the same on the north side.

Peter turned, glanced at the door opening in the wall and plunged through desperately.

Something wet and clammy enveloped his face and he let out a muffled cry, striking out blindly in the dark. The flashlight bounced on his chest, making crazy whirling patterns on the walls and floor. Peter dropped his gun and fell down on his knees, scrabbling wildly in the damp dirt until his fingers encountered something hard. He lost it; scrabbled again. He clawed at his face with his left hand, panic-stricken. Then he realized:

Draped across his face was a huge, damp spider's web. He suppressed an hysterical giggle. The darkness, the damp, it was getting to him. He swore at his own loss of control, steadied the flashlight and stooped to retrieve the gun.

But it wasn't the gun that he'd touched before—the gun lay a few feet away. What he'd touched was another dismembered skeletal hand.

Peter snatched the gun up, alert to danger. He played the flashlight around the room, gun leveled. The hand wasn't there by accident—the Sheriff's men would have found it. Was it a warning? A trap? Well, he couldn't go back, he reasoned, and gritting his teeth, he inched forward through another darkened doorway, expecting something to hurl itself at him any minute from the inky blackness…

Some fifteen minutes later found Peter standing staring at a blank wall.

He was shivering with the cold. He'd passed through six vacant rooms, each one a dripping, moist rectangle. The whole cellar was empty. And now he'd reached a deadend and there was nothing but a blank wall. The journey had played havoc with his nerves. His gaze was bright and feverish; his hand ached where he gripped the gun too tightly.

Peter played the flashlight around. Totally irrationally, he was nervous now about the opening behind him even though he'd just come through it. Then, something on the floor caught his eye and he knelt down.

A patch of dark stickiness was puddled by the wall. At first Peter thought it was blood. Then the sweet, sickly smell arose to his nostrils and he realized it was a piece of the ripe fruit, half squashed by the wall bricks.

He ran his fingers along the brick, examining the wall closely. Then he felt it. He trained the flashlight down and went on all fours to peer at the wall base. There was a series of cracks in the ancient mortar.

He unslung the rifle from over his shoulder and, gripping the barrel, used the stock as a prod. He heaved against the bricks at the base of the wall. They gave slightly. Peter unclipped the flashlight and positioned it carefully on the floor where its beam would illuminate the loose bricks. He held the .45 in his right hand, propped the barrel of the rifle under his armpit and heaved forward, training the .45 on the lower wall.

The bricks slid back another inch.

Peter knelt down and squinted at the opening in the wall, calculating madly. If the loose bricks were pushed right back they would leave an opening approximately twelve inches high by two feet across. Not very big, but perhaps big enough for someone—or something—to squirm through. Peter pondered for a while. He made a quick estimation of the number of rooms: they were roughly the same size and ran the whole length of the building—which meant...

With a sudden exclamation, Peter realized that hidden behind the wall was *another chamber* at least twenty feet long.

He made up his mind quickly, turned and marched out of the chamber with a determined air. He switched the flashlight off and soon his eyes grew accustomed to the faint light from the ventilation slits, giving him enough confidence to move through the adjoining rooms more rapidly. With the .45 at the ready, he padded through the darkness, ready to fire at the slightest threat. It did not come. And soon he emerged from the cellar door into the night air with a sigh of relief.

It was warmer outside. Peter was surprised to find that the sun had gone completely; the sky was already a deep violet with the hills silhouetted against it, black and brooding.

Peter went to the kitchen, this time without hesitation, and grabbed the sledge hammer from behind the fridge. He hefted it up on his shoulder, then cursed and slapped his head. The rifle! The fucking rifle! He'd left it on the floor in the cellar!! What an idiot he was!!

With his heart racing, he hastily strapped the flashlight to the barrel of the .45 with some duct tape, then he strapped the whole thing to his left hand. No one was going to wrest the gun away from him in the darkness, he thought gravely. Shit, he'd had enough!

With a bravado borne out of desperation, Peter ducked back into the cellar door and sprinted through the first dark doorway, his heart hammering. But fear had transcended itself to become a kind of wild abandon. He loped through the cellars, the gun ever at the ready, his eyes wide in the gloom.

By the time he reached the inner chamber, he was bathed in a cold sweat. He paused as he stood before the last doorway, breathing heavily. Then he whirled and threw the sledge hammer into the darkened room. It hit the earth floor with a thud followed by a sudden scurrying sound. Peter hurled himself through the door and ducked to one side, clicking the flashlight on with his left hand.

The light blossomed, illuminating the blank wall garishly; but the cellar was completely empty, save for the sledge hammer. The rifle had gone.

Still acting out his adrenalin surge, Peter ripped the duct tape off, tore away the flashlight and propped it on the floor at a slight angle so it illuminated the base of the wall.

The stones he'd moved earlier had been pushed back into place. This was it. Peter unstrapped the .45, jammed the gun into his waist band and seized the heavy sledge hammer. With a savage grunt, he drove it into the wall.

The hammer crashed into the adobe. Vertical and horizontal cracks radiated across the brickwork. Peter raised the hammer and swung it fiercely again. The jagged fractures deepened. He took a deep breath, raised the hammer high over his shoulder and swung it through the air with a wild cry.

Impact. A complete section of the wall collapsed.

Something white launched out through the opening on top of Peter. He yelled, clawed for the .45 and over-balanced, sending the flashlight flying. Enormous shadows leapt up on the walls as a bony shape lurched on top of him. Then the flashlight went out and the room was plunged into darkness.

Peter managed to grab the .45. He fired wildly. The .45 was loud in the confined space. Each flare revealed a brief glimpse of staring black eyes and an ugly white grin. But the thing was on top of him and the bullets spanged uselessly into the wall behind it…

CHAPTER TWENTY-THREE

Miranda woke, shivering. A gentle voice whispered to her soothingly in a strange language. Save for the dim light of a tallow candle on the bedside table, the room was dark. Miranda stared up at the odd, flickering shadows cast by the candlelight, momentarily confused. Then she realized she was lying on Miya's bed and the figure bending over her was Molly.

Molly wiped Miranda's naked body with something cool and damp, crooning in the strange tongue. Miranda relaxed; Molly's touch was gentle, healing. She allowed herself to be dried off, then sat up like a compliant child as Molly helped her into a cotton nightdress.

Molly turned her head and called out softly in that strange tongue and the door opened to reveal Miya's huge bulk. He slipped into the room quiet as a shadow and helped Molly to clear away the remnants of the ritual.

Something was missing, thought Miranda. It was the same feeling she'd had on waking up on board a ship to find the ship's engines had stopped. It was the same sensation: something was not there that had been there before. Puzzled, Miranda tried to evoke the feeling she'd lost. There! Fleeting, evanescent, it brushed her consciousness; less a feeling than a sound registering almost beyond the audible frequency. It had been with her so consistently, it was only because it had gone now that she realized it had been there at all. Its absence did not bring a sense of loss but relief, as if Miranda had been in pain without knowing it.

She began to cry softly. Miya was at her side instantly. "I've been very sick," sobbed Miranda, "Really sick and I didn't even know it."

Miya took her hand in his and spoke to Molly in their native tongue. She responded with a few guttural syllables. "She says," said Miya gently, "To thank you."

"Thank me?" whispered Miranda hoarsely, "I want to thank her." She took the old woman's hand in hers; again she felt that odd little tingle and the woman smiled toothlessly.

"No. She wishes to thank you," said Miya, "She says you are…a True One. There is no direct translation. But, because of you, she says she met her Guardian again and her Power is redoubled. This is the first time she has met her Guardian since she became a healer over sixty years ago. It is a great gift."

"Not more than she gave me."

"But there is something else," said Miya, "Something that is troubling her very much."

"Tell me," urged Miranda.

Miya hesitated. "You are very weak. Perhaps we should wait." He spoke to the old woman again. He nodded, then turned to Miranda. "She says your body is weak but your spirit is the strongest it will ever be. I will tell you now."

When Miya told her, Miranda gripped his hand and bit her lip until the blood welled over her lip and ran down her chin. Despite the old woman's admonitions to be strong, Miranda wept. Her body convulsed with great sobs of anguish.

She cried for hours.

CHAPTER TWENTY-FOUR

Peter writhed in the dark on his back with the weight of the nameless thing on his chest. Animal sounds bubbled through his lips as he lashed about wildly. Slowly, he realized that he was fighting needlessly; his struggles met no resistance. He stopped fighting the thing and cautiously reached up and ran an exploratory hand over it.

It was a skeleton.

Peter jerked his hand away...then reached out again with quivering fingers and touched the bony skull. There was a metallic click as his hand encountered a chain. His whirling senses slowed and he sat up cautiously and extricated himself from the bony embrace. He scrabbled around for the flashlight and, instead, found the .45. He knelt by the skeleton and peered into the gloom, trying to make sense of the dim shapes and fuzzy oblongs in the blackness around him.

There was just enough light from the ventilation slits for him to distinguish the wall section which had collapsed inwards from his final hammer blow. Lying across his legs was the bony cadaver, gleaming faintly in the dark, jaws wide open as if deriding Peter's panic. A grisly, smelly, long-dead skeleton, it had fallen on him when the wall collapsed.

Peter's heart slowed to normal. But he kept the .45 raised as he scrabbled for the flashlight in the loamy soil. He couldn't find it; perhaps it was buried beneath the wall.

He rose to his knees and peered into the gloom, wishing for the flashlight. As if in reply, the ventilation slits suddenly brightened. Moonlight poured in cutting milky swathes of light through the gloom. And Peter could see. He grunted in surprise:

As if spot-lit in a dance macabre, white, bony cadavers hung suspended from the inner chamber wall at odd, twisted angles, glowing faintly in the moonlight.

Peter edged forward. As he touched the crumbling wall, another portion fell and another skeleton clattered down in a shower of dust and fragmented adobe.

It was some kind of burial chamber, reasoned Peter. He counted five cadavers in all. But there was something else; glowing wanly in the gloom beyond.

He stepped over the broken wall, avoiding the crumpled skeleton on the floor, and into the darkened chamber. It stank. It stank so badly he stopped in his tracks, his eyes streaming, his throat gagging. He put his hand over his nose and tried to breathe through his mouth. It was only partially successful—he could still smell it: A mixture of decay, putrescence and animal filth mingled with the graveyard smell of damp earth and the cloying scent of over-ripe fruit.

Peter fought to stop himself vomiting. Breathing through his mouth, he moved forward into the chamber, still holding the .45. Something cold and wet brushed across his calf and he leapt back as if stung. The moonlight thinned and faded—probably it had gone behind a cloud—and the chamber was dark again. Peter could see something; but he could not identify it in the gloom that swirled around his feet like black ink as the moonlight faded from the slits. He stood for a moment, uncertain. Then the slits brightened again and revealed something whitish and luminescent just above the ground. Peter leant forward cautiously, wondering if the whitish blur was another cadaver. Then he realized what it was:

A root; a white root.

Extending from a damp, mossy wall like bony, white fingers was a mass of root tips like frozen, white worms. Peter was puzzled; he'd estimated the room to be at least twenty feet long and this wall cut across the room only ten feet in.

A growl broke the silence behind him and he whirled around. The noise repeated itself; an ugly animal growl; low, evil; unlike anything he'd ever heard in his life.

"Stay there, now!!" he shouted, "I'm armed!! Don't move or I'll shoot!!" He pressed his back against the wall. The damp soil pressed against his shoulders and the wet, bony roots poked into his flesh like probing fingers.

The noise came again, this time with a peculiar smacking sound. There was a flurry of movement, and Peter fired.

He missed. The bullet smacked harmlessly into the ground. The muzzle flash gave Peter a stark view of the earthen floor littered with bones and excrement. Then It was upon him.

Peter was born down by its weight; its awful stench full in his nostrils as his face was buried in its fur. His hands clawed at its matted back, thick and furry. His right hand lashed about wildly, firing the gun over and over until it was an empty, clicking weight.

He clubbed the heavy gun on the creature's back. The thing screamed. He clubbed it again with dull thuds of metal on flesh. Then Peter's throat was clamped in two bands of iron and he was fighting for breath. He twisted and writhed impotently, pummeling madly at the creature with the gun. But the grip tightened. His breath became a harsh bubbling noise at the back of his throat; a mist seeped down over his eyes. Then his vision began to darken. He could feel himself slipping as his senses clouded. Peter made one feeble attempt to get free—with all his might, he pounded and clubbed at the creature. Then his strength failed and he went limp.

There was a noise like a thunderclap. Light blossomed, searing Peter's eyeballs. A confusion of shouts and cries, vaguely familiar. The creature's grip slackened. Then all was blackness.

Peter came to slowly, his breath rasping in his throat. A dark shape hovered over him. For a moment he couldn't focus. Then the foul odor hit his nostrils and he realized he was still in the chamber.

"Easy now…easy," came an oddly familiar voice. Who?

The dark shape bobbed and resolved itself into Dooley's face, inevitably chewing. "Well, lookee here," said Dooley with a grin, "Ole Clint Eastwood himself. Good job I came, boy. You were near a goner." The Sheriff chuckled deep in his throat.

Peter sank back wearily. If he'd had any strength he'd have hugged the Sheriff—never had someone's irritating mannerisms been so endearing. Then nervous reaction set in and Peter began to shake involuntarily.

"Here, give the boy a blanket," said Dooley, "He got the chilly willies sudden like."

Despite the Sheriff's banter, Peter accepted the blanket and, wrapping himself close, stared around the chamber.

Two grim-faced men stood behind the Sheriff clutching rifles. Two incandescent lamps were slung from the roof beams, illuminating the entire chamber.

Peter felt like laughing and weeping all at the same time. He was alive! He looked down at the crumpled body on the floor next to him; the matted fur outline, the open jaws and glazed eyes. He tried to say something, but it just came out as a choking noise.

The Sheriff chuckled again. "Boy, you musta shit yoursel' wholesale when this sucker jumped you in the dark!" He pushed the body contemptuously with the toe of his boot and it slumped over, revealing the staring eyes and stubbled jaw of an old man.

"Jesus!!" exclaimed Peter, "Who?!! Christ almighty, I know this guy!! He stopped us on the road when we first came! He was as drunk as a coot!"

"Yep, that's him O.K.—Joe Bear. Loonie ole Joe," said Dooley spitting on the floor, "He cashed in his chips, boy—nearly took you with him."

Peter examined the man curiously. A stinking bear skin was draped over the man's body; the bear's head formed a grotesque helmet; the fur was lashed around the man's torso; strange ornaments hung around his neck and waist—dried flesh; human bones; and a row of dog's ears slung on a cord.

Dooley bent down and picked up a gun. "This is ole Cal O'Donnell's," he declared, "And this…" he picked up a wallet, "…is Ferris Ansell's. Looks like we done found our killer—and a right screwball at that."

Peter stood up. He was unable to take his eyes off the body. The man lay staring sightlessly at the ceiling, the eyes open and dark. There was something on his lips and Peter shuddered when he realized what it was: They were stained purple; juice dribbled down the dead man's chin.

The Sheriff's men gripped their rifles nervously. Peter didn't blame them. The chamber was creepy.

It was so large that it obviously extended much further than the width of the Mission rooms above it. Age-blackened timbers criss-crossed the ceiling, festooned with rusty chains. The cellar wall on the Tree side was a crumbling lattice of adobe pierced with tree roots. White and bony, they poked through the wall and arced a full ninety degrees to sink into the other wall like fat, white snakes seeking their prey.

"Sheesh!! Look at this!! What in hell is it??!!" cried Peter gazing down a narrow corridor cut in the solid soil.

Four niches had been cut into the west wall, each as high and wide as a man, running parallel to the longitudinal axis of the Mission. Each niche formed a narrow corridor. Peter peered down the first one. The lights did not penetrate far, but he could just make out some dim shapes at the other end. "What the hell's down there?" he muttered.

"Creepy, innit?" chucked Dooley, enjoying himself immensely.

For once, Dooley's manner didn't irritate Peter; rather, it made him feel much better in these bizarre surroundings. "Jesus, Dooley, I don't know how you keep smiling," said Peter, "I stopped having fun quite a while back. Now, what the hell is down there?"

"Check it out," said Dooley blithely. He lifted the slim black tube of his Sheriff's flashlight and thumbed the button. The beam sprang to life, illuminating the corridor.

The niche was about fifteen feet long and twelve feet high; for all the world like one of those gloomy corridors found between the book stacks of an old library. Peter whistled when he realized what it contained:

Human skeletons, each standing erect, facing the wall; their fingers hooked into the damp earth as if they had died trying to claw their way through the earth walls.

There were five in all. The Sheriff played the flashlight over their bony whiteness. The roots were everywhere. Thick, white fingers branching from one wall to the other, impaling the skeletons; passing right through the rib cages, the eye sockets, the open mouths and into the damp earth of the opposite wall. The skeletons were transfixed by the roots; locked irrevocably into their earthy coffin.

Peter studied the skeletons' stance: their arched backs; the bony fingers clawed into the wall of earth. "Christ, it looks as though they were trying to get out!" he said, "Did Joe do this?"

"No siree, not unless he did it a'fore he was born," said Dooley in grim satisfaction, playing the flashlight over the mass of entangled roots and bony cadavers. "An' ole Joe wasn't *that* old. Lookee here." He pointed into one corner of the room. "See that?"

An ancient and rusted trowel sat on top of an bucket covered with cracked and crumbling mortar. "These here suckers…" said Dooley pointing at the skeletons chained together on the floor, "…walled themselves in—a long time ago. Looks like suicide to me. These guys musta lived here when it was a Mission. Look." He lifted his hand and something glittered in the light. It was a crucifix on a thin chain. "This was around that first sucker's neck," said Dooley gleefully, "These guys were probably the Mission priests. Why, these dudes musta been dead eighty years, man!" A noise behind them made the Sheriff turn. "Hey, lookee here, " he said amicably, "If it ain't our Indian expert."

"Miya!!" said Peter, "It's good to see you!!"

"Miya?" said Dooley staring at Martinez, "Oh, yeah, I see," he muttered.

Peter clasped Miya's hand fervently. The big man, dressed in his Realty Agent's suit, responded with a warm handshake.

"You should be thanking this guy for your life," said the Sheriff to Peter.

"What?!" exclaimed Peter, puzzled.

"Well, ya must be in a right ole state still," chuckled the Sheriff, "If ya think I'd be running around dirty ole cellars in the middle of the night outta choice! No siree." He chuckled again and slapped his thigh. "Ole Martinez told me you was going off on some kind of Lone Ranger mission out here and when I heard that you was out buyin' up the whole goddamn gun shop, I hightailed it out with two of my boys."

Miya raised an eyebrow at the mention of guns. Peter shrugged. "Like you said, Miya, you can't do a thing round here without the whole goddamn town knowing—and am I glad."

"Yep, you were lucky, boy. We just got through these gates when we heard some shots. We booked it down the cellar and by the time we got to you, this crazy loon was a'tryin' to strangle you, just like he strangled the rest."

Miya began examining the body, the bear skin, the amulets and other paraphernalia strung around the dead man's neck.

Peter shuddered. "So you shot him?" he said to Dooley.

"Nope," said the Sheriff.

"I heard a shot," said Peter recalling those few confused moments before he blacked out.

"Nope. I shot above his head," said Dooley, "A warning, like. I was scared of hitting you. Then I smacked him hard as I could over the head with my ole Peace-Maker." Dooley shifted the wad of gum to his other cheek and said speculatively, "Looks like I hit him too hard. He just keeled over an' died."

Miya was now sifting through the mess on the floor. Unheeding of the smell of animal decay and feces, he examined each article minutely.

"I'm surprised you haven't jumped on Miya," said Peter wryly to Dooley,

"Interfering with the evidence before the forensic experts get here."

"He *is* the forensic expert," said Dooley dryly, "Joe Bear was an Indian and Martinez is our Indian expert. He's not here by accident." He pointed at the dead man. "This sucker killed at least two men. Now we got the messy business of deciding why and how, the motive and all that crap." He spat on the floor and sighed. "Beats me. The fucker is dead and that's that. In the old days we'd have dug a hole, dropped his body in it an' forgot the whole dang business. Now we got all kinda shit, ipso dipso facto an' all: motive, plea of insanity…" he shrugged, "But I gotta do it." He turned to Miya. "You figure out what made this sucker tick yet?"

Miya nodded. He stood up slowly, fingering a small object made of bone. He held it in the light. "This is a bow. A *Devil Bow* made from a human rib and wrist sinew." He handed it to Dooley.

"Kinda small, innit?" said Dooley turning it over and over in his hands.

"Well, it's only a symbol," said Miya. "It means that ole Joe thought of himself as a *'kitdongwe'*—a Death Doctor. They were believed to have selected their victims with this bow."

"Jesus," muttered the Sheriff, "Goddamn California! Why did I ever leave the South? Down there we got nice, clean murders—profit or passion. Here, it's always some goddamn voodoo cult or sumpin'!"

Miya examined the marks on the floor. "Joe was eating all kinds of crap…" Miya pointed to an earthenware pot, "Looks like he's been mixing up some real potent medicines." He dipped his finger into the pot and sniffed it. "Can I take a little?" he asked the Sheriff, "I'll be able to tell you what it is tomorrow."

"Sure," said Dooley, "I'll get the rest analyzed. But don't you tell no one—strictly off the record, hey? But, by the time those idiots down in the city lab get us the results, it'll be next Christmas."

Peter grinned at Dooley. He was beginning to see the man in a different light.

Dooley turned to Miya. "Look, I'm kinda pissed off havin' to hang around down here. Kin we figure what this boy was up to—apart from being crazy—and git?!"

"Yeah, I think so," said Miya, still carefully sifting through the articles on the floor. "See those?" He pointed at the three empty niches cut into the wall of solid earth, "Looks like Joe discovered this place by accident, then decided he was going to do the same with his victims as happened to these old priest guys down here."

"What do you mean?" said Dooley sharply.

"Well, look. These niches are freshly dug." Miya reached out and brought away a handful of fresh, crumbling earth. "He must have dug these out himself. He was probably going to stick some other bodies down here."

Dooley winced. "You mean, he was going to dig up these two suckers Ansell and O'Donnell and drag 'em down here as well?"

"Looks like," said Miya slowly, "His motive certainly wasn't profit. You see, he kept the gun and the wallet as Power Objects. The *Kitdongwe* thought that possessions of the dead gave them some kind of influence over them."

Peter was bending over a wooden trunk in the corner. "Hey, look at this," he cried. He pulled out an old censor, a Bible and a crucifix. "These must have belonged to the priests."

"Shit on this place!" said the Sheriff darkly, "I had enough already—priests, voodoo, skeletons! Let's go! I wanna beer and a good cigar to get the stench out of my nostrils." He turned and stomped off through the doorway. The deputies followed him eagerly, glad for an excuse to leave.

Miya was bending over the wooden trunk. As Peter turned to follow the Sheriff, Miya took something out of the trunk and slipped it unseen in his pocket.

Peter gazed around the kitchen. The cracked sink was still laden with dirty dishes, the dusty shelves were a mess of paper packets and cans of food. The very normal mess of it was a relief after the bizarre scene in the cellar. He took a sip from a cup of jet-black coffee and let out a deep sigh.

Dooley, who sat at the table with Peter and Miya, fumbled in his pocket and brought out a hip flask.

"Hey, you need some medicine, boy," he said, "Not Indian medicine, white man's medicine." He offered it to Miya.

Miya raised his hands with a sorry expression: "You know we Indians can't take our drink," he said morosely.

"That's O.K." The Sheriff winked, "I'll drink yours."

Peter allowed the Sheriff to pour a stiff shot of whisky into his coffee. He raised the cup and sniffed the pungent alcohol-coffee mix and downed it gratefully. The drink hit his belly with a warm glow and he sagged visibly in his chair.

"You are bushed boy," boomed Dooley, "You need some sleep."

Peter nodded wearily. Then a thought surfaced that had been nagging at the back of his mind. He stiffened. "Miranda! Miranda, how is she?!" he cried, half rising from his seat.

"Relax," grinned Miya, "She is sleeping the sleep of the innocent. When I left her she was out like a light. Why, I bet she sleeps for two days."

Peter slumped back, relieved.

"Take it easy, Riley," boomed the Sheriff, "It's all over—bar the shouting." He chucked and took a swig of whisky, "And there'll be a lot of that, you mark my words."

"What I don't get," said Peter tentatively, "Is why you're so goddamn happy!"

"Happy? Well, now thar. I gotta think about that one—a'fore I gets myself into trouble." The Sheriff scratched his head and replaced his hat, chuckling. "Just between you and me, it's like this: I've been hanging around the County for ten years, messin' with poachers and pot farmers, and now look, here we got a genuine serial killer, a real voodoo creep! And not only do I solve the murders—with, I may add, some help from you guys—but I manage to apprehend the sucker myself. And that ain't no mean achievement in mah book."

The Sheriff's boasting didn't bother Peter. Why should it? He owed his life to him, he thought. He said so in no uncertain terms.

"Well, sir, that's mighty nice of you. But even though I'm shootin' off my mouth, the truth is I wouldn't have done nothin' else. It is my job." He turned to Martinez who still held the sinew and bone bow in his hands. "Hey, Martinez, before this thing turns into the usual fiasco—the coroner, photographers, the press an' all that—maybe you could tell us what ole Joe was up to."

"I'm not sure," said Miya slowly, "The ornaments and rituals down in the cellar are kind of mixed up—which figures with Joe," he said slowly. "Joe never did know *what* he was. First he told me he was Pomo, then later he said he was Yurok and he spoke a kind of crazy mixed-up dialect." Miya sighed. "But this business here… I guess Joe always fancied himself as a shaman, the way he would flit around the country at night. And the Bear Doctor role would just about fit his ideas of being someone special." He stood up and gazed out of the darkened doorway, "Especially on account of how much he hated people." He looked at Peter. "I guess you're lucky. He'd obviously been living in this place for a while. Even before you came, he must've been down in that cellar cooking up his evil rites, half-crazed with his own power."

The Sheriff looked at him cautiously. "So what was all this bear skin business? Who in hell did he think he was?"

"The Bear Doctor was an old Indian tradition. It was known by Indians over the entire state from the Shasta to the Diegueno. Most of the Bear Doctors were harmless. But some of them weren't. They would dress up in a bear skin and travel at night, robbing and killing anyone they came across. Most people were terrified of them—the Indian people, I mean. The Bear Doctors were renowned as poisoners and some of them actually believed they could change themselves into the bear with all its ferocious strength and power." He paused. "They were generally thought to be indestructible, these Bear shamans, with the power of returning to life after death. I guess Joe must have been hyping himself up on something, 'cos he sure did have a lot of strength for an old man, didn't he?"

The Sheriff didn't reply. But Peter remembered those steel-like hands encircling his neck and he shuddered. "He sure did," muttered Peter, "I couldn't get him off me."

Dooley chewed thoughtfully. "Well, we got quite a case here. It's gonna put us all on the map."

Peter frowned. "Oh, Christ," he said, "Does it have to? I couldn't stand it! This place will be like Niagara Falls with tourists and photographers…"

"What can I do?" said the Sheriff with a shrug, "Make the County out-of-bounds to visitors? Gimme a break!"

"Can't you keep it low? Keep it to yourself?" asked Peter.

"Huh, with those two jokers downstairs?!" The Sheriff was referring to his deputies, "It's too late now. They're just itching to get back to town so they can scare the pants off their buddies with some blown-up version of what they saw. Tell you what, though," said Dooley, "I'll put up a road block when we've finished our investigation. That'll keep some of the rubbernecks out, though, take my word for it, they'll find their way through like flies to a freshly shit dog turd."

"You do have a turn of phrase, Sheriff," grinned Peter wryly, "Anyway, thanks." Peter stood up and walked to the door where Miya stood quietly gazing into the night.

The moon was high and clear above the sierra hill, bathing it with a silvery light. Moonshadows silhouetted the trees in little, dark clumps. Somewhere in the distance a dog barked and then an owl hooted.

"Well," said Peter staring at the moon, "It's good to get back to contemplating ole Mother Nature after all this supernatural business."

Miya didn't look around. "For the Indian, there is no such distinction," he said quietly.

CHAPTER TWENTY-FIVE

The next two weeks were worse than Peter could have imagined. Despite the Sheriff's genuine attempts to protect the Mission, Peter and Miranda were hounded by sensation-mongers, reporters, tourists and rubberneckers.

The story ran in all of the newspapers, including the 'Natural Detractor' which enlisted the aid of a psychic to prove 'that twelve priests had been imprisoned by visiting aliens who had sealed them in a cellar after poisoning them, to conceal their invasion from an unsuspecting world'.

As wave upon wave of sensation mongers descended upon the Mission, Peter became very cynical. Even Miranda was shocked. She made no attempt to defend her fellow man, as was her normal response, but fell into a grave and uncustomary silence when the subject was broached. Matters came to a head when Peter found that sightseers were detouring the Sheriff's road-block and traversing the hills on foot to spy greedily on the Mission.

Peter had returned from a day in the fields to find a complete stranger standing in the kitchen, firing away briskly with a flash-camera. Peter was irate. He ran out to the Jeep without thinking, grabbed the .45 and let off a few shots into the air. The man fled in terror, leaving his light meter behind. He never returned to claim it.

However, matters did not improve so, temporarily, Peter and Miranda moved out. Not to a motel, but to Miya's place.

"Christ!" said Peter one night, sitting in the sweat house with a naked and comradely Miya, "I really don't get it. Haven't these people got homes, families, jobs? Can you imagine driving a hundred miles, crawling on your belly across a field and sitting there all day just to catch a glimpse of a couple who were unfortunate enough to live in the same place as a crazy killer??!! I really, really don't understand. There is something I'm missing. Something about people that hasn't clicked."

Miya declined to comment, save to say: "It will not last. These things pass with time."

Of course, he was right. But to aid the natural process, the Sheriff put up a notice that the property was guarded by ferocious dogs (untrue) and that armed guards (untrue) would shoot trespassers on sight (untrue).

And so it was the unwelcome tourism gradually declined and finally,

Peter and Miranda were able to move back to the Mission. In a way, Peter could not be blamed for not noticing the change in Miranda. The furor of interest in the 'Mission murders' threw him completely—in fact, he was acting very atypically himself under the abnormal pressures. In a similar way, Miya had also changed. Peter never noticed the odd silences that would spring up between Miya and Miranda or the wordless, yet meaningful glances they would exchange. As for Miranda's subsequent depression, Peter put that down to 'post-trauma let-down' and her general distress over the unwelcome attentions of the tourists.

He couldn't have been more wrong.

AUTUMN

'*The success of a tree as an organism depends on the strategic location of its living cells. Imagine that by some sorcery, all wood, bark and non-living material in a tree—and even the ground which conceals its roots—were to disappear and leave the living cells standing in utter nakedness. A shimmering phantom would be revealed in which every tiny detail of the tree would be seen. The tree has lost its massive ruggedness. Its tall and slender cone is as transparent as a soap bubble; its interior void except for spectral, silvery ribbons of wood rings that run horizontally between the outer surface and the center of the trunk, fading out at various depths.*

The leaf canopy of this ghost is a silvery mist made by living cells crowded together in buds and leaves. The root system of the tree, at a casual glance, reflects the form of its canopy with its intricate network of branches. The 'foliage' of the root system consists of root hairs which alternately bloom and fade, undulating like a shimmering Aurora Borealis.

This is no pretty, imaginary vision. It tells the arrangement of the living cells in the tree's body.'

Rutherford Platt
The Great American Forest

CHAPTER TWENTY-SIX

Peter sat in the Mission kitchen with Miranda. Outside, it was raining, but that was nothing new—it was more of a surprise when it *wasn't* raining; it rained almost every day.

Peter, clad in a thick pair of woollen army pants, galoshes and a sweater gazed across the fields through the open door. The rain fell in misty sheets, gusting over the hills, cascading down the smooth face of the distant rock above the river.

The river was now, indeed, a river. It had swollen its banks to become four times its summer width. Even from this distance they could hear the roar where it dashed against the base of the huge rock and was deflected around it in a muddy torrent. And still it grew, for the rain was incessant, swelling the river more each day.

Peter loved it. After the aridity of summer, it was so rich. The grass was suddenly bright green and the hues of the hills were heightened by subtle nuances and fresh shades of color.

Peter listened to the drumming of the rain on the roof and sipped his coffee contentedly. "It's funny how it all turns out," he said to Miranda without looking up, "A crazy man living in our cellar and we never even knew it. Remember when we met him on the road, eh?"

Miranda didn't respond. She was playing moodily with a box of matches on the table. Her uncombed hair fell in rats' tails around her white face; her eyes were dark patches; her skin, blotchy. She looked ill.

Peter continued without noticing she hadn't answered. "Why, I bet you that he really responded to you being so kind. Crazy people do, you know, no matter how far they're gone. I've always said it, some part of them notices and responds. Why, perhaps it was your act of kindness that kept him away from us! Who knows…?" Gradually, sensing the silence behind him, Peter paused in his monologue and turned. Miranda didn't look up. "What's the matter?" asked Peter slowly, "Are you still not feeling well?"

"I didn't say that," said Miranda curtly, snapping a match in two and arranging it with the others on the table.

Peter gazed at her, and for the first time noticed how bad she looked. Of course he'd realized that she hadn't been feeling too good, but then the whole affair had taken its toll on both of them. Now they were back at the Mission, they'd done nothing but lounge around for two days and already *he* was beginning to feel better. But, if anything, Miranda looked worse.

"Miranda," he said anxiously, "Maybe we should go away down to Mexico or something for a few weeks, get some sun. You really look like you need a holiday."

"Oh, yeah?" she retorted, scattering the matches suddenly, "Here we go, Mr. Cause-and-Effect."

"Miranda!" said Peter, blinking at the harshness of her tone, "What is it?!"

"Miranda looks sick. Miranda goes on holiday. Miranda is not sick. Neat, isn't it?" she said coldly.

"Miranda!" Peter shook his head. "What have I done?! I was only thinking of you!"

"Oh, thinking of me, were you? Solutions, solutions—everything is easy for the man of solutions, isn't it? There's always an answer for you, Peter, isn't there?"

"Look, Miranda," said Peter, his face twisted in pain, "I don't know what it is I said or what this is all about, but if you'd only explain, I'll do my best to put it right."

"That's it, Peter," she said, standing up so suddenly that the chair fell over, "Explanations, answers. That's it. Everything has an answer in your neat, little, ordered world. And when anything goes wrong, Mr. Peter can fix it, can't he? Can't he??!!"

"Miranda, this isn't necessary."

"Necessary!! How the hell do you know what's necessary or not, Mr. Fix-It?!!" She was shouting now. Inexplicably, she suddenly burst into tears and ran out of the door.

"Miranda!!" shouted Peter.

Sobbing, she ran across the yard towards the old theater, her bare feet slapping on the wet gravel. Within seconds her hair was slicked down on her head and her thin dress plastered to her body.

Peter ran after her. "Miranda!! Don't!!!"

She ran into the theater and slammed the door. Peter looked over the edge of the windowless opening. Miranda lay crumpled on the hardwood floor of the stage. "Go away!!!" she shouted.

"Miranda, don't do this to me!!"

"*You*?! Don't do this to *you*?!" mimicked Miranda, "Huh! Leave me alone!!!"

"Miranda!!"

"Leave me alone!!!" grated Miranda through clenched teeth.

Peter dashed back to the house, wrapped two woollen blankets in an oil slicker and ran back across the yard to the old theater. He leant through the window. Miranda still lay crumpled on the stage crying quietly. "Honey!

Please! I know you don't want to talk to me, but you'll get really sick if you stay like that."

"Leave me!" she whispered.

"O.K.," he said sadly, "But look…" he tossed the bundle onto the stage by her side, "…here's some blankets. I'm not coming in, but please wrap up warm—please!"

He ducked down beneath the window and sat on his haunches in the pouring rain. The water ran down his head and trickled into his collar. He felt completely miserable.

Peter clenched his hands in exasperation. She was right. Mr. Fix-It. He could strip down a generator, build a silver machine—repair anything. But when it came to people, he couldn't do zip. He was swamped by an uncustomary sensation of helplessness and a vague nagging guilt. What had he done? This was not like Miranda; she didn't go around blaming people unnecessarily. There must have been something… He shook his head, bewildered, and stood up. He was drenched through, but he didn't even notice it. He raised his head cautiously and stared over the edge of the window.

Miranda lay on the ramshackle stage with the blankets drawn around her like a child. Her shoulders heaved beneath the blankets; she was crying quietly. The sight was like a dull blade in Peter's heart; his eyes prickled and a lump came to his throat.

But he knew better than to approach her just then. Head down, he walked to the Jeep and climbed into the front seat. Ever faithful, Peter knew that at that moment he could only do one thing for the woman he loved—leave her alone.

So, he left her alone.

As the Jeep roared off, Miranda, lying in her little cocoon of warm misery on the theater floor, didn't even look up.

CHAPTER TWENTY-SEVEN

Miya, very civilized in a neat dark suit and tie, gazed across his garden at the rain battering on the roof of the sweat house. He glanced up at Peter who sat across the porch from him bundled up in a thick coat, his hair slicked wetly across his head, his glasses steamed up, his feet thrust into fur-lined mud-boots. "Perhaps it's a good thing you came, Peter," Miya said slowly, "Before anything happens."

"What do you mean 'before anything happens'?" said Peter, "Between me and Miranda?"

"No—not exactly," said Miya quietly. "The situation has been difficult for me. I've not wanted to worry you or to frighten you, but I know there would come a time—and it's come now and I have to warn you."

"Warn me of what, Miya? Please, you're supposed to be my friend! Don't beat around the bush!" said Peter. He snatched his glasses off and wiped them furiously as if they were the offending objects. "Just like Miranda! She wouldn't tell me anything! Now you're doing the same! I don't know what you're talking about!"

"Obviously Miranda does," said Miya firmly. Peter raised his eyes to the ceiling. "C'mon, relax, Peter. You must admit, it hasn't been easy to discuss… shall we say, esoteric matters with you in the past—and that's why both me and Miranda have been so reluctant."

"Well," fumed Peter, "As I'm not a member of the local psychics club, perhaps you'll let me in on the act now!"

"Peter," said Miya, "Can't you see how difficult you're making it? Neither me nor Miranda have broached a matter of great importance 'cos you're not ready to listen. Now things have come to a head and you're still not prepared to listen! Where does that leave us?"

"You tell me," said Peter.

"Well," said Miya, "I'll tell you where it leaves Miranda. It leaves her out in the cold, sobbing on a damp floor 'cos *she* can't communicate to the man she loves."

The blow hit home. Peter sat back as though stricken and his face crumpled. For a moment Miya thought he was going to cry.

After a brief silence, Peter spoke. "I'm sorry. I've never been very good at…emotional things. And I am making it difficult. Please…nothing matters to me more than Miranda, even my own stupid beliefs—nothing. I'm ready to listen, just tell me."

"I'm sorry, I was so blunt," said Miya, "I didn't want to hurt you."

Peter shook his head without rancor. "I needed it. Go on, I'm listening."

Miya sat looking at Peter for a moment, then he said: "Perhaps you are. Look, I understand what Miranda is trying to tell you; she's doing it without words in the only way she can—with her emotions and, sadly, it's working. You know *something* is wrong, but not *what* is wrong. You see, she knows that as far as you're concerned, the situation at the Mission ended with the death of Joe Bear." Peter looked puzzled but did not speak. "Yes, I know what you think, Peter," said Miya, "You have a neat explanation for the events of the last few months: Crazy Joe Bear got some idea in his head that he was a great Indian Devil Doctor and killed two men to prove it. Right?"

"Right," said Peter slowly.

"You've got it all tied up neatly. And as far as you believe, over eighty years ago in a fit of religious fervor, those priests made some kind of suicidal pact, chained themselves together, walled themselves in and starved to death?"

"Right," said Peter puzzled.

"Well, I wish it was that simple," said Miya. "Wait a moment." He got up and went into the house, leaving Peter staring at the drizzling rain. He returned a moment later with a book in his hands and sat down. "This, Peter, is the Last Will and Testament of one Santos Valasquez, formerly of Spain; a neo-American immigrant and neo-Franciscan priest."

"Wasn't he the man who built the Mission in the first place?" asked Peter.

"Yes. And probably it was his remains that fell on top of you when you knocked the cellar wall down," said Miya without humor.

Peter stared at Miya and the book, then said slowly: "You told me that there was no more written last time you read out the account to me. Where did you get this from?" He picked up the book, gently turning the leather-bound volume over and over in his hands. Then he noticed the purplish stain on the cover and he handed it back to Miya hastily. "Christ! Did you get that from the cellar?"

"I did," said Miya.

"Wash your hands, then," said Peter with a look of disgust.

Miya nodded. "You'll be sure that I will—I do every time I touch this book," he said. "But first, listen—and I mean, *listen*." He opened the book and began to read aloud.

Peter gazed out at the rain, unseeing. As Miya's voice floated across the small, wooden veranda, it mingled with the steady downpour of rain; a rain that seemed to stretch across the years to blend with the rain of another time and another place, and the voice of a man long, long dead:

"'*I cannot but hope where there is no hope and in that hope there is a diminution of my fear, but, alas, my dream, as fortune would overtake me, becomes the substance of this nightmare. The dead do walk. It has been said; it has been shown; the evil-that-has-no-name. And I say it now in our final hour of hopelessness, for, if we had said it before and not tied our rational recourse to the glib explanations of the good and evil in man, we would not have come to this pass. But I say it now, for the Undead gibber long in their chains: Father Montez; Father Castille; Nino; Padua and Mantilla.*

Horror upon horror. I, who witnessed the Last Rights, I, who sprinkled the dust on the graves with my own hands, do watch them shriek and writhe in their chains in this dungeon which they dug for themselves.

What fools are men who will not admit the evidence of their senses. For months fear has stalked the Mission, since the first murders, and with the fear came that peculiar indolence; a sleep that is not a sleep; an apathy which has stopped us all from fleeing the horror of this place. I, who came upon the first body myself, the good Father Mantilla, with his throat wrenched and his mouth afoul with the vile nectar, and I who witnessed him not two weeks later, stalking the night air like the Foul Fiend himself. It cannot be!' cry our senses. But it is, it is. My only hope for my fellow man—my devotion to my Caretaker and the spirit of Our Lord Jesus Christ—is in this incarceration.

By my side lie the bodies of my companions, lifeless, it would seem. But upon the empiricum of the evidence of mine own eyes, they will shortly rise to gibber and shriek at this mocking wall of death with their companions following suit.

But it is too late. The mortar is set, the chains are tied and the key hurled through the narrow window shaft away from arm's reach. Already the pangs of poison claw at my belly. Within the hour, I join my Maker. But I die with a glad heart, knowing the evil is confined and that I, at least, will rise no more to walk undead like my wretched companions.

It grows dark and their shrieks are fearsome. But what can they do to a man do who is already dying? And who can hurt a man who is on the way to join his Creator? A foolish thought, but as the good light of day fails, a small candle would have been some comfort. I had not thought to bring it. Enough. For the sake of Jesus Christ Our Lord, Amen.'"

Miya's voice died away to be replaced by the sound of the rain hissing and thrumming on the porch roof.

Peter was silent for a long time, deeply moved by the dying words of this heroic priest. Eventually, he shook off the heavy feeling that had settled across his heart and asked: "What is it…you want from me, Miya?" His voice was soft and uncharged.

"Peter," said Miya, "There is something more to this business than a crazy, drugged-up loon who killed two men. Don't you see? The two diaries are irrefutable evidence of what really happened to these poor men. It's the Tree—it's dangerous."

"Yes," said Peter softly, "This fruit is…somehow very harmful."

"It's more than that. Can't you see, Peter?! Look, when the Indians talk about Huk—the Spirit Bird of the Tree with a red poison in its quills—it's not some simple metaphor!" He stood up in exasperation. "Fairy-tale translations of the old Indian myths have done more damage than good! I told you before, it's impossible to think of it in these terms." He threw up his arms in an unusual display of emotion. "Let's just say that, as you have an animus within you, a life spark, well, that is what the Huk is in the Tree. It's a manifestation of something older than man, something that is harmful to man."

"You're trying to tell me the Tree is… alive?!"

"That's not quite the way I'd put it, but it'll do for our purposes. And there's Miranda. Look, we haven't talked about what Miranda experienced with Molly Buckskin. We've never discussed her health or anything that happened, but I tell you, she is in great danger for sure, and we've got to do something—and now!!"

Peter's face was white. He stood up, no longer listening to Miya. "Oh my God," he muttered. He slapped his forehead, "Oh my *God*! I can't believe that I could be so stupid!" He stared at Miya, ashen. "It's the whole business: the strain, the murders, the whole goddamn business! We've been living in such a frenzy, such a crazy mess, I forgot!!" he cried out in anguish, "I forgot my wife took something that could harm her when she was pregnant! I, Mr. Peter Riley, *forgot*!!"

"Peter," said Miya, "There's something I've yet to tell you."

"Miya, I'm sorry!" said Peter. "Look, I've got to use your phone." He dashed into the next room and dialled a long-distance number. "Hello… Yes, David Gordon of the Bio-Chemistry Department… Well, that'll do…"

Peter stood nervously tapping his foot as Miya came through the door. "Peter," urged Miya, "I've got to—"

Peter held up his hand to interrupt Miya and spoke into the phone. "Hello… Yes, this is Peter Riley… Look, what do you mean? When will he be back? Oh, no! I can't wait that long, you see—" He stopped and listened.

"David told me to pass on a message," said the tinny voice on the other end, "He said he's been trying to phone you for weeks but in the end he gave up. He's sent you a full report in the mail and he wants you to get back to him. He says it's very urgent."

"Oh, my God!" muttered Peter.

"What was that?" said the tinny voice.

"Oh nothing, nothing. Thanks." Peter slammed the phone onto its rest, wrenched it up again and dialled the Mission. When the phone rang at the other end, he turned to Miya and said, exasperated: "The report on the fruit! I stopped collecting my mail when we got sackfuls of it from all the crazy people all over America and the report has been collecting dust at the Post Office all the time! Oh, shit!" He slammed the phone down. "Oh, shit, she isn't answering! She must still be in the theater!"

"Peter," said Miya, "I've got to tell you something."

"I know, I know," said Peter, "Oh, what an idiot I am, Miya! Please, I'll be back later. I've got to go to the Post Office!" He shook Miya's hand. "I'm sorry, Miya," he blurted, "I know you're only trying to help." He dashed out of the door.

The Jeep rumbled to life outside, then roared out of the driveway. Inside the room, Miya sank in the chair, pressing his thumbs into his eyes and realized he'd used Peter's abruptness as an excuse...

He hadn't been able to tell Peter, especially as he knew Peter would never believe it—until it was too late.

CHAPTER TWENTY-EIGHT

Miranda lay curled up in the blanket listening to the rain drum on the theater roof. It was so nice to lie like that. She'd cried herself into a state of numb clarity until she could cry no more. All that was left was that dull ache in her belly.

Wouldn't it be nice, she mused drowsily, just to lie like this, listening to the rain forever; through each day, through each night, on and on, until, one day, the rain would stop and the sun would come out bright and cheerful and she'd wake up to find it was all over and everything was right with the world again?

She held on to this lie, urged it to be true. But the lie, shoddy and useless, slipped from her grasp. It didn't happen like that; she had to do something herself.

Painfully, she sat up and faced the bleak Truth. Everything looked the same: the dilapidated stage; the open barn-like roof with its exposed cross-truss; the roof timbers thrumming steadily with the rain; the beaten earth floor where the spectators had sat to witness... What...? What performances had been played out on this primitive stage? Then she realized that in her need to drift away, to forget, to go to another time, another place, her mind was pulling her away from action.

She made her decision.

She stood up and threw the blankets off, strengthened by her resolve, and stared up at the roof supports.

The roof timbers were twenty feet high at their apex, but the nearest main cross strut—a beam of eight-by-eight fir—was only ten feet above the ground. That would do it.

She glanced across at the window and her mind flooded with the image of Peter leaning in to throw the blankets to her. Hastily, she shoved all thoughts of Peter from her mind. In this, she was alone.

She clambered off the stage and padded to the center of the earth floor and stood underneath the great cross-beam. She gazed up at the intricate structure of the roof struts. Odd, she thought, how vivid everything is; she could see every knot in the wood; every swirl of the grain; the places where it was scored or nailed—even the spider webs in the corners glinting with fire-flies of light, crisp and clear...

There! She shook her head, realizing she was side-tracking again. She turned and strode over to the far side of the building to where Peter's tool box lay. Alongside it sat a wheel barrow, a rusty spade, a garden fork and a coil of rope. She picked up the rusty spade and leant her weight on it to see if the grayish wood handle was rotted. It bent but did not give; it seemed strong enough.

Carrying the coil of rope, she returned to the center of the room. She whirled the rope end and tried to swing it over the rafter. She missed. The rope fell at her feet. She tried again, and after a couple of attempts, succeeded. This time, much more carefully, she threw the other end over and succeeded first try. Now the rope hung in a double loop with two ends hanging down. She knotted the two ends together and adjusted the height. She tested it by taking the loops in both hands and swinging on it with her full weight. It held.

In the ground, directly below the rope ends, she began to dig out the dirt floor with the shovel. It was hard going; the earth was packed so hard that she had to use the garden fork to break it up before she could shovel the dirt out.

It was slow work. But, somehow, it seemed right that it should be so. Like a ritual, it was right that she shouldn't hurry anything; each part of it had its own time, its own rhythm.

She became acutely aware of the time and place: the theater; the ground; the dull gleam of the fork; the sweat on her brow; and allowed herself the luxury of losing herself in the act of digging.

When she'd finished the hole, she almost regretted it was over. She sighed, went to the stage and began collecting pieces of broken wood. It was birch, old and well-seasoned; it would burn well but not too fast.

After a few trips, she had a sizable pile stacked next to the shallow hole. She selected some of the thinner pieces of wood and built a neat pyramid within the hole. Around this central core, she stacked some of the larger birch pieces.

She stood back and surveyed her handiwork. Satisfied, she took one of the blankets from the stage, wrapped it around her body and pushed at the warped theater door. It creaked open with a complaining rending sound and she stepped out into the cool benediction of the rain, hot from her labors.

She closed her eyes for a moment, allowing the rain to fall soothingly on her head. Then she walked across the yard, unhurriedly, savoring the coolness. Shifting gusts of rain shunted across the fields, ran in great gouts down the Mission walls and battered at the river. The river was up; she could hear its dull roar above the hiss of the rain, and, somehow, it seemed right that it was so, though she did not know why.

A strange serenity had descended upon her. She did not know why. Perhaps it was because she'd come to a decision; perhaps it was because the ritual had a certain rhythm of its own as ancient as the blood of Man. It was all beyond her power or ken, and what would be would be…

With an easy grace, she made her way to their bedroom. As she entered, she glanced up at the Kuksu portrait which seemed to stare at her knowingly. She gazed at the portrait's eyes for a moment, then knelt down by an old cedar trunk against the wall. She raised the trunk lid and took out the birch-bark skirt that Molly Buckskin had given her. She also took out an amulet, three bundles of dried leaves tied with raw cotton and a piece of folded paper. She closed the lid and carried her precious load to the bathroom.

She slipped off her work dress and showered, rubbing herself down with the pungent herbs. She dried herself carefully and slipped on the Indian garments. Without looking in the mirror, she brushed her hair, plaited it into two pigtails and secured it with a cotton headband. She looped the amulet around her neck, then unfolded the piece of paper carefully.

Within its yellow creases lay a coarse brown powder. She dropped it into a glass of water, then, reciting the words she had learned from Molly, she swallowed it. Its bitter taste brought tears to her eyes, but, repeating her solemn recitation, she washed it down with another glass of water.

When she'd finished the incantation she returned to the kitchen. She searched through the drawers on the table, found a polythene bag and wrapped the bundles of leaves and a box of matches in it. She folded this and put it into the pouch of her skirt and went out into the rain. Instead of turning towards the theater, she circled the house until she was beneath the Tree.

Grave-faced, she stared up at the huge trunk glistening yellow and black; rivulets of rain oozing down it. Naked from the waist up, barefooted, Miranda stood like a statue, gazing upwards. The rain beat upon her white skin, ran over her shoulders, her arms, her breasts. It coursed down her face in rivulets, dripping from her eyelashes; cold, damp. The wetness seeped into the waistband of the skirt, down her thighs and probed between her legs like clammy fingers. She shuddered, but, simultaneously, a warm glow kindled in her belly as the Indian herbs began to warm the core of her being. The glow spread through her loins and up into her chest and she no longer felt the cold rain.

She closed her eyes, raised her arms up to the Tree, the Wind and the Rain, and began to sway gently. Of its own accord, a sound emerged from her throat and, as she'd been instructed, she let it come.

Again and again the sound came; and though it came from her own throat, Miranda heard it as the voice of another. Miranda wailed; but it was a wailing as old as man: the grief-cries of womenfolk waiting for boats that did not return from a storm-tossed sea; the mourning cry of mothers who had lost their sons in senseless battles; the keening of wives with husbands lost to nameless causes.

It was no longer Miranda's wail but the anguish of all womankind for the millions that had perished mindlessly and uselessly through the ages, every one of them a mother's son. The wailing ceased. Miranda intoned that which Molly had written for her. She said aloud the Word that could not be spoken; she spoke the Unspeakable.

It was done.

She opened her eyes, and, without looking back, she turned and walked towards the theater. Her belly was glowing with the warmth of the medicine. She felt oddly light on her feet, almost happy.

Inside the theater, she unwrapped the polythene bag and took out the bundles of dried herbs and the matches. She lit the kindling, blowing at the tiny, yellow flame until it flared and licked at the worn birch boards. When the fire was crackling merrily, she broke open the bundle of dried herbs and sprinkled them on the fire and said the Word again, this time very softly.

The slow fire in her belly had begun to mount. Beads of sweat sprang out on her chest and shoulders. The fire subsided, smoldering under the dried leaves. She leant across and blew gently. The leaves caught and a cloud of acrid smoke wafted up from the blaze. Miranda inhaled deeply. The fumes bit into her lungs and she reeled back dizzily, her eyes red and smarting.

Her eyes were blurred with tears, but she returned to inhale the smoke over and over until her chest hurt and she couldn't see at all. When she could take no more, she stood up and groped for the dangling rope, tears streaming from her red eyes. She found it and, raising her left arm in the air, carefully tied one end to her left wrist. She did the same with her right wrist, until both her arms were suspended above her head.

She stood astride the fire, her arms in the air.

A slight wind wafted up smoke and she inhaled it again, still in a standing position. Then she slowly lowered herself onto her knees in front of the fire, her thighs open. The warmth of the flames licked the inside of her naked thighs like an insistent lover and she let herself drop towards them until the ropes grew taut and her arms were strung above her head. And so she hung on her knees, her breasts bare above the smoky fire, her feet behind her, her thighs open, as if offering herself to the flames...

Her thoughts began to tumble and spin. She swayed, letting her arms take the weight instead of her knees. The fire was just a plume of smoke now and she eased her knees closer to the shallow pit, keeping her thighs apart. She felt the smoke billow up her legs, caressing her thighs with a gentle warmth. It funneled up the skirt, and, trapped between her thighs, licked at her naked belly and genitals. It was pleasant, intoxicating. She had to struggle with her tumbling thoughts to remember... What...? Why...? Aah, yes, the Word; she remembered the Word; she had to say the Word one more time. She opened her thighs wide and, one final time, she said the Word.

When the first spasm hit her she couldn't believe the pain. She reared up on her heels; her body arched like a bow and her belly went hard as a rock. She was too shocked to scream. She hung, taut, her eyes bulging wide with agony. Then she went slack and swung back whimpering. The rope bit into her wrists unnoticed. Great beads of sweat oozed between her breasts and down her belly as she collected her racing thoughts: Surely not, she thought, panicked, not like this! It can't be...not this bad!

But, unbidden, the jagged pain lanced cruelly into her belly again. This time she bit through her lip to stop herself screaming. But it was no use; the scream was torn from her lips and she arched her back, every muscle and sinew in her body straining against the pain.

The pain gradually slackened, but this time, did not subside completely. Like fragments of broken glass, it pumped inside her belly in spurts. She moaned and swayed, dangling helplessly on the ropes, and before she had time to take her breath, another spasm hit her body and she was arching and twisting in agony again. Feverishly, she muttered incoherent pleas, snatches of song, nonsense phrases; torn from her lips by the white-hot agony stabbing deep into her belly.

It became worse; not as a stabbing pain but as a burning growth. Deep inside her, it mounted higher and higher. As it grew, she clenched her teeth and her eyes rolled in disbelief. She began to lash from side to side, the ropes abrading her wrists unnoticed.

"No!!" she whimpered, "Not that!!!" Then she screamed: "Nooo!!!"

She was flailing from side to side trying to escape the impossible, incomprehensible pain that swelled inside her. Her eyes glazed and rolled up into her head; her mouth fell open; her lips stretched across her teeth; her mind was a single shrill note of 'Nooooo!'. But it swelled with the awful sensation that her body was no longer Arms or Legs or Body or Breath or Mind, but PAIN, PAIN, PAIN; only Pain until...

...It burst; rupturing like an exploding balloon: Release; merciful release flooded Miranda. She sagged in the ropes and fell into a blissful darkness...

...A young-old woman padded across an azure sea and plucked two crystalline blossoms of red with a glassy 'spang!'. Taking one in her mouth, she placed the other in Miranda's. Despite its crystalline hardness, the flower was sweet and juicy. The young-old woman smiled and repeated a phrase over and over in a strange tongue. Miranda smiled, wetness running down her cheeks. She understood:

"You will be well, you will be well, you will be well," chanted the Indian woman.

Redness arose before Miranda's eyes, became green then blue. Then she fell into blackness again...

Miranda opened her eyes slowly, blinking away the tears, numbly aware of the wetness running down the inside of her thighs. Her arms hurt but she took a breath and, gripping the ropes firmly, she hauled herself upright, stood on her feet shakily and stared into the hole at her feet.

For a second, it did not register. Then her eyes widened in horror and a whimper broke from her throat. Her mouth fell open and her belly contracted in revulsion. She turned her head to one side and began to vomit.

As she crouched, heaving, something wet and sticky stole forward from the shallow hole, wrapped itself around her ankle and pulled at her foot with a gentle but insistent tug.

Miranda spat out the brackish vomit taste and reared away, alarmed. The stickiness retreated, slithering back into its hole. Miranda tore the ropes from her wrists, never taking her eyes off the thing in the hole. Molly had prepared her, but the actual sight made her tremble with horror.

As she'd been instructed, she ripped her skirt off and dropped it into the hole. Unheeding of her own safety, she kicked the burning embers in on top of the skirt, then snatched up the final bundle of medicinal leaves and threw them on top.

The leaves erupted with a 'whumph!' of orange flame. The thing in the pit let out a scream of pain that became a series of pitiful moans. Miranda clapped her hands over her ears, anguished. She pivoted and turned on the spot, agonized. She ran around in circles, unable to go and yet unable to look as the flames hissed and gurgled in the pit and the theater was filled with the awful dying noises of the thing.

"Oh my God!!!" moaned Miranda, "Oh my God!! No!!!"

The creature let out a final bubbling whimper and fell silent. Miranda listened to the crackling of the flames and whimpered herself. She closed her eyes and, with her bare feet, kicked fresh dirt onto the flames. Then gagging, she ran out into the rain.

Miranda rolled about naked on the wet grass, whipping her head back and forth, clutching her belly in paroxysms of disgust. The rain beat down on her, sloughing away the dirt from her breasts and the gouts and globules of blood on the inside of her thighs. And yet, Miranda felt that she'd never ever be clean again.

¤

From the hillside above, the woman watched the naked Miranda writhing in the grass. The woman sat in a lean-to of bark and grass; a small, A-shaped shelter that faced onto the Mission below.

Her nut brown face impassive, she sat with her hands clasped around her birch-bark skirt. At her feet was a semicircle of angelica and pepperwood leaves. As the girl twitched and writhed below, the woman muttered and intoned, waving her hands over the semicircle of herbs.

Eventually, the girl ceased writhing and lay with her legs open, letting the rain wash her clean.

The woman smiled; her face was transformed, showing that she was just a young girl herself. She picked up a pipe, lit it and proceeded to blow its smoke in four directions—East, West, North, South.

Then, after taking a few bites of persimmon, she settled back into her lean-to to resume her vigilance.

¤

Miranda opened her eyes and blinked away the rain from her eyelashes. It was done. The horror of the last few months melted away as she realized she had done it. She wept softly, but this time with a difference. She stood up, naked in the rain and enjoyed the cleansing sensation of the pure water running down her wet thighs.

When she was ready, she composed herself and returned to the theater and looked into the half-covered hole. This time, her face was impassive. She stared down at the smoldering, dirt-covered thing in the pit without emotion. It was done. And that was that. She recited the final words as she'd been taught and, taking the shovel, she threw the rest of the dirt into the hole until it was a heaped mound on the floor. Then she stamped it down flat.

She threw aside the shovel and, without looking back, walked out into the rain.

CHAPTER TWENTY-NINE

Peter shoved the canvas mail bag onto the table in the donut store and went to the counter to order a large coffee and two honey-glazed donuts. The frizzy-haired woman behind the counter eyed him quizzically, but Peter didn't take up the cue; he wasn't in any mood for gossip—though the woman obviously was, as the donut store was empty.

He stood by the counter—a semi-circular affair arranged around the baking ovens and glazing trays so that the customers could see the donuts being made—and watched as the frizzy-haired woman selected his donuts with a pair of out-sized tongs.

"Is that all, then?" she asked, her eyes boring into Peter.

Peter nodded noncommittally, keeping eye contact to a minimum, paid and carried the coffee and donuts—and the package—back to the table.

It had taken a half an hour of sorting through their 'fan mail' before Peter had located the package. He picked up the bulky package and hefted it in his hand. Good ole David, he thought, *this* felt formidable. The address on the return label read:

> *'Dr. David Gordon*
> *Department of Bio-Chemical Research*
> *U.C. Berkeley'*

He conjured a mental image of David; a thin, bespectacled Brit—the perennial scholar. Despite his youth, David was a rare phenomenon: a man who could have been famous and rich by virtue of his work, but who cared little for either riches or fame. David was a remarkable botanist and biochemist whose work for the rubber companies in South America had commanded a prestige and salary that could have set him up for life.

David had spent five years in a stinking, malaria-ridden hut on the Amazon, stricken down repeatedly with dysentery, giardia, even tubercular hepatitis, while searching for rare botanical species. David's specialization was that bizarre group of plants from which the psychotropic alkaloids were refined. By the by, he'd bred a couple of hybrid versions of the plant, *Hevea*. These new strains had improved the rubber economy so much that a major rubber company had financed him for five more years. David had chugged along happily with his studies of Indian poisons and medicinal plants. Simultaneously, much to the joy of his corporate benefactors, he'd collected a wide variety of *Hevea Brasiliensis*—the rubber plant.

Thus, by virtue of talent alone, David had attained a position only dreamed of by most research scientists: an attachment to a major university and almost unlimited funding from a major corporation.

Peter grinned at the thought: David couldn't have cared less. If he had ten cents and a paddle, David would *still* be down the Amazon, amoebic dysentery or not, pursuing new plants with the same zeal.

Peter unsealed the packet. A wad of computer readouts and lab analyses fell onto the table. He sifted through the documents until he found a hand-written letter from David. It read:

'Good Lord, Peter, you are the most elusive devil in the whole state, I swear it! I've been trying to get hold of you by phone for days. I send this little lot out of frustration. I had wanted to discuss this with you personally, but tomorrow I'm off down to Columbia for a date with the famous Hevea Brasiliensis once again. This time for United Consolidated (Rubber, that is). Incidentally, did you see my paper on Hevea Corymbosa in the New Scientist? Talk about pop-art science! But I digress...

Christ, Peter, where did you get it?! This stuff is amazing—and I mean that. The potential pharmaceutical uses are enormous. You must contact me as soon as I get back. I've included all the reports—I believe you're up to most of the jargon. But here's a (very) brief and unscientific synopsis written off the top of my head:

a)   The plant is unique, but it does share some of the neurotransmitter activation akin to the derivative from the Banistecopsis (see p.6). But it also contains an enzyme-blocking agent that renders the action quite destructive. It has an effect which is something like a cross between psilocybin and curare—in other words, it is a deadly poison.

b)   Its specific action is on the higher cerebral responses (see p.11), but, in large doses, it damages them. Also, a complex interaction takes place in the hindbrain which disrupts the autonomic nervous system in a bizarre way. The lab reports are shown on p.27. In small doses, it rendered our frog subjects drowsy, lethargic; larger doses killed them off—immediately. The amazing thing is that two of the frogs that died—and I mean dead, no heart beat, drastic drop in body temperature etc.—were pulled out of a

*freezer a week later and revived, though somewhat sluggish.
Closer analysis reveals no less than six highly-differentiated
active ingredients acting in a synergetic way, whose effects
we can measure but not duplicate. As it stands, the plant is
highly dangerous and should be treated as a lethal poison.
But get me some more and get back to me. You could be
rich!*

*The drug may be similar to that used by the Haitian medi-
cine men to assert some degree of domination over their
subjects. (There's a plant they use which I've tried to get
from them by hook or by crook for ten years—without luck.)
Anyway, this extract is the basis of the zombie myth in
Haiti.*

*Look, I've got to stop now—duty calls. I'll be back from
Columbia in two weeks. I suggest you read the photostated
(slightly sensationalised) report on Haitian Voodoo I've
included. However, the medical facts are, to the best of my
knowledge, valid and verified from reputable sources. Dr.
Nadem is an old friend of mine—he doesn't bullshit.*

xxx Love, David'

Peter's heart was pounding and the coffee stood untouched as he sifted
rapidly through the lab reports. He pulled out a copy of 'Haitian Voodoo' and
read it feverishly.

After he'd finished the article, Peter sat and stared through the coffee-
shop window, his mind whirling. Across the road was the local airstrip—just
a small runway with a few hangars and Quonset huts sprinkled around it. He
watched a light plane taxi along the wet tarmac. Suddenly, it lifted into the air
and pulled into the sky in a tight arc. As it soared higher, its wheels folded
under, transforming it in an instant from a creature of the land to a winged
creature of the sky.

Bizarre, he thought sitting in the bright sunshine contemplatively, zombies—the walking dead. But it really was no more miraculous or bizarre than
the flight of that huge, metal object slicing through the air. Seeing that huge
mass of steel and aluminum on the ground, who would believe that it could
fly? It seemed impossible. And yet, it was a daily event, almost mundane.

A primitive would gape, even kneel, awed by the God-like properties of
a race that could fly. Legends would blossom, stories be told, myths passed
on in the oral tradition. Embellishment, distortion and downright lies would
add to the total effect—and the mundane would be imbued with the myth of
miracle—a miracle that could be explained simply by the differential pressure
on an aerodynamic-shaped wing cross-section.

And in the zombie report, here it was again: a perfectly scientific explanation of the zombie myth; and an account of the age-old, tiresome distortion of fact.

He leafed through the lab reports again and saw how the old zombie legend could arise. This alkaloid affected the hindbrain: the metabolic rate was lowered; the heartbeat was reduced dramatically; the higher cerebral responses were rendered dysfunctional by a disruption of the neurotransmitters. This drug could effectively simulate death for the duration of a standard coroner's examination until the effects diminished.

The Haitian 'walking dead'—of which the reports were well-documented by bewildered relatives—were slightly brain-damaged. The damage to the higher cerebral responses made them particularly pliant and suggestible… In other words, a zombie.

Peter's mouth was dry. He ran a woolly tongue around his lips and took a swig of cold coffee.

Miranda had imbibed that drug but, fortunately, only a small dose. Her pregnancy had saved her when she took another dose; mercifully, though she had been 'non compos mentis', good old morning sickness had caused her to vomit—and inadvertently saved her.

From what? thought Peter, his face was grim. And God knows how the foetus had been affected. Brain damage? Mutation? Worse? He shuddered and once again cursed himself for his insensitivity. No wonder she'd been upset!

He scooped up the papers and stuffed them in their envelope. Slinging the mail sack over his shoulder, he went to the phone booth, slid it open, got in and closed it tight. The frizzy-haired counter assistant watched his every movement, bristling with curiosity. He turned away and dialed the Mission number, praying that Miranda would answer. He grew agitated as it ran on and on.

Then, suddenly, he heard Miranda's voice: "Hello…?"

"Thank God, honey!" he blurted out, "Are you alright?"

"Yes," she replied distantly.

"Are you sure?! I'm sorry I upset you so much. I realize now what it was. I'm such a fool! The baby! Will you ever forgive me?"

"I'll forgive you," came her voice. There was something odd in her tone.

"It's this horrible mess," said Peter biting his lip, "Honestly, honey, I wouldn't normally have been so…inconsiderate. But, look, I've got some real bad news…but it's got to be said…and maybe the phone's not the right way, but—"

"Say it," interrupted Miranda in the same odd voice.

"No. I'll come home. I want to be with you."

"Say it," said Miranda flatly.

Peter was silent; she sounded bad. "Miranda—"

"Say it, Peter," she intoned.

"Well…it's just that…I got the report back from David Gordon," said

Peter, desperately groping for some justification by using David's name, "The drug is dangerous—real dangerous…"

"Peter, say it," came the voice.

Peter gulped. "Well, I think we should be thinking in terms of… aborting the baby—for your sake *and* the baby's."

A sigh came down the phone. A long, drawnout sigh that Peter couldn't understand. There was a moment of silence, then Peter realized Miranda was crying. "Oh, Miranda, I'm sorry! I didn't want to tell you over the phone. God, please don't cry! I'm sorry you're so upset!"

"No, Peter," she said softly, "I'm glad you told me on the phone. It's O.K., it's O.K., don't worry. Come home." Then there was a click and the buzz of the dialling tone.

Peter pulled open the phone booth door and a rush of cool air hit him. He realized he was bathed in sweat. He walked out of the door without even looking at the counter assistant. She gathered up his untouched coffee and donuts and, tut-tutting to herself, crumpled them up in their paper napkins and threw them in the trash can.

CHAPTER THIRTY

Peter stood disconsolately by the swimming pool, watching the rain form intricate patterns on its surface. He stirred the water moodily with the long-handled cleansing net as though absently stirring a pot of soup. Peter was unhappy. Not only that; he was perplexed and bewildered. He'd always known his basic weakness—communicating his emotions—and now, added to this was the total impossibility of understanding the bizarre behavior of the opposite sex. Peter turned the facts over in his mind glumly and realized that he was getting nowhere with Miranda.

Last night, for the first time ever, Miranda had refused to sleep with him. She'd even refused to sleep in the same house and had bedded down in the camper shell of the old Ford parked behind the workshop. The Ford was ancient, but Peter, with his innate reluctance to get rid of anything mechanical, had kept it, despite its condition. Now he regretted his action for it seemed that, by default, the Ford was now Miranda's bedroom.

He'd tried to discuss the matter with her reasonably. He recounted a watered-down version of David's scientific report—a convincing argument for the necessity of an abortion. And she'd agreed.

Just like that. No 'yes' or 'buts' or tears. She'd agreed.

"O.K.," she said.

"O.K.?" he asked, "O.K. what?"

"O.K., I agree about the abortion." Then she kissed him warmly on the mouth, took her bedclothes and pillows and set up home in the Ford.

He followed her out like a lost puppy, standing hatless and coatless in the rain, but she just kissed him again and closed the camper door in his face without further explanation.

Peter's night in the bedroom had been the loneliest of his life. He tossed and turned and finally gave up all attempts to sleep. She was still sick, he was sure of it. The next day, Miranda appeared briefly from her camper shell boudoir, ate her breakfast in silence and refused to see a doctor. Then she returned to the camper and slept all day...

Peter pulled the long aluminum pole through the dirty water and stared at the workshop. The hood of the Ford protruded around the edge of the building, slick with rain. But he couldn't see Miranda, though he knew she was under the camper shell. Well, he thought morosely, perhaps it was to be expected—the whole affair had been such a strain on them both. And the prospect of an abortion was not something a woman would relish. Perhaps it was better she slept to get her strength up.

He squared his shoulders and swept the net across the rain-dappled surface of the pool, scooping up a morass of twigs and leaves. He decided he had to make an effort to cheer up. After all, if *he* was miserable, where did that leave them? Poor Miranda, she needed a breather and all he could think of was his own needs. He grimaced as he realized how self-centered he'd been. He dropped the pool net in exasperation, walked back to the house and phoned Miya and chatted for about ten minutes.

Miya seemed to respond to Peter's need to chatter aimlessly and was cheerfully gossipy without focussing on anything in particular. They arranged to meet late afternoon and parted amicably.

After the conversation, Peter felt much better. He returned to the edge of the swimming pool and stood watching the sheets of rain blow across the gloomy hills which were scarcely distinguishable from the gray sky.

Peter took a seat on the old, sodden oak bench overlooking the disused pool, feeling lighter, heartened at the prospect of seeing Miya. It was strange how much Miya had come to mean both to him and Miranda; even more curious when he thought how different their viewpoints were. He could understand Miranda's liking the man—she and Miya were very much the same. Miranda's preoccupation with myth and magic were subjects that Peter avoided like the plague.

And yet he, too, was drawn to Miya. He really thought of him as a friend. Yes, that was it: despite their differences, Miya was a true friend. Peter, in his thirty-five years on the planet, had made no more friends than could be counted on one hand. He had always been a loner. Perhaps then, mused Peter, a friend was someone who disagreed with your viewpoints, opposed your life style and was constantly at odds with your belief system and yet couldn't help but like you.

Peter grinned at his own definition. Well, as a piece of homespun philosophy it might be lacking, but it certainly summed up his relationship with Miya.

Peter resolved not to mope any more. He returned to the house, took a hot shower, dried himself off and donned a dry pair of long-johns, a thick pair of woollen socks, a heavy, waterproof anorak and thick woollen trousers. He thrust his feet into a pair of warm, fleece-lined rubber boots, whistling as he laced up the waterproof tongue, stood up and stamped his booted feet experimentally. His feet were warm as toast. This was the stuff! he thought, realizing that this simple procedure had changed his mood entirely.

He sauntered out into the rain ready to tackle anything, and proceeded to examine the disused pool and hot tub. His practiced eye ran over the filter system, the heater tanks, the inlet and outlet valves. Mmm, they were a mess, he thought with a certain satisfaction: the concrete path around the pool was filthy, littered with broken branches; the pool itself, muddy and murky, choked with dirt and leaves.

He made his decision: He would clear out the pool; put up some baffle boards to keep the leaves and dirt out; and clean out the hot tub and filter system. Now that was a meaty project! He paced the perimeter of the pool sizing up the problem.

The concrete path surrounding the pool was sheltered by a dense beech hedge. He gazed at the golden-brown beech leaves floating on the pool's surface. He nodded in satisfaction. The first thing to do was to build a fence inside the beech hedge to stop more leaves blowing into the pool. Then he would clear the pool and get the hot tub going. Peter felt better already and thought of how much Miranda would enjoy lying in the hot tub in the pouring rain.

Transformed into a man with a purpose, Peter clumped jauntily through the pouring rain to the workshop. Half an hour later, with the whirring chime of the Skilsaw still ringing in his ears, he was ready, and he trudged backwards and forwards from the workshop to the pool carrying stacks of timber on his shoulder.

Peter was happy. Happy to be working; happy to be doing something; and every now and then he would glance across at the rain-slicked hood of the Ford and think of Miranda—a Miranda wet and steaming, splashing around in the hot tub, shrieking with merriment as she dived into the freezing swimming pool, her naked flesh gleaming with health as she thrashed about in clear water.

Peter worked away steadily, realizing that this is what he'd been missing—*doing* something. He'd been sitting around helpless for so long, with bizarre incidents piling up on him one by one. And now, as he smacked nails into the six-foot fencing planks with dexterous blows of the framing hammer, he was happy. Once again, Peter was fixing it all up.

A sudden flurry of wind scooted the reddish-brown beech leaves across the pool's surface. Peter, hot from his exertions, pulled back his rain hood and allowed the wind to blow the cool rain across his face. He sighted a sixteen-penny nail, tapped it once to set it, then brought the waffle head of the hammer down with a hearty smack that drove the nail below the surface.

As the fence went up board by board, Peter felt like he was rebuilding his life again. Miranda would have the abortion; she would be healthy; the awful events of the past few weeks would fade; Miya was about to pay a visit—that would cheer Miranda up.

Shifting slightly on his feet to get a better swing, he drove in another nail with a satisfied grunt. He'd have the pool ready in a few days, he thought contentedly, well in time for Miranda to enjoy it while she was convalescing from her abortion.

Heartened by his task, Peter worked rapidly, and in less than two hours, the pool was sheltered by a handsome fence of new redwood boards. The double barrier of the beech hedge and the redwood fence was more than effective; the gusts of wind were completely stopped. The wind battered at the boards, but around the pool, all was still.

Peter surveyed his work: The fence should last a couple of winters until he put up something more permanent, he thought. Now for the pool—a major cleaning job! Glowing with his exertions, he strode over to the pool and grabbed hold of the aluminum handle of the pool net.

He frowned. The net end had dipped below the pool surface; the handle poked up at an acute angle, gleaming wetly. He gripped it firmly with both hands and pulled. Nothing happened; the net remained stuck firmly underwater.

Peter knelt, gripped the rounded concrete lip of the pool and bent over to see what was holding the net. The thick layer of leaves floating on the surface blocked his view completely so, cupping his palm, he scooped the leaves aside gently and put his face close to the patch of water he'd cleared. The rain dappled the surface, distorting the images beneath it. He frowned and leant his whole body out, shielding the surface from the driving rain. The pool surface steadied a little beneath the protective shield of his body, and he squinted into its depths.

He could see *something* weaving, clinging to the submerged net, but the eddies and whorls on the pool's surface made it too difficult to see any details. He grabbed the pole; took a firm grip with his right hand then, reaching forward with his left, he took a deep breath and pulled with all his might.

Mud billowed up to the surface; the pool slapped and slopped against the sides; and the pole gave slightly. Peter took a deep breath and, with a mighty heave, pulled again. Next minute, he was pitched forward into the pool.

The water hit him with an icy shock. As he went under, he glimpsed something wriggling on the bottom like a bed of thick, white maggots.

For a moment he hung on the surface face down, suspended by the air trapped in his thick pants and coat; numb with shock. There was a gurgling sound as air bubbled up; his boots filled with water; his body swung around in a lazy arc and, feet first, he went under. Realizing what was happening, Peter, coughing and spluttering, grabbed frantically at his boot laces. But still he went down.

He landed on something soft and yielding. He opened his eyes to see that he was up to his waist in a waving bed of maggoty, white vegetation that entangled his arms and legs. He jerked his legs frantically but he merely rose a few inches, to be sucked down again by the swirling, white mass.

Peter fought the temptation to open his mouth as his chest swelled and tightened. Desperate, he thrust his hand into the white mass and began tearing handfuls of vegetation from his ensnared feet. The torn vegetation floated past his face and he dimly realized what it was: Roots. He was trapped in a thick bed of sinewy roots.

Peter forced himself to relax. He let himself hang. Then, with all his strength, he struck out to the surface of the pool. He half rose from the tangled bed of roots; his hands cleaved the air above the pool, but his head never broke the surface as the roots pulled him back down.

This time he panicked. He struggled wildly, tearing up great handfuls of the roots until the water was a murky mass of dirt and broken roots. One leg came free, but the other remained trapped as his struggles began to weaken.

The deep 'thud, thud, thud' of his heart was too loud in his ears. His chest began to shudder and waves of redness ran across his closed eyes. His struggles became feebler as his chest swelled to the point where it felt as though it would burst.

He was suddenly grabbed under the armpits. With a rending of roots, Peter broke free and slid up to the surface. His head broke through and, with a choking cry, he sucked in great lungfuls of air, his eyes distended. He glimpsed Miya's face looming against the gray sky. Then he went down again and blacked out.

Peter came to retching on the concrete path, straddled by something large and heavy: Miya. Miya pressed his weight down on Peter's chest then eased off. He repeated the movement.

Peter racked and coughed, then began to breathe more easily. He sat up and spat out a mouthful of dirty water. "Oh, God!!" he sputtered, "I nearly had it then! You saved my life, Miya. Good job you came along when you did!"

Miya, dressed in an oil slick, Stetson hat and jeans, stared grimly at the pool. It was now a uniform, muddy gray speckled with the pelting rain. "Come," he said, "Come inside. You need to change your clothes." He turned and strode towards the Mission house without a backward glance at Peter.

Peter, still spitting brackish water, followed. He took a few steps, then nausea hit and he fell and retched at the side of the path for a good ten minutes. He stood up again and staggered weakly to the kitchen.

Miya stood at the stove preparing a hot drink. Peter stumbled past him into the bedroom and began to take off his wet clothes with some difficulty. As he eased off the sodden boots, he looked up through the window grille to see gnarled limbs of the Tree etched black by the rain. "Roots! Hell! Who'd believe they'd stretch that far?!" he muttered thickly. He threw his wet clothes in the corner, toweled himself down and put on some dry ones. Resisting the temptation to hop on the bed, he rejoined Miya in the kitchen.

Miya, strangely silent, was sitting at the table with a cup of hot tea in his hands. Then he spoke very flatly: "You're a lucky man, Peter."

"Yep…thanks to you," said Peter soberly, "Like I said, I was a goner… tangled in those roots. Did you ever see such a thing?! They must have been pushing their way up through the drainage ducts since summer! They were so thick!" Peter shuddered at the memory of the underwater struggle.

"What is it?! What happened?!" came a voice from the doorway.

And there was Miranda standing barefoot in the doorway, her face heavy with sleep, her clothes wet with her journey from the truck to the kitchen.

"Miranda!" Peter jumped up, "Are you O.K.?!"

Even though she had slept so long, Miranda's face was still lined with fatigue. She flicked a look at Miya who nodded imperceptibly. "Hello Miya. What happened then?" she asked sharply.

In a few curt syllables, Miya described Peter's near-miss in the pool. Miranda gave a cry and ran to Peter and hugged him. "My God, Peter! Thank goodness you're safe! It nearly got you, too!"

Grateful for the contact, Peter hugged her. Then, with his face buried in her hair, he said slowly. "What do you mean '*it*' nearly got me?"

"The Tree!! Thank God Miya came in time!"

"Wait a minute," said Peter soberly, "It's not that I'm ungrateful for what you did, Miya…" He turned to Miranda. "Look, Miranda, look…I fell in the pool—foolish that I was to be cleaning it out in these heavy clothes—and I got tangled in those goddamn roots. It was my own fault. I don't want you to get carried away with this now."

There was a heavy silence.

Miya and Miranda looked at each other; Miya impassive, Miranda weary. Sensing their bond, Peter flared with resentment. "Hey, wait a minute, you two! Don't go giving me any more of that crap now! And you, Miranda!" he said sharply, "It's really not very healthy to think like this you know!"

"Peter," said Miranda coldly, "You're lucky—and so am I. And the minute you realize that simple fact, then maybe we'll be able to stop this before something really terrible happens—maybe. And we can't do it without Miya's help."

Miranda's coldness, her support of Miya fed Peter's anger. His resentment grew white-hot. "Look you two, will you two stop this—*now*! I just don't like this kind of talk—it's not only crazy, it's downright unhealthy. And I mean what I say!"

"Unhealthy, Peter?!" hissed Miranda, her face taut, "Unhealthy?! You want to know about health?!" Miya raised a cautionary hand, but Miranda ignored it. Her voice was like a cold blade. "Peter, you go out to the theater, hey! Just go to the theater now!"

"Miranda," said Miya palliatively, putting his hand on her shoulder.

"It's O.K., Miya," said Miranda stonily, "I'm O.K., but Peter isn't. It's time Mr. Riley faced up to some facts!"

"What is this?!"growled Peter hoarsely, bewildered by the sudden turn of events.

"Go, Peter! You go to the theater. You'll see a spot in the middle of the floor. Go take a look!" said Miranda.

The bitterness in her tone subdued Peter. He stood up uncertainly, looking from Miya to Miranda. "O.K.," he said slowly, "O.K…I don't know what you mean by this, but I'll go take a look…if it helps, I'll do that…" He backed out of the kitchen and plunged into the rain.

Miya took Miranda's hand. She wasn't even crying; it would have been better if she had. She just stared ahead, white-faced. Miya made as if to speak; thought better of it and just put his arm around her gently. Closing her eyes, Miranda sagged against his shoulder, her eyelids trembling.

A few minutes later, Peter appeared at the doorway. He stood there with the rain drumming on his head and held something up to the light. "What does it mean?" he asked, puzzled, "I don't understand."

Miranda turned and gave a cry: In his hands, Peter held the beech-bark skirt; it was only half burnt.

"What is this meant to prove?" said Peter, "Could someone let me in on the big secret?"

Miya looked at Miranda's ashen face. "Is that all…you found?" he asked Peter slowly.

"Yep, just a hole in the ground with some burnt twigs and this, er, skirt thing. Oh yeah, there was a mound of fresh dirt by the hole like a gopher or something had dug it out…"

"Miya!!" said Miranda under her breath, "It wasn't dead!!"

"What? What's that?!" asked Peter puzzled.

But Miranda just stared off into the night, her eyes wild, muttering: "It wasn't dead! Oh God, no! No…not that!!!!"

CHAPTER THIRTY-ONE

Peter knocked at the screen door with redoubled force, feeling like Orphan Annie. He turned up his coat collar as the rain finally found its way down his neck and began to trickle uncomfortably through his shirt. "C'mon!" he muttered, "Answer!"

The small yard looked as miserable as he felt. Even in the dim light it was sordid: an aged refrigerator stood canted over on a mound of gravel; a rusting motor bike peeked out from under a crown of thick-leafed ivy winding around the handle bars; beer cans littered the wet ground.

Clutching the bottle of Southern Comfort tightly in his other hand, Peter knocked again. Southern Comfort was one of the few drinks that Peter actually enjoyed—in moderation. Moderation was not, however, the keynote of the evening. There is a time in every man's life when he's had enough—and Peter had decided he'd had enough.

Miranda had locked herself in the Ford truck after an uncharacteristic bout of hysteria. After a brief attempt to 'talk some sense into Peter', Miya had lapsed into a very inscrutable Indian non-communication.

Peter was sick of it; sick of the past and sick of the present. Miranda and Miya seemed hell-bent on frightening the wits out of each other, he thought broodingly, and he, Peter Riley, for once was fed up with their airy-fairy beliefs and dark references to God-knows what.

Peter tried to quell his annoyance. After all, Miya had pulled him out of the pool in a very timely manner. But Miya's complicity with Miranda seemed to add fuel to her fears, to exacerbate her tendency to resort to mystical interpretations of perfectly natural phenomena. She could do without it, reasoned Peter. It was making her hysterical at a time when she most needed to forget the horrible events of the past few weeks.

And so things had come to a head and an angry Peter had left 'to get a little air', deciding that he needed to kick over the traces. Thus, Peter had resolved to seek out the time-honored solution to man's insoluble problems— 'to get drunk with the boys'.

There were two major drawbacks to this idea: one, Peter didn't really drink; two, he didn't know any 'boys'. And it was because of this that he now found himself clutching a bottle of Southern Comfort, half-drunk, at the back door of the one 'boy' he knew: Sheriff Dooley.

Since the incident in the cellar, Peter had felt a curious affinity with Dooley. Perhaps it was the matter-of-fact manner with which Dooley had dealt with the murders. Peter needed that. Peter also realized—not without some personal discomfort—that he and the Sheriff did have something in common: a distinct lack of friends.

Peter knocked again, though not so impatiently—his Dutch courage was already beginning to fail him—when the light flooded on and Dooley's voice cut across the porch. "Who 'n hell is that, huh?!! Speak up!! Who is it??!!"

"It'sh…Peter Riley," said Peter, trying hard not to slur his speech, "Peter Riley!!"

There was a rattling of bolts and locks then the door creaked open. Dooley stood there, dressed in the same clothes he always wore, chewing. Peter wondered vaguely if he ever undressed. "What kin ah do for you, Mr. Riley?" said Dooley eyeing the bottle.

Peter's nerve failed him and he was suddenly overwhelmed with embarrassment. Probably he would have made a fool of himself by turning and fleeing, had not Dooley grinned and said: "Ah see… You got a belly-drinkin' problem."

"Eh?" said Peter nonplussed.

"A belly-drinkin' problem," repeated Dooley, "Worst kind. A problem that makes you so sick to your belly yer got to fill it full o' liquor to kill the fire."

"Well," said Peter encouraged, "I thought that…well, as I was in the area and…I don't know many people…maybe you might wanna drink…" He floundered and tailed off, hopping from one foot to the other nervously.

"So this is what you might consider a social call?" asked Dooley with an odd expression.

"Yep, it sure is," said Peter in a rush of words.

A look of delight crossed Dooley's face. "Well, step right in, sir, step right in. Sounds like a mighty fine idea to me."

Half an hour later, Dooley was a little more lubricated and Peter was on the way to being long-gone. During the course of the long, rambling conversation, Peter found out that he was the Sheriff's first and only social call in ten years.

Dooley, glad of an audience, grew more loquacious; Peter was delighted to find genuine interest in the Sheriff's pithy anecdotes. The stories rolled out, smoothed by the Southern Comfort: bears, muskrats; hunting deer in Colorado; the steelhead trout that Dooley had once shot with a thirty-ought-six from a moving pickup. "Got the goddamn thing when he leapt the shallows," he said slapping his thigh, "Luckiest shot of my life! Ah jumped in the water in a flash, a'gettin' mah best boots wet! Pulled him in with an ole net. Couldn't believe my eyes—ah'd just barely nicked his backbone! Now, if'n I'd hit him straight on, he'd still be kickin'; the bullet would'a gone right through. But he was rigid, man; plumb paralytic, quivering like a jelly and dead as a doornail!" He smacked his lips. "Ah measured him—'cos I always know afterwards fellers don't believe you. I pulled out this little Sears sixteen-foot tape I always used to carry here…" he slapped his hip, "…and that sucker was three foot one inch long! Man, it tasted good, just like chicken!"

The phone rang and Dooley carried on for a moment, ignoring it. It continued to ring. Finally, he picked it up in exasperation. He listened for a moment, perplexed, then he said: "O.K., Ben, slow down, slow down, dammit! Now, run that by me again real slow… C'mon man, no shit?! In this weather? I don't believe it! What are you doing there anyway…? O.K., O.K., I'm comin'…"

He slammed the phone down and filled his glass again, proffering the bottle towards Peter. Peter declined; he still hadn't finished the last glass and he was pretty far-gone. "Would you believe this goddamn County?!" said Dooley tossing his drink back, "People are so poor they'll even rob the dead!"

"What do you mean?" asked Peter puzzled.

"That was ole Ben Cook, the grave-digger. He's a loony old bugger, ah suppose you've got to be to do that job. I guess it's the only job he can get on accounta nobody else wants to do it…"

"What did you say about robbing the dead?" asked Peter thickly.

"Well, seems like he was hanging about up there near Crawley's field— that's where we bury the poor and those folks who got no one to pay their funeral expenses—and he sees someone moving about in the dark." He chuckled. "Don't surprise me none, 'cos I know that ole Ben goes up there to have a 'little hit by the moonlit crick', we calls it…" He laughed at Peter's puzzled face and translated, "That's to smoke some weed and poach a little. Don't harm no one. But the ole boy ain't quite right here…" He tapped his head and took another swig of liquor, this time straight from the bottle. "Yeah, see, he's very possessive about Crawley's field—like he owns it or sumpin', which he don't, of course. But most folks humor him. Who wants to own a pauper's graveyard anyhow? He's always sitting up there with a shotgun to scare courtin' couples off. And, by God, he does!" hooted Dooley derisively, "Though who he expects to be out in this weather beats me."

"But what was this about robbin' the dead?" asked Peter urgently.

"Well, he reckons that someone's been fiddlin' around with ole Joe Bear's grave—Cal O'Donnell's, too. Wants me to take a look. Now, sir, I ain't goin' out in this weather ter poke around no graveyard, no siree!"

The phone rang again. Dooley picked it up wearily. "Oh…yeah…O.K., Ben, calm down man. You bin drinkin' too, huh…? O.K., O.K., I'll come… Hold there…relax." He slammed the phone down with a sigh. "No rest for the wicked," he said, "The old coot is scared out of his wits. Wants me to come right away." He stood up and stretched. "Duty calls. When you gotta go, you gotta go." He showed his teeth in a wry smile. "Well, I'll be seein' you, unless you want to come pokin' around a graveyard in the middle of the night?"

The liquor burnt harshly in Peter's stomach and his mouth was sour. He suddenly regretted the dullness of his liquor-laden brain. "Well," he said slowly, "I'd like to come with you."

"Well that's mighty civilized of you," said Dooley, "You're welcome. Who knows what we'll find out there...?"

CHAPTER THIRTY-TWO

Miranda sat in the Mission kitchen staring at the open door. The yellow swathe of light from the room only penetrated a foot or so into the gloom outside. The rain seemed to leap into the doorway; flailing drops ghosted from the gloom and ran down the worn stone step in a miniature torrent. Miranda stared at the rain drops, mesmerized by their appearance and disappearance, as if each one were a tiny, cosmic event.

Finally, she broke the silence and said huskily: "Will you help us, Miya? Will you? Please?"

Miya, sitting as still as a statue, smiled. "You know that's what I'm here for. But I can't help you without Peter. He needs to…join with you. Two heads are better than one; and two hearts are more than a match for most eventualities."

Miranda sighed. "It's difficult. We're so different. That's why I love him, I guess. But at times like this I feel so exasperated! What more can we do?! He just won't accept the truth—and only that can save us!"

"Only wait," said Miya, "He will change. I only hope he doesn't do it too late…"

¤

The patrol car shifted to second gear, protesting, and chugged over the hill. The headlights stabbed up into the air, beading a thousand raindrops with crystal light. The car crested the rise and descended and the beam shot straight forward along the muddy road. Dooley muttered and pressed the gas pedal. The car roared and shot forward.

Peter cried out: "Sheriff!!"

A figure staggered across the muddy road directly into the path of the car. Dooley swore, slewed the wheel around and the car slid sideways with a high-pitched squeal, then bumped onto the grass verge and stalled. Peter was jolted forward in his seat belt. But the Sheriff, though cushioned somewhat by his large belly pressing against the steering wheel, was jerked forward and smacked his head on the windshield.

"Shit!!" cried Dooley, putting his hand to his head, "Shee-it!! Mother-fucker!!"

"You alright?" asked Peter.

"Just about!" snarled Dooley dabbing a cut on his forehead, "I kinnot get into the habit of fastenin' mah seat belt—and lookit what I do!" He jerked the door open, pulling his gun. "Who'd a thought there'd be some loon on this road at this time 'o night?!" He eased out of the seat and stomped around the car, sweeping the gloom with his flashlight angrily.

Reluctantly Peter got out of the car and joined the Sheriff.

"He's gone," muttered Dooley, "I musta missed him. Shit!"

"What are you so mad about?" asked Peter.

"Ah'm mad 'cos I missed him!" snarled Dooley, "Leastways, if'n we'd hit him, we'd know who the idiot was!"

Peter grinned as the wet, ill-tempered Dooley climbed into the car with a surly expression. "Now, I'm sure you don't mean that, Sheriff," said Peter whimsically.

"You'd be surprised," said Dooley dryly, "There's a lot of folks in this town I wouldn' mind hitting at sixty miles per hour!"

Fifteen minutes later, the car eased between the weather-worn cemetery gate posts. The headlights angled through the darkness for thirty yards, then failed to penetrate further.

"This is it," muttered Dooley, "I hope that fool Ben Cook makes it worth our while." He pulled a slicker from under the seat, gave it to Peter and eased his own slicker over his head. "Regulation issue." His muffled voice came from the crackling folds. "Keeps you from gettin' wet, but not from gettin' shot."

Peter gazed bleakly into the gloom and Dooley's remarks did not seem at all funny. He donned the slicker and got out of the car. The headlights illuminated a row of crude wooden crosses—a uniform gray in the car lights. Peter shivered. It was a drab scene. The graves were untidy mounds of dirt, quite unlike the neat, well-tended rectangles of an orderly graveyard. Peter commented on this.

"Ole Ben," muttered Dooley, "Kinda feeble in his dotage. He don't make much of a grave-digger. He just' does the minimum, see? No six feet under the old cold ground and all that crap for him. You're lucky if you get three outta him, I tell you—eighteen inches on a bad day. One night 'o rain and a high wind and half these suckers would be rollin' all over the field—bones, coffins, the lot!" Dooley chuckled sardonically, "Talk about the walkin' dead! These suckers'd be flyin'!! Uh uh, what's that?" He dropped his voice and cut the flashlight. "Something's movin' over on the edge of the field," whispered Dooley. "Peter, cut the car lights…easy like."

Peter reached through the window and flicked the column switch; the gloom sprang up all around them. Dooley listened carefully for a moment then motioned to the other side of the field. Peter could hear a faint noise; he nodded. Dooley drew his gun from the slicker, then, to Peter's surprise, he grinned, raised the gun in the air and fired once. A scream erupted from the other side of the field. Dooley shouted: "Git over here, Cook!! C'mon, stop assin' about!! Now!! Afore I fill your ass with lead!!"

A moment later, a dishevelled bundle of rags, dripping and sodden, skittered up to the Sheriff. "Jesus, Cook, what you doing out like this?! Why aren't you in your hut, man?" hissed Dooley. He thumbed his flashlight, illuminating the most leathery, toothless face Peter had ever seen.

"Sheriff, you gotta gimme a ride!!" blurted Ben, "I gotta get outta here!!! The corpses—they up and walked, Sheriff!! Believe me!! They got outta their goddamn coffins and walked!!!"

"Did you see them?" asked Peter.

"No I didn't! But they're gone! And how else would they go?! There's no one comes up here but me!!"

"You wanna lay off the booze and pot, Ben," growled Dooley, "You're gettin' paranoid!"

"I swear it, Sheriff!! You know I bin tending the pauper's plot for fifteen years now—it never happened before!!"

"There's always a first time for everything!" snapped Dooley. "Now, stop blatherin' and show me these graves."

Ben shook his head and pointed off into the darkness. "I ain' a'goin' back, not me! You go! There…just over there, by the fence line." Then he bobbed out of the light and scuttled off into the gloom mumbling to himself.

Dooley patted Peter's arm in the gloom. "See what kinda crap the ole Sheriff has to deal with?" he snarled. "C'mon, we're getting wet. Let's use the car. You sit in the back."

Peter nodded and got into the car behind Dooley. The Sheriff slewed the car backwards in a skilful manoeuver, then drove it forward between the gate posts at an angle, simultaneously flicking on the high-beams.

Blinded, Ben Cook was caught in the beam, jerking like a wet scarecrow. He shielded his eyes, moaning fearfully. The car shot up alongside him and Dooley jerked open the door and hauled Ben inside like a bundle of wet rags "C'mon, let's go. Ben, stop this crap a'fore I bop you one, uh? Ah mean it!" said Dooley savagely.

Ben stopped whimpering instantly. The Sheriff turned the car around and headed off to the far side of the cemetery, the car bumping and swaying across the sodden earth.

Dooley, Peter and Ben waded through the wet grass towards the far side of the plot, their shadows long in the light from the stationary car.

"This is it! This is it!" whined Ben as they reached two grave markers canted over at an odd angle.

Dooley clicked on the flashlight, played it over the grave—and swore. The soil had been swept back from each of the graves and the cheap pine coffin lids smashed open, the wood splintered fresh and white.

Dooley knelt down and hefted a rock at the side of the grave. "Look…" he said, pointing at the lines raked in the soil, "…whoever did it dug it out by hand, and they smashed open the lid with a rock. Must be some crazy," he said thoughtfully.

"I should think so," muttered Peter, "Coming up here in this weather just to dig up a coffin! Only a nut would be out in this—us included, I guess."

"No," said Dooley picking up a piece of splintered wood.

"No??" Peter looked at Dooley askance.

The Sheriff was shaking his head. "I mean, whoever it was didn't come up here to dig up no coffin," he said slowly.

"How do you figure that?" asked Peter, gazing at the splintered coffins. Peter wasn't drunk anymore, nor was he sober, but an unpleasant in-between; his head was muzzy and his throat sour and brackish.

Dooley flashed the light momentarily into Peter's face. "You look like you just climbed outta the grave yourself, boy!"

Peter nodded and winced; the movement made his temples pound. "Yeah. But what do you mean…'whoever came up here didn't come to dig up the coffins'?"

"Think about it. If you *came* to do this, you'd bring a shovel and a breaker bar, wouldn't you? Not scrabble about in the dirt with your hands." Peter nodded. The Sheriff was no idiot. "Whoever did it," continued Dooley, "Did it kinda spontaneous like. Sure you didn't dig 'em up yourself, Ben Cook?" Dooley suddenly flashed the light into Ben's terror-stricken rheumy eyes.

"No! No, I wouldn't do that!" spluttered Ben, "Not me—no!!"

"Huh, I wouldn't put it past you. Diggin' 'em up for barbecue, you ole ghoul!" snorted Dooley. "C'mon, let's get outta here." He turned and began stomping back towards the car, followed by Peter.

"Gimme a ride!! Gimme a ride!! Don't leave me here!!" yelped Ben running after Dooley.

Dooley stared stonily at the bundle of rags that hopped up and down in front of him. "Christ! Changed your tune now, haven't you?!" Dooley wrinkled his nose, "Do I have to ride with you again? You stink, Ben Cook! I bet you ain't had a bath in a year!"

"I'll roll the window down!" cried Ben unabashed, "I'll sit in the back!! Don't leave me here!!"

Dooley spat and nodded wearily. "O.K., O.K." They all got in the car; Ben in the back. "Don't wind the window down, Ben!" called Dooley, "It's too cold. I'll just leave the heater off." He glanced at Peter and grinned at what he saw. "Sweet as roses, heh?" Peter had his hands cupped over his nose and mouth, gagging at the stench that permeated the car. "Once ah found an ole rat caught under the springs o' mah armchair. Bin dead for two weeks," chuckled Dooley enjoying himself. He glanced in the mirror and raised his voice. "Smelled just like you, Ben!"

"Har, har…mmm," mumbled Ben.

Whether it was agreement or not was not Peter's concern—his attention was elsewhere. He coughed and gagged, tears in his eyes. "Oh my God!" he hissed.

Dooley chortled. "Folks reckon that you get to be like the things you work with—like farmers look like their cows and all that. Well, ole Ben is that way. He smells like those corpses he buries, like he's been dead three weeks himself!"

Throughout the journey, Dooley continued his banter. But Peter, who could barely breathe, didn't find it funny.

They dropped Ben off on the edge of the town and Peter took his nose from under his collar and slid open the window, taking great breaths of air. "Christ, Dooley, how do you stand it?!"

"Ah don't," grinned Dooley. He spat a stream of tobacco out of the front window. "It's the 'baccy. Reckon the ole nicotine must deaden mah nose 'cos it just don't bother me." He continued driving for a moment, then he glanced at Peter. "What're *you* agitatin' about?" he asked, "I can almost see your brain wheels a'smokin'."

"I was thinking," said Peter thickly, "These two men—Cal and Joe Bear—they were both involved in the murders, you know. It's strange, isn't it?"

"'*Involved*' is a peculiar word," said Dooley quickly. "But I guess it don't mean much," he shrugged. "You see, they was the most recent buried, that's all. And the way Ben buries them don't take but a few scoops to pull them suckers out. So, whoever the loon was who pulled 'em out …well, he could see they was fresh dug." He shook his head. "There's some weird folks around these parts, I tell you; cults and voodoo and all kinds a shit—makes your hair stand on end. Probably somebody using them bodies for some black magic rite or sumpin'."

"What I was saying…" said Peter slowly, "…was—why didn't they dig up all three graves?"

"Three?" said Dooley puzzled, reaching forward and increasing the speed of the wipers as the rain flurried across the windshield.

"Yeah…the other guy, Ansell—Ferris Ansell."

"Oh, yeah, I see. Well, ole Ferris went out in style," he chuckled. "You see, Crawley's field was bequeathed by a God-fearing soul—old man Crawley. He wanted to see that the paupers of the town got a regular Christian burial. But folks who can afford it get buried in the graveyard down by the church." He pointed down the high street, "That way!"

"So, who paid for Ferris Ansell?" asked Peter, "I thought he had no living relatives."

"He didn't. But there was a family vault; paid for by his two sisters—both beat ole Ferris to dyin' by a few years, so Ferris got to go in the family tomb, and that's that." He cast a shrewd glance at Peter. "You doin' some Sherlock Holmes thinkin', boy, I can see. What you gettin' at?"

"Maybe," said Peter, "Whoever did it—the bodies, I mean—also took Ansell's."

"It's a good theory," said Dooley, "But…" he suddenly turned the car to the left and slid into his yard alongside Peter's Jeep, "…I learnt in this job a long time ago, that when it's time to quit—quit." He cut the engine. "If ole Ferris has been took, too, there's nothing I can do about it right now. If he ain't been took, no sweat." He suddenly stuck his hand out. "Nice of you to come, boy, I appreciate it."

Peter shook his hand. "Yeah, it was good. At least at first. Can't say I like the last part so much."

"You're darned right," chuckled Dooley, "Messin' around in graveyards this time a night! Look, are you O.K. to drive or you wanna crash on my couch? Wouldn't wanna pull you in for drunk drivin' now. You sobered up or what?"

"Oh," said Peter abashed, "Sure, I'll make my way back. I'm O.K. Thanks—thanks a lot."

They both got out of the car and as Peter slid into the Jeep, Dooley stomped onto his porch, turned and, rocking on the heels of his boots, yelled: "Careful now! Be sure you don't run over any zombies!"

Peter waved back but he didn't smile.

¤

On the main street, all the traffic lights were red, blinking on and off for the night traffic. Save for Peter's Jeep, the road was deserted.

Peter cruised down the deserted street, his mind besieged with strange thoughts. As he cruised past a clothes' store window, his eye caught the stiff, waxy posture of a mannequin and it made him shiver involuntarily. Its open staring eyes seemed to follow him along the road. The alcohol had all but worn off, leaving him in a febrile state; the thoughts swirled and spun through his brain unbidden. He tried to stop them but a single phrase from David Gordon's report kept repeating itself over and over again:

> *'The semblance of death was so precise as to warrant a death certificate from a qualified medical practitioner. And yet, some of these so-called dead men were seen walking just two weeks after their burial…'*

Peter couldn't stand it any longer. He made his decision. He screeched the Jeep around in a tight U-turn and headed back towards the main grave-yard…

¤

"What do you mean, you only hope he doesn't do it too late?" asked Miranda.

Miya stood up and placed his hands on her shoulders. "I'm sorry. Sometimes I'm too direct, but it's simply that we—or you, at least—must get Peter to help us now, even if he is skeptical. We need him on our side. At the moment he's running around the town doing God-knows what, chafing with anger at us two. It's not a good situation. We should all be…" he put one hand in the other, "…united, working together, not fighting each other."

"So there *is* something we can do," said Miranda.

"Yes," said Miya, "But it's dangerous." Miranda looked grave. Miya smiled. "Well, no more dangerous than it has been so far—but still it's dangerous. And we need Peter to be here," he said softly, "I need the *two* of you here. Don't you see? It was the two of you that started it. I need the two of you to finish it."

"The two of us?" Miranda stared at him blankly. "I was the one who… seemed to trigger it off. Peter was just an innocent bystander."

Miya shook his head. "No, Miranda, it cuts deeper than that. Don't you see? It takes two to tango, I think the expression goes."

Miranda's face was drawn. "Poor Peter, at least I'm on my guard." Miya nodded. "Can you tell me?" she asked urgently, "Tell me what it is?"

"No," said Miya, "Not tell—I'll show you; it is almost time. When Peter returns he will be…more amenable then."

"How do you know that?" asked Miranda in open admiration.

"Oh, nothing psychic about that," retorted Miya, spreading his hands in a comic gesture, "But when a man storms off from his wife into the night, nine times out of ten when he comes back, the fire has gone out of his belly."

"I hope so," said Miranda, "It's getting real late. I do hope he's O.K." She dropped her eyes. "He's never done this kind of thing before."

Miya nodded. "Yeah, I guess he's not the type. But then, these are strange times."

CHAPTER THIRTY-THREE

Peter stopped the Jeep well before he reached the cemetery gates, and cut the headlights.

He felt lousy. He rubbed his eyes savagely and pummeled his cheeks, aware of his deep fatigue. What the hell was he doing, anyway? This was insane! He glanced up at the gates of the cemetery. The posts were surmounted by twin globes of light illuminating the entrance. In the light, the gates looked like giant spider webs covered in dew. God, it was like a scene from some Gothic horror movie, he thought, squirming at his own stupidity: Peter Riley poking around a cemetery in the middle of the night! To do what…? He promptly answered his own question: To prove a scientific theory, that's what.

As he thought it through, his resolve strengthened. *He* wasn't going to test some crazy theory about the living dead, zombies that walked in the night. Nope. He thought over the details of David's report. Nope, it wasn't insane—unusual, yes; bizarre, yes; but not insane. On the basis of a valid scientific report from an eminent scientist, it was quite reasonable to assume that these men had never been dead at all.

That did it. Peter grabbed the rifle from behind the seat and tucked the .45 into his waist band resolutely. No living dead here, he thought; no 'B' horror movie scare where the dead stalk towards a hero who fills them full of bullets and on they come, staring eyes, great gaping holes in their chests, clutching hands.

No, he thought, these guys *were not dead*. Shoot 'em and down they go. Peter suddenly recoiled from his own bloody frame of mind. That's what comes of hanging around Dooley, he thought. Still, it had its compensations; he did feel a lot better.

"O.K.," he said firmly to no one in particular, "This is it," and swung out of the Jeep decisively.

Wearing the slicker Dooley had lent him, Peter was able to walk up to the lighted graveyard gates with the rifle concealed. He reached the gate without mishap, then saw something that made his pulse quicken: Within the frame of the main gate was set a smaller gate—and it was wide open. Perhaps it was never closed, he mused. After all, this was a small town. But, this was no excuse to turn back now. He gripped the gun more firmly, stepped through the small opening and surveyed the graveyard.

A wet-slicked tarmac road curved out of sight into a veritable city of white crosses, stones, statues and obelisks that glowed faintly in the light. Instinctively, Peter struck off to the left, his feet slapping dully on the wet tarmac. The gates fell away behind him; it gradually grew darker. After only five minutes walking, the lights behind had almost faded completely and he had to resort to squinting. He grimaced, realizing that in his burst of bravado he'd failed to bring a flashlight. He stood for a moment, deliberating whether or not to turn back. But he couldn't remember if there *was* a flashlight in the Jeep, so, cursing his own muzzy head, he decided to go ahead.

He stopped at one of the graves and, peering closely, managed to decipher the name: 'Abbey'. Then the next one: 'Stephenson'.

"Shit!" he muttered—he'd thought at least they'd be alphabetical. He kicked himself mentally; of course they couldn't be! Or could they? He stood, uncertain, trying to remember how it ran from his infrequent visits to other graveyards. Then he realized he was standing in front of a direction board. He struck the palm of his hand on his forehead. "Get a hold, Riley!" he muttered. He bent over the board and read the inscription, which said simply: 'Family Vaults', with an arrow pointing to the right.

Jackpot!! He strode off to the right and rounded the curve to see the ornate colonnades of numerous vaults looming ahead, each as different from the other as custom-built houses.

Stopping at the first, he traced the name with his fingers: 'Roberts'. Then the next: 'Almass'; then 'Williams'. He flitted about trying to ascertain if there was any order in the vaults, decided there wasn't and began to move slowly along the dark wet facades, tracing out the names one by one.

Ten minutes later he found it: 'Ansell, Margaret and Dolores' And, newly etched in the stone, fresh and sharp beside the other names:

> *Ansell, Ferris*
> *May God have mercy on our souls*
> *As we lived together, so we sleep together*

Peter shivered. The stone was cold and damp under his fingers.

He stood facing the vault, which was no more than a large box—albeit a very ornate box with fancy cornices, molded figurines and cherubims. The vault was not much bigger than a garden shed. Three solid stone steps cut into the earth led down to the double doors of the vault; a black rectangle in the gloom below.

Peter put the stock of the rifle under his armpit and eased it up, with his right hand on the trigger. Without descending the steps, he leant forward and pushed left-handed at the door. His hand met thin air. Then he realized why: The twin doors opened inwards and one was already open. He drew his hand back sharply, suddenly feeling very exposed.

He glanced around, straining his eyes, peering nervously into the patches of gloom between the white gravestones. But all he could make out were the indistinct shapes of wet statues. His heart pounded as the shapes took on an air of menace. "Damn it!!" he muttered, trying to take hold of himself. He clutched the rifle more firmly, gritted his teeth and pushed at the other door. It swung back with a rusty squeal.

Now both of the doors were open, but all Peter could see was a jet-black rectangle. He put one foot on the first step and poked the rifle forward into the gloom, half expecting it to be wrenched from his grasp.

Nothing happened. Gingerly, he eased down onto the next step, paused, then ducking his head, he was inside.

The place smelled of mildew and a faint odour he couldn't quite place. He eased forward and was swallowed up by the gloom as his feet clattered on a stone-paved floor. He stood there, rigid in the dark, his heart beating so fiercely that he was afraid it was audible. His fingers hovered stiffly over the rifle trigger, ready for the slightest movement ahead.

His eyes grew accustomed to the gloom and he began to make out the rough shape of the room. To the left and right were the dim shapes of…coffins? He stepped forward and his knees struck an obstacle in the dark. He backed against the wall, chest heaving, but nothing happened. Then, in the faint light from outside, he saw he'd bumped into a raised stone slab. On the slab rested a coffin.

Then he saw a shape in the gloom; a dark patch in the corner the height of a man. He cried out in alarm, jumped forward and jabbed it with the rifle barrel. It fell over with a bang that made him leap back, his heart hammering even faster. It was only the coffin lid that had been propped in the corner.

Peter stood breathing heavily, waiting for his pulse to slow. He listened carefully, but the only sound was the hiss of rain and the drip of water. He inched forward and, lowering his face, tried to peer inside the coffin. He couldn't see a thing; it was inky-black in there. Slowly he reached forward with a trembling hand and felt inside the coffin: Something writhed, warm and soft, under his touch.

He screamed and fired the rifle involuntarily. It roared deafeningly. The muzzle flash revealed a frightened pack-rat leaping out of the empty coffin. Then all was dark.

Overcome with claustrophobia, Peter backed away from the coffin and stumbled up the steps, his chest heaving. The cool rain was an instant relief after the musty vault, and he leant on the door post of the vault allowing the hysterical laughter to well up. Frightened to death by an old pack-rat!! He giggled in nervous relief, resting his forehead against the cool wall of the vault.

He stopped giggling when something suddenly grabbed him from behind.

CHAPTER THIRTY-FOUR

Miranda peered out into the darkness. She was getting worried; the rain had not abated and there was no sign of Peter. "Maybe I should ring the Sheriff," she said to Miya.

"Mmm, he wouldn't thank you for that," said Miya, "What are you going to tell the Sheriff when you pull him out of bed at this hour? You had an argument with your husband, he lit out for town and you haven't seen him since?"

"But there's nowhere open at this time of night!"

"There's a couple of twenty-four hour truck stops up the freeway," said Miya, "He could be there. More likely he's sitting in his Jeep staring at the rain or he may even be asleep. But…" he said, "…if it makes you feel better, I'll ring around."

Miranda smiled thinly. "Perhaps it would be better if you did. He's never gone away like this before. It really upsets me."

Miya nodded. He went to the phone and began to phone around the all-night cafes. Miranda sat back in the chair and watched the rain sputtering into the light from the kitchen door. She sat for a long time, lost in her own thoughts.

Miya's voice gradually faded into the background as the rain seemed to grow louder and the buffets of the wind resounded like distant drums, low and even. The noises began to lull her: the hiss; the dull boom; and the regular pulse of the wind. Miranda gradually slipped into a half-doze…

Something brushed across her mind like the touch of moth's wing. She was awake instantly, straining her eyes to see into the darkness. Was there something out there?

The rain beat down in a relentless wash of sound but beneath it all Miranda thought she could hear something else. She held her breath and listened. Was it music? The lilting rise and fall of men's voices just below the hiss of the water? Or was she imagining it? It was so faint, she couldn't be sure. She sat stock still, listening, wondering if her imagination was playing tricks with her.

Miya's voice brought her back to the kitchen. "Nope," said Miya returning to his chair, "Not a sight nor sound of him." He caught sight of Miranda's face. "What's the matter? You O.K., Miranda?"

"Miya," said Miranda in a shaky voice, "I think there's someone out there."

"Did you see something?" asked Miya frowning, "It's very dark out there."

"I'm not sure… It's like I *heard* something… But, look, it's more a feeling," said Miranda agitated, "And it doesn't feel good."

Miya nodded. He stood up and went into the bedroom and returned with a flashlight.

"You're not going out there, are you?" asked Miranda anxiously.

"Just a quick look around the building. Don't worry." Miya smiled reassuringly as if he were merely going to check a fuse. Then, without hesitation, he plunged out of sight into the dark curtain of rain and disappeared from sight.

Miranda sat biting her lip, watching the doorway. Then, just as suddenly, Miya reappeared, making her jump. "Oh! Miya, you startled me!"

Miya was wet through. He stood dripping water on the kitchen floor. "Miranda, have you been down the cellar?" he asked sharply.

"No," said Miranda, "We've kept that door shut since…since the…" she tailed off.

Miya nodded. "Peter could have opened it."

"It's not likely," she said. "We pushed a log up against it to keep animals out."

"Well," said Miya, "It's open now." He went over to the corner, reached down between the fridge and the wall and withdrew a long-handled wood axe.

"What are you going to do? You're not going down there again?!" shuddered Miranda.

"What else?"said Miya, "If there's someone there, I'm going to find out."

"Don't go alone!" said Miranda leaping to her feet, "Please don't! I'll come with you."

Miya shook his head then he looked at Miranda's face and changed his mind. "O.K. then, come with me. But stay behind me, hey? Don't do anything foolish."

Miranda nodded. "Just a moment." She stood up and draped the blanket over a chair and, pulling a thick anorak over her cotton dress, she followed Miya out of the door.

They ducked out into the hissing rain, padded across the yard and down the steps to the cellar. The door was wide open; the log pushed back.

Miya stared at the patch of gloom that was the open doorway. "I'm not going to use the light," he whispered, "Here, you carry it. Don't switch it on until I say so. Our eyes will soon get used to the dark. O.K.?"

Miranda nodded, her face pale. Miya, wielding the axe in front of him two-handed, slipped into the doorway. Miranda followed. Fear welled up in her as the gloom closed around them, but she closed her eyes tightly and on re-opening them, she could see slightly. Miya touched her arm reassuringly and they began to make their way through the cellar.

Despite her fear, Miranda couldn't help but admire the cat-like progress of the Indian. Miranda, despite her bare feet, moved along to the accompaniment of loud rustles and bumps that set her teeth on edge. Miya was noiseless.

Within fifteen minutes they had threaded their way through the interconnected cellar spaces to stand in front of the gloomy black rectangle which led to Joe Bear's former hide-out.

Miya held up a cautioning hand to Miranda and then slipped silently through the final opening. Apprehensively, Miranda followed.

Miranda stood squinting into the dark slightly behind Miya; the flashlight at the ready. Gradually, she could make out the details. The adobe wall still lay in a crumbled mess where Peter had demolished it. Beyond it were the niches from which the Sheriff's men had torn the ancient skeletons from their imprisonment in the tangled tree roots.

Miya cat-footed forward and stepped silently over the broken wall, axe at the ready. Then, abruptly, he stopped. Miranda, close behind, stopped too. There, in one of the niches formerly occupied by the ancient skeletons, Miranda just made out a faint outline.

Someone was standing there…

¤

As the hand grabbed him around the neck, Peter's heart leapt and he would have whirled, but a harsh voice snarled: "Don't move or I'll blast you where you stand! Now turn slowly."

Peter did. It was Dooley.

"Shit!" spat Dooley lowering his .45, "Who do you think you are?! Perry Mason?!"

Though Peter's heart hammered in his breast, he said, relieved: "Dooley! Man, I'm glad it's you."

"So am I," muttered Dooley, "You goddamn idiot! You're gonna get yourself killed creeping around this time o' night!! I knew it musta bin you!" He holstered his gun. "Shit, ah should be home in bed and here I am running around graveyards again!! C'mon, let's git outta here!"

"But…!" protested Peter. He jerked a thumb behind him. "…Ferris Ansell is gone. It happened, just like I told you."

"I don't give a shit!" growled Dooley, "Like I *told you*, it don't matter a damn whether I find it's missing at two in the morning or ten a.m. the next day—'ceptin' that I get a good night's sleep! That's the difference! C'mon you idiot!"

Dooley strode away angrily. Peter followed reluctantly. He caught up to the Sheriff, who churned forward through the rain like a miniature battleship.

Peter began to protest again, but Dooley cut him short: "Shit, Peter! I gets a phone call from the ole Mrs. Howard who tells me she sees some loon with a gun sneaking into the cimitary and I knewed it was you—I knewed it soon as she said it on account of the way you was talking before you left."

"Well, why did you come out if you knew it was me?" asked Peter, hurrying alongside the Sheriff breathlessly.

"Why?! Huh! Lookit the way I just walked up behind you and grabbed you! Now that should teach you a goddamn lesson! Say it hadn't been me? Huh!! You could be dead, boy! That's what!"

Peter was silent for a moment. "Look, thanks, Dooley," he said softly.

Dooley snarled. "Best thanks you kin give me is to get home, git your ass to bed and git a good night's sleep! Then maybe I'll be able to get home to *my* bed before you git into even more trouble!"

CHAPTER THIRTY-FIVE

Miya reached out and touched Miranda softly. She jerked at the contact. He motioned her to stand to one side, pointed at the flashlight and made a gesture with his hand. Miranda understood; she stood aside. Miya moved forward, raising the axe above his head. He half turned, nodded to Miranda and she thumbed the flashlight.

Miranda let out a cry of horror.

Standing in the niche was Joe Bear—and someone else.

Miya stood with the axe poised, caught in the beam of light like a bizarre vignette in a wax museum of horror. He slowly lowered the axe and stepped closer to the niche.

Joe stood facing the damp black wall of earth, his hands raised at shoulder height, his fingers hooked into the soil in front of him; like talons. In exactly the same pose at his side were Ferris Ansell and Cal O'Donnell.

Miranda's hand trembled; the flashlight danced up and down, casting ghostly shadows over the bizarre trio.

"Hold it still!" whispered Miya sharply, "Miranda!"

"They're dead!" said Miranda in a strangled voice, "They're dead!! What is this…??!!"

Miya beckoned Miranda to move closer until she was staring straight up at Joe Bear. Joe's eyes were open, blank and unseeing, his fingers dug into the soil in front of him like pale worms.

"Look…" said Miya pointing.

Miranda stared aghast at the wall behind Joe. Where the Sheriff's men had left a mass of severed roots was new growth; white, maggoty fingers that filled the entire wall from top to bottom. Some of the roots had already bridged the gap to the motionless figures. Miranda stared, open-mouthed, at the slight indentations where the roots probed at Joe's shirt.

"This was what happened to the priests," said Miya softly, "The roots didn't grow through their bodies when they were dead, they grew through them while they were still living."

"*Is* he alive?!" whispered Miranda, unable to take her eyes off the figure standing silently, its fingers hooked into the wall.

"His body is," said Miya, "I don't know how much of his brain is left."

He reached forward and snagged a finger over one of the roots that snaked into Joe's back. The root came away easily, snapping like a succulent young bean sprout. Miya held it up and Miranda came forward and shone the flashlight on it.

The broken white tip oozed with blood.

Miranda swayed and put her head on Miya's shoulder to steady herself. "Oh, my God, Miya! What is happening?!!"

As if in reply, Joe Bear suddenly dropped his arms from the wall and grabbed Miranda by the neck.

Miranda dropped the flashlight, screaming, but her scream was cut short as Joe Bear's hands clamped around her throat. The hands squeezed harder. Miranda gurgled and sank to the ground held in an iron grip, her eyes bulging and her legs scrabbling beneath her.

She heard a dull thud; then another. The grip loosened slightly. Then there was another thud and Miranda wrenched free, gulping and choking as a dark figure slid down to the earth besides her. She lay twitching in the damp, cool earth, making horrible gasping noises.

"Easy, easy…" said Miya's anxious voice, "Take it easy…"

Miranda began to breathe more evenly. Miya put down the blood-stained axe and shone the flashlight on her throat. "C'mon," he whispered, "Let's get out of here. Here, lean on me." Miranda staggered to her feet. Miya grabbed the flashlight and the axe, taking Miranda's weight on his shoulder. He played the flashlight over the figure on the ground. "Don't look," he warned. But Miranda had seen it. She shuddered and looked away.

Miya gazed impassively at the crumpled body of Joe Bear. The head was canted at an odd angle, attached to the trunk by a single fragment of flesh. "C'mon, let's go," whispered Miya. He eased Miranda through the cellar door and helped her through the darkened rooms. Miranda whimpered in the back of her throat, but made her way as best as her tottering legs would allow.

By the time Miya had finished his work it was almost dawn and the pale light had begun to filter through the ventilation slits in the cellar.

Miya, despite Miranda's protestations, had left her tucked up warm and safe in the Ford truck by the workshop, then returned to finish his task.

Tired and dirty, Miya hauled the last brick into place. He had spent the whole night rebuilding the wall, carrying the large cinder blocks into the cellar one by one. And now the wall was almost finished, except for a two-foot gap at chest height. Miya stood back and surveyed his handiwork. When the last four bricks were in place, the wall would once again be an impenetrable barrier.

Miya gazed through the opening cautiously, taking one last look at the figures that had once been Cal O'Donnell and Ferris Ansell. Joe's grisly remains still lay on the floor but the other two men had not moved. They stood frozen in the same postures, their fingers hooked into the wall in front of them, the spidery mass of white roots at their backs.

Chanting sonorously, Miya took a package out of his pocket, opened it carefully and threw a grayish-white powder through the opening. He jerked free an amulet from around his neck and, still chanting, threw that in too.

He knelt down in the moist, damp earth and picked up three beer bottles he'd filled with gasoline earlier. One by one, he tossed them through the hole in the wall, still muttering as they crashed on the other side of the wall with a glassy tinkle.

He stopped chanting. It was ready. He took a bundle of dried moss and leaves from a pouch at his side and lit it with a match. At first it didn't fire up; acrid smoke billowed upwards. Miya raised the bundle first to the North, then South, East, West—and spoke the Words. He blew on the smoking packet until it glowed red-hot, and threw it through the hole. There was a 'whumph!' and a sheet of yellow flame belched outwards.

Miya squatted down on his haunches and waited until acrid smoke began pouring out of the hole, blue in the half-light. Then he buttered the last of the breeze blocks with mortar and slipped them into place with a few taps of the trowel. The wall was blank, unbroken.

The light grew as the morning sun brightened through the ventilation slits. Miya sat thus for a long time. Then he rose and padded softly out of the cellar.

Golden and healing, the sun was rising over the sierra hill. Miya took in a deep lungful of air and expelled it, eyes closed, letting the warmth sooth him. But still he could not erase the last sight of Cal O'Donnell and Ferris Ansell from his mind.

When he'd first seen them, the men had been standing as Joe had been—with the roots crowding behind them.

But in just the few hours it had taken Miya to close the wall, the roots had jabbed their bony white fingers into the men's backs. The tendrils had oozed out of their open eyes, nostrils and ears and had already plunged into the opposite wall, feeding like voracious, white worms.

WINTER

'Chemistry, probing the wonder of chlorophyll, stumbled over a fascinating fact that may reveal an evolutionary kinship between trees and human beings. If the single atom of magnesium is detached from the chlorophyll molecule and an atom of iron put in its place, the same numbers of atoms and their arrangement become a molecule of red blood.'

Rutherford Platt
The Great American Forest

CHAPTER THIRTY-SIX

Peter, sitting in the kitchen, stirred the thick black coffee and glanced up at a dishevelled Miya. "Technically speaking, you're guilty of murder," he said softly.

Miranda sat with her knees huddled to her chest. She pulled the anorak closer around her shoulders and said: "Are you talking to me as well, Peter?"

Peter's face sagged. He'd just learnt two unpalatable facts: the grisly contents of the cellar; and the fact that Miranda had aborted her baby. Peter knew Miranda was referring to the abortion, but responded with silence, gazing at his coffee as if the answer lay in its warm, black depths. His face was blank, his mind seething. Miranda had told him that she'd aborted the baby—that was all. She would not offer any further information. When Peter pressed her for details, she'd just stared at the table.

The silence became unbearable, but Peter could not meet Miranda's steely gaze. Eventually, he forced himself to speak. "No, I wasn't referring to that, Miranda," he said slowly, "You know I already realized that the...foetus might've been damaged. That stuff you ate was really toxic—you were lucky." He looked up at her for the first time. "If you'd have taken any more, you'd certainly be brain-damaged—probably irreversibly."

Miranda gave a weak little smile. "You don't think I am now?"

"No more than usual," said Peter wryly.

At the bad joke, Miranda's face softened and she leant forward to touch Peter's cheek. "Peter, no matter how weird I seem to be acting, I do love you, you know." Peter nearly burst into tears, but old habits die hard and he just hugged her gruffly.

Miya sat watching them quietly, then he stood up as if to go. "Don't go, Miya," said Peter slowly, "Please sit down." Miya sat down again and waited silently. Peter, running his hands through Miranda's hair nervously, continued in a haltering voice: "What I said then about...murder ...I'm sorry, Miya. You saved Miranda's life and you saved mine. I must seem like an ungrateful wretch. But..." he smiled wryly, "...I guess I'm just continuing with my conventional reactions to a very unconventional situation. It hasn't quite sunk in yet." He shuddered, "The thought of those three living dead *things* frying behind that bricked-up wall below gives me the willies, I tell you!"

Miya nodded without speaking. He watched Peter's face carefully.

"I know," continued Peter, "Especially after reading David Gordon's report, that those three would have been vegetables, hopelessly brain-damaged …though…" he frowned, "…I don't understand what happened to Joe Bear. He seemed to be in control—at least more than the others."

"To some extent, Joe managed to stave off the effects of the drug," said Miya slowly, "He used other poisons—some snake extracts that I found in his medicine bag. He was using the fruit the way the Hopis use peyote, the difference being that they know what they're doing and what they're doing it with." His face saddened. "Joe was an amateur and a fool. Now he's a dead fool. He just died a bit sooner than he would have anyway."

Peter nodded. "No jury would be able to convict you for killing a dead man, Miya." He sighed. "And they're not going to find out. The bodies are bricked up and nobody's going to bother with that wall—least, not while we're here."

"Are we staying, Peter?" said Miranda, murmuring into Peter's shoulder, "Are we staying here?"

Peter stared down at her. "I guess so. There seems to be something to finish here." He paused, then added sheepishly: "I'm still not so sure I agree with all the mumbo-jumbo surrounding it. Bizarre as the whole thing has been, I wouldn't be telling the truth if I said less than that. So far, it's all been explicable in terms of science—novel, perhaps, but nonetheless rational…" Miranda stiffened and withdrew her head from his shoulder. She sat staring at him, her face set. Peter became flustered, but with an air of desperation, plunged on. "Look, I'm just saying what's true for me. I'm not *trying* to be pig-headed or anything like that. I've got to say what I believe, even if it hurts the people close to me…" His voice died away. Miranda stared at him with a strange mixture of compassion and sorrow. Peter looked down at his hands. "What is it you want, Miya?" he asked.

Miya stood up. "Your cooperation."

"In what?"

"In destroying the Tree."

Peter laughed mirthlessly. "My God! Why don't you just ride into town, pick up the Yellow Pages and get a tree firm to do it? It's a big tree, but it isn't invulnerable."

"It's not that easy, Peter," said Miya wearily. He spread his hands out in supplication. "Look, Peter, I really want you to help. I really want your cooperation. I know that you're looking at all of this with…a scientific mindset, and…" he looked troubled, "…what I'm trying to say is that there *are* other ways of looking at it. They are not incompatible with your own views, just different."

"Convince me," whispered Peter. It was not sarcasm but a plea.

Miya nodded, recognizing Peter's torment. He strode to the doorway and looked out at the rain and the misty morning light on the hills. "Peter," he said with his back turned, "In terms of what you would call science, the tree, a creature which evolved four hundred million years ago, is not so different from man."

"How so?" frowned Peter.

"Man crawled out of the sea as a primitive organism an epoch ago and his weapon was motility," said Miya, still gazing at the flourishes of rain which danced across the vegetable garden. "He gained independence from the sea by becoming an air-breathing creature. But the price that Man paid is that he must constantly forage for the nutrition that once came to him easily, borne by undersea currents. Man can never be still. In comparison, Tree is a far superior adaptation, for Tree took the sea with him. Look..." he counted off on his fingers, "...of the forty or so elements used to build and maintain a tree, some are very rare—copper, manganese, mercury, cobalt, silver, tin. How do you think the tree gets these from the soil?"

Peter frowned. "I don't know—never studied it."

"I have," said Miya, "And it gets them by drawing up a vast river of water through itself; a minor sea. A tree absorbs and discharges hundreds of gallons of water every day so that, eventually, even the rarest mineral will be brought to the tree cells. Clever, eh?"

"I'm not so sure...where this is leading. What's the point?"

"This," said Miya suddenly, "If I were to talk about the Spirit of the Tree, the legends of the Pomo, the myths of the Yurok, you would yawn and head for the door, Peter. But your own science is only a myth and a metaphor to explain that which it cannot comprehend. Yet, I've just given you a scientific explanation to demonstrate that Man, a creature which is still composed of four-fifths water—the primordial element from which he arose—is not so different in essence from the so-called inanimate object you call a tree. Peter, both Man and Tree are of the sea."

"It's a big step from showing that life originates in the sea to imbuing a tree with some eternal spirit," said Peter dryly.

"Is it?" Miya laughed. "The trouble with scientific education is that while it is just a metaphor itself, the people who dispense it lack the ability to create the poem that the metaphor implies. But..." he held up a finger, "...a poem it is. Watch!" Miya struck a mock dramatic pose like a Victorian actor.

For the first time in months, Miranda laughed out loud. Peter stared at her and some of the tautness went out of his body.

"Not her—*me*!" retorted Miya, "Watch me!" He threw off his jacket and raised both hands. "So, Peter Riley!" he boomed theatrically, "I, Miya, will recite a poem. Not the myth of the Huk, the bird that lies within the Tree of Death, poisoning with its red-quilled liquid; not the legend of the Yurok or the Cheyenne; not the fable of the World Tree. No, Peter..." he paused dramatically, "...I will give you the white man's Myth of Organic Chemistry and show you how wonderful and terrible it can be!"

Miranda moved closer to Peter and placed her hand on his shoulder. Peter covered her hand with his and they both gazed at Miya. Miranda's eyes were bright and sparkling.

"So!" cried Miya, raising his hands to the air, "We have Tree…" He stood swaying, his palms upturned, "…a creature of serenity is this Tree, silent and unmoving. And yet, the very substance of its being is a story of violent energy; an ode of fire and water; vast forces; biting poisons; substances that would fry the liver and curdle the brain!"

Peter blinked nervously, but Miya continued: "I set the stage!" he boomed. "First, the players. Alchemy and the alchemical forces—the magical substances of the Medieval Age! I give you Nitrogen, Phosphorous, Potassium, Magnesium and Sulphur! And the stage is set…so our tale begins," cried Miya. "Nitrogen, a substance of vast force that contains within itself the possibility of awesome explosions and yet, alone, is a mere chunk of deadness. Phosphorous, a substance which ignites without fire, so that its very name means 'the Bearer of Light'. Thus, deep within the Tree we are in a world of explosive forces and spontaneous, flaring fires—and the battle begins: Potassium, which as Potash is a painful, searing caustic, is necessary to oust the poison of Sodium. Poison meets poison, snake bites snake, and from it springs life!" He paused dramatically. "Magnesium! A substance of mysterious, electrifying forces, origin of the ancient art of Pyrotechnics—the magic of Colored Fire. And last but not least, there is Sulphur, a voracious eater of metals, which becomes, with the addition of a little burnt wood and nitrogen, Vishnu the Destroyer, the instrument of man's inhumanity to man; the agent of multiple death—gun powder!"

Miya paused staring at the ceiling, his fingers crooked, his knees bent. He intoned: "Once more I repeat it: Nitrogen, Phosphorous, Potassium, Magnesium and Sulphur, things that crackle, burn, sear, explode, devour and kill. These fearsome elements are found in every living cell of Tree. Elements of death, they bring to Tree—Life!" Then he pointed at Peter and said: "Now, can you deny the white man's Myth of Chemistry which shows indisputably that within the very core of Tree is the Spirit of Fire??!!"

Peter swallowed.

"Well?" asked Miya.

"Well, not when you put it like that," spluttered Peter.

Miya suddenly bowed. "My case rests," he said quietly.

"Bravo, Miya! That was wonderful!" cried Miranda. She ran over to him and gave him a hug.

Miya's face became serious again. "I'm sorry to do that to you, Peter. I simply wanted to make my point—all knowledge is only a narrow perspective, a certain way of looking at things. In the end, our human explanations are only an approximation of a vast mystery, whether we use the myth of Science or the myth of Magic."

"Miya," said Peter, "You're quite a guy. That was very impressive."

"I don't want you to be impressed. I want you to help me," said Miya quietly.

"But," said Peter, "What is it you believe in? The myth of Science or the myth of Magic?"

Miya smiled for the first time. "Whatever does the job. I believe in that which works—and I don't question it," he said.

"O.K.," said Peter, "I'll help you. Just tell me what to do."

CHAPTER THIRTY-SEVEN

Peter grunted as a hand shook his shoulder. It was Miranda. He sat up and yawned. He could hear a yipping and slapping of feet on the wet earth outside, just audible over the hiss of the rain.

"Here." She gave him a hot coffee, "Drink this."

"What time is it?" asked Peter sipping drowsily.

"Two a.m.," whispered Miranda.

"Christ! How long has he been at it now?"

"Hours," murmured Miranda, "But he's called me."

"Called you?" asked Peter surprised. Then he realized that Miranda was bare-footed and clad in a birch-bark skirt.

"Yes, I'm to dance," she whispered, "I came to tell you that you must keep the fire going—don't let it go out. Perhaps we may go on for a long time. From now on, you can't sleep—it's very important."

Peter grinned and nodded. "Ah, well," he said, "I said yes, and I've got to keep my word. Here." He pulled Miranda close to him and kissed her forehead, "Dance well. I'm coming."

Miranda smiled gratefully and, hugging Peter a final time, slipped out.

Peter, still half-asleep, slipped on an oil slicker and a pair of waterproof boots and ducked out into the hissing rain.

Miya, dressed in a magnificent headdress of woodpecker feathers, a breech cloth and a chest plate of woven thongs and beads, was dancing around a fire. The fire had been lit near the Mission gates—as far away from the Tree as possible, but still in sight of it.

Orange and red flames whirled up into the dark sky. The rain fought fitfully against the huge fire and lost, hissing and complaining as it pelted the corona of flame.

Miya, bathed in sweat, slapped the earth, dancing fiercely, his eyes black and distant as he whirled and skipped, describing complex patterns on the steaming earth.

Like a bleached Indian maiden, Miranda danced at his side, twirling and stamping in a fair imitation of Miya's step. She was naked from the waist up, her sweat-slicked breasts bobbing wildly, tanned by the firelight.

Peter gazed at the half-naked bodies with a wry sense of his own acceptance. It did not seem bizarre. On the contrary, there was a certain incongruous familiarity about the scene and yet Peter had never seen an Indian dance in his life.

Shaking himself into action, Peter took the flashlight out of his coat pocket—for it was still quite dark—and went to gather wood, picking his way across the Mission compound. Within a short period, he had gathered a stack of wet two-by-fours which he carried to the fire.

Working this way, he soon cleared the compound of scrap wood, so he went to the deserted theater and, with a sense of grim satisfaction, took a sledge hammer to the creaking stage. The brief flurry of destruction did Peter good. Sweating and heaving, he brought the heavy hammer down again and again, smashing into the stage. Soon he stood amongst a splintered mass of hardwood and, breathing hard, he wiped his forehead, realizing how much anger he'd been repressing.

His gaze fell on a mound of dirt in the middle of the floor, illuminated starkly by the vast blaze outside. Miranda had been trying to show him something, he thought, but she'd suddenly clammed up. What…? Like a buzzing fly, the thought continued to plague him as he worked, but he brushed it aside and plodded dutifully backwards and forwards carrying armloads of splintered wood.

Within an hour he'd piled a small mountain of wood at the side of the conflagration, ready to feed the flames. Peter yawned, realizing how tired he was, and sat down by the warm, comforting glow of the fire for a brief rest…

Peter's head jerked up and he realized with a start that he'd nodded off. He panicked, thinking that the fire had died down. But though it was visibly lower, it was still blazing. Peter leapt up and began hurling fresh boards into the flames. The fire roared its approval and sent columns of sparks shooting up into the pale pre-dawn sky.

Miya and Miranda were still dancing; even more wildly than before. The freshly-fed flames leapt higher, illuminating Miranda's cavorting body. Her head snapped back and forth, her eyes fully closed; her plaits lashed at her naked shoulders as she whirled like an intoxicated Dervish.

Miya, with his back to Miranda, had his arms raised as he muttered and stamped. He faced the flames as if exhorting them; cajoling, pleading. Finally, he threw his head back and screamed; a series of high-pitched, yipping sounds that made Peter's skin crawl. Leaping alongside Miranda, Miya bowed his head and resumed dancing, his feet pounding the earth in a curious tattoo.

Miranda was long gone; oblivious to the heat of the fire, the sweat on her body, the sharp stones under her bloody feet. All was movement; all was rhythm. It was delicious. As if she were a puppet, her legs, feet, arms and head lifted and fell in an ecstatic rhythm of their own.

She heard a dull thudding and realized it was Miya dancing with her

again. Her own pace quickened—thud, thud, thud—indistinguishable from
the pulse of her heart, the pounding in her veins. Faster and faster; the dance
increased in pace and Miranda's breathing came in ragged gasps and her face
grew flushed.

Miya was chanting. The sound beat against her ears so liquid, it mingled
with the hiss of the rain and the crackle of the fire; merged and wove in and
out with a sinuous roll that counterpointed the buffet of the wind, the roar of
the fire and the thud of their feet.

A sheet of red drifted across Miranda's closed eyelids; she staggered, but
managed to regain her balance without falling. She turned once, twice in a
lazy circle, then she began to whirl; slowly at first, one hand raised in the air.
The whirling grew faster, swept up by the liquid syllables of Miya's chant.
The noises melded, splashed about her in undulating waves. Miranda's ears
began to roar and the thudding grew louder, louder until it was a huge hollow
boom inside her skull bones. Then, just as it threatened to burst her eardrums,
she seemed to lift from the ground and...

...There she was, gliding above the blue ocean with the long red flowers
soaring like glass pillars from the blue sea to an azure sky. Miranda skimmed
through the air; a white bird gliding effortlessly above the breakers crashing
on a sandy beach far below. A tiny figure alone on the beach lifted a diminutive arm and waved. Miranda dropped, plummeting through the air in a vast
arc and swooped yards above the beach and the young-old woman who stood
there. The woman smiled and beckoned, her face simultaneously wrinkled and
unblemished. Miranda skimmed around and came back in a long, slow curve
as the Indian woman reached forward, snapped off one of the glass sky-pillars
and threw it to the sky. The white bird swooped, intercepted it and caught the
blood-red flower in its beak.

The glassy red spire was ice-cold in Miranda's mouth; sour and rank in
taste and smell. Suddenly it melted and crimson dribbled down her chin.

Shrieking, Miranda plummeted from the sky, a bird no longer. Faster
and faster she fell, with the liquid dripping from her open mouth in blood-red
gobbets, to fall to the ocean. Each drop hit the sea with a booming explosion,
jetting a great column of bright red water high into the air. Then the entire
surface erupted and a vast sheet of flame gusted across the ocean to the
horizon, and Miranda heard a shrill yell: "*Canemilan Kale Kalemaleto!!*"

And all was Fire.

Miranda's eyes shot open to see Miya throwing his headdress into the
fire, screaming at the top of his lungs. His face contorted, the veins knotted
in his throat, Miya screamed over and over as he tossed in Ferris Ansell's gun
then Joe Bear's stinking bear skin.

Miranda glanced around fearfully. Something felt wrong. A sudden wind
had sprung up from nowhere, slapping the rain across the yard in huge sheets

that hissed spitefully as they hit the fire.

A vast groan rent the air. Miranda whirled.

It was the Tree; swaying and juddering, its huge, black branches waving madly as Miya, screaming defiance, finally threw his amulet into the fire.

Peter stood aghast, clutching a length of wood impotently in one hand, staring upwards. Miranda slowly backed away, too frightened to make a sound as the Tree lurched and heaved as if trying to tear itself from the ground.

Miranda realized what was happening, found her voice and screamed out a warning. But too late. With a screech, a huge branch swung around in an impossible arc and smacked Miya right into the fire.

For a moment, Peter did not move. He stared in disbelief at the shuddering Tree and the huge branch that had torn itself away from the main trunk leaving a raw, open wound in the bark. Beneath Peter's feet, the ground pitched and heaved as the Tree writhed, and he fell onto all fours.

Then Peter was up and running; vaulting over the fallen limb, dodging fallen branches. "Miya!!!" he shouted involuntarily. For Miya was slumped head first in the red-hot coals of the fire, one arm across his face. "Oh my God!! Miya!!!" screamed Peter in a anguish of impotence. He tried to plunge forward, but the heat snatched the very air from his lungs and drove him back with its oppressive force. "NOO!!" he screamed and lunged forward, his hair smoking and fizzy, and grabbed hold of Miya's arm. With a strength borne of panic, he slung the large man over his back and carried him ten paces before he collapsed in a heap on the ground. Peter beat desperately at Miya's smoldering body until his bare hands were raw and bleeding. But he did not stop until he'd extinguished the last spark and then, with a whimper of anguish, he rolled Miya onto his back.

Miya's face was untouched, but his arms, chest and thighs were a curdled mass of burnt flesh embedded with bits of ash and smoking wood.

Then Miranda was at his side. "Miya!!" she whispered urgently.

Miya opened his eyes. "You heard," he whispered, "*Canamilan Kale Kalemeleto*." Miranda nodded, her face taut. "Surround the Tree with fire and water—do it," whispered Miya. His eyes rolled up into his head and he slumped back.

"We've got to get him out of here," muttered Peter. A gust of wind made the fire flare, jetting sparks into the air, illuminating Miranda's face. Peter, seeing her expression, hissed urgently: "Miranda! D'you hear me?! We've got to get him to a hospital!!"

Miranda nodded slowly. She placed her hand on Miya's chest where the skin was black and crisped. She seemed very far away. "He will live," she said flatly, then stood up and gazed at the torn Tree which still twitched spasmodically like a limb-torn insect.

Peter had never seen such an expression on Miranda's face before. It was cold; so very cold. And behind her eyes, the venom of pure hatred.

CHAPTER THIRTY-EIGHT

"You can go in now," said the Doctor, "But not too long, eh?"

Peter, dressed in a green surgical gown and mask, nodded and held open the door to the side ward so that a similarly-attired Miranda could go through. He followed her in and they both stopped, uncertain: Miya's bed was completely enclosed in a plastic tent. Miranda gave Peter a sorrowful look and, tiptoeing to the tent, she lifted the flap cautiously.

Miranda exclaimed in surprise. Except for a pair of tiny briefs, Miya was naked, and, if anything, he looked worse than he had the day before. His skin had been cleaned and sterilized and, though it was no longer black, it looked even more horrible—like a freshly-flayed turkey.

Miranda and Peter stood ill-at-ease and stared, unable to find words for the occasion.

"Hey, you two," grinned Miya, "Never seen a barbecued Indian before?"

Miranda waved her arms helplessly. "I'd give you a hug, but I don't dare touch you," she said.

"Pity," sighed Miya, "It's a nice thought." Despite his cheery grin, the big man was obviously tired. Peter had never seen him so weak.

"You're very chirpy for someone who's just been pulled out of a fire," said Peter wryly.

"And why not?" said Miya, "I'm alive. You're alive." His voice changed. "How much do you weigh, Peter?"

"One hundred and fifty pounds," said Peter, "Why?"

"Well, I weigh two hundred or so," said Miya, "That was quite a weight-lifting feat back there—thanks. If it hadn't been for you, I'd be one helluva well-cooked Indian—not just barbecued!"

Peter went red. "I couldn't leave you to fry, could I, you old coot?!" he said, embarrassed.

"Good job, too. At least now we know."

"We know what?" asked Peter.

"What to do with the Tree," said Miya, "Fire and water—that's the way. It worked..." he grinned, "...only too well. I should have been more cautious. It's my own fault I'm here and yours that I'm not six feet under."

For a moment Peter was silent. Miranda could sense his inner struggle, but she waited. Then, finally, Peter spoke. "I owe you some kind of apology," he said slowly, "There's something going on back there that I don't understand —more than I imagined possible… The Tree is something unnatural—maybe supernatural…" he shook his head, lost for words.

"You white men," said Miya with a weak smile, "Forever trying to distinguish between the natural and supernatural, when to us Indians, it's so much easier—*everything* is natural."

"Even the Tree?" whispered Miranda gazing away into the distance.

"Even the Tree," said Miya.

"Fire and water," mused Peter, "In a way, that's what the Tree is made of…"

Miya nodded. "I'm going to be here for months, according to the doctor." He grimaced. "A lot of skin grafts, a lot of lying about doing nothing."

"You'd look better in bandages," said Miranda eyeing the oozing mess that was Miya's chest and thighs.

"Then I'd never heal. At least the white man has learnt something about medicine," said Miya, "The air is, itself, a healer. But it takes a long, long time. Waiting is all I can do."

"Then it's up to me," said Peter.

"Eh? What? What do you mean?" asked Miranda.

"Miya's going to be in here a long time," said Peter. "The Tree's going to bloom again. Its cycle will start again in Spring…if it's not stopped, that is. So, I'm going to stop it."

Miya stared at him. "How?" he asked softly.

"Fire and water of course," said Peter. He thought for a moment and added ruefully. "I may not be up on Indian lore, but I do know Fire and I do know Water. I can do it."

Miya stared at him long and hard through narrowed eyes. Then he spoke. "Yes, Peter, you do know about these things—more than most white men. Yes, you try it—but be careful. Tree is more cunning than the fox and it is much older than you."

The doctor's head popped around the curtain, cutting them short. "Time's up, Ladies and Gentlemen. I'm sorry."

Peter sighed, stood up and saluted Miya. "We'll be back soon, Miya."

"Be careful," said Miya. "Oh, one thing: just open that drawer over there…" Peter pulled the bedside drawer open. In it lay an amulet and a medicine bag on a rawhide string, the twin to the one Miya had given Miranda. "When Flame must cut like Knife, use it," intoned Miya.

Peter nodded gravely and tied the amulet around his neck. Miranda touched her lips and gave Miya a warm farewell smile and, pushing aside the curtain, stepped outside the tent.

"Peter," said Miya as Peter turned to follow.

"Yes," said Peter pausing at the flap, "What?"

"Use Miranda—you'll need her."

Peter thought for a moment. "I can't promise that. Let me think about it.

It's very dangerous…"

"Use her," said Miya fiercely. Then spent, he sank back into the sheets; the fire ebbed from his eyes and his face was suddenly drawn and gaunt.

Peter gulped, a lump in his throat, as he realized that Miya had been faking nonchalance to hide his intense pain. "Thanks," he said huskily.

But Miya's eyes were closed and he did not reply.

CHAPTER THIRTY-NINE

Peter turned the harpoon gun over in his hand.

"An' this here is the reload," said the salesman pointing at a catch, "Just do that…that's it…pull it back here and…yep, that's it. You've got the hang of it. Pretty powerful, too. And this tank is light in or out of water." He slapped the tank of compressed air with a metallic clang.

"I'll take it," said Peter, "But haven't you got any spare harpoons?"

"Some," said the salesman, "How many do you want?"

"Fifteen," said Peter.

"Fifteen?" said the salesman. He scratched his head and looked around the Sports Store. "Fifteen! You planning to lose that many?"

"Nope," said Peter, "But I got my reasons."

"Well," said the salesman with the air of one who knows when not to ask questions, "I'll see what I can do…"

Miranda sat in the Jeep outside the hardware store until Peter struggled out with his load and dumped it on the seat. Together they ran through Peter's checklist of equipment and, working rapidly, stowed each article carefully into the back of the Jeep.

"That's it?" said Miranda when they had cinched down the tarp over the Jeep bed.

Peter sat at the wheel staring down the street through the rain-streaked windshield. The traffic lights blossomed green, yellow and red flowers, distorted by the rain. "There is one thing," he said, "But I've got to go and pick that up personally."

Miranda looked at him sharply. During his time as a self-made engineer, Peter had formed many contacts in the business—Miranda knew Peter could lay his hands on many illicit substances. Miranda also knew that, if it didn't hurt anybody, legality had never bothered Peter very much—he was much too practical for red tape. "What is it you need to pick up personally, Peter?" she asked shrewdly.

Peter seemed far away, staring through the windshield at the huddled figures scurrying along the sidewalks clutching their collars. "Oh…a compressor," he said absently.

"You need to pick that up *personally*?" said Miranda steely-eyed, a hint of sarcasm in her tone. "Quite the absent-minded scientist act… C'mon, Peter, I may be dumb, but not that dumb. What is it?"

"You're not dumb," answered Peter.

"Don't change the subject," said Miranda.

Peter squirmed in the seat and looked at his hands. "Couple of crates of dynamite," he said, "Getting them off Jerry Livingstone."

Miranda put her hand on Peter's knee; her palm was hot, his knee damp. It suddenly felt close inside the Jeep. Peter rolled down the window and breathed in a lungful of cold air and sat watching the rain drops splashing into the puddles on the tarmac.

"Are you going to blow the Tree up?" asked Miranda slowly.

Peter shook his head. "I don't know…" he said hesitatingly, "That could be a very bad mistake, throwing bits of Tree all over the place. It might…regenerate somewhere else through spores or something. Who knows? No. I've got to destroy it in where it stands, like Miya said, with Fire and Water."

"So, what's the dynamite for?" whispered Miranda putting her hand on his shoulder urgently, "C'mon, Peter, this sounds very dangerous."

"Never you mind," said Peter, "That's for me to sort out."

Miranda jerked away and sat upright. "Peter! You're going to do this alone, aren't you?!!"

"Miranda," soothed Peter, "Please! We've been so lucky so far. I'd hate anything to happen to you."

"Oh!" she said sharply, "On the other hand, I'd just love something to happen to you, wouldn't I?!"

"Miranda," said Peter softly, "It could be very dangerous and it's better I do it alone—really."

"Oh, yeah, Mr. Clint Eastwood?!" cried Miranda, hurt and angry.

They argued all afternoon; in the wet and steamy confines of the Jeep; in a roadside cafe. The argument flared up again, redoubled, when Peter revealed that he had booked Miranda into a cheap motel. Miranda ranted, cajoled, pleaded, railed, but Peter would not budge.

Finally, by dint of sheer exhaustion, Miranda realized she'd lost. Peter had only been this adamant on a couple of previous occasions and Miranda knew that once Peter decided something like this he would never give in; he was as impenetrable and intractable as his namesake—the Rock.

The Jeep pulled up under the garish sign of the motel. Peter sat with the engine ticking over and pointed at the red and green sign which, as usual, announced 'Vacancy' and 'No Vacancy' simultaneously. "That is irrelevant. Your room is booked for an indefinite period."

Miranda glared at the L-shaped collection of ugly rooms. "The car ports are empty," she said sarcastically, "There's obviously lots of room in the motel. And no wonder—it's crummy! Just the place to learn your husband's blown himself to kingdom-come!" As if to underscore her point, the driving rain began to overflow the motel's inadequate gutter system and gushed down the damp adobe walls in multiple rivulets. "Huh! It's probably damper than anything in there—probably full of mildew!"

Peter didn't rise to the bait. He sat patiently, the engine running, waiting for Miranda to get out.

Miranda wound down the window and stared at the forlorn collection of newspaper vending machines chained together like robotic slaves. The headline on the local paper read:

Floods in Chesterville; five drowned.
Experts say more rain to come

"Well," said Miranda, "It's good that we're parting in ideal conditions—at least if you don't blow yourself up, there's a chance you could get drowned."

Still Peter did not respond. Miranda had assailed him with sarcasms for the last two hours and he wasn't going to be swayed now.

Miranda could stand it no longer. She knew he'd sit there all day and night if necessary. So, with a snort of annoyance, she leapt out into the rain and dashed into the motel office without even looking back.

Peter let out a great sigh and eased the Jeep into gear. He turned it around, peering out of the open window, hoping to catch a glimpse of Miranda and wave goodbye. But she didn't emerge from the office.

He'd won his point, but it didn't make him feel good. He consoled himself with the grim thought that if he'd given in to her demands, he'd feel much much worse. He sighed wearily; but he turned the Jeep and roared off towards the freeway. He had a couple of cases of dynamite to collect.

CHAPTER FORTY

Peter gunned the Jeep down the country road. His face was set in a scowl. The trip to get the dynamite should have taken two hours. In fact, the road conditions had been so bad, it had taken twenty-four. Peter had spent the night sleeping in the Jeep in a lay-by because the road had been so badly flooded. The police had blocked the road off and, despite protestations from the line of stalled traffic, they wouldn't allow anyone through until they'd pumped out the road surface to ensure that no one got marooned. The flooded road had taken most of the night to drain.

Peter glanced up at the sky. It hardly seemed like eight o'clock in the morning; it was as dark and gloomy as if the day were just ending.

The Jeep skidded sideways across the rain-slicked road. With a curse, Peter wrestled with the wheel, righted the Jeep and eased his foot down again. The Jeep swept along the wet road with a high-pitched hiss, a plume of white mist billowing behind it. Peter eyed the sky warily, wondering if he'd be able to get into the Mission. He'd heard that the Mission road frequently collapsed into the river in the rainy season. He prayed fervently that it didn't happen this year.

Peter reached the turnoff to the Mission road without mishap. He spotted a large flatbed in the lay-by there and slowed down. The flatbed bore the legend 'Manlow Truckers, CA'. Peter nodded in satisfaction and pulled the Jeep over. This was the trucking company he'd phoned the day before. He parked on the gravel lay-by, got out and inspected the vehicle roped onto the bed of the truck.

It was a curious vehicle made of sheets of rivetted iron —basically two large iron buckets joined together. It was, in fact, an All-Terrain Vehicle. Peter had built it himself. It looked crude but it served its purpose—though it lacked any esthetic appeal with its boxy design.

Peter examined it closely. The two large containers were joined by a central shaft. The rear articulated independent of the front. In the front bucket was housed the engine and the driver's seat; in the rear, a passenger seat and storage space. For amphibious travel, the exhaust poked up three feet in the air. With its huge rubber wheels and rudely-welded joints, the vehicle resembled a crudely-shaped beetle more than a vehicle—but it did the job. It could negotiate a forty-five degree incline or a rocky stream bed with equal ease. It also served as a boat, although the sea-board tended to be a little low for comfort and its pace was, to say the least, ponderous.

Peter finished his examination. The vehicle looked O.K. It had obviously been loaded by professionals and secured very efficiently.

Peter knocked on the cab door. After a moment, the window rolled down and the tousled head of a sleepy driver appeared over the edge.

"Huh?" said the driver drowsily.

"Peter Riley," said Peter. He pointed a thumb at the flatbed. "The ATV—it's mine. You were delivering it to Aloe Vera Mission."

"Oh, yeah," said the driver sheepishly. He swung open the door and climbed out, grinning apologetically. "Just catching a few z's. Drove down last night but I had to wait at Chesterville—road's flooded."

"Don't I know it," said Peter with a grin, "We must have been in the same convoy."

"You could have saved me a trip," said the driver jokingly.

"What? And drive that thing down the freeway at twenty miles per hour?!"

"Well," said the driver slowly, "You're going to have to drive it anyway." He indicated the Mission road curving away between the trees. "I got a report that the road to the Mission is washed away. Nothing bigger than a Volkswagen kin get through, so they say."

"Shit!" muttered Peter.

"Look," suggested the driver, "Why don't we unload the ATV, dump whatever you've got in the Jeep in that, and you can drive it the rest of the way? Leave the Jeep parked here, eh?"

"Good thinking," agreed Peter.

An hour later, after much sweating and heaving, the ATV was unloaded from the flatbed.

The driver waved goodbye to Peter. "Gonna be O.K.?" he shouted from the flatbed cab.

"Sure," replied Peter waving back, "Take it easy yourself."

The driver winked and engaged the gears with a hiss of air-brakes. The flatbed rumbled off into the gray rain and was soon lost to sight.

As the noise of the flatbed faded, Peter became aware of the rain as a tangible presence. Everywhere there was water. He glanced up at the trees. Every tree, every leaf was sodden. The rain fell in vast sheets, relentless, as it had been for days. Even at this distance Peter could hear the crash and hiss of the swollen river where it over-ran its banks, swirling through the undergrowth, dragging trees, branches and sections of bank along in its path.

Conditions were lousy and he was alone, he thought. The realization did not comfort Peter, but he shrugged: he had a job to do and he would do it because there was nothing else left to do. He climbed into the makeshift seat of the ATV and, after a few tries, coaxed the engine into a throbbing roar. He reversed clumsily, unused to the vehicle's low gearing, and, pressing the pedal to the floor, began to chug towards the Mission at a steady speed of twenty miles per hour.

Peter rounded the curve of the mountain and slowed down, filled with apprehension. Perched precariously on the side of the road ahead was a red and white 'Danger' marker. The road was almost impassible at that point. A huge section of the road had slumped into the river below; there was barely enough room, even for a small vehicle.

Peter stared morosely at the river raging just a few feet beneath the crumbling road. The meandering stream of summer had metamorphosed into a raging torrent. Rocks which had formerly concealed the summer trickle were now themselves hidden beneath the surface of a great, muddy rush of water. Borne on the surface of this vast brown gout, logs, tree branches—even entire trees—swept by at dizzying speeds, battered against the narrow walls of the ravine.

The river thrilled and frightened Peter simultaneously, so fierce was its energy. And though the rain still fell in great sheets, in comparison to this restless tumult, the rain seemed so insignificant that Peter hardly noticed it was raining at all.

He eased the ATV cautiously up to the fallen section of the road, slowed to a crawl and rode the ATV up as tight as he could to the rock face. For a second, the off-side wheels clawed at thin air, raced, then caught and the vehicle lurched, slewed—and he was across.

A movement caught his eye. He turned in his seat to see the 'Danger' marker topple into the torrent. Quicker than his eye could follow, it whipped out of sight to reappear a moment later fifty feet downstream as a splintered mass of white and red. Then it was gone.

Peter suppressed an involuntary shudder, thinking that, but for a very narrow margin, that might have been his own fate. Then he pressed the pedal to the floor and gunned the ATV until he rounded the corner and brought the Mission into sight.

Now, from this distance, the Mission's most distinctive feature was not the Tree but the river. More than five times its original width, it girdled the northern flank of the Mission in a vast, muddy arc that had taken with it an entire tract of land, some farm equipment and one of the outbuildings.

The massive rock which had perched above the river, was now half submerged beneath it, flecked with foam where the river battered angrily at its base.

Peter nodded in satisfaction. He wouldn't have wanted it any other way.

¤

Above the Mission, the woman sat on the hillside, snug and dry in her lean-to of bark and earth, a blanket of animal skins thrown around her shoulders. With a face as stiff as mahogany, she watched the beetle-like vehicle crawling through the rain towards the Mission. Closing her eyes, she began to chant. She was still chanting softly when Peter stopped the ATV outside the Mission gate and peered into the yard.

¤

Peter eyed the remnants of the bonfire warily; the ashes were black and sodden, driven into the muddy ground by the rain. The broken limb lay where it had fallen, stark across the wet ashes like a great black anaconda waiting to strike.

Peter moved cautiously with a slight hint at self-reproach at the absurdity of the situation. But Miya's fate was still too fresh in his mind for him to take any chances.

To his satisfaction, the loss of the limb had been a severe blow to the Tree—a good third of its trunk had been badly damaged. Running down it from top to bottom was a gaping wound from which oozed a thin, reddish sap, pooling in a sticky mess at the tree base.

Peter, reluctant to get too close, sidled around the fallen limb in a wide circle as he took stock of the yard: a tangled mass of dying branches littered the ground like dead soldiers strewn across a battle field. But though a good third of the Tree had been lost, the remainder stood ugly and erect—and somehow, thought Peter uneasily, *waiting*.

He got into the ATV, backed it up a few yards and then, accelerating as fast as he could, drove it through the gate, slewed around the fallen limb and headed for the far side of the Mission at full throttle. Even at maximum velocity, the ATV was painfully slow and Peter's nerves were taut as it crawled around the huge mass of the fallen limb.

Peter jammed the accelerator to the floor, fully expecting a mighty branch to come crashing down on the vehicle, crushing it like a cockroach. The engine whirred and protested; Peter's neck prickled with anticipation and…

…Nothing happened. The ATV reached the far side of the Mission without incident. Peter cut the engine and for a moment he sat there, gathering his whirling thoughts, sheepish at his own bout of nerves.

He looked up at the Tree and the sight of it obliterated the momentary feeling of sheepishness. Like an ugly black hand, it hovered above the Mission, ready to seize his home and crush the life from it. And, for the first time in his life, Peter was filled with such an intense loathing that he knew what it felt like to want to kill.

His mind flooded with images: Miranda's white face; Miya's battered body; the sightless, staring eyes of Ferris Ansell—and a red tide rose up inside him; hot, urgent. He stood up in the seat and, screaming at the top of his voice, hurled a stream of obscenities at the usurper that had tried to take his wife, kill his friend and drive him out of his home…

Finally, his anger spent, Peter whirled the ATV around and set out for the black rock, his heart full of grim resolve.

¤

On the hill above the Mission, the Indian woman heard the shrill cries of anger and hatred. She paused in her chanting, and smiled a slow, mahogany smile.

CHAPTER FORTY-ONE

Peter gazed across the thick, swirling torrent thoughtfully. To fall in was certain death; to be whipped away in a flash and battered on the rocks below.

His destination was the huge black rock, big as a house, which reared up from the muddy torrent on the opposite bank. It was no easy task; somehow he had to get his equipment across to the other side. He squatted down, drawing the hood of his anorak around him, and pondered the matter.

His eyes fell on the machine at his side and he patted it affectionately. Cleansed by the rain, it gleamed like new, bright yellow and red. A compressor —this he knew, this he could understand. Every machine was a docile beast ready to do Peter's bidding. Peter could solve any problem to do with machines. Well, here was a problem—a big problem—and this time, Peter and his Machine were going to fix it for good.

Peter gauged the distance across the muddy swirl by eye; it was at least a hundred yards. He trudged off through the rain, his feet and ankles slushing wetly through the grass, and returned a moment later with some extra-large hose couplings. He screwed them deftly onto the compressor hose. Despite the cold cutting into his hands, Peter worked quickly and soon the hose was long enough to reach across the river.

Scrabbling in the back of the ATV, he selected the equipment he needed—a hammer, drill, masonry bit, charges—and stuffed them into his backpack. He'd already strung up the fire caps, so all he had to do was to plant the charges and thumb-in the detonation caps. He grinned sardonically at the absurdity of his thought: That was *all* he had to do! He stared at the muddy torrent… It was the understatement of the year. First of all, he had to cross the river. A young madrone tree swirled into sight, smashed against the rock, splintered and whipped out of sight downstream. Well, he thought ruefully, this time Peter's *gotta* fix it—no way out.

Laying the harpoon gun on the ground, he coupled its hose to the compressor. With a few tugs of the ignition cord, the compressor started, roaring into life in a cloud of oily smoke. Peter tweaked the choke and carburetor expertly until the blue smoke disappeared and the machine purred away like a contented cat.

Praying that everything would hold, Peter set the compressor to maximum pressure. While the pressure was building, he began coiling a half-inch nylon rope in a very careful neat circle at the water's edge. His precision was by no means excessive: there was over one hundred and fifty yards of slack in the pile—but the slightest snarl in it and it would tangle and fail to reach the opposite bank.

He finished looping the rope and, satisfied with his work, tied one end to a grappling hook. The other end he knotted to the ring at the bottom of the harpoon. The compressor coughed and chugged. He glanced at the dial: the pressure was up; the needle hovered near the red. Mentally crossing his fingers, he opened the valve connecting the compressor tank to the harpoon gun. With a whoosh! of escaping air, the gun twitched in his hand. It bucked and swayed with a pressure it was never designed to withstand. But though it leaked at one joint with a high-pitched hiss, it held.

Propping his elbows on the edge of the ATV, Peter aimed the harpoon gun at a young scrub oak on the opposite bank of the river just behind the rock. Peter breathed in, out, and on the next intake, depressed the firing button. The harpoon leapt across the river, rope trailing. But the rope snagged and the harpoon plunged straight down into the water. The coil of rope sitting on the ground sang and puttered as it unwound rapidly. Desperately, Peter jumped on it and held it down with both feet. Grabbing the taut rope, he began hauling it in hand over hand. The harpoon surfaced and he pulled it in and stared at it ruefully. It was warped and bent as though a giant hand had crushed it. Well, he thought, one down, fourteen to go. Good job I bought a fair supply of harpoons...

He tried again—three more times. Each time he lost the harpoon to the river and he began to realize he was going about it in the wrong way.

Then he had an idea. Instead of the nylon rope, he looped a double thickness of thin fishing line on the harpoon ring. He sighted the gun at the oak and fired one more time. This time, unhampered by the long rope, the harpoon flew straight and true, thudding deep into the wet earth behind the scrub oak.

Knowing that too strong a tug would pull the harpoon out of the soft earth, Peter began to feed the fishing line through the harpoon eyelet with the gentlest of tugs. The line, invisible to the naked eye against the muddy river, nevertheless snaked across it, passed through the harpoon ring and back to Peter's hand. The nylon line grew taut as he pulled in the slack, and the rope at his side rose and began to inch through the air. Peter couldn't help but grin at the illusion. It was as if the rope inched through the air above the river with no visible means of support.

He stopped grinning when the rope, on reaching the eyelet, snagged. A worried Peter tugged gently. The harpoon quivered and loosened slightly in the soft earth. Peter grimaced; he didn't want to pull the harpoon out. Taking up the slack on the fishing line, he tugged again, holding his breath. This time, the rope popped through the eyelet and curved around, heading back towards him inch by inch. Peter hauled the nylon fishing line hand over hand, until the rope finally arrived at his side of the river without mishap.

He grunted in satisfaction: "Whew! Done it!"

The white rope now looped across the river, draped over the branches of the scrub oak, ran through the eyelet of the harpoon and doubled back across the river to where Peter held both ends in his hands.

Peter fastened one end of the rope to the ATV, the other end to the grappling hook. Lashing the rope and the grappling hook to a chunk of two-by-six, he hurled them as far as he could across the river. The bundle was snatched downstream immediately. Peter saw the harpoon on the opposite bank judder in the ground as the current snatched the buoyed grappling hook downstream and jerked on the rope. Peter hauled in the rope, hand over hand, as fast as he could and, to his relief, managed to pull the grappling hook up onto the opposite bank.

The harpoon suddenly gave, pulling free from the earth. But, no matter; the rope was still hooked through the scrub oak's branches. Swiftly, Peter pulled at the rope until the grappling hook snaked up into the branches of the tree and, mercifully, caught.

Peter untied the rope from the ATV and glanced around, searchingly. A little further along the bank of the river stood a tall Californian Bay. Keeping the rope taut, Peter walked backwards to the tree and, hauling himself up into the lower branches, looped the rope as high around the trunk as he could.

He scrabbled up through the crisp, dark-green foliage, his nostrils full of the crushed leaf smell, sharp and tangy; a heady menthol. He crouched on a stout branch and tied the rope tight around the trunk. Wiping his hands on his trousers, he tentatively lowered his weight onto the rope. With a 'twang!", it gave. He grunted, and to tighten the rope, wrapped it around a branch for security and tried again. This time as he lowered his weight onto the rope, he kept a wary eye on the grappling hook snagged in the branches of the scrub oak on the far side of the river. The rope sagged; but even as he leant his full weight on it, the grappling hook held.

Well, this is it, he thought. He ran through a mental checklist, remembered the compressor hose and, dropping to the ground, he tied a thin, nylon line to it. Swinging the heavy backpack onto his shoulders, he went back to the Californian Bay, shinnied up onto the first branch and contemplated the task that lay before him.

Twenty feet above the swirling surface of the river, the rope rode straight and taut across. Peter eyed its arrow-straight line ruefully, knowing it would give as soon as he put his full weight on it. He wondered how far down it would go once he was in the middle—and that was the point of no return. Well…he'd just have to find out, he thought.

Snagging a short safety line to his backpack, Peter eased himself out onto the tree limb, belly down, then, clutching the rope, he swung out into the air.

The rope dropped a few feet; the trunk of the young scrub oak bent; the grappling hook held. Peter, still hanging over the solid ground, waited a moment until the rope stopped swaying then, as rapidly as possible, he began to swing hand over hand along the rope. With a conscious effort, he resisted the desire to look down. But though he did not look, the river made its presence felt as an angry roar beneath his feet, berating this insect man for defying it. Then, with the sheer effort of the climb, Peter's world shrank to the pain in his arms as he gripped, swung, gripped, swung. With every swing, the pain in his arms increased and Peter was only halfway across when he realized he wasn't going make it. His hands were raw and the dull ache between his shoulder blades had become a silent shriek of agony. Desperately he hung in midstream, too exhausted to move forwards or backwards.

He seemed to hang for an eternity, deliberating what to do, when his dangling foot accidently dipped into the rapidly-moving water. Peter was jerked sideways as if he'd been kicked by a horse. Pain wrenched through his shoulders and he cried out loud as the backpack sagged, pulling him down with its relentless tug. No, he thought frantically, he was going to fall!! His hands were losing sensation; they were slipping from the rope, his palms raw and bleeding. His foot caught the muddy torrent again. He was flipped sideways, juddering and bouncing on the rope. Reflex made him grip the rope tightly in a final desperate attempt to hang on.

Then, with a desperate lunge, Peter swung his feet up into the air, wrapped both legs around the rope and dangled upside down, both arms and legs around the rope. The pain in his shoulders subsided immediately and Peter let out a gasp of relief. But relief was only momentary. The ache in his shoulders told him that this new position would not offer him respite for long, so he began to move forward again. Dangling upside down like a sloth—and just as slow—Peter inched painfully across the river towards the opposite bank.

A sudden noise made Peter stop. He craned his neck just in time to see the grappling hook vault through the tree branches with a tearing sound—and the rope went slack. He hit the water and a great icy hand snatched him and hurtled him a hundred yards downstream before he'd even realized he'd fallen.

A terrible roar filled his ears as he bounced up and down on his back, bewildered by his viewpoint: a jumbled montage of sky, water and rock. Then he realized he wasn't moving downstream at all but was juddering up and down on the water in the same place like an anchored watersled, smacking against the surface with a repeated force that threatened to knock him senseless. The grappling hook had somehow re-snagged onto something and Peter was now strung out at the apex of a neat 'V', thrumming up and down on his back like a hooked fish.

He went under, but immediately surfaced again, coughing and spluttering, and as the pounding resumed again, Peter knew he couldn't take this punishment for long. The sheer speed of the water kept him bouncing on its surface, but the pounding was taking its toll and he began to black out sporadically.

His vision began to dim; red circles formed behind his eyelids and he made a desperate decision: He reached above his head and clicked open the release on the safety line.

Twang! Peter was propelled downstream like an arrow from a taut bow string. He went under, surfaced and impacted a nest of branches that cracked and snapped, raking his body with cruel force. He grabbed out wildly, missed, then passed out again.

Peter came to in a panic and realized he was wedged in the stationary branches of a large madrone that lay half out of the water. Though its roots were still embedded in the bank, the madrone was playing a fierce game of tug-of-war with the river. The river, with relentless force, was slowly dragging the madrone further into its path. Even as he watched, the trunk of the madrone creaked and slithered across the muddy bank, sucked further into the river's grip. Heedless of his torn hands and nails, Peter hauled himself through the branches with a speed born of desperation. Finally he felt solid earth beneath his palms. He sagged on his belly and, with the rain battering his head and shoulders, blacked out again, just as the madrone slipped off the bank and swirled out of sight into the dirty brown torrent...

Someone was tugging at his backpack. Peter peered up through bleary eyes. It was a piece of fishing line—the line attached to the end of the compressor hose. It had held. With his remaining strength, Peter wound the line clumsily around a young sapling and then sank back, spent.

¤

The Indian woman went back to her place in the bark and grass lean-to on the hill above the Mission. She was wet through; her legs smeared with dirt and mud. Scrabbling around in a woven bag, she located a small packet and unfolded it carefully to reveal a pungent-smelling salve. Gingerly, she began to smear it on her torn and bloody hands. Gradually the balm took effect and the fire in her hands began to die away. Opening her hands, she studied the fresh rope burns and nodded in satisfaction; they would heal. Then she resumed her cross-legged vigil, staring at the bedraggled figure lying insensate on the river bank below.

¤

Peter stirred and raised himself up on one elbow. His face hurt. He put his hand up to his jaw and winced with pain—he could hardly move it. Then he stared at his hands; lacerated in a dozen places, red blood oozed across his palms, watery and thin in the driving rain. He examined his thigh. His left trouser leg was ripped open, revealing a long, bloody gash.

Despite the pain in his jaw, Peter was filled with jubilation. He'd done it! He'd crossed the river! The realization of his success lent him a fresh wave of strength and, crawling to his feet, he began to pick his way crab-fashion along the steep bank towards the rock and the scrub oak.

At the scrub oak, Peter stopped, puzzled. The grappling hook was wrapped twice around the base of the tree, firmly anchored. He shook his head in wonder. He'd seen the grappling hook jerk free with his own eyes! This was well nigh impossible! What a fluke! Christ, he thought, if it hadn't happened, he'd have certainly been a goner! He shielded his eyes from the rain and gazed across the misty fields to the Mission and the brooding mass that hovered over it like a tarantula.

What a charmed life! he thought. This was the third time he'd almost had it. Peter Riley, who'd never suffered anything more than a cut knee or blistered palm! He grinned and immediately winced ruefully—his jaw was, without a doubt, fractured. He touched it gingerly; it was a huge, swollen lump. Well, he thought, no time for mere details like broken jaws, you don't jump into the fire then complain about the smoke. Miranda's image flooded into his mind and, with a brief burst of exultation, Peter raised his fist and shouted out loud to the sky. "Yeah, I'm going to do it! I'm going to do it!! Someone up there likes me!"

He never knew how true it was...

CHAPTER FORTY-TWO

The safety line bit into Peter's waist, chafing through the thick layers of clothing.

He was drilling the last hole. He positioned the gleaming drill-bit against the wet rock, leant on the air-drill with all his might and thumbed the 'Start'. The drill whined and protested, biting into the granite with faint puffs of smoke. Just inches away from Peter's feet, the water snarled and licked like a hungry animal waiting for him to make the slightest mistake.

Peter was crouched in the lee of the huge rock, his weight on the taut safety line fastened to the scrub oak. The air hose arced gracefully above the muddy, brown water and snaked over the opposite bank to the compressor. The compressor broke into an intermittent chugging as the pressure dropped, but Peter did not even glance up. He concentrated on the air-drill, forcing the protesting bit into the granite by leaning his whole weight on it.

It was tough going; his hands were numb; his chest burning with the pressure of the drill handle against it. Despite the pain, he pressed harder with his chest until, eventually, the bit sank deeper into the wet rock and finally it was deep enough. With a sigh of relief, he slung the drill onto the bank and rubbed his bruised chest. He fished about in the backpack and, taking out the charges, he tamped each one into the holes he'd drilled and carefully secured their detonation caps.

It was slow going. He glanced up at the grayish sky; it was nearly ten a.m. on the second day of his labors and he still hadn't finished, nor had the rain abated.

Hauling himself up on the rope, he climbed up the bank, his feet sucking and gurgling in the wet earth. He reached the scrub oak and unclipped his safety line.

He had another decision to make. He gazed broodingly at the swirling brown mass that separated him from the opposite bank. The line, now carrying the twin loops of the air hose and an electrical wire, was still stretched in a low arc across the river. He thought about it briefly: the rope was now firmly affixed at either end but... He shook his head. No sir, he was going around; he wasn't going to chance it again, even though the line was as steady as a rock.

Then he hesitated. Going around meant cutting across country some eight miles to the County Road, crossing the bridge and trudging back again—a round trip of sixteen miles in all. It was going to take some time.

Torn between the two alternatives—one dangerous; the other time-consuming—he equivocated, weighing up the possibilities. As he did, a dead animal—a cow, a dog, he couldn't be sure—suddenly bucked up on a crest of water, smacked dully against the base of the rock and whipped out of sight. He was left with a brief impression of staring white eyes and bloated flesh. Any doubts about his decision disappeared in an instant: He was definitely taking the long road—no matter how long.

Slinging his backpack over his shoulder, he threaded his way through the wet manzanita and headed cross-country towards the County Road...

From the safety of the workshop, Peter eyed the Tree. He was cold, wet and tired. In some vague way, he had the feeling he was working against time. The journey across country had taken a lot out of him, but he was on a roll; it was unthinkable to stop now—even though the events of the next few hours were totally unforeseeable.

For Peter, this was something of a precedent. Practical Peter was accustomed to working within a set of known parameters and here he was setting up a situation in which all hell may break loose and he didn't even know what particular form that hell might take. With a self-reminder that in his acceptance of the Tree as adversary, logic had been thrown out of the window, Peter pushed his misgivings aside. He was going to do what he had to do—and let the morrow bring whatever it would...

Spitting on his hands, Peter began hauling the five-gallon containers of gasoline out into the yard one by one, grouping them around the pile of ropes, tackle and pulleys already stacked there.

The centerpiece of the equipment pile was a curiously archaic device. With its polished rosewood surface and shiny brass connections, it looked like a quaint piece of Victoriana. But its quaintness belied its deadly functional simplicity: The box was an old but perfectly functional detonator. From its center rose a shiny brass plunger; twin wires ran through the wet grass. They were long, traveling the whole width of the field. They were looped over the rope across the water. On the opposite side of the river, the wires were connected to the charges sunk in the rock. As a precaution, Peter had pulled one of the connecting wires off its brass ferrule on the detonator—he did not want a premature explosion.

Peter eased the last of the five-gallon containers into place, wrinkling his nose at the rank smell of the spilled gasoline.

He set the harpoon gun on a tripod to give it a little more stability, slotted a harpoon into the gun barrel and looped a thin nylon line through the harpoon tip. Kneeling down, he sighted along the gun—it was aimed it at the Tree's trunk.

Peter was half amused by his own precautions; but, having decided to act, Practical Peter was taking no chances. He wasn't going to get anywhere near that Tree—not ever again.

Carefully sighting the gun, he pressed the trigger. With a hiss, the harpoon leapt forward and buried itself into the trunk with a dull thunk!. Peter almost expected the Tree to emit a howl like a wounded banshee. But nothing happened. Getting as bad as Miranda, he thought wryly. But the self-reproach was without conviction: the memory of Miya's burnt and battered body was still far too vivid to be a comfortable thought.

He slotted another harpoon into the gun and fired again. Thunk! The second harpoon thudded into the Tree two feet from the first. It was an easy shot, but Peter wanted to ensure a fairly even spacing.

Gradually Peter moved in a wide arc around the Tree, loading and firing the harpoons until he'd plunked ten of them into the Tree's trunk. They encircled the black-green trunk, bristling like a primitive necklace.

Hands on his hips, Peter surveyed his handiwork dispassionately. That had been easy; the next step was a tad more tricky.

He tied one end of the thin line to a nylon rope, as he'd learnt to do at the river, gently pulled the rope along with the line until the rope passed through the eyelet of the harpoon and hauled it back again across the intervening space. Still holding the rope, Peter mounted a low step-ladder and tied the rope around an eight-foot post he'd firmly embedded in the earth. He plucked the rope experimentally; it let out a taut twang. Satisfied, he descended the ladder and carefully hooked the handle of a five-gallon drum onto the pulley. The rope sagged beneath the weight of the heavy drum, and the pulley lurched and swayed close to the post.

Mounting the ladder again, Peter began working the five-gallon drum along the rope in gentle jerks. The pulley swayed and inched along the rope, rasping and squealing. The drum progressed forward in a series of jerky stops and starts until, finally, it bumped against the distant tree trunk. Peter released the tension on the rope and lowered the distant drum gently to the ground at the base of the Tree. Then, by dint of several flicks on the rope, he managed to disengage it from the drum's hooked wire support. Mounting the ladder, he repeated the whole process with the next oil drum.

It was a slow process but it was safer than getting near the Tree. Despite his fatigue, Peter never took his eyes away from the Tree for more than a second. Nor did he ever get anywhere near any of the overhanging branches. Once during his labors, the Tree moved, the branches tossing up and down. Peter froze, ready to run. Then it stopped and Peter decided it had been the wind. Nevertheless, his hands were clammy and shaking and he had some difficulty handling the next pulley.

Eventually, he lowered the last drum into place, and the Tree, bristling with a collar of harpoons, was surrounded by a rough semicircle of gasoline cans leaning against its base.

Peter sloshed through the wet grass to the edge of the surging river one more time and checked the detonator wiring. Everything seemed O.K., but he realized his stomach was a knot of tension and his neck was stiff and aching: It was almost time.

At a safe distance from the Tree, he circled back to the ATV, climbed in, reversed it with a noisy roar and drove it to within easy access of the Mission gate.

Just a few too many unknowns, a few too many variables, thought Peter darkly. He didn't like it. He swung his leg over the edge of the ATV and, skirting the fallen limb, approached the huddled pile of equipment.

He was tired; fatigue was beginning to mist his eyes; every bone in his body ached; and his broken jaw was a dull, throbbing fire. But he rubbed his eyes and, mustering his strength, began to fill empty soda bottles with gasoline using a plastic funnel. The '60s strike again, he thought as he stuffed the mouth of a bottle with a rag and hefted it in his hand. The time-honored Molotov cocktail.

In this manner, he manufactured six of the crude incendiary devices. Satisfied with his work, he stood up and took one final look around.

Across the fields, the river was a great brown muddy gush. The sierra hill was almost lost to sight where sky and earth melded in a bleak grayness that arched over Peter's head, giving him the claustrophobic sensation of standing under a vast dirty-gray bowl. It was a mistake to stop. His awareness of his body redoubled: his aching temples; the throb of his broken jaw; the stabs of pain from his gashed thigh; the weariness in his joints. It was oppressive. Peter was filled with a sudden yearning for clarity and renewal; the warm sun; spring flowers; the buzz of insects. He recognized this as a symptom of his fatigue, took a deep breath and tried to shake the feeling off. It was too late to stop now.

"Peter, you look so tired!"

He whirled, his heart racing.

It was Miranda. She stood, guiltily defiant, in a raincoat and galoshes far too big for her. Nevertheless, her face was determined. "I came to help," she said quietly.

Peter opened his mouth to protest. A flood of accusations crowded to his mind: dire warnings; ire; exasperation. But the words met the tide of sensation rising in his breast, ebbed and receded. He was simply glad to see her. He took two swift steps forward and she was in his arms, sobbing quietly. Holding her very, very tight, he murmured meaningless words of consolation.

Miranda pulled away gently and gave a great sniff. "Oh, I'm sorry, Peter. Sorry! I came to help not to…fall apart. You know, I've been eating my heart out, Peter! I've been so worried! God, I couldn't let you do this by yourself, love."

He looked into her large blue eyes; frowned at the dark circles that rimmed them. Once again his breast welled with the familiar feeling of amazement that such a lovely creature could be as enchanted by him (so it seemed) as he by her. He cradled her head against his shoulder and, staring up at the gaunt, black claw of the Tree, said: "We can do it—and we'll do it together." Miranda hugged him wordlessly, trying to stop the tears streaming down her face. "Cry if you want to—it's O.K. for now," he whispered.

She cried, but not for long.

When she stopped crying, Peter explained to her exactly what it was they had to do...

CHAPTER FORTY-THREE

Raising the rifle to his shoulder, Peter glanced at Miranda. "Ready?"
Miranda, with a Molotov cocktail in her hand, nodded.
Peter squeezed the trigger and the rifle bucked against his shoulder. He fired again, the shots loud against the hiss of the rain.
Gasoline gushed in twin spouts from the holed container at the base of the Tree. Peter began to fire more rapidly, ejecting the brass cartridges with dexterous flicks of the lever, blasting away at the other containers. Gasoline jetted in steady streams from the bullet holes. Despite the rain, the air was filled with its acrid stench as it gushed out and pooled around the base of the Tree.
"O.K.!" shouted Peter, "Now!!"
Miranda flicked a lighter, holding it close to the gray-soaked rag in the soda bottle.
Nothing happened. She cursed. She flicked the lighter again.
"Hurry up!!" cried Peter, "We don't want the rain to dilute the gas!!"
"It won't work!!! Oh God!!" muttered Miranda, flicking the lighter again and again with a nervous, fumbling motion.
Peter dropped the rifle and grabbed the bottle from her. "Here, try both hands."
Holding the lighter in both hands, Miranda flicked it with her thumbs. It worked.
A yellow-black flame suddenly coiled up from the rag. Peter, caught off guard, yelled and tossed it reflexively toward the tree trunk. It fell and smashed onto the ground twenty yards short. A sheet of yellow fire rippled across the ground but failed to reach the pool of gas.
"Shit!!" said Peter. "Quick, hand me another. We'll have to get closer—!"
He was cut short by a deafening roar. He was flung forward, taking Miranda with him. They fell in a sprawling heap, Peter laying across Miranda's body. He raised himself on his elbows, half turned and peered over his shoulder.
A great blast of heat slapped his face. He shielded his eyes and let out a whoop: The tree trunk was girdled by a wall of yellow flame. "Got the bastard!!" he screamed above the roar of the flames, "Quick, Miranda, the

other bottles!!"

Miranda grabbed another Molotov cocktail and hurled it into the blaze. Peter followed with two other bottles in quick succession. The bottles exploded in a series of whumphs! Fire rippled along the length of the fallen limb. The air was suddenly hot in their lungs and their faces prickled with heat.

"Got it!! Got it!!" shouted Miranda excitedly.

The flames roared and hissed around the base of the Tree, licking up to engulf the lower branches in an orange corona.

"We got it!! We got it!!!" screamed Miranda, dancing up and down in an unholy glee.

Peter's heart was hammering. "No," he shouted, "This time we do it Miya's way. Fire isn't enough."

"Fire and water! Fire and water!!!" screamed Miranda, her face demonic in the flare.

"Yeah!! And that bastard Tree is going to get it. C'mon, start the ATV!!!"

Clumsy in her galoshes, Miranda flip-flopped out of sight behind the oily flames on the burning tree limb. Peter heard the ATV chug faintly into life behind the wall of flame. Then Miranda, her face blackened with soot, re-emerged through a cloud of oily, black smoke. "O.K.!!" she shouted, "I'm ready when you want!!"

Peter nodded and, kneeling over to the detonator, re-attached the loose wire. He twisted the brass screw down on the terminal thread. and gave it a final tighten. It was ready to fire. All he had to do was depress the plunger.

Miranda's scream rent the air behind him: "Oh God, Peter!! Look!!!"

Peter leapt up. Miranda's eyes were wide with horror; her face garish in the orange and yellow flames. He followed her pointed finger. With an exclamation, Peter began to back away instinctively.

The Tree was moving.

Beneath Peter's feet, the ground trembled as the huge limbs shook and juddered. The juddering increased, rattling Peter's teeth. He fought for balance, clapping his hands over his ears as an unearthly keening whine shredded the air, assaulting his ears.

In a grotesque parody of movement, the black limbs danced and swayed, flailing up and down like a human being, as if the Tree was trying to beat out the flames.

"Look out!!!" cried Peter.

An entire section of the tree limb, beating at the air in agonized strictures, broke loose. It whirled through the air, impacted the Mission wall and fell with a rending of broken branches.

"Get back, Miranda!! For Christ's sake!!" screamed Peter and, desperately, he flung the last Molotov cocktail into the flames.

Sparks shot up from the circle of fire, fed by the freshly-fallen limb that lay broken and splintered around the base of the Tree.

"Peter!!!"coughed Miranda, her eyes red-rimmed and streaming, "Hurry up!!" The Tree writhed and heaved like an agonized animal, "Do it!!!!" urged Miranda.

Peter backed away and stumbled over the detonator. He knelt down, coughing and spluttering. His eyes were streaming with tears and he had to fumble blindly for the detonator handle. "Christ, where is it?!!!" he muttered frantically.

Up in the higher limbs, the flames vaulted with a sudden crackling and the creature skittered along the branches, leaping from one scorching limb to the other. It raced to the end of the largest branch and hopped back and forth in agitation. Then the entire branch fell into the flames in a great cascade of sparks. The creature made a desperate leap in midair, landed on the ground with a thud, rolled and scuttled into the concealing smoke…

The heat was so intense Peter could hardly breathe. Blinded by the smoke, his chest heaving, he resisted the urge to run. Then his hand suddenly encountered something hard and unyielding: the detonator! His hands tightened on it; he bunched his shoulders…

But before he could depress the handle, something struck him on the chest, knocked him sprawling and mounted his inert body.

Peter glimpsed something that looked like a giant crustacean; its carapace cracked and pitted with old burn scars. It reared over him and he caught a brief flash of its maggoty underside before it clamped over his face. He seized it with both hands, terrified, trying to pull it off as hundreds of white tendrils wriggled and probed at his flesh. Then something wet and sticky coiled around his neck and tightened. Worm-like tendrils forced their way into his throat. He could neither see nor breathe. His face was plunged into a seething, wriggling, fetid mass; his nostrils filled with a peculiar stench—a mixture of earth, decay, burnt flesh and scorched wood.

The tentacle tightened around his neck. He scrabbled to get his hand under it, but the wriggling white worms continued their frantic probing into his nostrils, into his mouth, at his eyes, his ears.

Miranda screamed again and again as Peter rolled on the ground clawing at the hideous mass clamped over his face. Without thinking, she grabbed a shovel and jabbed it at the creature's scorched carapace. The creature let out a peculiar bubbling noise, but its grip tightened.

Miranda went totally beserk.

Screaming and yelling incoherently, she jabbed the thing over and over using the sharp point of the shovel. Peter stopped struggling and went limp. With all the force of sheer terror, Miranda swung the shovel in a mighty arc, striking the creature from the side, barely missing Peter's head. The creature lost its grip and rolled off Peter's face. With a scream of rage, Miranda brought the edge of the shovel down in a mighty blow that cleaved open the creature's carapace. A gout of greenish liquid gushed out of the split, mixed with a spurt of bright red. The two liquids ran together in a sticky stream; the creature jerked spasmodically and the tentacle slackened.

Peter's chest heaved; then he was breathing again, coughing and spluttering; he choked in a lungful of air, his hand on his throat. Through a red haze he heard a high-pitched noise and he squinted through tear-blurred eyes to see an insane Miranda lashing at the creature, her face contorted in a fury that was barely human.

Then the ground reared up between them and Peter was knocked backwards by a great, knotted mass. He tried to scrabble to his feet but the earth shifted beneath him again. Like a subterranean creature, a huge gnarled root burst up through the soil. Peter screamed: "Miranda!!!!" But he couldn't see her; the space between them was suddenly full of quivering roots which were rearing up through the wet earth like black-green snakes.

For the first time in thousands of years, Tree moved; in the throes of its agony it moved as a final, desperate act for survival.

The sides of the Mission collapsed and folded like a cardboard box as huge knotted roots tore through the earth beneath it. The swimming pool buckled and warped, thrusting up a small mountain of blue tile. The Tree flexed once, twice, then reared up on its entire root system and a vast underground network tore itself from the earth, extending far beyond the Mission and half way across the river. Like a giant, predatory insect, Tree rose and showed itself in all the terror and might of its enormous bulk.

Clinging to the underside of a huge root, Peter rode up into the air, disorientated by the bucking earth and the tumultuous noise. His hands slipped and he fell, dropping with a thud into a moist trough of heaving, white roots. He jerked away, rolled, and encountered something warm and dirt-covered. It was Miranda. "Miranda?!!! Miranda!!" Frantically he brushed the dirt from her eyes and mouth.

Miranda coughed up a mouthful of black dirt and sat up, eyes wide with shock. But, nevertheless, alive.

Peter's foot caught something solid. It was the detonator. The earth heaved and fearful of losing it, Peter cried out: "Miranda!! The detonator!!"

But Miranda was staring down at something that lay in the trough of earth a few feet away against the white roots—a squirming crab thing that oozed red and green.

"Miranda!!" shouted Peter. He scurried forward on all fours and grabbed the detonator before it was lost in the heaving roots.

Without taking her eyes away from the creature, Miranda cried out, anguished.

"What?!!!" shouted Peter still scrabbling for the detonator handle.

She shouted it again, louder: "Do it now!! Please!! For God's sake,

Peter!"

Praying that the line had held, Peter rolled onto his belly and pressed the plunger. It slid slickly into its socket and Peter sagged across it, spent. For a second, nothing happened. Then, from the distant hillside, there came a deafening roar as the rock exploded...

The lower half of the rock disintegrated into a cloud of smoke and orange flame, hurling tons of granite fragments high into the air. The crown of the rock slumped and slid into the muddy river. The airborne fragments followed, raining down into the water. The huge rock slid forward with a ponderous grace and then toppled over, blocking the river completely.

The river battered against this obstacle like a thwarted beast. But the gigantic rock blocked it irrevocably and, with a hiss of rage, the river changed course and seethed across the Mission grounds in a twenty-foot high wall of solid water. It smashed through the outbuildings, carrying them with it, then swept over the Mission in a tide of refuse: broken trees; torn buildings; and crumpled fencing.

Peter had just finished roping himself to Miranda when the water hit them. They were hurled upwards, borne on the muddy tide and smacked against the bole of the Tree. Peter's breath was knocked out of his body; he fought for consciousness. Then flood hit fire and his vision was obscured by the huge clouds of steam that gushed up from the flames.

Like a predator seeking its prey, the flood water eddied uncertainly around the yard. Huge waves slopped between the arches of the roots seeking an avenue of escape. They found it and, with a roar of triumph, surged out of the yard and down the Mission road.

Peter clutched Miranda, unable to fight the force of the water. They were carried helplessly on the crest of a muddy wave towards the Mission gates. They went under, coughing and spluttering. Something hit Peter in the back with a sickening thud. He scrabbled at it feebly, then realized it was the wooden sign from the gate. Peter seized it with both hands and, kicking desperately, he managed to pull himself across it. "Hold on!!" he yelled. Miranda seized the wooden sign and, clinging desperately to its bobbing mass, they were born on the muddy tide along the Mission road.

With a roar that sounded like jubilation, the surging water turned abruptly to the right and cascaded down the rocks to join its brother in the ravine below, back to its original course.

Peter lay amid a tangled heap of mud, broken trees and roots. He stirred feebly and raised himself up on one elbow. Miraculously, they had been thrown up onto a small hillock at the side of the road. Miranda, face down, lay a few feet away, still roped to him. Her clothes were torn and bedraggled; her boots gone; and across her legs lay the Mission sign, pinning her to the ground.

Peter pushed himself upright just in time to see the river join its old course, tumbling thunderously down the ravine, bearing huge chunks of burnt and broken timber. "Miranda! Wake up!! Miranda!" he urged, shaking her shoulder desperately. He parted her hair where it was coiled around her neck in a matted swathe and, with trembling fingers, felt for a pulse. She was alive!

Miranda stirred, then sat up as if waking from a dream, gazing around in bewilderment. They were beached at the base of the mountain which reared above the Mission road. Beside them, the river, seeking its lowest point, tumbled in a muddy cascade into the ravine. Miranda stared at it, mesmerized. Then her eyes lighted on Peter's face and she realized what they had accomplished. She threw her arms around his neck and began to murmur his name over and over again into the sodden material of his ragged coat.

"Look," he whispered, "Look, Miranda! Look what we did!"

Still holding onto him fearfully, Miranda gazed across the Mission lands.

From the sierra hill to where they sat, the water lay in a great unbroken sheet. The Mission building was completely submerged, its presence only revealed by eddies on the water's surface. The new river now ran straight and true along the path of the submerged Mission road at the base of the mountain.

Miranda was staring at the Tree.

If the Tree had been mighty, the root system was mightier. The scorched and blackened branches, frozen in an impotent gesture clutching at the air, seemed feeble compared to the vast root system that rose up from the water like a giant banyan.

The root system wasn't *on* the Mission land—it *was* the Mission land. Its huge bulk stretched from the mountain to the base of the sierra hill, fully a mile in diameter. Reared up out of the water, its roots formed caves, inlets and arches through which the river swirled and sucked, tearing greedily at the helpless Tree. Like an ancient beast in its death throes, the Tree shuddered as the rabid water tore at the top soil, carrying tons of the precious black earth into the ravine.

The Tree's desperate act of survival was its own death blow. The tender roots, torn from their haven in the soil, wriggled feebly beneath the water, vainly seeking purchase. But the water forced its way into every crevice until, with a ponderous grace, the Tree succumbed. It settled, slipped sideways and slipped again with the faintest of noises; it could have been a moan or a sigh—or even just the wind. But one thing was certain: Tree was dying.

The huge mass slipped again, canting at an acute angle so that some of its charred upper branches dipped into the muddy brown water. Shards of wood and splintered branches beat against its blackened limbs in dull, slopping thuds.

Then, with an agonized screech, the Tree toppled over and fell into the water, tearing vast tracts of muddy earth with it. The water, as if incensed, rose in a fresh tide of anger. A wall of water rose around the drowning Leviathan and swept towards the submerged County Road, a filthy morass of charred bark and splintered wood.

"Let's get out of here!" shouted Peter, "C'mon! We'll be swept away!!" He pushed away the sign with a grunt of effort and helped Miranda to her feet.

Miranda stared down at the sign. The wood surface, cleansed by the river, glistened smooth and wet; the letters etched bold and clear. Miranda mouthed the word dumbly: "'Calavera'."

"C'mon!!" yelled Peter, "Miranda, let's go before it hits!! C'mon!!"

Miranda stared at the sign, glassy-eyed, until Peter pulled her away forcibly. They scrambled up the bank seconds before the river roared over the spot where they had been lying. As if angry at missing its prey, it threw gobs of mud and broken branches upwards, splattering the retreating couple. They reached the safety of a narrow ledge and threw themselves on its stony surface, exhausted.

The river raced beneath them. Replete with filth and refuse from the dying Tree, it tumbled over the ravine onto the rocks below with a mighty roar.

To Peter, it was as though all the filth was being swept away from their land, from their life and deposited in the ravine to be carried far, far away. He put his arm around Miranda and they sat with their legs dangling above the new river, staring at the Tree which lay in the middle of a reddy-brown lake like a toppled giant.

Miranda pointed at the heavy oak sign caught by one end on the river bank below. The sign began to swing off the bank, dragged by a tide that surged along the ground where just moments before Peter and Miranda had been. Miranda looked at Peter and mouthed the word: "Calavera?"

"We never knew," said Peter.

Miranda said it again: "Calavera?" as if she didn't dare say it out loud.

Peter nodded dully. "Yep, that's it," he whispered, "It is Spanish and it means 'Death's Head'."

Miranda took Peter's hand in hers as the sign—all that was left of the old Mission—was finally dragged into the water and thrown into the ravine and rendered into a splintered mass by the raging water. Miranda lifted her face to the sky, and although he could not distinguish her tears from the cleansing rainfall, Peter knew that she was crying.

As the rain ran over Miranda's face, washing away the filth of the Mission yard, Peter held her tightly and spoke of the creature that had leapt from the Tree; asked if she knew what manner of being it could have been; asked if Miya had ever talked of such a thing.

Miranda could not tell him; not now, not ever. Instead, she clung to him, lifting her head to the cleansing rain and sobbing as she never had before.

And for once, Peter knew that her tears were answer enough, so he let the matter be and rocked Miranda like a child until the rain had washed away all the filth and her hair hung limp and clean in strands of dully-shining gold and her face was pure again.

Eventually, she stopped crying and just clung to him. They stayed like that for a long time. And she never had to tell him that the creature was their own child, horribly mutated by the Tree's rabid toxins...

¤

On the hillside above the Mission, the Indian girl stood impassive, staring at the submerged Mission and the giant, water-logged corpse of Tree. And in the manner of one who loves all Life, whatever its purpose, she muttered and chanted Tree's secret name and, in a final gesture, she lifted her arms to Sky, Rain and Fire, telling the tale of Tree's life and asking forgiveness for its death.

When she had finished, she broke down her lean-to and, lighting some leaves, scattered the ground with ashes from the smoking herbs. Then, throwing a blanket around her shoulders, she strode off across the hills to seek out her father and share the news.

¤

Like a living force, River raged along the ravine, over-running its sloping banks by some thirty feet. It tore hungrily at the trees, ripped away groves of manzanita; lofty madrones fought vainly with the current and succumbed, adding to the crackling wall of detritus.

For seven miles River ran without loss of power, sometimes paralleling the County Road, sometimes engulfing it. At the Widow Jenkins' property, it swung around in a wide arc, taking giant bites from the dark-brown earthen banks. Vast chunks of green-topped earth collapsed into the water as River crept closer and closer to the Widow's house, threatening to undermine the very foundations.

But here there was provision for flood. A concrete breakwater jutted out from the banks, laden with rocks, stones, rusting car bodies, old bedsteads and a wall of concrete sacks placed there by the foresight of the County authorities.

River dashed up against this motley bulwark, failed to dislodge it and, chastened, swirled around it and emptied into the vast bowl of Miller's Valley, a flat, undercut plain that demarked the progress of a vast glacier millions of years before. There, the River spent its force and ebbed out to become a placid lake fed by tributaries from the rocks all around it.

In the summer it would dwindle and diminish to a large pond where cows and horses could munch in a leisurely fashion on the succulent green weeds at the water's edge. But for now it was a huge brown lake, restless and turbulent, tugged hither and thither by the currents that seethed into it from the flood waters.

It was here that the creature was finally deposited.

Battered, bleeding, oozing its sticky life fluids, the creature, almost torn in two, scrabbled into the quieter shallows.

Feebly, it squirmed through the mud like a giant crustacean and surfaced on the edge of Widow Jenkins' land. The creature dragged itself painfully, inch by inch, oozing a thin stream of green and red. It reached land and toppled over into a ditch, its white underside bloodied and wriggling like a hundred dying maggots. It heaved frantically with its dying strength and, managing to right itself, it crawled into the undergrowth at the edge of the Widow's garden.

It didn't get very far. Its movements became slower and slower. Reaching a patch of mulch by the side of the white clapboard cottage, it stopped altogether. With a weak spasm, the creature settled into the mulch, tried to move forward once more but failed. Then, with a final gush of its life fluids trickling into the moist earth, it died, mewling piteously.

Inside the house, the Widow, dozing in her armchair in front of the fire, raised her head at the strange noise. Then the wind buffeted the house, she stretched her legs, warm and cozy, yawned and nodded off to sleep again...

Trudging down the sandy road with his arm around a sodden and dishevelled Miranda, Peter chortled happily. Miranda glanced at him, puzzled.

"What is it, Pete?"

"Hell," he said, "You know something?! I've just had a good idea! Remember what you said about not being grown up but acting like a kid when you moved to a new place?"

"Yes, I remember it well," she said with a wry face, "That seems so long ago."

"Well, that's it," he said. "To hell with the Mission! We've got enough money. If there's one thing you've taught me, it's this: let's go play! To hell with clearing up that mess! Let's leave it to the grown-ups!"

"Peter!" For the first time that day, Miranda laughed and Peter grinned broadly at his success in cheering her up. "But where?" she asked.

"The sun!" he cried, "The sand, the sea... Hawaii!"

"Hawaii?!" cried Miranda, "Oh, God! The sun again!"

Peter, looking roguish, pointed a finger to the sky. "When the summer won't come to you, *you* go to the summer. C'mon, we've been out in the rain too long!" And, grabbing her hand, he began to pull her until, finally, she burst out laughing and they ran, hand in hand, through the rain towards the main road and civilization.

CHAPTER FORTY-FOUR

The mechanical excavator raised its giant claw and brought it down with a crash, rearing on its telescoping pods like a bucking bronco. It raked a vast mound of earth backwards, righted its bucket and scooped it up. The machine dropped off its pods, slewed backwards on its tracks with the warning-reverse piping and shot forward to dump tons of earth and rubble at the side of the river.

Sheriff Dooley, hat in hand, stood scratching his head, enjoying the watery, morning sunshine that filtered down from a blue sky flecked with scudding, white clouds.

The sierra hill was a bright emerald; budding oak and manzanita were etched out in dark relief against the fresh green richness. Life was bursting out from every swollen twig and branch. The buckeye trees at the west end of the Mission were in bloom; their fragrance filled the air, carried across the fields on an early morning breeze that still held a slight chill of winter.

Dooley gazed around the Mission yard, chewing thoughtfully. The Mission was a buzz of activity: construction men dug, cleared, sorted and hauled away vast mounds of rubble; chainsaws tore through iron-hard wood with a screaming whine as dour-faced woodmen sectioned the stark limbs of the monster Tree.

The Mission was an unholy mess. Not a building remained standing. The swimming pool was a muddy mass of buckled blue squares and knotted roots. The vegetable garden was now a muddy marsh embedded with broken rock, tiles and splintered foliage. The Mission building was a battered ruin of crumbled masonry with the broken spurs of roots protruding rudely between fallen brickwork.

Dooley fingered a postcard in his top pocket and stared moodily at the construction boss who stood chatting to a dark-skinned Mexican wielding a giant chainsaw.

Expertly, the Mexican lopped off sections of the tree stumps. They fell in neat concentric discs, each stained red in the center like fresh madrone heart. A couple of trucks stood by, one already loaded to the brim with sections of the wood, ready to roar off down the Mission road. The road was clear; the river had been restored to its rightful path.

The construction boss noticed Dooley and came sauntering over. "Well," he said, staring down at the muddy objects on the ground, "What do you make of it? Creepy, isn't it?"

Dooley stared, unmoved, at the three battered bodies laid out on a wooden pallet. They were more skeleton than corpse; their withered flesh hung in strips from peeling bone—and one of them had been decapitated.

"Naah," said Dooley slowly, "Not really."

The construction boss shot him a puzzled look. "What do you mean? We've just unearthed three bodies from a collapsed house and you say it ain't creepy?! Look at that one—it's got no goddamn head!! These suckers didn't die in the flood—no way, man!"

"Nope, you're right," said Dooley chewing methodically. He spat expertly on the ground and continued chewing.

"Well? What then?" said the construction boss, a small, pock-faced man of about forty, "Didn't we do the right thing to call you?"

"You did," boomed Dooley, clapping him on the shoulder, "You sure did." There was a sudden change in Dooley's manner. "I'm right glad you did, Mr. Murphy. Now I can complete my report."

"Complete your report?!" said the construction boss, perplexed, "What do you mean?"

"This here's Cal O'Donnell," said Dooley pointing at one of the corpses, "This is Joe Bear and this is Ferris Ansell—or what's left of them. They were buried in Fall of last year, but some sucker dug up the bodies—a local crazy is what we all reckoned—and for some unknown reason, dumped them in the river."

"Dumped them in the river? How do you figure that?"

"Well," said Dooley, impassive, "How else would they find their way here? Washed down in the flood, weren't they!!"

"You think so?" said the boss, scratching his brow, "It don't look like that to me. Looks like these suckers had been under the house for a time. And where's the goddamn head to this one?!" He pointed at the headless torso. "Looks like it's been chopped off like an ole log!"

"Huh," chuckled Dooley, "That there's ole Joe Bear. And, right enough, it happened just like I said it would."

"What do you mean?" said the construction boss puzzled.

"Well, ah always did say if his head were'n' sewed on tight he was so dopey he'd lose it somewhere—an' he did, huh, didn' he?!" Dooley cackled at his own joke and slapped the construction boss on the back. "I was right, were'n' I?!"

"If you say so," muttered the construction boss.

"Look," said Dooley, "I examined them bodies and they'd definitely been swept downstream and that's what I've put in my report—ties the whole case up, sort of. When the coroner comes, I'll have these dudes out of your way in no time. Then the whole affair will be neat as a pin—a finished job, so to speak. Just like the fine job you're doing here."

The construction boss shrugged. "We're getting well-paid for it, right enough. But I'll be glad when you get these things outta here—they're giving my boys the creeps."

"They'll be outta here in no time at all." Dooley cocked an ear, "In fact, sounds like the coroner's on his way now." He knelt down and drew a muddy tarp over the grisly remains. Something dropped out of his shirt pocket and fluttered to the ground unnoticed.

The construction boss snatched it out of the mud and wiped it off. "Hey, you dropped this." It was a postcard; a picture of azure seas, palm trees and bleached white sand. "Hawaii, eh?" grunted the construction boss appreciatively, "I could do with a stint there after this winter. Worse downpour we've had for years." He proffered the card to Dooley. "Friends out there?"

"Yep," said Dooley. He took the card and pocketed it, slipped on his sunglasses and stared at the construction boss, his eyes hidden by the dark circles of glass, "Real good friends. Be seeing you."

Then he strode off to meet the coroner's van and fake his report.

CHAPTER FORTY-FIVE

The Mission clean-up was nearly finished; most of the men had packed up and driven out to join the slow convoy of outward-bound trucks.

The construction boss sat smoking a final cigarette, watching the sun set blood-red over the darkening greens of the fertile hills as the foreman finished up for the day.

The foreman eased the chainsaw expertly through the huge limb and stood back as a section three-feet wide crashed to the ground. "Reckon that'll do it for today, huh," he said.

"Quite a Tree, hey, Jed?" said the construction boss, "I've never seen anything like it."

"Yes sir. Should fetch a nice price for the owners," said the foreman, wiping the sweat from his brow with a handkerchief. He shivered slightly; a chill was creeping though his bones as the earth lost its heat with the dying rays of the sun.

"Nope," said the construction boss, tossing his cigarette down, grinding it into the dirt, "They're not going to get a cent."

"What?!" said the foreman puzzled, "This wood is harder 'n walnut or oak! In fact, it's one of the hardest woods I've ever cut! An' there must be thousands of board feet here!!"

"Well, whatever…" grunted the construction boss, "Our instructions were to clean up the property, get rid of the Tree whatever way we wanted—burn it, sell it—anything. The owners don't want it." He slapped his palm against the limb. "Suits me. It's a nice little bonus. Ah already made a deal with a saw mill for the trunk. We just got to get it there."

"Quite a problem," said the foreman eyeing the Tree's huge bulk. He slipped his coat on and together they trudged off to the truck, ready for a hot meal and a shower. "What're they offerin'? Got a price yet?"

"Naah. I don't even know what to tell 'em," said the boss, "They won't set a price on it until they see the wood. I couldn't find no one who knew its name."

"No sir," said the foreman, "It's an strange specimen, alright. Funny leaves, bright red flowers… But I tell you, it sure carries a lot of fruit."

"Edible?" queried the construction boss, getting into the truck.

"I guess so," said the foreman. "I came down here one summer. This sucker was so thick with fruit you couldn't get a finger between it. But I never did try none." He started the engine and eased the truck out between the shattered walls of the Mission. The sun had dipped down now and the landscape was bathed in a deep blood red that drained the foliage of its green. "Yeah. This isn't the only place where this Tree grows, though," he said revving the truck.

"Oh?" said the boss, "Mind if I smoke?"

"Nope," said the foreman. He continued: "There must be at least twenty of these suckers growing down on Widow Jenkins' property. Shot up from nowhere they did. They're already in bloom. Pretty thing, too—brightest god-damn flower you ever saw."

"Must be the water, eh? She lives right on the edge of the stream, don't she? That'll do it."

"Naah. More like TLC," said the foreman with a chuckle.

"TLC?" queried the construction boss, puffing at his cigarette and star-ing at the darkening valley as the light slowly ebbed from the spaces between the rocks and trees.

"Yeah," grinned the foreman, "Tender Loving Care. You know how it is with widders. If it isn't cats, it's somethin' else. Why, she looks after those plants like they was babies!"

"Yeah, I know what you mean," grunted the construction boss.

"Why," said the foreman, easing the truck into gear as it chugged slowly away from the Mission towards the mountain road, "Come late summer, early Fall, there's gonna be so much fruit out there, I don't know what she'll do with it…"

The boss was silent as the truck bumped and jolted over the muddy track that, for a while, had been a river of destruction. Then he spoke: "She'll prob-ably stick it in jars an' sell it—you know what widders are…"

"Yeah, I know what you mean—waste not, want not!"

¤

On the hill overlooking Widow Jenkins' place stood an Indian. The sun was high in the noon-day sky and he shielded his eyes with his palm and stared narrow-eyed into the valley below, taking in the curve of the stream, the neat garden and the curl of blue smoke rising from the prim clapboard house.

The skin on his arms was twisted and gnarled with burn scars and his open shirt showed the scars of multiple skin grafts.

A young Indian woman—the man's daughter—stood at his side. She was dressed in moccasins, a suede skirt and a fringed buckskin jacket. Around her neck was slung an amulet and at her side, a medicine bag. She stared down at the garden, her face serene, her eyes calm. Above her eye was a jagged scar that ran down one temple; but this did not mar the handsomeness of her young-old face. "It is so, isn't it, Father?"

He nodded, staring down at the garden. "It is so," he said with a tinge of regret. He had loosened his tie and slung his suit jacket over his shoulder. Even dressed for the Real Estate office, he looked no less an Indian than his daughter.

Her eyes ran over the scarred and warped flesh on his bare arms and her hand went instinctively to her brow. She ran a brown finger along her own scar: Tree had marked Father as it had marked her, she thought. They both knew the consequences of its wrath; but it had been a small price to pay.

"Come," said the Father, circling an arm around the girl's slim shoulders, "Once again, we have work to do."

She smiled at her Father and, cat-footed, they began to make their silent way down the hillside towards the Widow's house.

Once again, they were going to help the white man against the forces that surrounded him; forces he did not know of or understand.

Unacclaimed; in a culture that didn't even know they existed, without accolade or approval, Kuksu and Maru descended towards Tree to do what they had to do, as they always had done—alone.

THE END

BIBLIOGRAPHY:

The Pomo Indians of California by Vinson Brown and Douglas Andrews, 1969. Naturegraph Publishers, Inc., Happy Camp, CA

The Great American Forest by Rutherford Platt, Prentice-Hall, N.J., 1965.

The Californian Indians, compiled and edited by R.F.Heizer and M.A. Wimpole, 2nd Edition, Univ. California Press, 1973.

Planet Earth - Forest, Time-Life Books.

Trees, by James Underwood Crockett, Time-Life Encyclopedia of Gardening, Volume 10.

Northern California 100 Years Ago, compiled by Skip Whitson, Sun Books, Albuquerque, 1976.

Discovering California, edited by Bruce Tinson, California Academy of Sciences, 1983.

Almost Ancestors - The First Californians, by Theodora Kroeber and Robert F. Heizer, The Sierra Club, 1968.

Franciscan Mission of California, by John A. Berger, G.P. Putnams Sons, NY, 1941.

Indians of California - The Unchanging Image, by James J. Rawls, Univ. of Oklahoma Press, 1984.

Teachings From the Ancient Earth, edited by Dennis and Barbara Tedlock, Liveright, NY, 1975

The Master Book of Herbalism, by Paul Beyerl, Phoenix Publishing Co., Custer, WA, 1984.

Yurok Myths, by A.L.Kroeber, Univ. California Press, 1976.

American Heritage, October 1976, Volume 27, #6.

Spirits, Heroes and Hunters from North American Indian Mythology, text by Marion Wood, illustrations by John Sibbick, Schocken Books, NY, 1982,

Old California Houses - Portraits and Stories by Marion Randall Parsons, Univ. California Press, 1952.

A Natural History of Western Trees, by Donald Culvoss Peattie, Houghton, Mifflin Co., Boston, 1953.

Organizing to Beat the Devil (Methodists and the Making of America) by Charles W. Ferguson, Doubleday, 1971.

Tales of the North American Indians, selected and annotated by Stith Thompson, Indiana Univ. Press, 1966.

Indian Tales, written and illustrated by Jaime De Angulo, A.A. Wyn Inc, NY, 1953.

The Great Religions of the Modern World, edited by Edward J. Jurji, Princeton Univ. Press, 1946.

Romance of the Highways of California, by Commander Scott, Griffin-Patterson Co., CA. 1946.

The Pollen Path - A Collection of Navajo Myths, retold by Margaret Schevill Link, Stanford Univ. Press, 1956.

California Inc., by Joel Kotkin and Paul Grabowicz, Rawson, Wade Publishers Inc., NY, 1982.

American Indian Mythology, by Alice Marriott and Carol K. Rachlin, Thomas Y. Crowell Co., NY, 1968.

Warriors of God, by Walter Nigg, Alfred A. Knopf, NY, 1959.

American Catholics, by James Hennessey, S.J. Oxford Univ. Press, 1981.

Historic Spots in California, by Mildred Brooke Hoover, Stanford Univ. Press.

The Wild Stories of America's Beginnings, by Tere Loftin Snell, National Geographic Society, 1974.

The Tree at the Center of the World (Story of California Missions), by Bruce Walter Barton, Ross-Erickson Publishers, Inc., Santa Barbara, 1980.

The Golden Era of the Missions, 1769-1834, by Paul Johnson, Chronicle Books, 1974.

California Gold Mines, by Friedrich Gerstaecker, Bio-Books, Oakland, 1974.

Myths and Legends of California and the Old Southwest, compiled and edited by Katharine Berry Judson, A.C. McClurg and Co., 1912.

History of California, the Works of Hubert Howe Bancroft, Volume 1, 1542-1800.

About the Author

Prem Willis-Pitts is a colorful character with the kind of diverse background which lends itself to passionate storytelling. Raised in a Liverpool-Irish ghetto, he traveled around America for 17 years collecting material. Author of a wide array of award-winning works which encompass radio plays, musicals, biographies, screenplays, T.V., journalism and novels, he has literally hundreds of scripts to his credit. Always multi-tasking, he is currently working on a children's book and a graphic science-fiction novel with cover illustrator, Ron Houghton, as well as a Shakespearian musical and his next novel—a science-fiction comedy. Otherwise, he is "free on Sunday morning between 10:00 a.m. and 10:15 a.m.!" He lives in Denver, Colorado, and welcomes e-mails from his readers: pwillis9@aol.com

Other books by P. Willis-Pitts:

Between the Shadows of the Night
Chariot
The Link Trilogy:
Book 1: Orphans of the Last Dream
Book 2: Children of the Link
Book 3: The Dreaming Stone
Cassie Jallassie's Adventures in Space & Time:
Book 1: Androids, Arachnoids and Alien Malls
Book 2: In Search of the Android Libido

Short Story Collections:
Starry, Starry Night, Speculative Fiction of the Heart
The Sacred and Profane, Specualtive Fiction of Sex & Religion
Masques, Speculative Fiction of Nightmare & Illusion

Non-Fiction:
Liverpool, the Fifth Beatle, An African-American Odyssey
The Roots of British Rock Guitar
The Fire and the Rose
Lost in America: A Limey on the Loose